A BRUSH WITH EVIL

ART OF THE DEAD *series*

More books may be ordered through booksellers or by contacting:
JS Books Publishing
7301 Ranch Road 620 N Suite 155
Unit 300
Austin, TX 78726

info@jodysummersbooks.com

ISBN: 978-1-7331775-4-2 (sc)
ISBN: 978-1-7331775-5-9 (ebook)

Printed in the United States of America JS Books Publishing rev. date: 09/22/18

A BRUSH WITH EVIL

ART OF THE DEAD *series*

JODY SUMMERS

I would like to say thanks again to all the friends and relatives
who have supported my writing efforts.
It's those people who see you through those dark days . . .
And keep you going

CHAPTER

tabula rasa- (tăb'yə-lə rä'sə) from the Latin *tabula*, tablet and *rasa*, erased. Defined as: The mind before it receives the impressions gained from experience or a need or an opportunity to start from the beginning.

Early September

Beakers and test tubes bubbled in every direction containing solutions of various colors and consistencies. At first glance the scene was reminiscent of Dr. Frankenstein's laboratory, but then again, at least for the last several generations, every chemical lab tended to draw those images from people. Elliot was leaning over a larger triangular shaped beaker. He was observing the solution inside drift from a scarlet to a light pink when he heard the door to the lab open. The low hiss of gas flames burning underneath many of the containers was the only other sound in the lab. Elliot was so engrossed in the surprising color change that he neglected to look up, completely uninterested in whoever was interrupting his work.

The flame glowing brightly *above* a beaker to his left was burning steadily. Elliot ignored it. Microwaves passing through and generating a flame from saltwater was, to him, more of a curiosity than a discovery.

His real interest was what those same microwaves could do when they passed through a human body that had been infused with molecules of gold. Unfortunately, gold molecules had an inconvenient tendency to bind with anything else but cancer cells. That tendency was the last hurdle he was trying to overcome. The gold could be injected directly into a tumor and would work pretty well that way, but it wasn't an even distribution which made the effect of the microwave's erratic and potentially dangerous. Additionally, if the cancer cells had not yet produced a tumor then there was currently no viable way of utilizing his microwave/metal concept.

The news about the by-product of his research had been all over the media, the fact that certain radio wave frequencies when passed through saltwater released hydrogen. But that effect was just that, a by-product. Elliot was in the business of curing cancer, or at least he hoped he was. And as far as being a fuel, the device consumed more energy than it produced anyway. To make it worse, the news that little device had garnered had brought him more than just a little unwanted publicity. About four months before he had agreed to an interview as a possible means of acquiring some much-needed financing, and to spread the word about other possible applications of his technology in the cancer field, but it hadn't worked as he had hoped.

"Good afternoon, Elliot," a voice uttered from the direction of the door.

The voice froze Elliot in his tracks.

Not again, he thought. That voice was connected to the worst consequence of his increased visibility in the media. He had to restrain a sigh before responding.

Without turning from his work, Elliot replied, "What do you want, Arthur? I'm busy."

A sudden cramp afflicted his right shoulder causing him to drop the glass pipette he was lifting from his work bench. It fell to the floor with a crash of exploding glass as Elliot spun around to face his visitor.

"I just wanted to talk to you for a moment."

The visage of Arthur turned Elliot's stomach no less than the sound of his voice. He was a skinny, oily, black-haired crow of a man with a hawk-like proboscis to complete the picture.

His crystal blue eyes, however, reflected an unusual intelligence and intensity countered by a gait that spoke of an individual with no grace or physical prowess. And that was before one even began to interact with the sociopathic mal content. Aside from his gaunt, stark appearance that, to many people, brought to mind the works of Edgar Allen

Poe, and his unusual clothing choices, Arthur was unremarkable, at least on the outside. On the inside his mind moved at an amazing velocity and his intelligence was higher than even his ego would believe. Still, there was only one characteristic that he cherished, one very unique ability with which Elliot was unfortunately very familiar.

"About what now?" Elliot assumed that his tone of voice was going to cost him, but he couldn't help it.

"I think you know, Elliot. Now why don't we sit down and chat?" As he spoke, Arthur moved over to the only empty work bench and sat.

"Do I have a choice?"

"Come on. That's no way to treat your business partner."

"You're not my partner. You're my bane." Another spasm, this time in his neck, caused Elliot's head to swing painfully to the left. He looked up in time to see a squint of pain cross his visitor's eyes which satisfied Elliot to no end, and that little bit of satisfaction, even more than his own pain, caused him to relent his verbal antagonism as he crossed to the table Arthur had selected.

Elliot sat obediently at the small relatively empty lab table across from his unwanted guest and remained silent.

"So, is there any progress on the research?" Arthur asked softly.

"No, there's not. As I've told you before. I'm severely limited as to what I can do with my available resources. I need more money to make progress."

"So where were you last week? You were gone from the lab for two days."

The question caught Elliot by surprise, and somewhat unnerved him. He hadn't known that his movements were being tracked that closely. A new fear assailed him.

"I just took a little time off to try to clear my head," he answered.

There was a long pause while Arthur stared at him.

"Come on, Elliot. We both know that you don't take time off. Where were you?" Arthur's tone had a coldness reminiscent of a viper's gaze.

"I was here in the city. Well, at the beach really. I just wanted to relax a little. Sometimes it helps to give me perspective."

"Two days' worth of perspective change? You're lying, and if you don't tell me the truth, I'm going to make you tell me. You understand?"

Elliot did understand, and he didn't have the time or the inclination to spend the rest of the day working in pain, nor did he have any intention of telling this lunatic where he had been.

"OK fine. I got a call from an old friend from my hometown who found my number and wanted to visit. She said she was feeling nostalgic."

"She? Oh my, I don't think you have time right now for a new *she*. You have work to do, and I don't want anything to slow you down."

"She won't. She was just passing through on her way overseas." Elliot's pulse was ratcheting up. Lying was not exactly in his wheelhouse.

"Overseas. Does this lady have money? Maybe if she likes you, she would be interested in an investment." The sharp spark in Arthur's eyes further alarmed Elliot.

"That's absurd Arthur. You can't just ask someone out of the blue for several hundred thousand dollars for a research investment."

"That depends on how much they like you and your work, now doesn't it? Also, it's a bit different when I ask, wouldn't you say? Is she coming back through?"

"Not that she mentioned."

"Too bad. Well, I'm sure you'll let me know if that changes. I'll let you get back to work. I know you have a lot to do. I don't imagine you'll be needing any more time off, either." With that Arthur stood and strode smoothly out the door.

Elliot's pulse was racing. He continued to just sit for a moment, the sounds of bubbling and humming from the equipment in the room seeming to resonate with his pounding heart. He didn't need Arthur meddling in his personal life. How did he ever get himself in this situation in the first place? All he wanted to do was help people.

Moments passed as he considered. He was going to get another call from her, and he was excited about it. In fact, he was somewhat surprised he hadn't heard from her already. They had first met over a week ago. It was already September. But no matter when she called next it had to be kept from Arthur. Had he really been followed or was Arthur simply monitoring his comings and goings to the lab? Didn't that man have anything else to do with his life? Thinking about it, Elliot decided maybe in his situation, he didn't.

Damn! He thought as he finally rose from his chair and moved back over to his work bench. His thoughts returned to his work. If only he could get those gold molecules to bind where he wanted . . .

CHAPTER

Early April
Five months earlier

"Well, I, for one, think it's a great idea," Sean said. His head swiveled to the window of the trailer. The rain was coming down heavy and the outside lights were making interesting patterns in the early evening darkness.

Since their return from Germany months ago and their decision to rebuild their arson-razed home, Kira had only done a few paintings for her business, Canvas of Life. Her amazing, quasi-conscious art style had led her to extraordinary revelations once she began applying it to paintings which included cremains, the ashes of the deceased.

Memories, emotions, and even experiences from the deceased whom she was memorializing impinged on her conscious and subconscious at various times while the work was underway.

She had almost decided to give up the whole business after her run in with Sean's adopted dad, Jason, and then her own crazy cousin.

She wanted to give people peace but wasn't sure the cost was worth it. The only reason she had even considered it was Sean had convinced her that he could and would be there to help her if she needed. But now she was waffling.

"Why, Sean? Why do you think it's such a great idea?"

"Come on, Kira. You're works are an incredible gift, and you don't have to worry about anything strange on this one. According to his wife he'd been an architect his whole life with very little else to interest him other than puttering around the house and walks in the woods with her. How damn spooky could he be?"

Immediately Sean could sense the turmoil his words were eliciting, but there was less fear in those sensations than confusion. It was exactly the response for which he'd hoped.

"Well, I guess you're right," she relented. "I just don't want to have any more of those crazy experiences. They were too horrifying."

"But even then, look at all the good you did, Kira. For that matter, ask yourself this: if you don't use your gift, what else would you like to do with the rest of your life? Besides, this will be a good chance for me to practice sharing your visions with you."

Her hesitation stretched out, and Sean sensed he'd won the battle. Then another thought surfaced seconds before Kira caught his gaze and softly spoke.

"Raise our children?"

Shock invaded Sean's consciousness. Why hadn't that thought crossed his mind before? He'd truly never even considered children, but now that she had expressed the thought, he realized the possibility excited him. It made sense. They *were* getting married next month, after all. He was so stunned; he didn't know what to say.

Obviously reading his features Kira asked, "Does that sound good to you?"

Sean had to mentally shake himself to verbalize an answer. "Er . . . of course it does. I had just never really thought of it before. Of course! It sounds wonderful!" He abruptly swept her into his arms. "Wait," he said pushing her back to arm's length, "Are you pregnant?"

"No, silly." She laughed. Then her face abruptly changed as she reverted to the previous topic. "On the other hand," she said as she riveted his gaze, "I guess child rearing wouldn't command *all* my time."

She looked up into his eyes, and he thought his heart would melt all over again. "Anyway, I suppose it will be fun to see what it's like having you there with me while I'm painting."

"That's my girl," Sean said as he gave her another huge hug. His thoughts divided between the novel concept of having children with her and being curious as to what it would be like to follow her into her trance. Essentially that's what it was: a trance; but Kira didn't like that word, and so Sean made a point not to use it. Instead they both just euphemized the experience to "while I'm painting" or "my painting

7

mode". That was fine with Sean. If it made her more comfortable with what she could do, then they could call it anything she wanted. It wasn't as if he didn't appreciate the feelings. He was still dealing with the growing scope of his own abilities, and he could well understand her fear. He was still learning how to control the newest facet of his talent. Easily sensing emotions was bad enough, this new ability to garner thoughts as well, was much more troublesome. It started with their chase of Kira's cousin, Poena, but only with Poena and Kira. Now it was apparently expanding. The trouble arose not only because of how all those thoughts made him feel as though he was spying on someone's most inner privacy, but also because of how all that information made him feel personally. It wasn't the picnic everyone seemed to think it would be, reading other people's thoughts. How many times had he thought about the reality of people's inner struggles? It continually amazed him how many casual notions flashed through people's mind that you'd rather not know. The random thought that shocks or horrifies you, that you quickly discard, ever so thankful that no one else knew it was there. The first time he'd snagged a horrific thought crossing Kira's mind, one that he'd even sensed her immediately reject, he had recoiled at the ugliness of it and reconsidered what he knew of her. It wasn't until a bit later when he'd had time to consider how similar horrible thoughts crossed his own mind on occasion, and how horrified he would be if she was privy to those, that he resolved to find a way to better filter what he was noticing. Nevertheless, it was a new consideration, and an exclamation point on the oft quoted phrase, "what evil lurks in the hearts of men." It was definitely going to be a learning experience to understand when and what he should discard.

"I'll give her a call and tell her to send the ashes," Kira said, interrupting his introspection, "I can start next week. I don't have much left to do for the wedding preparations anyway, since we're having it here and we have most of a month left"

"You never cease to amaze me, Sweetie," Sean answered proudly then thought for a moment, "At least we have a month as long as the new house is finished on time," he continued. "I tell you what, I'll stoke up the fireplace and we can have a glass of wine on the bear rug while watching the storm . . . and maybe practice getting you pregnant."

"That sounds wonderful." The gleam in Kira's clear blue eyes greatly augmented her simple statement.

The trailer that served as their residence until the completion of the new house had come with a faux fireplace that Sean thought was pretty worthless so he had replaced it with a cylindrical, antique, wood-burning stove inserted in the same space with the exhaust pipe extending up through the existing shaft. The result was a picturesque source of heat. It worked amazingly well, and the front door of it could be left open to watch the flames if one wanted. Sean had already decided that he'd find a place for the old antique in the new house when it was time.

As far as the bear rug was concerned, it was a bear Jason had shot and one of the few of Jason's belongings that had survived the fire. Both he and Kira had agreed to keep it. To Sean, it was a concession to remind him that the terror Jason had visited on others wasn't truly done under his control. Besides, it was just too lush to give up; at least it was once they got the smoke smell and the soot out of it.

Sean was finishing tending the wood stove when Kira sauntered back into the room wearing a dark blue silk robe, with two glasses of wine in one hand, a comforter over her shoulder, and a pillow under her arm. Her appearance this way was becoming a ritual sort of foreplay that they both loved. It had started from a whim in Kira's old French Quarter apartment, a whim they had both enjoyed so much that she kept repeating it.

"Well that didn't take you long," Sean said as he admired her walking toward him. Her curves were still as perfect as the photos he had seen from her modeling career, and he felt blessed all over again to have her in his life.

"I didn't want you to change your mind," she said with an inviting look dancing in her eyes.

"Not likely," he answered.

Kira handed the glasses to Sean before setting the pillow down, and as she spread out the comforter her robe fell open.

Sean was sitting below her in a perfect position to view the smooth skin, uninterrupted by any further clothing. He slid his arms inside the garment and had her in a tight embrace by the time she snuggled in beside him. Her thick chestnut hair fell heavily on his shoulder and face, and he lost himself in the feel and smell of her.

"Where did the wine go?" she asked playfully.

"Wine? What wine?"

With that, his mouth took hers and their sounds were covered by the crackling of the fire while the rain fell unattended.

~

"Sean, the ashes have arrived," Kira called from the other end of the trailer. It was two days after their bear rug tryst.

Those words always marked the beginning of a new adventure, either large or small, Sean reflected. He was just getting out of the shower for the second time. He'd been working in the barn and the smell of horses had been following him around like a smitten hound. He'd wanted to part with that fragrance before settling in with Kira. He walked down the hall towards her as he answered.

"Great, Hon. That was pretty quick, coming from Alabama. So, when do you want to start?"

"Now, I think. I'm afraid the longer I wait, the more likely I'll be to chicken out."

"Now it is then," he replied. His feelings of pride for her were swelling by the moment. He could sense how scary this was for her, and her resolve to forge ahead warmed his heart.

~

Sometimes it was still a struggle for Kira to deal with Sean's abilities. Now that he was getting to the point where he could sense thoughts as well as emotions, it left her feeling a bit naked . . . all the time. A feeling she gotten over once already.

Still, he had developed a knack for being discreet about what he shared of his perceptions and what he kept to himself. That little bit of the unknown kept her world bearable. It wasn't even that she minded him being able to read her so well.

Hell, most of the time she relished the closeness, but there were always those occasions when something terrible slid through her mind, some unbidden thought that she found appalling. Those were the moments that she wished she could exorcise and hoped fervently that Sean missed. He'd never commented or even reacted to one of those thoughts before, but Kira couldn't delude herself into believing that he'd never snagged any of them. Maybe she should talk to him about it. Then again, maybe she shouldn't.

"I think I'll make some coffee while you set up. Do you want any?" Sean offered.

"None for me, thanks. It'll give me the jitters."

"OK. Holler when you're ready."

"I'm sure you'll be back before then, Sean."

Kira sat down on a chair beside her easel. This wasn't the stool she utilized when painting but a lower chair that would allow her to mix. She prided herself on being able to use the entire quantity of ashes in a painting so the entire loved one was in the work. Inevitably she had to first pour out the entire contents of the urns sent to her, to determine the size the work would be. Frequently it was quite large.

She had a large stainless-steel bowl set out for that purpose and filled it with the ashes. It was not only the volume of the ashes that she had to assess but their consistency as well. She had already discovered that not all ashes are created equal. Some seemed finer than others and some had a slightly coarser texture. She had wondered what could possibly cause the difference and had read a bit about cremation to find out. When she ran across something about the remaining bones being put through a hammermill to grind them up, she had discontinued the line of thought entirely. There were some things she didn't need to know. All she needed to discern was how best to work with it to achieve her ends.

She selected a measuring cup she kept handy and scooped some of the ashes into another smaller container. After a brief pause, she reached for her blue paint. She sensed there would be some sky in this picture, so she decided to begin there.

If she later decided the sky should be cloudy or dark, she could easily change from the initial blue. As she began to mix, a few gentle images floated through her mind. This was a small bit of her ability that she'd never really described to anyone.

Her decision as to what she was going to paint came from the images that she received as she mixed. The process seemed much more supernatural than just the painting itself, and as a result, Kira had kept the secret more jealously than any other. It only happened, however, with the first mix. None of the successive interactions with the cremains centered on a setting and somehow it was an unusually eerie sensation. That was why she was careful to do the first one with Sean out of the room. If he hadn't volunteered to leave for a few minutes, she'd have suggested something to get him out of the room anyway.

Buildings. She was getting images of buildings. Houses, actually. Beautiful Victorian homes, to be more precise. Mrs. Dentner had told her he was an architect but not what kind of buildings he did. Surely, he must have designed houses because the images she was getting in fleeting succession were gorgeous.

Movement from the kitchen caught her attention, and she quit mixing. The images popped out of existence, but it was fine. She knew where to start. She set the bowl down and reached for two more, then began pouring a small volume of ashes in each.

"You about ready?" Sean asked while walking into the room with his steaming cup. Kira stared briefly. She never tired of looking at his strong face, hazel eyes, and near black hair.

"Almost. How about you?"

"I'm ready when you are."

~

Sean sat in an easy chair facing the canvas, and as he did, he sensed a flicker of a thought from Kira . . . something about a secret. He almost probed reflexively but stopped himself. If she wanted to have a secret, then she could have one. To distract himself he sipped the steaming coffee and let his thoughts shift to how beautiful Kira looked even in white baggy pants and a beat-up blue T-shirt that drooped off one shoulder. It was an excellent distraction.

Kira was moving her stool in front of the easel and applying some paints to her palette. She finally moved to her standard painting position, left hip on the stool, right leg standing on the floor. She shifted nervously and glanced back at Sean.

"Well, here goes," she said.

Outwardly Sean just smiled in return, but as she settled onto her stool, he closed his eyes, leaned back into the chair, and began focusing on her thoughts.

Victorian Homes? How had she come up with that idea already? It didn't matter. It wasn't his job to decipher how she decided content only to mentally shadow her through the experience.

At that instant Sean got his first surprise. The entire quality and flow of Kira's thoughts changed suddenly. They became smoother somehow, then blurry. His eyes popped open, and he caught a brief glance of her hand holding the brush up to the painting before closing his eyes again and being swept away. He had sort of tried this exercise with Kira before, and had actually accomplished it briefly in previous emergencies, but not since his senses had become so much more acute and never with such conscious forethought.

At first, Sean had the sensation of his thoughts being swept along in a fast river current, all blur and speed. Then the moving sensation dwindled, and the first image appeared. It was of an older man sitting at a drafting table working with a pencil and a T-square. Sean had some odd sensations of the man's thoughts before another image replaced the first. It took him just a second to understand the change. Now he *was* the man sitting at the desk and that man's thoughts were mingled with his own. It was as if two people were inside his head, both clear and distinct from the other. Numbers, angles, load bearing walls, direction, and diffusion of light all blinked through his mind like old familiar friends, and all the while his hands kept working with the T-square and the pencil. There was a sensation of great satisfaction. Then it occurred to him that he wasn't aware of Kira anymore. No sooner had the thought entered his mind than it was dispelled, and he did feel Kira there with him; but she was there with him inside the man they had seen. Now there were three people inside his mind. It was amazing.

Her mind was a warm familiar kernel in a swirl of new experiences. He let his thoughts settle down, pointedly attempting to affect nothing. He was here to experience, not to intrude. It felt as though Kira had no interest in intruding either. Sean sensed that she was doing exactly as he was, merely experiencing thoughts and watching events unfold.

Sean was relishing in the reality of it all. He knew where he was, and he knew how it was happening, but it felt so real. The room was warm, the T-square had the usual notch in the top side, the smells were the customary scents of paper, leather, and pencil lead all of which nestled in his mind as facets of the familiar.

It seemed impossible that Kira was still sitting on her stool with her hand gently creating brushstrokes on canvas. All of a sudden, another thought struck him. If events as innocuous as these felt this real what must it have been like for Kira to be in the mind of a killer as he committed murder? Much less *be* the one being murdered. The horror of it caused him to mentally recoil, and his eyes popped open.

As he did, he heard Kira gasp and turn abruptly on her stool, lowering her paint brush and fixing Sean with a look of concern.

"What's wrong, Sean? Why did you do that? As a matter of fact, what did you do?"

Sean needed a second to clear his mind and understand what had happened. Apparently, when he became horrified, some reflex he did not understand caused him to bolt out of the trance and somehow drag Kira with him.

"I don't know, Kira. I was there with you then I suddenly had a thought of what it must have been like for you to be in Jason's mind. The realization shocked me so much that I bolted out of the scene and apparently pulled you with me. Could you feel me there?"

Kira had a wistful look on her face for a moment before answering.

"Yes, I could . . . sort of. It was the strangest sensation. Everything was going about as usual. I was there in Mr. Dentner's mind, but I was also aware of this odd, comforting sensation in the back of my mind and somehow, I knew it was you. It felt good, Sean."

"Mr. Dentner?"

"Yeah, the man at the architect table. That was Mr. Dentner, Charles Dentner, the man whose ashes are in this painting."

"But how do you know that?"

Kira smiled playfully. "Experience, my dear, experience." Then her grin broadened. "But in this case, Mrs. Dentner told me. This is how it always is or some similar variation of it. Barring, of course, some of the odd dealings with your dad and my cousin."

"Wow," was all Sean could get out for a few minutes.

He felt Kira continue to watch him slowly absorb all this new info, sitting there patiently on her stool.

"Well, we already proved one thing," She said, "You certainly seem to be able to drag me back out of my painting mode when you want to."

"Yeah, right. If I can just figure out what the hell I did."

"You want to try again?" Kira asked.

"Sure. Just let me get a drink of water. I'm thir ..." Sean stopped dead in mid-sentence as his eyes landed on the mantle clock. Kira followed his gaze then began laughing.

"Yep, that's one of the other things you'll have to get used to. Time goes by a lot quicker out here than in the vision."

"Good Lord. I guess so. We were in there together for an hour and a half?"

"Yep. Look at my painting, Sean."

Sean glanced back at the canvas, noticing it now for the first time since opening his eyes. Kira had already roughed in the sky and outlined a home with a huge set of windows. Inside the windows was the vague outline of a man sitting at an architect's table.

"I paint pretty quickly, too, if you'll recall."

"I see that. I knew you were fast before, but after being inside with you it's even stranger. It felt like we were in Mr. Denton's mind for a couple of minutes at most."

"Dentner, his name is Dentner. I know. Weird, huh? I will say this, though. It was comforting to know you were there. It would be even more so if there was something scary going on."

"Have you ever tried to change what was happening in there?"

"Yeah, I did a couple of times with Jason, but it didn't work. I finally decided that since I am just viewing the past, there is nothing to change, so I quit trying."

"That makes sense."

"Come on, let's do some more."

Sean went and grabbed some water then reseated himself and followed her into her painting mode once again, but this time he was prepared for the different sensations and the time passed somewhat uneventfully. The only exception being that Kira discovered a hidden safe in the Dentner home which proved to be quite lucrative. When they were done Sean was certain he could add some great variations to their own new home.

The entire experience bolstered Kira's confidence and encouraged her to continue with her work. The new wrinkle of having Sean there with her as she painted was the thing that tipped the scale.

~

Three days later Kira presented Vera Dentner with the finished product.

Kira flourished the sheet from over the painting and Vera's jaw promptly dropped.

"Oh, my Lord! Kira, this is incredible. This house was one he hoped to build for us and never managed to complete. You've shown me in detail the one dream we never got to finish together. How could you have possibly done this?"

Kira could only smile as Vera's tears flowed. As a result of her gratitude Vera voluntarily doubled Kira's stated price.

The uplifting experience served as a glaring example of the good she was creating and a poignant reminder of why the risks were worth it.

CHAPTER

Early April

The cricopharyngeal muscle, pharyngeal muscles, the nasopharyngeal tonsil, Arthur reviewed the information in his mind as he sat in the stuffy waiting room. He had spent the morning committing the biology of the human throat to memory.

In truth, he had spent the morning the same way he spent most mornings: at the Los Angeles library with the table around him covered in medical texts. It was an obsession derived from his continual pain. Knowledge was power.

Passers-by gave him strange looks, for this method of study screamed of the pre-internet era. Arthur was so used to getting odd looks from just his appearance that the onlookers went totally unnoticed

He was always scanning through volumes replete with images of the human anatomy, including the skeleton, muscles, major organs, nervous system, everything he could get his hands on, and by utilizing his eidetic gift, committing hundreds of them to memory. This morning he had focused on the throat. He hoped that if he could learn enough about human anatomy, he could unlock the key to ending his ever-present pain. And so, to that end, Arthur studied incessantly. If his twisted ego had not stood squarely in his path for so many years, Arthur could have been a renowned researcher. His facility for absorbing raw information was only matched by his knack for snatching tidbits from one area of expertise and applying it to others.

The information from earlier this morning was still floating through his head in meticulous ordered fashion as he sat impatiently in the doctor's waiting area. A man sitting in a chair across from him coughed loudly. Arthur almost grimaced. He hated being forced to sit in a waiting room with a bunch of sick people. He hated being forced to do anything. He'd already been waiting for twenty minutes. He figured he would continue waiting for several more. These places were always inefficient. It disgusted him. What a waste of money. But his body dictated that he be here. It was just one more thing his wretched mother had cursed him with: disastrous genetic makeup. Of course, that idea completely ignored his various mental gifts.

At least his pain was tolerable today. The pervasive aches that plagued his slight frame were more bearable than usual. Fibromyalgia the doctors called it. As far as Arthur was concerned it was just pain.

He had been studying the disease and the ways to treat it. There were still too many doctors that were skeptical about its causes or even, in some cases, its existence. That thought sparked anger in him as it usually did, mostly towards his mother, but to the doctors as well. Idiots. If he could just make them feel what he was dealing with for five minutes, their skepticism would flee like a shadow in the night.

He had already tried most of the medical remedies, and the only thing that seemed to work for him was Vicodin, but he wasn't interested in being in a pill-induced fog all the time. He had read of homeopathic remedies that were supposed to have good results, but he hadn't availed himself of that option just yet. So, for now he simply lingered in a limbo of pain. He only resorted to the Vicodin when the headaches assailed him. To make it worse all this was separate from and in addition to the persistent ache in his head.

At first, he thought it was connected to the Fibro, but he came to realize that this was a different kind of pain and happened on days when his body felt otherwise great. And it was that deplorable little development and his attempts to stop it that had prompted today's visit. Surrounded by the vile dregs of humanity with whom he was forced to interact.

A woman's voice pulled him from his thoughts.

"Mr. Cannes?" A slender nurse with brunette hair called into the waiting room. He rose from his seat being careful not to touch anything he didn't have to and proceeded after the nurse. The sway of her hips as she led him down the hall reminded him of his mother's slutty gait and he wished he could just slap her. The more attractive the woman, the greater his desire to do them harm. She indicated a door with a smile and small gesture. It was all he could do to not spit on her rosy little cheeks. Arthur slid by her through the entrance with an iron grip on his will power.

"Please have a seat, Mr. Cannes," the doctor said.

A snide remark came to Arthur's mind, but he managed to leave it unvoiced as he acquiesced to the doctor's request and sat. Wordlessly he turned his icy blue eyes on the doctor and let them convey his question.

"The results came back from the MRI, Mr. Cannes. I'm sorry to have to tell you this but the Chemo didn't work. . . ."

Arthur's face remained expressionless. It was the result he had surmised after all. "So, is it something that can be treated with surgery?"

~

There were very few reactions that the doctor hadn't experienced in his years as an oncologist, including passive acceptance. Still, there was a coldness exuding from this patient that gave passivity a slightly new twist.

He decided his best course would be a similarly impassive attitude. On some level he knew sympathy would be unwelcome.

"Unfortunately, surgery is out of the question. It is too deep inside your brain to access."

The doctor searched his eyes again and saw nothing beyond the simple question. It was surprisingly unnerving. Prior to today he would have sworn that no patient's response to bad news could surprise him, but this guy left him feeling uncomfortable somehow.

~

Arthur's anger began to rise like magna from a volcano.

"You're kidding me, right? You put me through that damnable chemo for nothing and you just tell me I'm done? Is the rest of your life as impotent as your medical abilities? First one doctor tells me he can't help my fibromyalgia and now you're telling me I'm basically dead."

19

His voice had been rising along with his temper and now it morphed into images of hurting the man. An image of grabbing the idiot by the throat came into his mind. It was such a clear image. In his mind his fingers just reached up there and began to squeeze. At that instant Arthur realized that the doctor really was beginning to gasp. He raised his eyes to the doctor's neck and saw the choking reflexes wracking the doctor's body. Was he doing that? How could that be? All he knew was that the arrogant physician was in pain, and he liked it. Words began to pour out of Arthur's mouth.

"You tell me I have cancer and chemo will help; you lied. The other doctor told me exercise would help my fibromyalgia. He lied. What is it with you doctors? Do you just tell people what they want to hear to get their money then send them on their merry way?"

By now the doctor was on the floor clutching his throat evincing terror. Staring at the red-faced idiot on the floor Arthur realized he would have to find his own solutions.

"Fuck you," he said simply.

With that Arthur stood and left the examination room leaving the oncologist still coughing, dumbfounded, and terrified.

~

Arthur was an emotional storm of rage, astonishment, and satisfaction as he absent-mindedly marched toward his apartment. Idiot doctor. He'd just have to fix this himself. He was smarter than that kindergarten oncologist anyway. But what about that choking? Had he done that? He knew he had . . . somehow. He had done something similar when he was a child but never since then. Was it tied to emotion? The power of it thrilled him, and he was still angry enough to want to try again.

Arthur's gaze was intense as he noticed the stray cat in the alley up the street. It gave Arthur an idea.

The wary animal surprisingly allowed him to pick it up and bring it into his house.

Arthur sat in the shadows. His pale blue eyes seemed to glow above his prominent nose and angular face. The fickle play of the minimal light that filtered through the partially closed blinds and across his features gave his face a distinct Picasso-esque quality. Picasso angles in black and white.

But the cat didn't care. It sat there on the tattered ottoman staring back at Arthur as only a cat can do. Cats don't lose staring matches unless they get bored. It mewed plaintively as its tail swished lazily back and forth.

Arthur's gaze intensified and his brows knitted slightly. Seconds passed with both frozen in that bizarre frame. Beads of sweat slowly appeared on Arthur's brow. He struggled to clear his mind of all the distractions. Thoughts of his ugly childhood, his weak and simple-minded mother, his poor circumstances, the idiotic doctor, his infuriating pain, and his anger at the world in general, all were forcibly focused. Concentration was what he needed, focused, intense concentration. He'd been studying biology for weeks. It was human biology, sure, but he felt confident the cat had muscular similarities. He had the knowledge, and now he was certain he had the ability. Two incidences could not just be coincidence. He had to learn to use his anger, to control it. He could do this, but he needed to practice until it came easily.

These mental battles had to go away if his ability was ever going to be of any practical use. He had at least one disease to cure that couldn't wait, and he knew he'd need help. He imagined he'd need a scientist or a research team to do the work for him. This would be his tool of persuasion.

Drawing on his anger, he focused on the nerves along the spine. The ones that so often plagued him to distraction. Allowing for the cat's anatomy he chose some near the tail. He envisioned them being pinched.

Suddenly, the cat screeched, jumped, and twisted simultaneously. It was one of those extraordinary aerial acrobatics that are forever being replayed on the internet. As it turned in the air it seemed to try to bite its own tail. Regardless of what it intended in mid-air, when the animal's feet regained the ground, it was already running. Arthur saw the animal flash out of sight and into the kitchen. He next heard a bump and a crash, and then silence.

"Damn," Arthur said out loud. The cat had found another way out. But a sardonic smile slowly crept onto his face as he sat there alone on the couch. Then he whispered as the frightening grin grew even larger, "It worked."

CHAPTER

Early May

"Sean, the ashes have arrived."

It was a familiar call, even after just three times. Kira was still very selective as to which commissions she'd accept into their lives, for that is what truly happened. When she painted a portrait, she was letting the life of the deceased into her and Sean's lives, however briefly.

Now, though, with Sean available to be there with her if needed, she was truly beginning to enjoy her business again. She was still reveling in the wonder of it all. Having a future husband who could help her with her work was beyond her dreams. There was the other side of his gift though. His growing ability to read thoughts was still disconcerting.

It still left her with that bit of a naked feeling, and although he was consciously teaching himself how to filter that gift and not willy-nilly receive everything from everyone he was around, it still sometimes felt like an invasion. Even if he was filtering, she never knew when or how much was getting through. It had been a strange lesson to learn that a person could be so frightened of their own thoughts. That sensation of dread of unbidden thoughts seemed to be growing inside her, especially the dark ones that skip through your mind unbidden before you have a chance to evaluate them yourself. The only thing that was saving her from running scared at the thought of it, was their love.

Sean made her feel safer than she'd ever felt in her entire life and somehow that made it bearable, maybe even comfortable or almost comfortable; unless, of course, she ever wanted to give him a surprise party, or a surprise of any sort for that matter. That was a worry for another day though.

They had set the wedding date to correspond with the finishing of the house. It was something they had tentatively decided months ago, but now it was getting close enough that she could hardly stand it. Some of the hints they had taken from Mr. Dentner's plans in his painting had made the building schedule a bit more chaotic and expensive, but it was worth it. His layout for the wraparound porch was glorious, but what had really cost them some extra time was the little secret passage that had led to the hidden safe Kira had discovered while she was in 'painting-mode.' Sean had been simply smitten. He'd been like a kid with a new puppy and simply would not let go until she had agreed to let him incorporate a secret passage into their own new home.

It was set into the library, Sean's favorite room, and was triggered by a little lever behind one of the moldings for the bookcase. When pulled it would allow a three-foot section of the bookcase to swing in, revealing a passage to the right, going up to the master bedroom and another going down into the basement/storm cellar.

The upstairs passage came out behind a section of mirrored paneling inside the master bathroom closet and the basement passage featured a section of wall that would slide sideways to enter the basement. It was truly ingenious but as far as Kira was concerned, it was just silly. Still, it was worth having just to see the childlike excitement on Sean's face.

And the construction would still be completed in time for the wedding, so they didn't have to move the date which made them both happy. She couldn't believe that in two weeks she'd be Mrs. Kira Easton. The name sounded weird in her mind, but she was as giddy as a schoolgirl going to her first dance.

"So, when do you want to get started on it?" Sean called from the bedroom of their little trailer.

"Probably not until tomorrow," she answered.

"Do you want me with you?"

"Nah. These ashes are from a friend of one of my old modeling friends.

She said he was a computer geek of some sort. Ought to be pretty boring."

Kira heard laughing coming from the bedroom.

"Fine," he finally said, "I'll figure on working on the house then. What was the guy's name?"

"Shane. His name was Shane Chang."

~

Kira didn't get to the painting for two more days. While she worked, Sean stood inside the barn currying one of the horses. He had already fed them, and they could probably go without the extra grooming, but it was something he loved to do. It calmed him and the horses loved it so much that he found it almost narcotic. He'd become aware of the fact that the horses' simple sensations flowed into his awareness just like the ones from people. Only these sensations were never clouded with thoughts, and they were always simple and straight forward. This surprising caveat to his ability had made it extremely easy to train the animals. They simply understood one another. It was also such a welcome respite from the crowd of thoughts that churned through his mind when he was around people.

At least he was managing to learn control. Now, when he was in a crowd of people, it was more like standing on a downtown street corner. The cacophony of the blended sounds of the city weigh on your auditory sense, but very quickly you learn to tune out most of it, to the point that most of the sound slithers by your awareness like so much white noise.

Only those particular sounds that have some significance to you emerge through the filter like the sound of someone calling your name, for instance, or a car horn close enough to signify danger.

He was even learning to do the same thing with Kira, to give them at least a modicum of proprietary distance from her most intimate thoughts. In her case it was more difficult simply because he was interested in so many of her casual thoughts. Still, he'd learned the hard way that there had to be boundaries.

Things had been substantially smoother for both of them since that decision.

He thought about just how smooth everything in their relationship really was. He'd always heard marriage was hard work, but he couldn't imagine it being a problem with Kira. Just under two weeks. He grinned.

Sean drew the curry brush gently across the horses' flanks enjoying the sensations and letting them carry other thoughts away.

~

As she was mixing the first batch of ashes with paint Kira got an image of a large computer screen, but it was what was on the screen that shocked her. The image was so fast and so shocking that she doubted what she thought she had seen, so she had to wait until her first session of actual painting to confirm her suspicions.

Her palate prepared, and canvas in place, Kira skooched her hip up onto her stool until she felt comfortable. She cleared her mind and lifted the brush to the canvas. At once her thoughts floated away as they always did to that other place from which her incredible creativity flowed. This time, as occasionally happened, images flew before her like flash photos, chasing each other across her mind's eye. A man of boyish appearance sitting in a chair before a pair of huge computer screens, another image of the same man from a different angle, allowing the opportunity to see the rapt expression on his face, a close up of that same expression giving it a maniacal quality, and another flash back to the computer screens.

"Oh my God!" Kira exclaimed, coming abruptly out of her vision and nearly falling off her stool.

~

The thought shot into his brain like an arrow and his hands froze on the horse's mane.

Oh my God.

It was from Kira.

What was happening?

The new painting.

Sean dropped the brush and raced for the trailer causing the horse to dance back nervously.

"What's wrong?" Sean blurted as he exploded through the back door. Kira was still sitting on her stool, but her palette was on the floor, and she had her face in her hands.

When she didn't answer immediately, Sean stepped closer and put his hands on her shoulders.

"Kira, what's wrong?"

"The painting . . . this computer guy . . . he's disgusting."

Sean was actually a bit relieved. Disgusting was much less ominous than what he was imagining. Having lived through the experiences with his adopted dad, Jason, and Kira's cousin, Poena, "disgusting" certainly qualified as a relief. In a much softer tone, he sought to comfort her.

"It's OK, Sweetie," he whispered. As he held her, the revulsion she was feeling twisted in his stomach, and he had to clench his teeth as a moment of nausea swept over him. There was definitely a downside to being this connected to someone else. Then, through her mind, he got an image of what she had seen. The computer screens in her vision swam into his mind and he was accosted with a brief image of a sexual scene; but not just sex, violent, lurid sex interlaced with torture. The image sluiced away as quickly as it had come, but it was enough for him to understand.

"Ugh," he said, "I'm so sorry, Honey. That is revolting."

She evinced no surprise whatsoever at his casual display of mind reading.

"How can people do these things?"

It was a rhetorical question and Sean knew it. They had both seen so much worse. Still, being witness to other people's depravities from the inside was not an experience he would wish on anyone. So, he well understood.

"Why don't you take a break and we'll get some coffee?"

"Sean, how can I finish this painting? I don't want to have to look at that anymore and I'm certainly not about to reveal this side of the man to his loved ones."

Sean was thoughtful for a moment as Kira followed him into the kitchen.

"Maybe you don't have to Kira. Maybe you can learn to filter what comes to you in your visions just like I filter thoughts coming from others."

Kira stopped in her tracks and looked back up at him. "Do you think I really could do that?"

"I don't know why not. I do it every day, and I'm not so sure that what you do is that different from my ability . . . except for the painting part," he added with a playful smile.

Now it was Kira's turn to have a thoughtful moment.

"And the fact that yours are from the living," She barely whispered.

After two cups of coffee and a lot of bantered ideas, Kira agreed to try again with Sean there and see if he could help direct her from inside.

For Sean, the experience was very similar to his other ones with Kira: first the blurring of thoughts, then the images beginning from the outside of the subject, then suddenly, as the subject himself. No sooner had he become part of Shane than the images popped up on the two huge computer screens. It was like a scene from a modern-day horror movie. Sex and violence blended together in rapidly moving images. Sean was instantly repelled. He tried to close his eyes, but Shane's wouldn't obey. He tried to distance himself and intentionally remembered the images of watching Shane as he entered the trance with Kira, then suddenly he was there— back out of Shane's body and seeing the scene from the side, a perspective that didn't include being able to view the screens themselves. A moment of reflection told him Kira was there with him.

Sean's tension abruptly faded. How had he done that? He relaxed even more and let his senses take in other details of the scene inside the house. The computer desk was made of black metal and looked ultra-modern; more like a table really with some roll away wire drawers underneath. As he continued to relax, he sensed Kira doing the same. Sean was experiencing just a touch of smugness at what he'd been able to accomplish when his perspective suddenly snapped right back inside Shane and his view of the revulsion on those computer screens.

There was a mental gasp in his head from Kira as Sean steeled himself and focused his concentration. It might have taken just a few seconds, but it seemed like much longer before he managed to yank himself and Kira back out of Shane again. This time he didn't let his concentration slip, and he and Kira stayed put until she brought them both back out.

"How did you do that?" She asked, wide eyed.

"I'm not sure. I just focused my thoughts and remembered the images we saw as we entered the vision." The word "trance" kept coming to Sean's mind, but he was diligently trying not to use it around Kira.

"I don't think I could ever do that by myself," she replied, a touch of awe in her voice.

"Sure, you can. You just need to practice. Don't forget I've already had a lot of practice at filtering stuff coming into my mind. I have to do it nearly every day now."

Sean's gaze shifted to Kira's canvas, and he was amazed all over again at the extent she'd already completed. Kira was just shaking her head.

"I don't know, Sean. I think I'd have to have you there."

"We'll work on it on some other painting. One that isn't so gruesome."

Kira sat staring at her canvas for another few moments before turning back to Sean.

"The more I experience what goes on in other people's heads, the more I'm glad I don't know any more than I do. I don't know how you do it, Sean."

Sean's smile looked a bit like a grimace. "I do it because I don't have any choice."

"But I do," she answered. A moment later, she got up off her stool and came over and gave Sean a big hug. "I love you," she said. Her feelings washed over Sean like a blanket fresh from the dryer. For a few moments the world was perfect.

~

Kira's first sensation was that she was cold.

Next her eyes popped open, and she tried to rub them only to find her arms were restrained. As her eyes shifted to see what was holding her, she realized she was naked and strapped down to the bed, arms and legs splayed out to the four corners, held there by ropes of hemp.

What the . . ., she thought, *Did Sean . . . ?* Then a bolt of fear coursed through her belatedly. Her eyes canvassed the room. It was her and

Sean's bedroom, but where was he? She was just about to call out his name when her attention was drawn to the ceiling. There on the ceiling where two Asian eyes staring down at her. Even without the benefit of any other facial cues she was certain they were leering.

Before she could form a cogent thought beyond the fear, the eyes began to grow. She screamed and it seemed like the power of her scream acted as fuel to those eyes and they began to grow, larger and larger until they encompassed almost the entire ceiling. Her scream grew in power to match as her mind imagined saliva dripping from unseen fangs beneath those eyes. She struggled with the ropes but to no avail. Finally, her terror found words.

"SEAN!"

"Kira!" Sean answered sitting bolt upright in bed and grabbing her.

Kira's eyes opened in the same instant as her realization that it had been a dream. A horrible dream. She hadn't had a fearful experience like that since trying to paint for the FBI months ago.

"Kira?" Sean said again this time with a question in his tone, "Are you alright?"

As often happened, Kira's fear led to anger, and her next words were harsher than she intended. "And just how the hell are you going to protect me from *that*? I don't want to have nightmares like that anymore. It was Shane from the painting."

Sean was unfamiliar with having Kira angry at him and for a moment he was unsure how to respond. "Well I . . . ," he began spluttering.

Kira immediately recognized his distress and that she was the cause of it. "Oh Sean, I'm sorry. I didn't mean to take it out on you. It just scared me, and I'm getting so damn tired of being afraid like that."

A wave of relief washed over Sean's features further illuminating how much distress she had caused him.

"It's OK, Kira. I can only imagine what it must be like to have to deal with that repeatedly. As for protecting you from it, that's a whole other question. I'm going to have to think about it, but I bet I can find a way."

The determination in his voice was more cathartic than anything else he could have said or done. "I bet you will," she said as she leaned over to kiss him.

29

CHAPTER

Mid-May

"Err-a-errr-a-errr," the rooster crowed.

Sean stood outside and smiled back at the house.

Why do they do that? He wondered, glancing over to the rooster on the fence, by the barn. *Maybe to establish a territory,* he thought in passing. It was 5:30AM on the day of his wedding, and he'd been up for forty-five minutes taking care of horses. It was already hot outside. This would be their last time waking up in the trailer, and he'd been careful not to rouse Kira when he slipped out. It had only taken twelve months, and the new house was now nearly finished. It was a picturesque, modernized, expanded version of the old farmhouse.

The view from the tall-ceilinged, two-story house was now commanding. They had not only fitted the place with a beautiful wrap-around porch, courtesy of Mr. Dentner, but it also displayed a massive upstairs deck, one side of which held a large, trellised-off, hot-tub, all accessible from the master bedroom. The construction was of cedar and stone and was a successful blend of old-world craftsmanship and design, and modern conveniences. Large intricate bathrooms, big fireplaces, and an expansive kitchen marked the structure. The iron stove that Sean loved so much was still looking for a place to live. Kira wasn't nearly as fond of it.

~

Sean and Kira stood hand in hand in front of their massive stone fireplace. Both had agreed that the cedar beams arching overhead and the flames crackling in the fireplace were the perfect backdrop for the ceremonies. It was too hot for the fire but they both wanted the ambience of it, so they simply cranked up the AC to handle the extra heat. A couple of frilly tablecloths were their only concession to traditional wedding decor.

The Baptist minister was standing with his back to the fire while John and a female friend of his were standing on one side, with Aubrey, Sean's birthfather, on the other. Kira had no other family, so those three and the minister were all the witnesses that either needed or wanted.

The warmth of feelings welling inside Kira felt as though they might burst through her skin, and the knowledge that Sean was aware of every one of them warmed her even more. No longer was she afraid of his abilities. It was just one more facet of being in love with this extraordinary man. She could no longer imagine being in love with anyone else. And this was their day. After all their trials they were finally going to officially tie the knot. Kira felt for the hundredth time that her heart would burst from love.

She turned her gaze back to John, the quintessential old country Sherriff, but he was so much more than that to her. She was happy to see the smile on his badly scarred face. The scars he had received saving her life. His happiness was a welcome sensation. She could almost feel it herself. Maybe some of Sean's abilities were rubbing off on her.

~

Sean waited patiently for the minister to begin. He was relishing in the dance of emotions coming off Kira, John, and Aubrey. He tried delicately to curb the amount of actual thoughts that wafted into his mind from the others.

Right now, all that was flowing into his awareness was warmth and happiness from Kira, from Aubrey, and even John and his new girlfriend, Sarah. Behind and beneath all of that were his own emotions which often seemed to be lost in the flow of everyone else's. Separating them out was a skill at which he was slowly improving. He was happy, happier than he could ever have imagined.

Kira was the undisputed love of his life, probably even the only love of his life, and after all they had been through together, they were finally getting married. It was a joy he could never have imagined even as recently as two years ago.

"Dearly beloved," the minister began.

I'm proud of you, son.

The thought coming out of the blue was a shock. It was so clear and . . . directed. Sean knew that Aubrey's senses weren't as acute as his own, and he couldn't enter other people's thoughts like Sean was learning to, but there was certainly no doubt that this was an intentional thought coming from him. He had nearly glanced over involuntarily, but Aubrey was slightly behind him and it would have been unseemly. Regardless, the shock dissipated almost as quickly as it had arrived, and Sean was left with a lingering warmth. That feeling, from a parent, was such a new experience to Sean that its impact was quite powerful. It momentarily distracted him, leaving a wistful smile on his face. He saw and felt Kira notice the smile and return it, thinking it pertained to her. That was just fine. In fact, it was perfect.

"I do," Sean heard Kira say, followed shortly by his echoing declaration. Sean was a little surprised. The flow of other thoughts and his own had distracted him sufficiently enough that the minister's beginning words had slipped by him completely. He was just thankful that Kira had the first response. Her words had brought him back to his surroundings just in time.

The next few seconds disappeared in a blur of excitement until Sean heard the minister finally say, "I now pronounce you man and wife."

And then the kiss. Mental bliss gave way to the physical.

CHAPTER

Mid-May

Arthur sat on the beige beach blanket with his knees pulled up and his oily black hair blowing in the salty Pacific breeze. His seemingly translucent skin didn't lend itself well to exposure to the sun, but he wasn't here for a tan, hence the beige umbrella stuck in the sand beside him. He was here to practice his micro-telekinesis, as he called it.

After the unintentional incident with the doctor and the successful trial with the cat he had begun to practice using his gift on smaller objects but with greater precision. At first, he began with chess pieces, practicing for hours to move the pieces smoothly and accurately around the board. Once he'd mastered that, he began working with larger items. He was soon dismayed that the size and weight of the objects he could move was very limited. Try as he might he could never manage to maneuver anything weighing more than a few pounds, or larger than a small bicycle, or further away than about a hundred feet. This put a serious damper on his ideas of opening bank doors or stopping cars. But his knowledge of anatomy had given him ideas of how to use his ability creatively and he was satisfied that he could still accomplish all his goals with the abilities he had. So, he began to go smaller, practicing on rice grains and later salt crystals until he got to where he could thread a needle half way across the room using only his mind. He was ready.

~

Many people stole furtive glances of him as they walked or jogged by, for his appearance was somewhat striking. This was first due to his odd choice of clothing, then due to the predatory quality of his ice-blue eyes. His yellow pants looked like the women's modern version of capris, fitting his gaunt body tightly and stopping at mid shin. He wore a cut off T-shirt in a pale green with purple letters on the back proclaiming, "You're living proof the gene pool has a shallow end." All purchased at a thrift store. He could care less about his clothes or his appearance at all, for that matter.

The soothing ebb and flow of the waves here, just north of Venice Beach, typically had a calming effect on everyone, but it had no effect whatsoever on Arthur, any more than did the herds of bikini clad beauties that ambled in every direction. As a matter of fact, seeing all these women around him made his anger rise like bile in his throat.

All his life he had only been spurned by women, starting with the worthless mom he had been raised by who refused to believe he was so frequently in pain with no apparent cause and couldn't seem to make it three days without bringing home some new man. As the years went by, he developed a deep and abiding hate for all women. Misogynism barely touched the surface of the feelings he harbored; psychopathic loathing was probably a closer description.

All Arthur wanted right now was a place where he could sit comfortably and practice without anyone being the wiser.

He had first tapped into his ability when he was in grade school and a bully began making fun of his eyes. This wasn't such an unusual occurrence and would have gone by as a non-memory in Arthur's life had it not been for the fact that this particular bully didn't just want to humiliate him, he wanted to hurt him. Arthur recognized the quality in the boy's eyes. It was something Arthur often felt himself, but he was too small and weak to act on the impulse.

The boy's name was Mike. He was a redheaded, heavyset boy and just plain mean.

"Hey pussy, why don't you go home and play with your momma?"

Arthur was furious, but he knew better than to let this boy draw him in. If he had a bat or a rock, he would have attacked the boy like a crazed badger, but without any weapons against the bigger kid, all he could do was remain quiet.

"Cat got your tongue, wimp? Or are you just plain chicken?"

Arthur managed to keep quiet but unconsciously backed up a step. The movement screamed *prey* to the aggressive kid and he charged.

He shoved Arthur hard enough to cause him to fall backwards smacking his rump on the playground blacktop. Arthur jumped up quickly and retreated to the sandy area around the swing set all the while hearing the taunts of what a wimp he was. Arthur's fury built like a thunderstorm but no plan to strike back came to him.

Mike wasn't finished. He wasn't satisfied with the reaction from either Arthur or the gathering crowd. Suddenly, the redheaded tough guy barreled toward Arthur through the intervening swing set. Arthur backed up, desperately wishing that the boy would trip over the swings, wanting it so bad he could see it happen in his mind's eye.

At that instant one of swings danced sideways entangling the boy's legs and causing him to plunge face first into the sand surrounding it. There was apparently at least one rock that had made its way into the sand, designed to soften such falls, for when the boy raised his head, his mouth was bleeding and his front tooth was broken.

At seeing the copious amount of blood spreading across his face Mike screamed like the coward he truly was and raced inside the school.

Arthur ignored him. He was still staring at the dangling swing which continued to sway gently. The small crowd that had gathered to watch the spectacle quickly scattered as Arthur stood there staring at the swing. Consequently, none of them noticed the dancing swing that had acted as Arthur's savior suddenly go still, and Arthur's eyes went wide. He *had* done it himself. With a quick glance to assure he was no longer the object of any of the attention to which he had become so accustomed, Arthur focused on the swing again this time trying to cause just a small motion, but nothing happened. What he had been too young to understand at the time was the connection between his anger and his ability. And so, his gift had lain dormant for years, until six weeks ago at the oncologist's office.

Arthur smiled at the memories.

Focus. He had to focus. He was here to accomplish something today and these useless thoughts were burning daylight.

The previous evening, he had seen a news interview with a young scientist named Elliot Drake who was doing work on a cancer cure. He had accidentally stumbled across a fascinating potential energy source but that wasn't what Arthur found interesting.

The work was promising, and he decided right then that Elliot was the man he'd been looking for. He would have to persuade him to work for free, however, and that was the purpose of Arthur's visit to the beach today.

His first studies had been with joints and today he was working in particular with ankles and knees.

He focused on one of the passing beauties. It had to be a woman. Women were the source of his loneliness, the very center of every reason he felt so insecure. Even after his mother, women had always looked on him with disdain, and he hated them all. Therefore, it was on them that he most desired to unleash his wrath. The anger they ignited in him made his practice easier.

As the memorized image of a foot and ankle joint took shape in his mind, a tall, svelte brunette slowly ambled across his field of vision. Her blowing hair must have stretched nearly to her waist when not being playfully rampaged by the wind.

But all Arthur could register was the haughty expression of superiority on her face. It was time to remove that.

Some of the smaller bones in the foot are the cuneiform metatarsals which connect at the top of the foot just below the ankle. With an expression on his face resembling the result of eating an overly tart pickle, Arthur visualized the center metatarsal moving down . . .

A small, sharp scream emanated from the unsuspecting stunner as she dropped to the sand grabbing her foot.

Arthur smiled. The scream caused his mental image of her foot to dissipate so the woman's distress at once subsided. After a brief moment of massaging, she picked herself up off the sand with a quizzical look on her face, took a moment to recover her dignity, and continued on down the beach with a noticeably abated amount of swagger in her strut and a parade of strangers' gazes following her curiously.

The excitement swelled inside Arthur, followed by an overwhelming exhaustion. Not only had he accomplished what he had intended, but he'd been able to watch as that snooty bitch got taken down a few pegs. Now he was paying the price. His efforts to use his gift these days seemed to drain his energy disproportionately to the manner in which he used it, and a sharp pain had started up in his head.

Apparently, even small uses of his gift drained him badly, and he was going to have to find a way to deal with that if he was ever going to really make use of what he was now learning.

Still, the weariness didn't dim the elation at his success. Briefly, it occurred to him that he wasn't sure which sensation was more pleasant, his successful effort or the way it immediately affected the haughty woman. He didn't have time for that crap, though. He had more things to practice and needed something for his headache.

Soon enough he'd be ready to meet this scientist.

CHAPTER

Mid-May

Reception music was echoing through their big new house, and the food and drink was flowing among their tiny party. Sean and Kira spent quite a bit of time dancing while the other four got to know each other. Eric, the young minister, was a high school friend of Sean's, and he was glad to stay and socialize. Aubrey had never really come to know John, other than a couple of phone calls when John had contacted him to let him know he'd found his son and a brief interaction after. They were deep in conversation while Eric and Sarah discussed the wedding and weather.

Kira and Sean finally emerged from their private interactions, an extended slow-dance, and decided it was time to mingle with their friends.

"Come on Sean! Let's go talk to our guests."

"But I like holding you," Sean complained playfully.

"We've got the rest of our lives for that," she answered, "Starting with tonight."

Sean grinned at the insinuation and let her lead him over to their kitchen counter where everyone was mingling by the food.

"So now what?" John said, addressing the newlyweds as they approached.

"I guess more food, drink, and conversation," Kira answered brightly.

"No. I mean what are you two going to do with your lives now? The house is finished, barring a few odds and ends, the adventure is over. What's next for you two?"

"More of the same," Kira chimed in "or at least more of the same for me. I think Sean's got some flying and martial arts lessons in his future."

"But I thought you said you were done with painting after the last experience with Poena?" John asked.

A familiar pang of guilt visible to everyone flashed through Kira as she focused on the scars John had received on her behalf.

"Well, that was before Sean realized he could join me in my visions and pull me out if I need him to."

"What? When did this happen?" John asked.

The look on John's face was obviously surprise, but Aubrey's was an almost sly grin possibly mixed with a certain amount of paternal pride.

"I've done some more paintings in the last few months. It's given Sean and me the chance to practice when the stakes aren't so high. He's amazing at it."

"You mean he actually goes into your visions with you?"

"Yep, and he can help me change my perspective during the experience or drag me out completely if need be. He's already done both. We're thinking that in most cases he'll just have to go in with me on the first session to see what it's like, and if it's normal I can do the rest without him."

John's amazement wouldn't seem to subside. "How did you know you could do this, Sean?"

"I didn't until we first tried."

~

Sean didn't have to catch any of John's thoughts to sense the concern flowing from him. John had become very close to Sean and Kira in the months following their adventures and many of his opinions these days seemed to fall into the "parental concern" category.

His thoughts were interrupted by a strong thought from his dad.

Can we talk in private a moment? wafted into Sean's mind.

Sean smiled as he turned his head. Aubrey was the only one who intentionally directed unspoken thoughts towards him. He kept expecting Kira to do it, but for some reason she didn't, or at least she hadn't yet.

It wouldn't hurt to remind her of that, he thought. *It could be useful sometime*, as his dad apparently already knew.

"Excuse me," Sean said, "I have to grab something from the truck." Kira was now talking with Eric and John was ensconced with Sarah again.

"I could use a breath of fresh air," Aubrey offered, "I think I'll follow you if you don't mind."

A quick turn of the head and a gracious smile was Kira's outward response. Sean caught a flash of her thoughts, however. *What's that about?* Came clearly from her as he and his dad angled toward the back door. The perception made Sean smile. His sweet new bride didn't miss much.

It was Mid-May, in Kansas. The air was pleasantly warm, the skies were blue, and a surprisingly gentle breeze blustered just enough to bring the smells of grass and hay to Sean's nostrils while shooing away any lingering mosquitoes.

Sean didn't really need anything from the truck, but it was parked out by the barn, so he ambled slowly in that direction and waited for his dad to bring up whatever that thought was that was lurking in the back of his mind. Sean thought he could have grabbed it if he'd probed a little more, but he didn't want to. He liked to let people share things with him in their own time. Besides it was a good exercise in filtering, and he needed as much of that as he could get.

"So, do you know what I want to talk to you about?" Aubrey asked.

"Not till you tell me. I try not to do that by accident."

Aubrey smiled. "I can't tell you how proud I am of you, Sean."

The sensation of that emotion washed over Sean like a warm tropical wave. It was a wonderful sensation and unlike thoughts, Sean still didn't have any filter for the emotions of others. He felt most all of those, most all the time. It was one last hurdle he wished he could cross because even those sensations were dismaying and unnerving when he was in a crowd.

Suddenly the sensation of pride from his dad changed to sadness, and Sean turned to him sharply.

"What is it, Dad?"

"I thought you weren't reading my thoughts?" He asked, smiling.

"I'm not. This is an emotion. You suddenly got sad."

The gentle smile slipped from Aubrey's features as he said, "Yes, I am a bit sad."

"What's going on?" Sean's concern was turning to anxiety, and he was on the verge of going to get the thought from his dad's mind, but Aubrey was quicker.

"I'm dying, Sean."

The words hit Sean like a hammer. "You can't be," he stammered out, "I just met you."

"I know, son, and I'm sorry, but I am. It's a brain tumor. It's inoperable."

"Wha . . . when did you find this out?"

"Actually, I just learned two days ago."

"And you didn't want to tell me sooner because of the wedding?"

Aubrey smiled. "That's right. I don't want to ruin your wedding day. The only reason I'm telling you now is because I was getting increasingly concerned that you might pick it up from my mind, and I didn't want you to learn about it that way."

"There's no treatment possibility?" Sean asked in a near whisper.

"Well, there is one specialized radiation option, but the risks are so high that I'm just not willing to jeopardize what little time I have left. If there are any mistakes with the radiation targeting, it could take out brain functions."

Sean grimaced slightly, an emotion that Aubrey didn't miss. "I guess I understand where you're coming from on that. I think I'd make the same decision. How long do you have?"

"I'm not sure, Sean. Maybe a year, or a bit less."

Sean's features became stern with concentration. "So, then what are you going to do?"

Sean could sense that Aubrey wanted to say more but felt that any additional show of emotion would further upset Sean, so Aubrey's dry comment was of little surprise.

"I'd like to spend as much time with my new family as I can without becoming a burden."

"No problem, Dad. You can use one of the spare bedrooms and stay with us."

"No. I can't. I'm not going to be trundling through the house with a couple of newlyweds. I can stay in town at the hotel."

"If you're going to do that you may as well go home." Sean could sense the tension, and he could also feel his dad's conflict. There had to be a better answer. Then inspiration snagged him.

"What am I thinking? You can stay in the trailer! It's empty. It has everything you need, and it's close."

"Perfect," Aubrey answered, and Sean felt the tension dissipate like air from a punctured balloon. At the same instant the wave of sadness hit Sean and tears formed in his eyes.

"In the meantime, though, we're going to look for other possibilities, Dad. I'm like Captain Kirk. I don't believe in the no-win scenario."

Aubrey smiled. "You're a Star Trek fan, too?"

Sean sensed Aubrey's warm sensation from their familial connection, and the recognition of his own similar feelings served to strengthen his flow of tears.

"We better get back to our guests," Sean said, turning Aubrey with his arm over his shoulder.

"Wait," Aubrey said producing a handkerchief from somewhere and dabbing at Sean's eyes. "We can't let the guests see you crying, and don't you dare let this ruin your wedding night. I apologize again for telling you now."

Sean managed a smile. "I don't think you have to worry about the wedding night."

Aubrey smiled back. "Alrighty then. Let's go have a drink."

~

That evening in bed after enough passionate intertwining to exhaust them both, Kira lifted her head from Sean's chest and asked, "OK, what's bothering you? Did your dad tell you something upsetting when you went outside?"

"I thought I was the mind reader here," he asked, kissing her on the forehead.

"I don't have to read minds to know something is weighing on you. I just have to be in love."

Sean's answering smile was weak at best. "Well, I at least wanted to wait until tomorrow to tell you so I wouldn't ruin our first night as husband and wife."

"What is it, Sean?"

He felt her concern crescendo and knew there was no avoiding it any longer. "Kira, my dad is dying."

"What? How? It can't be. You just found him."

The wave of horror from her flickered through him causing him more discomfort than his own sadness.

"That's what I said. It's a brain tumor and he said it's inoperable."

"Then he's going to have to stay with us," she offered.

It was the kind of selflessness that Sean expected of her, but it still warmed him. "That's what I told him," he answered thinking that he was repeating himself.

"But he said he wasn't going to crowd a couple of newlyweds."

"Then he can stay in the trailer," she answered immediately.

"That's what I told him."

They both froze staring at each other at the second repetition of those words. Seconds later they both began laughing. It faded quickly, but it was at least enough to dissipate the tension. They discussed the details of Aubrey residing in the trailer for a few more minutes before the lovemaking started all over again. It seemed awkward at first with the news of his dad still lingering, but they were young and in love and the sadness couldn't hold sway for long. Their ardent passions were sufficient to push the sadness away for at least a little longer.

Even so, heavy hearts chased them both into sleep.

CHAPTER

Mid-June

Lisa's heart was heavy. With her money and her connections, it hadn't taken her long to get results. Barely a week had passed before she found the right firm to hire, a company called, generically enough, LA Investigations, but their address was Beverly Hills and their reputation was extraordinary. Within days they began hunting down her birthmother.

The investigators had informed her that, unlike decades gone by, the records of adoptions weren't nearly as inaccessible as they had once been. That didn't always make it easy, however. In Lisa's case the mother herself had taken steps not to be found. She had used a false name when she rushed into the hospital heavy with labor, according to an old retired nurse that the investigator on the case, Christopher, had interviewed. That had slowed them down because at first glance there was no reason to anticipate a false name, so Chris had spent some amount of time ferreting out that dead end.

Once he did, however, and partially owing to the fact that Lisa was only in her thirties and there were people left alive to talk to, Chris managed to find out Lisa's mother's real name.

As it turned out her name was Annabelle Kravitz and not the Penelope Parsons she had given to the hospital. Once Chris established her real name it was just a matter of time until he located her in Savannah, Georgia. Interestingly, Annabelle was a nurse herself, and that combined with her somewhat less than common name had allowed Chris to track her through national nursing association databases.

Lisa was getting more and more excited with each of Chris' reports. She was actually going to meet her mother. Would Lisa look like her? Would they have anything in common? Would her mother even want to meet her? After all she *did* use a pseudonym at the hospital. Maybe she really didn't want to be found.

It was two days after receiving the information about finding her mother that Chris had called Lisa with the bad news.

"Good morning Miss A, Chris Hynes here."

"Good morning, Chris, and can't you call me Lisa?" Lisa had been trying repeatedly to encourage Chris to call her by her first name, but he continued to resist. It made Lisa feel old. Her voice was a little groggy as it was only 8AM on the west coast, and she was anything but a morning person. But it was 11AM in Savannah which is where Chris was.

"Yes, Ma'am. I'm afraid I have some bad news for you."

Lisa's heart nearly froze in her chest. There weren't too many options for what this bad news might be, coming at this juncture from Chris. She tried to steel herself, but there was a tremor in her voice that she could hear.

"I'm listening," she almost whispered.

"I've located your mother in a cemetery plot on the outskirts of Savannah. She died eighteen months ago. I understand it was a mugging, and Annabelle fought back. The assailant hit her in the head with the butt of his gun and ran. She bled to death before the police finally arrived."

"Oh my God."

"I'm sorry Miss ... uh ... Lisa." There was compassion in Chris' voice. He was a younger agent and not very experienced in relaying this type of news.

A soft whimper began from Lisa and to his credit Chris waited quietly on the line while she composed herself. He didn't have to wait too long.

"Any other leads on my father?" She finally asked in a reasonably composed tone.

"Yes, Ma'am, one of our other agents is running down some information on him in Denver. We should have an answer on that in another few days. Also, we've found a close friend of your mom's who we're told might have access to some of her personal affects."

~

A week later she received an unexpected call from Chris.

"Hello?" Lisa answered in what, to Chris, probably seemed like her normal sleepy voice.

"Good morning, Lisa. This is Chris. I have some rather surprising news for you."

The agency had already told her that her father had passed away as well from lung cancer. Therefore, Lisa's mind snapped to attention at his words and the drowsy sounds dropped abruptly from her voice. "I'm listening."

"We just found out you have a full brother."

A tingling warmth radiated through her at the amazing news. For a moment she couldn't even speak then she finally asked, "How is that possible? And does he know?"

CHAPTER

Mid-June

Sean had kept his honeymoon plans secret from Kira. She loved surprises and since she had already been all over the world, anywhere Sean might pick was just fine with her. Besides seeing how excited he was to be getting to plan a surprise for her was almost as good as whatever the surprise itself was going to be.

They had had to wait almost a week after the wedding to leave on Sean's surprise honeymoon. He said it was the best scheduling he could get for what he wanted to do, given the wedding date. When they did finally leave Sean had ushered Kira out to the car with nothing in his or her hands.

"Sean, don't we need luggage?"

"Yep. Already packed and in the back." Kira's surprise was growing by the moment and she could see Sean was relishing it.

"You packed my suitcase, too?" Surprise battled curiosity both on her features and in her thoughts.

"Yep," he answered as he opened the door for her and kissed her before she could get in.

"Do I even get a hint?"

"Nope, but you can guess if you want." Mischief colored his tone heavily along with a little boy smile that made Kira smile back.

"You'll tell me if I guess?"

Her curiosity was so powerful now she could practically see it hanging in the air. Sean wasn't much better. Just by his movements she could see that he felt as giddy as a school kid on the first day of summer vacation. "Maybe. It depends on how quickly you guess something."

Kira was quiet for a moment thinking. "Hawaii?" she finally ventured.

"Nope."

"Paris?"

"Nope." His mischievous grin broadened and touched his hazel eyes.

"Ah come on Sean, I want to know."

In response, Sean just turned toward her and grinned.

Silence reigned for a few minutes as the truck tires crunched on the gravel road before Sean finally added, "You're really going to like it."

Kira just grinned back. "Fine. I'll wait.

A few minutes later, when highway 69 intersected with 435 Sean took the ramp to the east.

"This isn't the way to the airport," Kira observed.

"No, it isn't."

"We're not going to the airport?"

"Nope."

"So, we're driving somewhere for our honeymoon?"

"Partially," Sean answered cryptically.

"OK I'll quit asking."

They both enjoyed the urban scenery going by as Sean navigated them up by the Chiefs stadium and onto Interstate 70 east.

~

Sean had been managing to stay out of Kira's head as he had been thinking about details he had in place for their trip, so it caught him a bit by surprise when Kira spoke up again on a completely different topic.

"Sean, you know I wouldn't really quit doing my paintings, right?"

He turned to her to observe the sudden serious look on her face. "I didn't really think you would but some of your comments lately have made me wonder."

"Well, I understand that, but if I can't express my fears to you then who can I tell?"

Sean smiled. "I certainly understand that."

"And anyway, with you being able to join me in my visions, some of those concerns are gone. Besides I don't think I could live with myself if I quit offering my abilities to the public. For all the fear I've . . . we've had to endure, the responses I get from my paintings are too wonderful to stop."

"And your courage is merely one more reason that I love you," Sean replied.

Kira leaned over and grabbed his shoulder and kissed him on the cheek. "And your ability to understand is just one more reason I love you . . . now where are we going?"

Sean laughed out loud. "Nice try."

The time flew by as they continued east talking about everything from previous paintings, to plans for the future, to their new home. At length Sean took a turn as they approached the outskirts of St. Louis.

They had already passed the airport exit on the west side of St. Louis when Kira tried again. "So, you're taking me to St. Louis for our honeymoon?"

"Briefly," Sean answered with a broad grin.

Kira's curiosity peaked when Sean passed the I-55 cutoff and proceeded toward downtown St. Louis. Her head swiveled from side to side looking for a clue and she felt Sean's eyes on her, drinking in her curiosity.

She held her questions in check until Sean exited at the Laclede's Landing exit. The streets promptly turned to brick cobblestone and the antique buildings lining them made Kira think of the French Quarter.

The next turn brought them back to concrete roads and when Sean finally turned in to the Hyatt Regency hotel Kira couldn't contain it any longer.

"So, we were coming to St. Louis after all," Kira began.

"Well, yes. Briefly, like I said."

"Come on, Sean," Kira pleaded. "Tell me."

"Well, we're staying here tonight, and when we get checked in, I'll tell you the rest."

They checked into their room which turned out to be an ultramodern suite on the top floor with clean lines, muted but tasteful earth tones, and a magnificent view of the Mississippi river, much of downtown St. Louis, and the famous Arch.

Sean was conspicuously quiet as he opened the door for Kira and motioned her into the room. Champagne was in an ice bucket on a nearby table and two glasses. A small plate beside it featured strawberries and chocolate.

"Oh Sean!" Kira gasped. "This is magnificent." She turned to kiss him, but he held her back much to her surprise.

"A toast first," he said smiling broadly again.

Kira smiled back and accepted the glass he offered after popping the cork on the Dom Perignon.

"To the most amazing wife any man could ever wish for," Sean stated holding up his glass.

"To the most extraordinary husband to share incredible adventures with," Kira responded.

"I'll drink to that." Sean answered. They hooked arms and drew the fine crystal glasses to their lips.

Upon setting down the glasses Sean swept Kira into his arms and kissed her deeply. Four hands promptly began seeking clothing fasteners as they side-stepped towards the king size bed. Their ardor was enough to raise the temperature in the room as their passion for each other found release in their intertwined bodies. The next few hours flew by in fevered intensity each seeking and finding more and more ways to delight the other.

Kira rolled onto her back in a breathless collapse. "OK, now I want you to tell me where we're going."

Sean laughed out loud. "OK, that's a dirty trick. Your curiosity really is killing you. Isn't it?"

"You said you'd tell me once we got to the room," she pressed presenting him with a marvelous faux pout.

"Fine," he said, letting his own breathing return to normal. "We're taking a Riverboat cruise down to New Orleans for a several-day stay at the Royal Sonesta in the French Quarter."

"Oh Sean," Kira exclaimed delightedly, while she rolled back on top of him "That's where you stayed when we first met."

"Yes, it is," he answered simply. "Unless, that is, you work me to death before we ever make it to the Riverboat."

"Oh, I think you'll be able to handle it. Otherwise what's the use in marrying a big, strong country boy?"

Their carnal play resumed at a fevered pitch. It was a testimony to their passion that Kira didn't even think to ask any more details about the trip before they both fell asleep, exhausted, in each other's arms.

They awoke at 7AM the next morning and Sean told Kira they'd have to be to the dock by 9AM. They showered and dressed quickly. There was little to pack as Sean had packed an extra small suitcase for them both just for this night. The breakfast downstairs was wonderful but hurried. Still, they made it easily to the dock by 8:45AM.

"Whew, that was a bit of a rush," Kira said pulling her long thick hair up into a ponytail.

"True, but it's about the only rushing we *have* to do the entire trip. Unless of course we change some plans."

Before Sean could say anything else, Kira looked up and saw their transportation. "Oh my gosh! It's a stern-wheeler!"

Sean beamed. "Cool, huh? I've always wanted to go on one of these things."

"Me too!" Kira answered. "I've never been on one before."

"You're kidding?" Sean replied displaying earnest surprise. "I didn't think I could possibly come up with anything you hadn't done before."

"Ah come on. You started the trip out that way."

"What?" The puzzled look on Sean's face delighted Kira.

"I've never been on a honeymoon before, especially one with you." That earned her a kiss before Sean picked up the two large suitcases and began to make his way to the gangplank.

Kira had to walk fast to keep up with his animated gate. She could tell how excited he was and not for the first time she found herself wishing she could sense emotions like he could.

The sternwheeler was a magnificent anachronism. It's four levels were a brilliant white with the sternwheel itself, along with several accents, painted bright red. Images of Mark Twain's world could not be avoided when gazing on the lovely old river cruiser.

They boarded and were promptly greeted. A fresh-faced young porter with a smattering of freckles took the suitcases from Sean with a quick, "follow me please," whereupon they both had to hurry to keep up.

They settled in for the seven-night trip down to New Orleans which included stops in Memphis, Vicksburg, Natchez, Mississippi, and Baton Rouge before reaching port in New Orleans.

It was a magnificent sojourn. All of the passing scenery was so deeply reminiscent of history that it made Kira nostalgic about all of her recent changes, not the least of which was her new marriage to this extraordinary man and how that, and her new career, had made her former life seem like a dim memory. But for all the lovely sights, nothing lit up Kira's eyes like the French Quarter coming into view as they prepared to dock in the Crescent City. It was late afternoon.

"Being back here almost feels like coming full circle, doesn't it Sean?"

~

Sean could see, hear, and sense the excitement and contentment emanating from Kira. The sensations flowed over him like a first sip of delicate champagne and elicited a curious look from Kira that finally jolted him back to the moment and a reply.

"It really does," he said simply, but the grin on his face belied the simple response.

They took a cab to the Royal Sonesta and checked in.

"We have time to take a shower if you want and to change, but I have a fairly early dinner reservation at Arnaud's this evening," Sean said as he moved the bags onto the portable stands by the wall.

They both opted to walk to Arnaud's after freshening up, and Kira's clear blue eyes sparkled at all the familiar sights and smells around her. Sean felt the entire trip was worth it just for these few seconds of sharing her private revelry. He hadn't really considered all the new feelings he would have as a result of being a new husband, but everything beyond Kira's delight was simply icing on the cake. He couldn't get the grin off his face as they approached the wrought iron gate that protected the gorgeous mahogany and brass entrance to Arnaud's. Sean reached for the door to open it for his new bride but was foiled by the conscientious doorman who must have perceived their approaching shadow. They entered, both sporting giddy grins, and approached the hostess station.

"Reservations for two under Easton," Sean said to the hostess. With a quick glance down at Kira's hand the alert woman responded. "Right this way Mr. and Mrs. Easton."

Kira grinned at the appellation and glanced up to see Sean smiling back at her as he took her hand and followed the hostess to their table.

The evening lighting offered a golden glow to the white ceilings and linen tablecloths that draped over the small tables, adding to the patina of history that infused the entire restaurant. The hostess stopped at a little table by a window and two tables away from the three-piece jazz band that was setting up for the evening.

"Perfect," Sean said as the hostess pulled Kira's chair out for her and laid the menus on the table.

"Your server will be here momentarily," the hostess offered and left with a smile.

Sean and Kira sat, their hands reaching across the little table to hold each other's, eyes locked.

"This is perfect, Sean. Coming here was a brilliant idea."

"I'm glad you like it Mrs. Easton. We're going to hit Pat Obrien's one of these evenings as well."

"Of course, we are," she answered, as she leaned across the table and met him for a kiss.

~

The entire rest of the honeymoon was a whirlwind of joyous memories, shared new experiences, and love making. A week later they began their six-day trip back up the Mississippi and although it was equally wonderful, they still both thought the three weeks they'd allotted seemed way too short. When they finally off-loaded back in St. Louis Sean sensed from Kira what he was already feeling. Not even a lifetime would be enough.

Late June

The first challenge Arthur expected was to actually be able to find Elliot and the lab where he worked.

Then there would be the obstacle of getting him alone. Next, he would just have to hope his abilities were honed enough to compel Elliot's cooperation.

As it turned out finding the lab was easy. Its name had been included in the television broadcast and, much to Arthur's surprise, there was an address listed for it on the internet. Arthur had scouted the place for days and had been unable to detect anyone else going in or out of the building besides Elliot. Did he really work alone? After spending some more time working on his skills, he decided the time was right.

It was mid-morning on a Tuesday when he knocked on Elliot's door.

~

"Come in," Elliot called across the room. He was in the middle of a tricky experiment and he wasn't expecting anyone. He made no effort to keep the annoyance from his voice. Additionally, he was a touch curious. No one ever came to his lab.

A skinny, pale man in a ridiculous shirt stepped into the lab and closed the door behind him. When he spoke, his voice was surprisingly melodic in contrast to his gaunt appearance, but his tone seemed vaguely malicious and, for some reason he couldn't name, it raised the hairs on the back of Elliot's neck.

"Elliot Drake I presume?"

"Yes. And who would you be?" Elliot answered coldly.

"You can call me Arthur."

Elliot turned back to his experiment and lowered the flame under the cylindrical beaker. "What can I do for you, Arthur?"

"I'm interested in your cancer research," Arthur stated flatly.

"Are you a researcher?" Elliot asked, still without turning around.

"No," Arthur answered, "I am a brain cancer victim."

Now Elliot turned abruptly. "A victim?"

"Yes. I have terminal brain cancer, and I want to use your research to try to effect a cure."

Elliot's mouth sagged. The idea that a cancer patient would hunt him down for a potential cure was astonishing, especially at this stage of his work's progress.

"Arthur, my research is just that, research, it's not ready for clinical trials much less human ones, and even if I wanted to try helping you, it's illegal. Frankly, even if it wasn't illegal, I would need more money to procure materials to try it."

"Let me put it to you this way," Arthur began, "I'm dying and I don't give a damn about the legality of it, and I'll try to help you with the money issue but you're going to help me."

"Oh really?" Elliot answered feeling his ire rise. "Why the hell would I do that? Are you threatening me?"

"As a matter of fact, I am," Arthur stated and at that moment exercised his ability to constrict a particular vein in Elliot's brain.

"Aaah!" Elliot responded reaching for his temple with both hands. It felt like he was being hit with a ball peen hammer. The pain was so sudden and intense that Elliot couldn't even think to form a reaction. A couple of seconds passed before Elliot could speak. "Did you just do that?"

"Yes, and that was just a small example of what I'll do if you don't help me. Think about it carefully. I'll be back." With that Arthur turned and marched straight out the door.

Elliot stood still, continuing to rub his right temple and trying to fathom what had just happened. He had a horrible feeling that his life might have just taken a turn for the worse.

CHAPTER

Late-July

Lisa had all the information she needed. She had Elliot's number and his schedule. All she had to do was screw up the nerve to make the call. A full brother! It still seemed just impossible. And maybe even just as incredible, he had no idea she existed either, at least that was the information she got from the detective agency.

Her glance took in the whole room. It was a quaint little beach house but full of memories; it had been a place of refuge from a time gone by when life had been full of struggle and hope. Now it was more of a memory than a home, but she had kept it all these years anyway. Though she didn't come here much anymore, making this phone call from here gave her a sense of reassurance. She got up from the tall kitchen stool and crossed into the den, plopping down on the plush leather couch with her phone clutched in her hand. She took a deep breath as she pulled the small scrap of paper from her front pocket. She read the number again, noticing the slight tremble in her hand. It was another slight shock to find out that her unknown brother lived nearby in LA. What were the chances of that? She wondered briefly if this was a good time to call him. It was 10AM. Was he too busy to talk in the mornings? Would he even pick up? Maybe she should wait and call him in the evening? No that wouldn't work, her husband would expect her to be home, and she really wanted to make her first call from this place.

It occurred to her that she was looking for excuses to put this call off. *No*, she thought. She'd put it off long enough. A little more than a whole month of procrastination was ridiculous, and she was not going to allow herself any more time for excuses. It needed to be now, and she was going to do it.

With an increasing tremor she punched in the number. Three rings later she was ready to hang up and was just about to hit the button when someone answered:

"This is Elliot."

The voice was strong, and Lisa immediately detected a note of detachment as though he was preoccupied, along with a hint of annoyance. Sometimes she wished she was a little less intuitive.

"Hello, Elliot. I'm sorry to bother you at work. My name is Lisa Anderson and I got your number from a detective agency I hired. I believe I have a bit of surprising news for you. I . . ."

"Look if this is some kind of a sales call, I really don't have the time or the interest so . . . "

"No. This is not a sales call," Lisa could feel her pulse accelerate. This wasn't going as she had hoped. She hesitated until realizing he might hang up. "I'm your sister," She blurted out. The ensuing silence seemed to stretch out forever. She desperately wanted to say something to fill the silence but had no clue what to add until he responded.

"What do you mean my sister? I don't even know who my father is. You couldn't possibly be my sister."

Now Lisa didn't hesitate, "Your mother was Annabelle Kravitz and she passed away in Savanna, Georgia just recently. And I can tell you who your father is as well." She hurried on before he could respond or she lost her nerve, "But if it's OK with you I'd prefer to tell you the rest of the story in person."

Another interminable silence lay across the phone connection. Lisa was beginning to wonder if he was still on the line when he finally responded.

"Um, yeah. My mother passed away? I haven't seen or heard from her in years. If this is for real, I'd be glad to meet you . . . I guess when and where?"

Lisa hadn't considered the possibility that he would want to meet right away. She had envisioned getting to know him on the phone first.

"Um . . . wow. I . . . uh let me look at my calendar," she pulled the phone from her ear and scanned through her calendar app before continuing, "I'm booked pretty solid for the next three weeks on some major projects. How about the last week in August?" This was not the first time that her success had interfered with her personal life. The long pause caused her to fear him backing out.

"Uh . . . sure. That would be fine. I'm actually pretty buried myself."

Lisa was certain she heard disappointment in his voice but at least he wasn't pulling away.

"OK. Great," she responded.

The arrangements were made to meet at a Starbucks near the end of August and only when she hung up the phone did she realize that tears were streaming down her face. She had talked to her only brother.

CHAPTER

Early August

The woman screamed and yanked on the wheel of her mother-of-pearl colored Audi A8 causing it to swerve sharply into the right-hand railing that blocked vehicles from colliding with the cliff side. The car struck at such an angle that it rebounded back into the far-left lane and was clipped by a large navy-blue Acura SUV. The entire mass of metal careened into the left side railing slow enough by this time for the rail to stop both cars.

Arthur turned away and began walking back down the sloping side street. He was smiling broadly. It was another successful trial. He gave no further thought to the fate of either driver. If the woman was dead, so much the better; it would be one less beautiful, arrogant, female on the planet to mock his existence.

His goal this time had been to see if he could restrict the blood flow to the optic nerves at a distance of seventy feet or so and, judging by the woman's reaction, he had either accomplished his goal or something very close to it. He was finding himself able to affect smaller and smaller portions of the human anatomy. Additionally, it seemed that the smaller the object he was trying to manipulate the greater the distance at which he could affect it. Next time he'd have to try something from a hundred feet.

The bright sunlight warmed his back as he continued down the hill to his car. Sirens were already approaching in the distance. One of them was surely an ambulance.

Good, he thought. *If I'd only started a little sooner, I wouldn't have missed the morning traffic and could have produced a much bigger collision.* All in all, though, he felt tremendously cheered.

Not only were his own experiments going well, but the sniveling scientist was making progress, too. He imagined he'd be cured of this damn death sentence in short order. Apparently, some foundation had donated some funding for his project and his experiments were proceeding well. Arthur decided to go buy himself a bottle of champagne to celebrate. It was a wondrous day.

CHAPTER

Late August

Lisa arrived at the Starbucks early. She was trying to mentally prepare herself. Calm herself was more to the point. In all her years
she wasn't sure she had ever experienced this level of excitement and
nervousness at the same time. The long wait hadn't helped abate her
anticipation. She had hoped that being buried in her work would distract her, but it had done just the opposite. And to make matters worse
her decision to wait to tell her husband about the whole development
until after this meeting was weighing on her.

She wanted to be sure Elliot wasn't a creep before she made him an
official part of her life by telling the man she loved. But the decision
was haunting her a bit. Telling him always seemed to make things real.
Fortunately, he had been as busy as she was and they had barely had
time to talk for the last several weeks, but it still bothered her. Honesty
had always been a hallmark of their relationship and though she wasn't
telling him any lies, keeping this from him still smacked of deception.
And now, to top it all off, she just found out he would be leaving for
work again and wouldn't be back for about two weeks. So, the news
would have to wait even longer. It was torture.

She glanced down at her Grande mocha trembling slightly in her
hands, then back up at the door he would be entering. The sounds and
smells of Starbucks were familiar to her and this was an area of town
where she would be less noticed. She'd picked one of the overstuffed
leather chairs back in the corner. It was as far away as she could get
from everyone else and still be able to see the door. There was a second
identical chair next to her and a little round table in front. She glanced

at her phone on the arm of her chair; 3:15PM it read; the time Elliot would arrive. Elliot Drake. Her brother. The words sounded strange in her mind. She'd been testing them out repeatedly, but they still felt foreign.

She marveled again at the possibility of having a full brother out there all these years and having no idea.

The door opened and her heart skipped a beat, but it was two women who didn't even glance her way. A little stab of disappointment clutched at her heart and she took another sip of her drink. She had barely set the cup down when the door chimed again as it was opened.

She fixed her gaze on the tall, lanky, blonde-haired man as he paused at the front door. He gazed around the store until his eyes locked on hers. It was Elliot. They both knew it the minute they locked eyes, and a smile bloomed on his face as he walked purposefully in her direction. This was the moment she had been waiting for and fearing at the same time. What if he didn't like her after they met?

"You must be Lisa," he said as he reached out his hand. She stood out of reflex to take his offered handshake, though her blue eyes remained locked on his brown ones.

Like our mother's, she thought.

"Yes. Elliot, it's so great to finally meet you." Lisa stared into Elliot's eyes momentarily. "You don't recognize me, do you?"

Elliot looked confused, "I'm sorry, should I?"

"I'm actually glad you don't. I should start by telling you that my real name, or rather my name now, is Angelie. I changed it from Lisa when I began acting. I'm a musician and an actor. I've done quite a few movies." Understanding swept through Elliot's eyes.

"Ah. That explains it. I'm a science nerd who doesn't really date and rarely leaves my lab. I don't even remember the last time I saw a movie."

~

Elliot stared into Lisa's eyes. Emotions were not his strong suit but meeting this person whose eyes, he now realized, were just like his in shape, though blue instead of brown, was having a rather profound effect on him. It had been many years since he had thought of family, since he didn't speak to his mother and had had none besides her left, but now he realized there was a part of him that was more than intrigued to meet someone genetically related to him. Moments later when his coffee arrived Elliot noticed another similarity. He had a tendency to rotate his silverware horizontally in his hand when he held it, and after he stirred in his creamer he looked up and noticed Lisa doing the same thing over her second cup.

"Where did you learn to do that?" Elliot asked.

Lisa looked down at the motion her right hand was playing on the spoon. She promptly stopped and looked back up at Elliot.

"I don't know," she said. "But I think I've done it most of my life."

"Me too," he responded. "I don't know where I learned it either."

That little connection seemed to speak louder than words and made the conversation flow noticeably better.

~

Lisa had the distinct impression that a missing piece of her life was finally fitting into the puzzle. After a mere twenty minutes Elliot excused himself.

"I'm sorry to have to rush off Lisa . . . er Angelic . . . What would you prefer I call you anyway?"

"Why don't we just stick to Lisa? It seems more appropriate somehow."

"Great. Lisa, I have some experiments I need to get back to, but maybe we could get together again soon for a longer conversation."

"That sounds wonderful. I know just the place. I'll email you if that's OK."

"Sounds great. I'll look forward to it. I really am excited to get to know my only sister," he said as he scribbled his email on a card.

"I know the feeling," she responded.

With that he stood, and she mirrored him. He reached to shake her hand, but she stepped in to hug him. "We've got a lot of catching up to do," she virtually whispered.

He pushed back; his eyes gleaming. "I look forward to it," he said, and turned to walk away.

Tears welled in Lisa's eyes as she watched him go. "I have a brother," she murmured to herself.

~

The entire encounter affected Elliot so profoundly that he realized halfway back to the lab that going back there would be futile. It never occurred to him that finding out he had a sister would affect him so acutely.

As an additional surprise, he realized that talking to her for the first time on the phone had nowhere near the impact that meeting her in person had elicited. Even with the specter of Arthur looming over him he decided to take the rest of the day and tomorrow off to consider the ramifications of his new discovery.

CHAPTER

Early September

A rthur listened to the door of Elliot's lab close behind him. He was convinced now, more than ever, that Elliot's work was going to be his salvation.

He just had to find a way to get Elliot some more money since the miserable nerd had already blown through the foundation money and hadn't been able to raise any more himself. That was his next problem.

In the meantime, he needed Elliot to be more motivated. Who was this woman he had been to see? The bug he'd planted in the lab had kept him much more informed than he would have expected. Who knew Elliot spent that much time in the lab? Still, he had gleaned nothing about the woman. Maybe Elliot was telling the truth when he said she had left the country. Arthur doubted it. He felt certain Elliot would be going to meet this person again and when he did Arthur would be there. Maybe this would be the leverage to assure Elliot's complete cooperation.

Arthur walked down the street with a smile on his face that would have scared most children. His pale blue eyes gleamed with an unholy light.

It's working, he thought. All those years of suffering at the hands of women and life, and now he was getting his revenge.

It was just beginning to occur to him that there might be some monetary reward to figure into his efforts. He could do more than just hurt these haughty bitches; he should be able to earn a living from them as well, maybe even some sexual gratification.

Not to mention the fact that a financial windfall could also be used to hurry up Elliot's efforts toward a cure for his cancer. A walk to the beach would give him some time to think and maybe even spot some new targets.

How was he going to get money from these women and not get caught? Finding the wealthy ones in this part of the world was not the issue.

They were all rich or married to someone that was. But getting to them, finding them while they were alone, *that* was the trick. And was he just interested in taking the money that they were carrying or was there some larger goal he could aspire to? Getting into their homes maybe . . .

~

The next couple of months were spent settling into their new home, getting Aubrey moved into the trailer, running the farm, and generally acclimating themselves to their new life as man and wife. The days were already getting intermittently milder while they became shorter and Autumn was on the verge of asserting itself over the summer heat.

In the interim, Aubrey made it his mission to get to know Kira better. Anytime Sean was busy with the horses or working elsewhere, Aubrey would steal the chance to talk to her.

"It really doesn't bother you that Sean can read your thoughts?" He asked her.

Kira was busy cleaning up the kitchen, but she turned and gave Aubrey a tender but appraising look. Prior to him moving into the trailer she hadn't really had the chance to interact much with him. But now she was finding his increased attention not only interesting, but charming. As she answered his question, she considered the fact that he too, could read her emotions, which was fine with her because she was feeling increasingly close to him. She almost absent mindedly finished her rendition of her adjustment to Sean's abilities and turned back to smile at him.

"That's great. You two are just wonderful together. I'm so happy you found each other."

Kira stared for a second and smiled. "How are you feeling today?"

"Oh, I'm fine," he answered blithely.

With another quick gaze she decided that he was probably telling the truth. He was spending so much more time with Sean that she imagined hiding his feelings wouldn't even enter his mind.

Also, Kira had noticed the increased intensity of the conversations between he and Sean and the smiles that always resulted. It made her heart warm to get to see her new husband's new-found familial joy. Maybe even a bit jealous.

"Have you tried to think a thought to him yet?" Aubrey offered interrupting her mental meandering.

"What?" Kira asked turning to him again.

"Think a thought at him. I tried it at the wedding. It works well."

"Really?" she responded. "I'll have to remember that." A smile blossomed on her face as she considered it.

"I'm going to head back out to the trailer," Aubrey said somewhat suddenly. And before Kira could question if he was feeling OK again, he slipped out the back door.

CHAPTER

Early October

Angelie was dead. Brian Paré broke into sobs again. The sound echoed in the huge, window-lined den of his Laguna Beach Estate. It had been three weeks since his Angelie had died, but he was still wracked with pain. For a couple of successful movie stars, they had experienced what so many seek and never find. True love. Her sudden passing had been such a shock that he had mostly isolated himself in their beautiful home. He only left to tie some loose ends to which he was already obligated.

At least the isolation had the positive effect of separating him from the media and as a result the myriad of articles running in the tabloids didn't have any of those detestable pictures of him breaking down. When it came to private emotions the media had no heart whatsoever.

The more pain they could capture on film, the more tabloids would run it. No regard was given for how much emotional damage that might cause the poor saps who stared out from those publications with reddened eyes, tears, and horror on their faces. The public should get to see! Right?

Well, Brian had resolved they weren't going to see him that way, and lately that included most of the time. He would be perfectly fine then something would sharply remind him of her and he'd breakdown all over again. The doctors had called it a heart attack . . . but she'd always been so healthy.

He raised his head from his hands and glanced over at the tremendous fireplace. The urn sat on the floor to the left of it as a sort of decoration. The urn itself was a work of art in fine china with gold leaf trimming.

At least that sight wasn't still causing him to break down, but he did have a lingering sense of wrongness when he looked at it. Angelie wouldn't have wanted to be in an urn, even though she had requested cremation, she hadn't specified what she wanted done with the cremains.

Maybe I should just scatter the ashes somewhere, Brian thought for the thousandth time, but he couldn't bring himself to part with her. Maybe someday he'd be able to, but certainly not now.

Wiping his tear streaked face on his sleeve, he walked toward the kitchen to pour himself a brandy. He took it and went into the den to sit down at his computer. Brian had a habit of checking out the obituaries for any actors that might have passed away when an Ad popped up on the screen: Canvas of Life- Memorialize your loved one in a painting using their ashes.

"That's it," he said out loud reflecting the weight of his epiphany, and with no further thought he reached for his phone.

~

The phone call came in after 5PM. Sean was still out in the barn, so Kira answered while frowning at the Los Angeles area code that she recognized from her modeling days.

"Hello?" she began tentatively.

"Is this Kira McGovern?"

Kira thought briefly about correcting the caller with her new name but thought better of it. She didn't even know who this was at this point. "Yeees?" she replied tentatively.

"I'm calling about your Canvas of Life business . . . is this the right number?"

Kira had completely forgotten that she had forwarded her business line to their home phone earlier in the day. She promptly modified her tone, removing the suspicion pervading it.

"Yes, this is the right number for Canvas of Life. You'll have to pardon me, I was in the middle of something, and momentarily forgot I had my business line forwarded. What can I do for you?"

"No problem. My name is Brian Paré, and I was wondering if I could meet with you about doing a painting for me."

Kira was shocked. She wasn't a big movie buff, but she knew enough to recognize one of the highest profile names in the movie industry.

"Angelie? Is this about Angelie?" She finally asked, "I was so sorry to hear about your loss."

Even over the phone Kira could hear the strain in Brian's voice. "Yes, it's about her. I was hoping you might come and visit my home and discuss it with me. I feel like it's something that should be discussed in person, and I can't travel very easily as you might imagine."

The idea of going to the movie star's home qualified, in Kira's mind, as an adventure of the highest order, and she focused on trying not to sound overly excited when she answered.

"Um, well, I don't usually travel to my client's homes, but let me check with my husband."

"I have a better idea," Brian offered, "Why don't you and your husband both come? And bring your materials as well. As a matter of fact, if I can talk you into it, I'd love to have you do the painting here in my house. You can both stay here while you work, if you'd like. You and your husband could mix business with pleasure. My house really is a rather entertaining place to hang out. Or if you would feel more comfortable with it, I can pay for you both to stay at a hotel nearby and have you driven here every day."

He stopped speaking rather suddenly and Kira was too flabbergasted to quickly respond.

Brian must have read the hesitation as a negative indication, so before she could respond, he added, "Mrs. McGovern, I can pay you $200 thousand for the painting. Please say yes."

"Brian," she began breathlessly, "that figure is many, many times what I normally charge. I don't know if can . . ."

"Please, I have been suffering with conflicting thoughts of what to do with Angelie's ashes for weeks now. She absolutely would not have wanted her remains to be in an urn, but I just can't bring myself to scatter the last remnant of the only woman I've ever loved and have nothing to show for it or to visit. If your work can solve that dilemma it is worth much more to me than what I'm offering."

His impassioned plea tipped her over the edge. How could she say no? The opportunity was just too big on too many levels to let pass.

"When would you like us to come out?" She finally offered.

"Whenever you like. As soon as possible. Just tell me."

"OK. Let me talk to my husband about times, and I'll call you back this afternoon. Is that OK? Oh, and one more question if you don't mind me asking?"

"Sure, anything."

"What was the cause of death?"

"She had a heart attack."

There was just a touch of ice in his tone that caused Kira to respond hurriedly to his answer.

"I'm sorry to have to ask, but I seem to end up having a connection to the person whose ashes I'm painting with, and if there were any strange circumstances surrounding the death I prefer to know ahead of time."

"I understand," he replied, but again his tone implied otherwise, so Kira rushed to change the subject.

"Alrighty then. I'm sure Sean won't have an issue with this, and I'll get back with you as soon as possible with a schedule."

"That's perfect. And thank you, Kira. I'm very excited to have this done." I simply love the concept.

They said their goodbyes and when Kira put the phone down, she felt like she had just awakened from a dream. "So, let me get this straight," she began, out loud to herself, "Sean and I are supposed to fly out to California and stay at one of the most famous actors in the world's house, and I am supposed to do a painting for him of one of the most famous actresses ever for which he's going to pay me a fortune, and I was hesitating? What am I, crazy?" She laughed at herself and jumped up from her seat.

"Sean!" She yelled as she flew through the back door towards the barn.

~

Sean had just come back from riding one of the horses he was caring for and was now removing the tack and starting to curry the horse down when he heard the yell. Instinctively he reached out with his feelings, though just the tone in her voice told him she was excited about something and not in distress. He was just setting the curry comb down when she rounded the corner and flew into his arms. The embrace was short lived, however, as she immediately pushed back.

"Whew, you smell like sweaty horse!"

"Ya think? Since I've just been riding and grooming one, I'm not surprised. What are you all excited about?"

"How would you feel about us taking a little time and go to Hollywood and stay in a movie star's house? Maybe a week or two?"

"What are you talking about? Stay at a movie star's house? How did you come up with this?"

"One of the biggest movie stars in Hollywood just hired me to come to his house and do a painting for him of his deceased wife, but if you don't want to come I can . . ."

"Of course I want to come! When are we supposed to go, and who is it?"

His sudden shift threw her off balance. "Um, well . . . I guess as soon as possible. Is that OK?"

Sean paused to think a minute. "Yes. I'll have to call my flight instructor and cancel a few lessons but that's no biggie. The weather forecast is looking pretty nasty anyway. And then we'd need to ask John to check in on Dad from time to time, I wouldn't want him stranded out here alone. But since he's still feeling pretty well, I don't see why not! How long are we supposed to be there, and are they paying you any extra to do it there, I hope?"

Even as the words were coming out of his mouth, his other senses were picking up the intense excitement that was still wafting off her. It was all he could do to wait to let her tell him.

"Well, as to your first question, it is Brian Paré."

"Angelie's husband?" Sean interrupted.

"Yep. And as to your last question, he *is* offering me a bit more than I usually get: $200 thousand to be exact."

Her words hung in the air while Sean tried to swallow. His eyes continued to widen during the silence, however, and for a moment he looked like a frog trying to swallow an oversized bug.

"Two . . . you have to be kidding!"

"Nope. It's true. I didn't ask him for it. He offered. And then insisted."

"Good Lord. This is like getting a paid vacation after winning the lottery. When do we go?"

Before she could answer, Sean added, "Wait a minute. Did you ask if there were any strange circumstances surrounding her death? How did she die?"

"Sudden heart attack, and yes I did. Should be smooth sailing."

"Great," Sean said, smiling broadly, "In that case, when do we leave?"

Kira melted into him. "Did I mention I love you?" But his response was smothered by her kiss.

CHAPTER

When they stepped off the plane two days later Sean and Kira were greeted by a man in a chauffer's outfit holding a sign up that said "Kira McGovern".

"Did you mention to this guy that you were married?" Sean asked.

Kira could hear the discomfort under the humor in his voice. She may not have Sean's gifts, but it wasn't difficult to be sensitive to Sean. He was open, straight forward, and transparent in almost all instances. It was one of the many attributes she loved about him, and frankly his instinctive transparency made it *so* much easier to accept her own unwilling transparency via his mental gifts.

Mental gifts, she thought. How did she ever manage to find a person with abilities such as his?

If anyone had asked her if such a thing existed prior to meeting Sean she would have told them that they watched too many movies. Now she was married to a veritable psychic. Who was she kidding? If Sean was a psychic, she was a medium and judging by her experiences with her cousin, Poena, it ran in the family. It was all too crazy, and she hated the labels. The entirety of it made her former worldwide modeling career seem mundane by comparison.

The meandering of her thoughts had extended the timeframe since Sean had asked her the question.

"Hello? Kira? Are you in there?"

"I'm sorry, Sean. Of course, I told him I was married. I just didn't correct him on my name at the time."

"You don't like being an Easton?"

Sometimes Sean was still so much of a little kid, and she just loved him for it. She loved seeing the world again through his innocent eyes.

"Of course, I do! I *love* being an Easton, Sean. I'm thrilled about everything involved in being Kira Easton, but I spent quite a bit of money on advertising when I started Canvas of Life, and I just wasn't in the mood to correct Brian when I talked with him on the phone."

Kira wasn't quite sure if she heard a harrumph issue from his mouth or not because at that same instant the gentleman holding the sign addressed them.

"Mrs. McGovern?" he asked again politely.

"Actually, it's Mrs. Easton now," she answered holding up her ring finger.

She could almost feel the tension wane beside her as the words left her mouth. Maybe she *was* developing a bit of Sean's abilities.

"Yes, Ma'am. And this must be Mr. Easton?"

"That's me," Sean interjected.

The chauffer's smile was surprisingly genuine as he said, "My name is Jackson, and I'll be your driver. Your car is waiting, if you'll follow me."

Sean turned to Kira and raised his eyebrows then spoke in a near whisper, "We have a *car* waiting for us."

Kira nearly giggled.

~

The scenery on the way to Brian's house was California classic. Bad traffic and palm trees faded into rolling hills and pacific views. They were heading for Laguna Beach and the ride took longer than they had expected. The sun was low in the sky when the chauffer pulled onto the natural stone driveway. The house was predictably on a cliff with expansive views of the pacific as well as Catalina Island.

Sean's head was shifting from side to side as he tried to take in all the breathtaking visuals. Kira could see the little kid awe in his expression, and it tickled her so much that she had to grab his arm and pull him in close.

"Beautiful, huh?" She asked.

"Incredible is more like it."

Kira smiled again but it faded. The entire scene brought back memories of her modeling days, and those memories were always a mixed blessing at best. She'd already seen her share of exotic places and multimillion-dollar domiciles.

If Kira thought that Sean was excited before, she had to reevaluate now. The wonder on his face at even the appurtenances of the exterior of this mansion were reminiscent of a boy seeing his very first puppy.

"Kira, look at this driveway. It's all laid stones. Just the driveway must have cost a fortune."

"No doubt," she replied continuing to echo his smile.

The house was a white stucco, ranch style affair, whose main feature was the size and quantity of windows. It was obviously designed from the ground up with views to the pacific as its main attraction. Palm trees, brilliantly colored foliage, and a meticulously manicured lawn lined the stone driveway as the chauffer slowed, stopping just short of the garage door.

"You may enter through the front door, and I'll bring your luggage," Jackson said as he opened Kira's door for her.

"Thank you, Jackson," Kira answered then saw the expression on Sean's face. "Don't even think about tipping him," she said as she smoothly led him down the stone walkway toward the front door.

"Why not?" He asked as Sean turned his gaze up at the copper awning that overhung the porch.

"Because this isn't a hotel, and it would be an insult."

"Oh," Sean replied meekly as the front door seemingly opened by itself.

A wizened and stoic face stared out at them dressed not in some sort of tux but rather in a fairly casual, open collar white shirt and sandy sport coat. "Come in please Mrs. McGovern and guest. We have been expecting you."

"Easton," Sean said, "and I'm her husband."

"Yes, Sir. I'm sorry, Sir."

Sean's annoyance melted at the man's exaggerated politeness. "Oh, it's no problem," he said evincing his embarrassment at his own outburst.

"Please make yourselves comfortable, Mr. Paré will be with you shortly. May I get you something to drink? A soft drink or a cocktail maybe?"

"Maybe a couple of vodka tonics," Kira suggested.

"Yes Ma'am. I'll be right back."

When Kira turned back to Sean, he was still busy taking in the surroundings. They were seated on a heavy leather sofa that faced one set of the expansive windows. The ocean could be seen in the distance. It was a low-ceilinged room with one wall of bookshelves and a plush cream color rug. Around the edges, where the floor could be glimpsed, inlaid dark wood could be seen framing some sort of colored tile.

All in all, it was grand but not pretentious, Kira thought. That lack of pretention boded well for their working relationship with Mr. Paré.

The tinkling of ice cubes alerted Sean and Kira to the butler's return. They thanked him for the beverages and Kira's eyes roamed the massive room as she took her first sip. It was then that she spotted the urn sitting as a centerpiece on the table.

"There it is, Sean."

"There what is?"

"Angelie's remains."

"Oh," he said as his eyes followed her gaze across the room. "Nice urn."

"Aren't they all?" She replied.

"I just meant—"

"Good afternoon, everyone," Brian said as he breezed into the room, "I see Coulson has already gotten you beverages. Good."

Brian swept into the room with the grace of a dancer. His hair was black and reminiscent of Cary Grant down to the dark eyes and the cleft chin. It was no wonder the world found him so attractive.

"It's so nice to meet you, Brian," Kira replied as she flowed across the room toward him with an easy grace.

~

Sean watched her move across the floor and all of a sudden, he was reminded that his lovely new wife actually *was* an ex-supermodel, and in the same instant he felt inexperienced and out of place. Almost as a reflex he found himself reaching out to grab Brian's thoughts.

My, this woman is beautiful, floated into Sean's mind, and he had to stifle a wave of jealousy. After all, Brian's thought was just the simple truth, and there was no reason that the thought shouldn't have crossed his mind. Still, he couldn't help but stay to capture a few more thoughts.

If she's just as talented as she is beautiful then maybe, I'll get some peace from this whole thing.

"And you as well," he said taking her proffered hand. "I don't believe I've had the pleasure of meeting—"

"My husband," Kira interjected, "Sean Easton. This is Brian Paré."

"Nice to meet you, Sean."

Boy, she found herself one handsome farm-boy.

"Er . . . nice to meet you too, Mr. Paré." Sean was too flustered by the thought he had just garnered to maintain a semblance of composure. His ill ease came across as fluster at being in the presence of a star, which Brian was probably used to, but Kira was giving him a hard look. Before he got himself any deeper Sean took a deep breath and shook Brian's hand.

"Brian, please," he said smoothly as he returned Sean's slightly firm-er-than-necessary grip.

Brian abruptly turned his gaze back to Kira, and Sean caught a glimpse of something still lingering in her eyes.

Oh shit, he thought to himself, *she knows I was reading his thoughts. How does she know that?* He was still puzzling that one out as the conversation moved on. At this point he was just a fixture.

"So, Kira, do you think you can do something memorable with my Angelie's ashes?"

"I'll do my best, Brian."

He smiled and Sean had the thought that this particular smile was one he'd seen him use in many of his movies. It was his 'charmer' special. But that thought only led Sean to consider how much he actually *liked* this guy's movies. They were typically irreverent action films with at least a touch of humor, which reminded him that he really was in a movie star's house. Even though he wasn't the biggest fan of Hollywood, he *was* taken in by the idea of really being in a movie star's home.

"I'm sure you will," Brian responded smoothly, "Do you have any idea what the subject of the painting will be, or am I supposed to suggest something?"

"Well, you are more than welcome to suggest something, but

normally the topic of the painting comes to me when I'm actually working with the ashes."

"Really? This whole concept is just fascinating. How did you ever come up with the idea?"

They moved to a couch to sit, and Kira went into a rendition of how she had come up with the idea to use her mother's cremains. Sean was quickly tuning out as she went into detail on the story he knew so well. His gaze slid absently towards the massive bank of windows that showed the ocean in the distance over the roofs of some other homes.

"The view is amazing, isn't it?"

Sean's head snapped around to face Brian.

"Sorry, I've just heard her story so often and the view *is* breathtaking." His embarrassment faded instantly under the combined weight of both Brian's smile and the sensation of warmth radiating from the man. Sean was a bit taken aback to realize that Brian liked him. Maybe he was fond of farm-boys.

"Well, listen," Brian began, "I know you two have had a long trip and must be tired. Besides, I don't want either one of you to feel like you have to entertain me.

Please consider yourselves at home in my home. I'll have Coulson show you to your room"

"That's very considerate of you," Kira interjected, "We appreciate your gracious hospitality."

"Nonsense," Brian answered, "I'm the one dragging the two of you out of your homes to come here. The least I can do is make it comfortable for you. I actually have to run into the city to reshoot a scene they botched.

"Coulson can make dinner for you whenever you like, and Jackson will be here to drive you anywhere you'd like to go. Also, if the shooting runs late I might just stay the night there, so make yourself comfortable. Feel free to take a late-night dip in the pool. It's beautiful at night."

"Thanks again, Brian. Oh, and where would you like me to set up to paint?"

"You're the artist. You tell me."

Brian's 'charmer special' smile was there again, but as much as he expected it, Sean couldn't sense any falseness about it. Grudgingly, he accepted that he liked this guy as well.

"Well, if it's alright with you, I think I'd like to set up in here. I like the open space and the lighting is good."

"Perfect," he answered, "I'll have Coulson bring your supplies in here. Now if you'll excuse me, I really need to be heading to the studio."

With that, he angled toward the door and Sean and Kira found themselves standing there alone. Sean looked at Kira, but she was already moving toward the table with the urn on it. Sean followed quietly behind her. She hesitated in front of the table, and Sean stepped up beside her. She was reaching for the urn when Sean spoke.

"Kira, what do you—"

A sharp intake of breath from her cut him off, and she quickly replaced the urn back on the table.

"Oh my God," she breathed.

"What is it?"

"Fear and sorrow," she said.

"What?"

Kira turned to look into Sean's eyes. "Those ashes . . . when I touched the urn . . . Sean, it wasn't the emotions themselves that scares me, it's the intensity of them.

It was almost overwhelming. Oh Sean, what if she didn't die naturally?"

"But Brian said she died naturally. Of a heart attack, right?"

"I know he did."

Sean and Kira's eyes locked for several seconds.

Sean held a pensive expression for a moment. "Kira, you've never gotten a sensation from just touching an urn before. Why do you think you did this time?" For several seconds more they just stared at each other.

"Oh shit," he said finally, catching her feelings then her thought.

"I'm not doing it."

"And what are you going to tell Brian? Are you going to tell him that you're going to pass on his $200 thousand because you think his wife was the victim of foul play and you're too scared to see it through and find out what really happened? Hell, with an answer like that *he'll* probably haunt us for the rest of our lives. Not to mention he won't believe you."

Kira was silent for a moment as she absorbed the impact of his words.

"But, Sean, I don't think I can do it. Maybe we can just lie."

"Kira, I absolutely don't want you to do anything that you're really afraid of, or that might cause you harm. I love you too much to risk you for any reason, but you'll have me this time. *We* can get through it. You know I won't let anything happen to you. Besides, I can't think of a lie that would explain giving up that kind of money for a couple of weeks of work."

A sickly smile crept across her face. "I guess you're right. Alright, I'll try. Who knows? Maybe fear and sorrow were simply her response as she realized she was having a heart attack."

Sean sensed the mountain of fear blazing through her and he was awed by the courage she was showing. "I love you," was all he could get out.

"I love you, too."

~

Coulson brought them a meal on the back deck by the pool.

It was a deep blue, natural looking, stone lined affair, with a waterfall on one end comprised of a pile of flat stones and a vanishing edge on the far side. The views were as magnificent as any post card Sean had ever seen, even better than those from inside the house. They were both pensive as the sun set over the pacific. The sky just above the sun was burnt gold and the sun had dipped into a light indigo background just above the deep blue of the distant sea.

The orb itself was a variegated masterpiece changing from yellow to gold to blue to purple as it dipped into the ocean's deep azure. Sean could feel not only his own edginess but sense Kira's as well, and he knew it would be hard to sleep. Inadvertently, he snagged a thought from Kira.

I don't know how I'm going to be able to sleep.

Sean had to smile at their coincidence of thoughts. "Sorry, Kira," Sean said, "I snagged that thought. I was thinking the same thing. I have a good idea, though. Why don't we go for a swim? That should help us both sleep."

Kira ignored his admission of thought reading and responded directly. "That sounds like a great idea if the water's not too cold. And if it's not, I have an even better idea."

Sean was pleasantly surprised although initially timid of Kira's idea to skinny dip, but when she dropped her towel by the pool about fifteen minutes later, there was no way he was going to hesitate. His bathing suit was quickly forgotten by the edge as he dove into the tepid water and swam briskly over to Kira. The darkness had completely enveloped the pool area and the stars were rapidly transforming the sky into a tapestry of glowing pin pricks.

"Oooo, you feel gooood," he said pulling her close.

"You too," she answered returning his strong embrace. They kissed and a few seconds later she asked, "Do you think we can do this without drowning?"

Sean's smile encompassed his whole face. "I just love a challenge. On the other hand, there is a shallow end."

With that Kira wrapped her legs around him and enveloped his grin with her mouth.

~

Walking by the crackling fireplace toward the staircase, Kira smiled at the physical and spiritual warmth of their new house. It was getting late and Sean was waiting for her upstairs. They had had a wonderful evening, and she was looking forward to a good night's sleep. Her gaze lifted to the staircase in front of her, and she noticed something was wrong. The steps weren't carpeted; they were bare wood and in need of painting like some old farmhouse.

Hadn't she seen those somewhere before? She continued forward and put a foot on the first step. It creaked loudly, and she was again struck by the wrongness of it. The steps in her house were brand new. They couldn't be squeaking.

It was when she took the second step that something grabbed her from behind by the hair, and abruptly yanked her back.

"No!" she screamed. She was falling backward but twisting herself to try to see her attacker. Her head wouldn't turn far enough to look directly back, but she did catch a glimpse of one gloved hand . . .

"NOOOO!" Her shriek seemed to come from her very soul, and the volume increased by the second. Surely her head was about to strike the floor.

~

A monumental gasp rasped itself down her throat as Kira sat bolt upright in bed. Sean's arms were around her in a second and his sweet voice was echoing in her ears.

"It's OK, Kira. It's OK. I'm here."

Her fear melted in the warmth of his closeness, then abruptly turned to anger.

"Dammit, Sean! I don't want to *deal* with this anymore!"

"What? Did you dream about the painting?"

"Not this one. I had a nightmare about Jason, complete with gloved hands dragging me off a staircase."

Sean just sat there for a moment holding her and stroking her hair. He felt guilt. He had brought this particular nightmare into her life. How many times had he done exactly this, held her and soothed her after some terrible nightmare or vision? He understood her feelings, could deeply feel them with her as a matter of fact, but he could not imagine these horrific experiences actually stopping her from expressing her gift. Every bad experience she'd dealt with since beginning this business had led to a positive benefit for someone.

In her case, dealing with the dead gave the living some very positive relief. On the other hand, who was he to force her to continue to live through these horrific experiences? It made him feel selfish.

"I'm sorry, Honey," was all he could get out.

He felt her relax in his arms and felt the tension drain away.

"I'll be OK," she said with her head on his chest, "It just gets tiresome being afraid of sleeping."

"I wish I could do something more to help," Sean replied.

"You do. You always do. You're there to wake me up, or there when I do wake up to make me feel safe and remind me of what's really important."

"And what's that?" he asked feeling both intrigued and proud of her at the same moment. His courageous wife.

"Why you, of course, and helping others when I can."

"Why don't we just try to go back to sleep?" Sean suggested, "And maybe I'll just sneak into your thoughts, and see if I can't help keep the demons away."

Kira lifted her eyes up to him without moving her head from his chest. "That sounds wonderful."

Sean slid back down on the pillow and Kira remained attached to his chest. It was bare moments before he heard her breathing settle into a peaceful sleeping rhythm. His eyes were closed, but he was concentrating. He hoped he could do exactly what he suggested. The thought crossed his mind that maybe he could affect her thoughts and guide them away from those fearful places.

Who am I kidding, he considered, *reading someone else's thoughts is one thing, changing them is another.*

Moments later Sean's breathing matched Kira's.

CHAPTER

The sunlight filtering through the massive bedroom windows roused Kira earlier than she would have liked. She was greeted with Sean's face on the pillow beside her, eyes wide open and smiling.

"Good morning," she offered.

"It worked?" he asked trying not to accost her with his morning breath.

A mild look of surprise graced Kira's features. "Apparently it did. Thank you."

"You're welcome."

Kira just lingered there a moment absorbing the look and nature of Sean's light hazel eyes. They weren't just beautiful because of their hue; it was the kindness and lingering innocence that drew her like a lodestone. It occurred to her that she should do a portrait of him and then felt a flash of guilt that she had never thought of it before. She didn't do many portraits, but that didn't mean that she couldn't, especially of Sean. She truly believed she would never tire of looking into those eyes. She had another brief guilty moment as she realized that his experiences with her were costing him some of that innocence.

"I don't want to get up yet," she offered rolling her back to him and snuggling in. His arm slipped around her chest in mute agreement.

Her thoughts were still wrapping themselves around her new circumstances. This entire experience so far was bringing the worst of her memories to the fore, and it wasn't pleasant.

Being in the opulence of Brian's house reminded her of all the smug, self-important, haute couture fashionistas she had spent so much of her life enduring. The whole setting reeked of fake personas and plastic people. She hated it. It was getting away from that world that drove her to New Orleans in the first place and ultimately back to painting. On top of those unpleasant memories, her new escape had led her to some very terrifying experiences, and now she had an unwavering certainty and rising dread that she was heading straight into another one.

"It's OK, Kira," Sean whispered into her ear.

"I know, Honey," she responded reflexively.

Of course; she reminded herself he could sense her feelings even if he wasn't reading her thoughts. She was continually amazed at her own acceptance of her husband's remarkable gift. Was he reading her thoughts now? Did she care? Wait. Maybe she could try something.

Sean, she thought sharply.

"Yeah?" he answered immediately. Then paused and said, "Wow. That has to be the first time you've tried that. That felt like a train whistle in my brain."

"Really?"

"Really."

So, it's easier for you to read my thoughts when I am purposely directing them at you? This is wild, she thought.

"Yes. Much easier," he answered matter-of-factly, "And it really *is* wild, isn't it? Imagine how it feels on my end. When you direct them to me like that, I can't really filter them out. It's almost like you're shouting at me."

"I'm sorry. I didn't mean to shout at you."

Sean laughed. "You didn't really shout at me. It just felt like that and don't worry about it, but it is a good thing to know that you can pass me messages like that. Who knows when that little trick might come in handy? My dad is the only other person that has tried that. He did it at the wedding to get me to go outside with him so he could tell me about his tumor."

"That explains it," Kira answered, lifting her face up to his, "I saw you turn to him abruptly, and then you both made excuses to leave the room. I wondered at the time what was going on. He told me he'd tried it at the wedding, I should have figured that was why. Now I get it."

"I actually noticed you notice. You don't miss much, do you?"

"Well, he also mentioned it to me at the house." She smiled back at him and continued, "Not to mention, in my previous life it was a good idea to pay attention to what was going on around you."

"You want to go for a morning swim?" Sean said, changing the subject.

Kira returned his devilish smile. "Well, the water was warm."

Moments later splashing sounds and laughter emanated from the pool area.

They found their clothes before Coulson found them with breakfast on a tray, or maybe he had been waiting . . . either way his timing was perfect. Brian was nowhere to be found.

"I guess Brian did stay in town last night," Kira remarked.

"So, are you ready to give this a try?" Sean asked over a bite of omelet, ignoring her observation.

"As ready as I'm going to be. Are you ready to be there with me?"

"Always," he replied with such a small hesitation that Kira wondered if he'd been reading her thoughts, but it didn't matter.

"Great. Then why don't I meet you in the study in about fifteen minutes?" Kira was just finishing the last of her orange juice. Sean had finished just a bit before her.

"I'll take a quick shower to get the chlorine off, and I'll see you there." Sean's smile was a little too mischievous for Kira, but she let it go. She had plenty of other things to think about.

CHAPTER

Arthur walked down the street pointing ignoring everyone around him. He was again wearing a smile that would frighten children, and it was becoming a regular aspect of his countenance. His pale blue eyes gleamed with latent malevolence.

His headaches had abated somewhat, in fact this particular morning most of his aches and pains were remarkably absent. The unusual lack of pain directed his thoughts to the future, a topic he seldom allowed himself to consider. He now believed he would find a way to get the money Elliot needed and this cancer would be taken from him. So, what next? If he could get the money for Elliot then he could he could get more, and if he had all the money he needed, what did he want to do next? In his mind's eye an image of a woman falling down screaming blossomed. His smile widened. There was a whole world of women he could torment, and he knew with certainty that, given time, he could find more and more satisfying ways to do it. Would it be possible for him to learn to slice flesh with just his mind? What an interesting thought. Maybe he could even learn to extract a tooth with his ability. His broad smile now actually included a few teeth. It was a smile only a shark could love.

He looked up from his pleasant train of thought. The Hammer Museum sign confronted him.

That should be a good place to find wealthy women, he thought. He dimmed his feral grin and turned for the entrance.

Kira had a stool set up by her canvas and her paints were ready for her to pour in the ashes. She was dreading this, and it was the first time she had ever dreaded starting a painting. Sure, she had dreaded continuing them once she knew the horrors they held but having this sensation at the outset was a new experience. She glanced nervously back at Sean who was sitting quietly on the nearby couch.

"It's, OK," he offered, "It'll be OK, really."

She didn't reply other than to return his smile. That warm smile helped immensely, and she turned her head back to the blank canvas; it was just another tabula rasa waiting to be created. Her hands trembled slightly as she reached for the urn. She had a tiny amount of off-white oils in her small mixing bowl just awaiting the addition of ashes. Due to her trepidation, she had decided to allow Sean to be with her for the first mixing. She assumed he knew her little secret anyway, and it was a fair trade for the peace of mind he gave her. She glanced again at the shiny off-white mixture sitting in the bowl. She found it interesting that she was drawn to that color rather than some shade of pale blue. It signaled to her that this scene was going to be one of the indoors rather than out. The urn was heavier than usual, no doubt some indication of the amount of money Brian had spent on it, rather than its contents. Some of the gold accents were likely real gold.

Time seemed to almost grind to a halt as she tentatively tipped the urn up. Ever so slowly a slender stream of fine ash slid from the container into the stone mixing bowl.

Nothing happened.

Kira slowly put the urn back on the floor and began to mix in the paints. These ashes were finer than usual, and the mixture smoothed quickly.

A bedroom. A large bedroom. Then a flash to an even larger room.

Kira could see it in her mind's eye and immediately recognized it as a living room in some sort of beach house. The image was followed by sensations of warmth and happiness . . . and loving expectation then . . . HORROR!

Kira gasped and backed off her stool still holding the mixing bowl. Sean was off the couch so fast that he even managed to catch the stool before it hit the floor.

"What is it?" He nearly shouted at her as he grabbed her shoulders.

"I don't know," she answered in a shaking voice, "There was happiness, love, then . . . something really bad."

"Did you see what it was?"

"No, just the sensation and it was strange. Of all the sensations I've ever received when I was painting this was maybe the strangest."

"That's a pretty strong statement given some of what you've seen. What do you mean?"

"I don't really know. It just felt different somehow. Removed, sort of . . . I . . . I don't know. But whatever it was, I think it happened in a living room. At any rate that's going to be the scene for the painting unless Brian has some big objection. Did you sense anything?"

"I only felt those emotions you described go through your mind very fast. I think I was actually off the couch before you gasped. Whatever it was, it was strong."

"What shocked me was the sudden change from warmth and love to horror. What could have possibly happened to cause that? Do you think Brian could be involved?"

"No," Sean answered sharply, "If he was harboring something like that, I think I would have sensed it immediately. All I got from him was the profound sense of loss for Angelie."

"I agree with you. If it was Brian, I don't think that the sensation I got would have seemed so removed. It would have felt more impending or something."

They both stood there silent for a moment.

Kira's curiosity and sense of obligation were waging a serious battle with her most basic survival instincts. Fear was engaging its grip.

"Kira. If you really feel there is some danger, then stop. But I think we can do this. Don't you think we need to find out what this is about? There is something here that Brian needs to know, something that Angelie needs as well, to be at peace."

Kira gave no notice to the fact that Sean's comment was a response to her unspoken thoughts. She took a deep breath and decided that now was not the time to let her childish fears command her decisions.

"You're right." With the bowl still in her hands she said, "Could you move my stool back up a bit?"

Sean complied and she resolutely moved to sit on it with only a slight adjustment. They spoke no more words as she deliberately reached for her palette and scooped some of the grayish white mixture onto a corner of it.

"Well, here goes."

Kira's hand reached slowly up toward the canvas. As her brush touched its surface, she had the abrupt sensation of the bottom dropping from beneath her. It was the exhilarating falling sensation you get the second your car drops over the tip-top of the highest roller coaster incline. The feeling of acceleration increased as colors and light began to flash around her. She felt like her roller coaster car had just dropped through the tube of a spinning kaleidoscope.

Fear began to replace the sense of exhilaration as her speed continued to increase. A scream was beginning to form in her mind, the precursor to it escaping her lungs, when she suddenly plopped onto something soft in a brilliantly white room. She was on her back looking up and two huge crystal blue eyes appeared on the ceiling above her. Her first thought was of Shane Chang and her visions of his pornographic escapades, but she quickly dismissed the idea. This was different. These eyes had none of that leering quality, but they did hold some sort of looming menace in their pale blue depths. Kira's mind kept trying to complete the face that might go with those eyes to try to glean something else about them or this vision, but they suddenly disappeared. The searing white light around her slowly resolved into a large living room. As though some dense fog that obscured her vision had quickly dissipated. The room was huge and amazing.

CHAPTER

Kira made a deep sigh and leaned back from the canvas, barely looking at all the progress she had made. "Sean, I need to get out of here for a while. Why don't we go to an art museum?"

The look on Sean's face told Kira of his unenthused opinion of her suggestion, but she wasn't daunted. She had anticipated this. Before he could respond she added, "OK, I can see how that idea strikes you, but I have a compromise. There's a new exhibit in town of Leonardo da Vinci's works.

It includes not only his art but his inventions as well. Did you know Da Vinci had drawings for everything from helicopters to bicycles to siege engines and even guns?"

Now she saw the curiosity spread across Sean's face. It made her smile inside and out.

This must be what it feels like for him, she thought excitedly.

"OK," he said, "That does sound interesting. When do we go?"

"I'd say now. It opened at 10AM."

"I'm ready," Sean said, his smile continuing to bloom.

"Well I'm not. Give me fifteen minutes and we'll be out of here."

"Where is it?"

"It's called the Hammer Museum, and it's over in Santa Monica. Brian did say Jackson could drive us."

"In the limo?"

"I guess so. I didn't ask which car he was going to drive."

"Cool," Sean said. "Brian sure seems like a nice guy." Kira was about to respond when Sean added, "And extremely sad."

The compassion in his expression touched her. She walked over and kissed him gently on the lips, wrenching his attention to her.

"I'll be right back," she said.

Kira stepped quickly away from Sean moving toward their bedroom. Her own thoughts were a jumble. There was a touch of excitement to be here with Sean

and a heavy dollop of fear about the painting she was doing, but underneath it all there was a growing sensation of fulfillment. It must be what Sean sensed about her, and why he kept urging her to stay with her new business, but who would have ever dreamed of all the strange directions it could take?

~

Jackson had pulled up when Kira stepped out of the side door of the house. She wasn't surprised Sean was waiting in the limo. She had seen the excitement on his face when they rode in it from the airport. Limos were old hat to her, but she loved seeing the kid-like fascination in his eyes as he explored all the vehicle's nooks and crannies.

"Look Kira!" he said as she eased into the vehicle, "The screen between us and the driver goes up."

His eyes shifted to her body, and she promptly knew what he was thinking. Some things didn't require Sean's skills to glean. She was wearing a blue pleated skirt and a white spaghetti strap top, and it now occurred to her that her fashion choice wouldn't preclude easy access. She nearly made herself blush.

"Yeah," she replied as she slid next to him, "You can't see through it either. There are any number of reasons why they include privacy as a feature in these vehicles."

Sean's eyes briefly danced across her body again before locking onto hers. He reached for her, planting his lips passionately on her mouth, then her neck. It was definitely going to be a nice ride to the museum, and after all, they were newlyweds.

~

The Hammer Museum was a several-story stone obelisk of a building. Its sleek horizontal lines of light and dark marble screamed of ultra-modern, as did many of the museums around the country. Most visitors must enter through the parking garage several stories underground, but Sean and Kira's mode of transportation allowed them to bypass that experience.

"When would you like to be picked up?" Jackson asked as he opened their door.

Kira looked for the knowing expression on the driver's face as she applied the final touches to reassemble herself from their frolic. She detected nothing and Sean answered for her much to her surprise.

"I think you can come back in about three hours," he said then offered her a questioning look.

She merely smiled and nodded as she took the hand Sean was offering to help her from the vehicle.

The museum was rather crowded which Kira attributed to the popularity of the Da Vinci exhibit. Sean was exhibiting his usual expression of wonder at experiencing something new.

"Sean, have you ever even been to a museum before?"

"I've been to the Science Museum in Union Station."

"Kansas City?"

"Yep."

"Nothing else?"

"Nope, that's the only one. This is really cool though."

Kira smiled as she shook her head. The depths of her new husband's inexperience never ceased to amaze her, and she just loved it.

~

The warmth of Kira's tiny hand felt wonderful as she led him through the museum. The crowd was increasing as they went, and the weight of people's thoughts on his awareness was increasing accordingly. Sadness. Wonder. Awe. Emotions flowed to him like rivers to the sea. He opened himself to them for a moment. It was a new endeavor for him to take everything in for a few minutes and then begin to filter things out until he had quieted the torrent of perceptions. On the occasions he considered how he did this, his only conclusion was invariably bafflement. He had no clue how he managed it, but he did.

One child was exceedingly unhappy to be here. Sean thought for a second about how he knew it was a child. Then he smiled. A child's thoughts were just as recognizable as were their distinctive little voices.

When Sean turned to find the object of the feeling that had snagged his attention, he saw a boy of around seven who appeared to be on the verge of tears.

He must be the one. Sean's gaze shifted up to the parent where he sensed concentration on one of the paintings. The mother was oblivious of her son's discomfort.

A flash of anger from another source seared his thoughts, causing him to jerk his head around abruptly. A man standing behind a young woman who was gazing intently at a sculpture was furious at something. Sean concentrated some more. The couple had just finished a fight before arriving. It was about him never indulging any of her interests. That was why he was here, but he certainly wasn't happy about it.

"What is it, Sean?" Kira asked.

Sean smiled as he turned back to her and dimmed the incoming mental deluge. "Oh nothing. Just snagging thoughts from some of the people here."

"I thought you could filter that stuff out now."

"I can, but sometimes I don't want to. I'm trying to practice letting things in or keeping them out when I want. So, I was just kind of practicing."

Having to explain this to her made him feel a little sheepish, but not so much as to consider lying. Especially with his gift, it was important to be as honest as he could at all times. When he could *take* the truth from her it seemed horribly unfair not to offer the same back. It was a promise he had made to himself early on. Never lie to Kira.

"OK," she replied simply.

Sean sensed the satisfaction coming from her at his explanation and loved her all the more for it. He could only imagine what it must be like to have a relationship with him that included a gift like his. She never ceased to amaze him with the depths of her acceptance.

"The Da Vinci exhibit is on the third floor. We'll have to take the elevator."

Sean let her lead him as the steady trickle of less urgent thoughts gurgled through his awareness. His attention slowly turned to the paintings and sculptures in the galleries they were passing.

"I don't get these," Sean said as they walked.

Kira followed his gaze into a gallery of modern art paintings and smiled. "What don't you get?"

"Most of those just look like splashes of color on a canvas. What's the purpose?"

"Like which one?" She asked as she slowed to a halt with a sly grin on her face.

The question forced him to be more specific, so he picked the first one on his left. He drifted slightly toward it as he pointed.

"This one looks like a few lines of bright colors that were applied too heavily, so they ran down the length of the canvas. What makes that art?"

"How does it make you feel?" She asked, catching him off guard.

"Well, I don't know. The colors seem bright and happy, but the dripping seems kind of sad."

"Like blood dripping?" she prompted.

The suggestion unnerved him. "Uh. No. Maybe like tears."

"So, you've already had three different sensations from this painting."

"I have?"

"Yeah," Kira answered, "You've experienced happy from the colors, and sad and tears from the style by looking at this work of art."

"But I . . ." Sean paused as he continued to stare. "I guess I did."

"That may well have been the artist's only purpose. And if so, it worked for you."

"Well I . . . I'll be darned. That's cool." He turned to Kira, their eyes locking. "Thank you for that."

Kira just smiled, but Sean sensed the warmth of satisfaction coming off her like the waves of heat from a newly lit fireplace.

They stood there a moment longer before Kira gently began to pull him toward the elevator again.

"Doesn't it overwhelm you?" She asked, returning to their previous topic. They stepped into the elevator. By happenstance they had it to themselves.

"The painting?" He inadvertently reached out to her. Her meaning was there in her mind clear as a bell. In her eyes he watched as she saw him snag that understanding from her. She smiled knowingly before he spoke. She had remained silent intentionally.

"Not now it doesn't. Now that I have some control over it it's similar to the sensation you'd have at an outdoor market or festival. You can hear all the snippets of conversations going on around you, but you don't have to *listen* to them.

Without that filter I don't believe I'd be able to think for myself at all when I'm around others. It would be maddening." It felt good to voice the realization that had been floating around in his head for a few weeks. There was so much to adjust to while his abilities seemingly continued to grow.

Kira was quiet for a moment unconsciously nodding her agreement with his description.

They stepped off the elevator and turned to the right. The giant gallery loomed before them. The size of the room was itself inspiring. As Sean's eyes took in the exhibit he gasped softly.

"Oh my gosh!" He said as Kira turned to him. "I knew, generally, what Da Vinci had done but this . . ."

"Impressive isn't it?"

Recreations of DaVinci's work were interlaced around the room with actual drawings from the artist and inventor. Overhead was a replica of the wings he had designed to allow a man to fly. They were connected to a mannequin of sorts. Another replica, this one of his Aerial screw, a precursor to the helicopter, nestled in one corner. His rendition of the personalized war tank in another. Sean's head was rotating back and forth trying to take it all in at once.

"It's amazing, isn't it?" Kira asked as she watched him.

"Incredible! I knew he painted the Mona Lisa, and I've seen a few of his drawings but this . . . this is fantastic."

Sean's frank enjoyment was interlaced with the sensations of joy coming from Kira. It was a double whammy of joy that left Sean feeling giddy.

"I could stay here all day," he said dreamily.

"Then let's do."

More and more people crowded into the exhibit as Sean and Kira strolled around.

~

With new resolve and a wisp of a smile on his face he opened the big glass door of the museum and stepped inside.

The first thing Arthur noticed was the air conditioning. The warm humidity permeating LA disappeared with the clicking of the door behind him.

It immediately put Arthur in a better mood. He took three steps forward trying to decide where to go and then he caught sight of the Da Vinci display poster.

Perfect, he thought and with a slow casual gait, he made his way to the elevators. This was going to be fun.

~

Sean's attention kept gravitating back to Da Vinci's inventions more than his art and Kira, for her part, was glad to follow him around and watch his rapt expression wax and wane from display to display. As the crowd continued to swell, Kira reflected on the many times she had seen this exhibit before, but more than the continual change of exhibits, just being here with Sean made it all seem new.

While he studied a diagram for a submarine that Da Vinci had drawn but never built, her eyes drifted across the crowd and down to a Picasso display just a few steps down the hall. She closed her eyes for a moment and considered Sean's words about tuning out a crowd and as she concentrated, she realized she could make out any number of conversations around her, something she had been completely oblivious to before shifting her attention. It was a profound reminder of what we miss every day.

Upon opening her eyes, her attention promptly fixated on a tall slender man who was dressed a little too shabby for the venue. He had black oily hair and a sharp jaw line. Her gaze lingered for some reason as the man's head swiveled toward her until his ice blue eyes found hers. She averted her gaze abruptly, feeling somewhat embarrassed that she had been staring. Still, there was something strange about the guy that seemed to go beyond his mere appearance. She chided herself for the stupid thought, but a tiny shiver snaked its way down her spine.

She sidled closer to Sean and slipped her arm through his. He responded by pulling his arm free and slipping it around her waist. His attention never wavered from the card he was reading in front of another of Da Vinci's stunning foresights into the future.

~

Arthur's awareness flowed across the crowd briefly, looking for a likely target. He loved museums but the crowds today were weighing on him. He felt claustrophobic.

His eyes continued to scan, however, and stopped on a beautiful brunette who quickly averted her gaze just as he saw her.

Before he could decide, however, a noise from someone close by distracted him, diverted his attention, and his eyes locked on one of the Picasso paintings. He didn't know much about art, but he had heard of Picasso and now he was finding that he very much liked the man's work. His twisted images seemed to capture the essence of Arthur's opinion of people and the world in general. He attempted to discern a few of the more obscure patterns and color arrangements for another moment or two before glancing casually to his left and noticing a blonde with a haughty expression. The quality of her expression ignited his anger. It seemed to embody his opinion of women. Haughty, arrogant, uncaring, entitled, simply by reason of their beauty. He began to concentrate on one of the lower vertebrae in her neck.

~

Sean suddenly grabbed his forehead and swiveled his head to the left.

"Ow!" he exclaimed, evoking a sharp look of concern from Kira and the nearest of the crowd.

"What's wrong?"

"I don't know. Someone is thinking something . . . but . . ."

Pain lanced through Sean's mind like an electric shock accompanied by a woman's shriek from across the room. He instinctively began to survey the sensations of the people around him. Waves of thoughts drifted to him like the delicate tinkling of wind chimes in a gentle autumn breeze. Except for one. One thought struck him like the clang of a great steel hammer on an iron anvil ringing painfully through his mind. He grabbed his head with both hands and gasped sharply.

"Sean, what's wrong?" Kira asked as she reached for him.

By this time Sean's eyes were closed, head descending towards a standing crouch.

Kira was getting frantic.

"Come on let's get out of here," she said, while leading him away from the crowd who thankfully was continuing to stare at the lovely young woman on the floor still screaming and clutching her neck.

"Wait," Sean said, lifting his head back up, a look of grim determination in his eyes. He let his gaze wander, but it was not without purpose. The pounding in his head had a source, and he believed he could locate it. *There*, he thought.

One man on the edge of the crowd was not reacting with the shocked surprise and concern like everyone else. As a matter of fact, he seemed to be concentrating and suddenly Sean caught a clear thought.

. . . seventh cervical vertebrae 3 millimeters left and down . . .

Sean was stunned. That thought was clear as a bell, but it was vastly different from anything he'd ever experienced before. His eyes shifted to the poor woman on the floor still holding her neck.

"What is it?" Kira asked having watched Sean's abrupt change in demeanor.

"That man is causing that woman's pain, and I'm going to try to stop it."

Kira was too flabbergasted to respond as Sean's look of determination hardened.

Stop it! Sean thought, trying to put as much force in the mental command as he could. He wasn't even sure how he could do that, but he felt that if he bent his will on the thought it would somehow have more power.

STOP IT!

~

The thought hit Arthur's mind with the jarring effect of a rock to the temple, causing him to stumble a step and completely lose focus.

The girl on the floor abruptly stopped screaming.

Arthur looked up and around the room. He immediately saw a man staring at him. He was apparently with the girl he had noticed earlier.

Though Arthur glared back at the man, he was too shocked to give any more consideration to the extraordinary situation or precipitate another attack on his attacker. He simply turned and marched back to the nearest bank of elevators, his anger continuing to rise, though now at the obstruction of his objective rather than at the girl.

~

In response to his attempt to project a thought, the clanging in Sean's head abated immediately, as did the screaming from the woman on the ground.

He took a step in the direction of the lanky dark-haired man who was quickly retreating, but the sudden onslaught of the stricken woman's pain overtook him.

The force of the other thought had been blocking his awareness of her emotions, but now, with it gone, the full weight of her pain nearly overwhelmed him before it subsided, or he could distance himself from it.

~

Kira was beside herself. She had watched the interchange from the outside and had no notion of what might be going on, but Sean was acting in a variety of ways she had never experienced before, and she was too dumbfounded for a couple of moments to do more than hold his arm and watch.

~

As the stricken woman was helped to her feet by a couple of other men, the crowd began to break up.

Sean shook his head and straightened to his full height.

"Wow. That was unbelievable," he said.

"What was? What happened? And are you sure you're all right"

Suddenly her extreme concern came to the fore, and he felt a little embarrassed for leaving her in the dark.

"Yeah. I'm fine now. Kira, that was the strangest thing I've ever felt. I know it sounds crazy, but I think that tall oily haired guy was causing that woman's pain."

"You already said that much. What do you mean?" Kira asked with incredulity thick in her voice.

"Just what I said. That guy was doing something with his mind to cause that girl to hurt. I think he was moving one of the vertebrae in her neck. I could feel the thought first then caught it specifically when I focused on him."

"Moving a bone in her neck with his mind? Sean, that's crazy!"

Sean turned to look at her. "With all the things we've gone through you can say that?"

Kira paused a moment, then smiled. "I see what you mean, but for that matter the stuff we've gone through is crazy too."

"I feel like we ought to report this to someone, but there's no way anyone would believe me. It just feels wrong to do nothing," Sean said.

"I don't know what else we can do?" Kira was feeling somewhat bewildered by the situation and when she looked up the entire crowd had dispersed leaving her and Sean standing alone near the middle of the huge hall. "Let's get out of here," she said pulling gently on Sean's arm, "if you're OK."

"Yeah. I'm fine now. Let's go."

CHAPTER

With his hands stuffed stiffly in his pockets, Arthur marched down the street trying to understand what had just happened to him. He was a walking confluence of rage, curiosity, and frustration.

I felt that guy's thoughts in my head . . . Arthur thought. *How is that possible? I think that he even caused me to stop what I was doing. Well, maybe I stopped just out of surprise.* Arthur pondered that line of thought that for a moment . . . *no, that's not how it felt.*

He remembered distinctly hearing the voice in his head telling him to stop . . . and then he just did.

What kind of person could do that?

The irony of him even asking himself that question wasn't lost on Arthur; it was just that he had never stopped to consider that if he had unique abilities then it was possible that someone else might have some as well.

The afternoon sun was beginning to make him sweat, and the pain in his head from his little encounter was beginning to make it difficult for him to think. Arthur decided it was time to find a cold drink somewhere. Then he could go back to his apartment and figure his next move. Running into that guy was certainly just a random chance, and he had other things to do besides worry about another person out there with some sort of abilities.

~

The ride back to Brian's house in the limo was a strained silence.

All either of them could think about was the incident at the museum, but neither wanted to talk about it in front of the driver. It was a measure of their discomfiture that it never occurred to either of them to ask Jackson to roll up the slide window again. Even the gorgeous ocean views rolling outside their window couldn't drag their thoughts from the shocking episode.

Jackson opened their door in front of Brian's house and seemed not to notice their demeanor. Sean knew better. The front door was unlocked as usual and Brian was nowhere to be seen. By unspoken agreement Sean and Kira marched straight back to their bedroom. Sean walked to one of the huge windows while Kira shut the door.

Turning to face him she walked as far as the bed and sat down.

"Telekinesis?" She asked as she sat down on the bed.

Sean turned to her. "Yeah. I guess so. I think I would call it micro-telekinesis. Kira, the thought I caught from that guy was, 'seventh cervical vertebrae 3 millimeters left and down.'"

"That specific?" She asked.

"Those words exactly."

"How did you stop him?"

"I told him to stop."

"But I didn't . . ."

"With my mind."

"You ordered him to stop with just your mind?" The look on Kira's face was not unfamiliar. She had worn that expression on any number of occasions regarding either her own abilities or Sean's.

"Yeah. Only I don't know if that's what made him stop or just the shock of hearing my thought so strongly."

"You think he *heard* your thought? Have you ever done anything like that before?"

"Only with my dad or with you while you're painting" Sean replied in a distracted tone.

Kira paused for a moment in thought then said, "I keep thinking we should be telling someone."

"I know what you mean," Sean answered, "but I keep coming back to the same conclusion we had at the museum . . ."

"No one would believe us," she finished for him.

"Right," he agreed.

They both remained quiet for a few moments gathering their thoughts. Sean's shoulders swung back to face the panoramic view from their window while Kira's head remained down with her mouth to her fist and her elbow propped on her thigh.

She was still reeling from the adrenaline rush of the entire experience, while Sean's mind was busy rerunning the entire episode trying to understand just what he'd done.

CHAPTER

The next morning Kira woke up early and made her way to the den. She stared at the canvas sitting on the easel across the room as she walked toward it. She was going to do this. She had her nerve up again and her curiosity was beginning to kick in as well. The thought crossed her mind to wake Sean, but he was sleeping so soundly she decided to leave him be. The morning sun glittered on the waves in the distance, but variegated shadows still danced across the den. The north and west facing windows wouldn't allow for any strong lighting in the room until later on in the afternoon. That was perfect for getting started.

The little director's chair beside the easel was the perfect place to mix some more paint and ashes. She took her time mixing and trying to decide if she wanted to wait for Sean. In the end she decided to dive in herself.

Moving away from the director's chair and settling in on her stool, she raised her paintbrush to the canvas:

~

"... and so, we commend her spirit to God."

"Lisa heard the words and realized they signaled the end of the service, but at first, she couldn't move. She could barely believe it was over. Just five years after her adopted father's passing her adopted mother was now gone as well. The hole in her heart seemed to want to open up and swallow her utterly. Even if they had never understood her very well, her parents had been wonderful.

They had provided her with morals, values, and enough support, even in their lack of understanding, to allow her to follow her dreams, which is just what she had done. Her music career had blossomed, and she'd made them proud.

"Come on Hon, we should go."

Lisa turned and smiled at her fiancée. "Go ahead," she said, "I'll be just a few minutes behind you."

With that, he nodded briefly and turned to go. Lisa turned back to the gravesite.

"Goodbye, Mom," she whispered. Thoughts churned through her mind, memories both good and bad; but at this moment the one thing that stood out in her mind was not the similarities she had with her wonderful parents but the differences.

They had told her she was adopted when she was very young, and at that time it didn't have an impact on her life. She had only known her adopted parents. To her, at that age, the information about other parents was just that, information. It was curious but had no emotional impact. It was like watching a story on TV. It just wasn't real. But as the years had meandered past, she began to feel the weight of the differences. She watched her friends closely when she was with them at their houses, and she noticed the similarities in appearance and even mannerisms between them and their parents and siblings. Slowly she had come to realize the real impact of her being adopted. She had no brothers or sisters, so she had never experienced being around anyone biologically related to her. Innocently, Lisa had brought this up on one occasion to her mother who, being sweet spirited, had appreciated her concern and said she would help find them if that's what she wanted. Lisa, however, could feel the hurt coming from her mother as clearly as if it had been shouted in her face, and she wasn't about to cause her mother pain, so she dropped the idea and never brought it up again.

The wind had picked up and now a cold raindrop splashed on her nose bringing her sharply back from her reverie. It was at that instant she made the decision. She would find her birth parents. With a brand-new purpose in her heart she turned and walked back to the waiting limousine.

~

Kira gasped and leaned back from the easel.

That was incredible, she thought. *Who's Lisa? Was she some connection of Brian's deceased wife or a relative of hers?*

The astonishing detail of her painting experiences never failed to amaze her. She had been smoothly and comfortably in the head of whoever this Lisa person was, and Lisa wanted to search for her birth parents. Kira was familiar with living the perspective of the subjects of her work, but it was still startling to experience this Lisa woman in such a way. The only time it had happened in the past was with people to whom the subject was very close, like Jason's victims. This perspective also forestalled any opportunity for Kira to see what Lisa looked like. Additionally, there was a different quality here than any of her other previous experiences in that she wasn't afraid. In the past, she had only lost herself to another's perspective when their fear had gripped her so completely that there was no room left for her own self-awareness.

But here, she had lost herself to the seemingly mundane. If anyone had asked her if it was possible to have an encounter this profoundly different from all the others she had already experienced, Kira would have adamantly told them they were nuts. But here it was. Her next thought made her snicker. Here she was expecting something from an experience that was so extraordinary that nothing should ever be expected.

She had a sudden pang of guilt at not including Sean. Not because it had been a bad experience but because it had been such a good one. Also, Sean would have been particularly excited about the adoption aspect of the vision.

For a moment Kira just sat there thinking and looking out the window at the ocean far below. The scene was as idyllic as any postcard she had ever seen. Her mind supplied the sound she would be hearing if she was closer of the waves crashing on the surf and the constant breeze blowing in from the sea.

She wrenched her attention back to the canvas in front of her. The desire to get right back into the painting was powerful, but she was now determined to wake Sean. He absolutely *had* to be here for this. Belatedly, she placed her brush down, stood up from the stool, and set her palette on the chair.

Sean was in that state between dreams and wakefulness, balanced on the edge of sleep. His mind was battling a problem. It was a replay of the confrontation with the guy at the museum. How could anybody do that? And he meant that in several senses. How could someone have an ability like micro-telekinesis, as he'd come to think of it, and how could someone do something to deliberately hurt someone that way? Even injure them seriously. What was the reason? Not that he hadn't seen evil before, he certainly had with both Jason and Poena, but was there an evil presence involved here, or just another aberration of a mind?

Those were the instances he'd seen before, and he surmised that he would find one or the other to be the case here.

Replaying the scene in his head, Sean felt again the power of the thought and the concentration that the guy had utilized to actually move a specific bone in that poor girl's neck. For him, the sharp sensation of her immediate pain had been a great distraction to the attention he had been able to focus on the guy. How had he stopped him? By mentally telling him to stop? He wasn't capable of something like that, was he? Maybe the guy's own ability created some sort of special connection that allowed Sean to have an effect on him. Maybe while he was in the act of using his own abilities, he was vulnerable to someone else's thoughts. Anyone's thoughts? Surely not. Sean had to accept the possibility that he *had* done something, but what? And how?

The images of the event were replaying again and again through his mind with his eyes still closed. His ears registered a voice.

"Sean?"

Kira was standing over the bed leaning in to kiss him when Sean opened his eyes. He grabbed her suddenly and pulled her into the bed on top of him, eliciting a little scream from her in the process.

"Stop! What are you doing?" she squealed.

But Sean was busy nuzzling his face into her neck and kissing, which elicited a further, if somewhat subdued scream from Kira because he was tickling her.

"Stop," she said again, her tone hardening slightly. A smile still sat squarely on her face, however, softening her words.

Sean sensed both her delight and the seriousness lurking behind it. He released her abruptly leaving her lying beside him and took on a somber expression.

"What?" He asked simply.

"I had another session with Angelie's painting."

Fear lanced up through Sean, but a quick read of Kira's emotions told him it wasn't something bad . . . but it was something curious. He stopped just short of reading the thought.

"So, tell me," he stated, fixing and intent gaze on her.

Kira hesitated momentarily, pondering the fact that Sean *asked*, rather than *read* her. "It was the strangest thing, Sean. When I began the thing, I slipped into the person of someone named Lisa and I was completely there. I was so thoroughly inside her mind that I just barely noticed myself being there. The only other time that happened was with Jason's victims and that, I believe, was because of the power of their fear. But this was different. There was no fear whatsoever. She was experiencing her mom's funeral, and then she decided to hunt down her birth parents."

"Her birth parents?" Sean echoed. If he had been intrigued before, he was now doubly so, and he sensed Kira seeing it in his eyes.

"I thought that might tickle your fancy a bit. But I want to go in again, with you. It really was an amazing experience, and I want you to feel it with me."

"I'm in," he said, "That bit about her mother's funeral must have struck a chord with you as well." Sean stretched. "Can I shower and get a cup of coffee first?"

"Sure," Kira answered smiling brightly.

"Will you join me in the shower," he asked, "Please?"

Kira leaned in and kissed him. "Absolutely."

After a delightful and extended romp in the massive, multi-headed shower, Sean and Kira were ready to get back to work.

Kira sat down at her stool. This was the most excited she had been about a painting session since her very first commission for Louise. She glanced over at Sean who was settled comfortably on the couch near-by.

"Well, are you ready?" She asked as she mixed some more ashes with a touch of brown hues.

"Always," Sean answered smiling.

"Alrightythen," she said as she lifted her brush.

~

Sean felt the rushing sensation he had experienced before and the blurring of thoughts from Kira. Then suddenly he was looking out through another pair of eyes and detecting thoughts that were neither his nor Kira's. He focused for a moment and could sense Kira there, too. Her presence was a rather muted thing, but it was there like a steady beacon of familiarity sitting placidly on the shore of this thoughts.

Sean took what felt like the mental equivalent of a deep breath and abruptly felt the other person's words and emotions flow into his mind:

~

Lisa was excited. Her meeting with Elliot at the Starbucks had gone great despite its brevity. She was still taken by their physical similarities and the fact that he had their father's eyes. She wasn't sure how much of their mother either one of them had as the detective agency hadn't been able to send her photos. When she asked, they sent ones of her father and said they could get some of her mother too, but it hadn't happened yet.

"Hi Elliot, this is Lisa." She spoke quickly into the phone.

"Hi, Lisa."

"Listen, I just wanted to tell you how excited I was to meet you today, and I'm even more excited to get together with you again when we have more time. The only problem is I have a filming schedule starting up and it may be a few more days before I can get away."

"That's no problem," he responded. His words were even and metered, but she could still detect the note of excitement in his voice. "Just call me when you have time, and I'll check my schedule. I'm pretty bogged down at the moment as well."

"OK great. I'll call you as soon as I see a break coming."

The next week slid by in a blur of action and it took her longer to call him again than she'd wanted. Finally, after almost two weeks, their schedules meshed, and they were able to set a time the second week of September. He had actually conveyed a little urgency to meet up when they last spoke, which Lisa found strange but took it as a good sign.

And really, it didn't matter. She was so excited. There were a thousand questions she wanted to ask. And she was particularly glad he had agreed to meet her in this place. It may not be her home anymore since she and her husband had bought a much bigger place together, but it still felt like home and the perfect place to really get to know her newly found brother.

~

Kira leaned back from the canvas, and Sean opened his eyes. They both just sat there for a moment in their relative positions and tried to assimilate what had just happened. Sean glanced up at the clock on the wall and his eyes widened somewhat. He next glanced at the painting in front of Kira and registered another noticeable shock. Kira, however, was the first to speak.

"Did we just sit here in front of this canvas for three and a half hours?"

"Did we just experience two weeks or so of another person's life while we sat?" Sean replied.

Kira's eyes drifted to the canvas in front of her. "And did I just manage several days' worth of painting in that space?"

"And who the hell is Lisa? And is it a coincidence that she is an actor as well?"

Kira's eyes remained locked on the canvas, and her brows furrowed. Sean sensed her considering his question, but no answer was forthcoming to either of them.

The painting consisted of a large living area. The perspective seemed to be from someone in the room looking expectantly at another about to enter it, as the main feature on the canvas was a door. Also visible in the scene was a glimpse of a dining table off to the side and the edge of a kitchen through it. The detail was exquisite. There were blank rectangles of what must eventually become paintings or pictures of some kind adorning the walls, and an oblique view of a massive credenza and matching china cabinet were partially drawn.

Kira stood and stretched. Three hours in the same position had made her feel stiff if not outright sore They were both a little too dumbfounded to speak and Kira knew Sean was sensing her thoughts anyway. It wasn't hard to guess that Sean was experiencing the same feelings that permeated her.

"I'm pretty sure *that* has never happened before. Am I right?"

Kira managed a smile back at Sean. "Yep. You'd be right about that. Even with Jason the time frame that I experienced was never more than a few minutes to an hour. This was so far beyond that, I almost feel like I became this Lisa, whoever she is, for a while there."

"Me too," was all Sean managed to respond at first.

Silence ensued.

Sean finally tore his stare away from the ocean view and looked back at Kira. "Let's go grab a bite of lunch and go for a walk somewhere. I need to get out of here and think."

"Perfect idea."

At that point Kira realized she was still holding her palette and brush. She abruptly set them down and followed Sean out the door with a backward glance at the canvas resting on its easel.

Arthur continued to walk and sweat. He was almost back to the beach again. He hadn't slept worth a damn the previous night but had finally given up on yesterday's puzzle with the guy at the museum. His thoughts shifted instead to what he *had* accomplished. Prior to the interference he had successfully moved the precise vertebrae that he had intended. It had not only caused the pain he wanted, but he felt certain that without that guy's interference, he would have been able to paralyze her at least for some period of time. He had questions about what things he could move that would stay moved and which would return to their original position when he quit focusing.

He suspected the answer might be some of both; still his abilities were definitely growing. Well maybe *growing* wasn't the right word, refining, more accurately described it. There was still the question of how to use it in fashions other than just for pleasure.

He had accomplished several things already that really needed doing, but not everything had worked out the way he'd hoped and there had to be more he could do. Elliot was still progressing slowly in his little lab due to limited funding, and Arthur didn't have the lifespan to wait. There had to be a way to derive a monetary benefit from his gift. He had yet to solidify any strategy for extorting large sums of money from wealthy women, however. In the meantime, he could just continue to refine his abilities on whatever targets presented themselves.

The crashing of the waves intruded on his senses along with the voices of people. It was a low surf. The waves were two to three feet, just enough to interest the serious surfers. The bright sun, however, still made the foam gleam a brilliant white and drops of water splashing in the air shown like diamonds.

There were always people on the beach. He hated the crowds, but sometimes they were simply a necessity and the sound of the surf did help to dull their noise. He turned his gaze from the waves and the happy people, and his eyes fell on a little, portable hot dog stand with a bright red roof and an image of a giant hot dog attached to it. Those stands typically served frozen lemonade as well.

Perfect, he thought.

Arthur stepped up to the little stand, whereupon a diminutive gentleman of Indian persuasion greeted him kindly. He was wearing a white apron over a blue shirt with a LA Dodgers baseball cap tilted back on his head.

"May I help you, Sir?"

The lilt of his English annoyed Arthur, and he briefly considered doing something to the man. He resisted, however, because he would then have to go behind the counter to get his own food and drink, which would not only draw unwanted attention but would be cumbersome as well. For the moment he restrained himself.

"A hot dog and a frozen lemonade."

The vendor smiled. Everyone smiled at the sound of Arthur's voice. It was a melodic high tenor with a velvet quality that led most people to assume that Arthur was a singer. He had never sung a note in his life and wasn't even particularly fond of music.

"Yes, Sir, coming up."

The man turned back to the little cart and lifted the lid from a small steam table. He used tongs to retrieve a hot dog and deposited it in a bun retrieved from another container, then passed it back to Arthur with a napkin.

"That will be four dollars, Sir."

Arthur stood there considering again whether to at least do something simple like shifting a bone in the man's wrist, then decided it wasn't worth the effort. He'd rather practice on a woman, anyway. He reached into his pocket and realized he had left his wallet at home.

What the heck, he thought, focusing his thoughts on a bone in the wrist of the hand the man was extending. The man abruptly screamed and grabbed his wrist with his other hand. Arthur was fairly certain the bone would move back in place in another few seconds but by then he would be too far away to chase. Arthur walked briskly away as the man continued yelling. It was time to go back to his apartment and think.

CHAPTER

"So, where do you want to go?" Sean asked as they hopped in the car. Jackson was again at the wheel and was about to ask the same question anyway.

Kira smiled that mischievous smile of hers.

"Jackson, can you take us somewhere where we can eat and walk around to enjoy some scenery? Anywhere is fine, just surprise us."

"Sounds good to me." Sean replied.

Jackson began to drive, with a small, uncharacteristic grin.

Sean still couldn't get used to the idea of being chauffeured around everywhere, but he sensed that this wasn't particularly new or unnerving to Kira.

The modeling world, he thought, as he turned to look out the windows.

"This sure brings back memories," Kira said.

"Good or bad?"

"Both actually. It seems like modeling was always a somewhat uncomfortable mixture of both."

"How so?"

Kira seldom talked about her years as a model, and Sean took any opportunity he could to learn more about that part of her life. It was as foreign to him as he imagined farming was to her, and he felt like it was important to know that side of her, too. For that matter, as far as he was concerned, every side of her was important, and he couldn't imagine not wanting to know every facet of the life that had made her *her*.

As the thoughts rambled through his mind, he glanced down at the ring on her finger. It was still difficult to believe he was married.

"Well, on the one hand you have the sensation that everyone loves you simply because you are pretty. That, in itself, can be disconcerting because it makes you overly concerned with your appearance ALL the time. Then there are the people you work around. You have to be able to trust them, but there is always this nagging sensation that all they really want is whatever being with you can gain them. You know, connections, visibility, opportunities, and of course sex, if they think it's even a possibility. It's all very wearisome and eventually lonely.

Then there's the issue of privacy. Have you ever thought about the fact that the photos you see on the covers of most of these sleaze magazines depict someone that looks surprised and often annoyed or angry? That's because they are. The more successful you are, the more the photographers or paparazzi hunt you like a prime gazelle in the African veldt. Those photos can bring them several months' salary if they get a decent one.

So, everywhere you want to go, the grocery store, the drugstore, a movie, anywhere, can become a nightmare of weasels popping out of the bushes or zooming in on you with tremendous telephoto lenses to try to capture that one valuable image.

So, what happens is, you become trapped in your own home and have people do everything for you that requires being around the public. It really is the quintessential golden cage."

Kira fell silent gazing absently out the window, and Sean sensed the bittersweet nostalgia grow like a cloud inside the limo.

"Wow," he finally said, "I never thought of it that way. No wonder you wanted out."

Kira turned and smiled at him. "But I have you now and you're waaaay better than any phony public career." She punctuated her statement with a lingering kiss that lasted long enough to have Sean trying to remember how to roll up the privacy screen.

"We're here," Jackson said over his shoulder. "This is Venice beach and probably as good a place as any to enjoy the local scenery and grab a quick bite. If you'd prefer somewhere else . . ."

"No. This is great," Kira answered, "Come on Sean; let's go watch the crazy people."

"Do you want me to wait?" Jackson asked.

"No, just meet us back here in a couple of hours."

Kira seemed to take charge which, in this instance, was fine with Sean.

CHAPTER

Brian parked his Porsche in the garage noticing that the limo was gone. He surmised that Jackson had taken Sean and Kira somewhere. Brian knew very little about art, and most of what he had learned, he learned from Angelie, none of which included anything about the artistic process as it pertained to painting.

He dropped his keys on the kitchen counter as he entered from the garage and decided to go check on Kira's progress. Hopefully she had at least started. His thoughts wandered as he strode through his huge house. The reshoot he had just come back from had been grueling, and he still had a headache. At least it was done, and it had taken his mind off Angelie for a little while.

Once he was home, however, he could never escape her. Her absence was like an open wound that just wouldn't heal.

As he entered the huge den, his eyes lifted to the expanse of windows on the far wall. The sight of the ocean stretching out in the distance never failed to relax him. It felt like that blue undulating carpet reaching out to the horizon was a direct link to the rest of the world and always made him feel small. It was a welcome reminder of what a tiny speck we are in this great big world and as such, the world doesn't revolve around any single person, as his agent would have him believe.

He crossed the room, lowering his eyes to the canvas on the easel at the far side. It was turned slightly away from him so he couldn't yet see its surface. Vague anxiety slipped over him at the thought of the canvas still being blank. Brian had high hopes that Kira's work would help assuage the pervasive grief that beleaguered him. If she hadn't made any real progress it would be somehow disconcerting.

Glancing again quickly at the ocean in the distance, Brian swung around to face the canvas . . . and stopped cold.

"Oh my God!" The words slipped out, and his mouth hung open. Not only was the canvas not blank, a substantial image was already there and, what's more, he recognized it. It was the image of a living room he had seen before, years ago, when he had first met Angelie. Even though portions of the painting weren't finished, there was no mistaking the room. But how? How could Kira have drawn a scene from a dead woman's past? There were no photos of that house anywhere that he was aware of, and even if there were, Kira certainly hadn't been privy to them.

The living room actually still existed. It was the entryway to the house Angelie had owned before they met, and she had kept it even though they never used it. Come to think of it, Brian realized that he probably owned that house now, since Angelie didn't have any other family.

How would Kira have picked that setting? And maybe more important, why? It was where Angelie had been found, but nobody knew that, and he certainly hadn't told Kira. It was crazy. His eyes slid back up to the canvas whereupon he noticed rectangular patches on the walls. They were perfectly geometrical, vertical rectangles of lighter paint as if someone had pulled paintings off the wall leaving the discoloration in the spots where they had hung.

He just shook his head in wonder. From the moment Brian had decided to hire Kira, he had been skeptical of her abilities. Sure, he had read the testimonies about her revealing details of the departed to the surviving loved ones that they had been unaware of, but he hadn't really believed it. Hoped, yes. Believed, no. Well he certainly believed it now, but that just brought on another question. Not just the *how* could she have done it, but *why*? Why that scene, and what else was she going to draw in there?

Brian was by no means an art critic, but he'd been around enough wealthy people to have seen some masterpieces, and the work of art in front of him definitely did *not* suffer by comparison. The texture of it was amazing for one thing. He could only imagine that it was the result of adding the ashes to the paint. Angelie's ashes. The thought stole the joy from his experience as the burgeoning sense of loss again came crashing down upon him.

His next thought was that he wanted to talk to Kira. He even reached for his phone before deciding against it. If they left for a while it was most likely because she needed a break, and he didn't want to interrupt her peaceful time. He couldn't imagine how many hours she must have slaved over this canvas to accomplish so much. As an actor he knew how important your down time could be and how upset you could get if someone interrupted it. No, there would be time enough to talk to them when they got back and for now, he had nowhere else he needed to be.

He turned to the bar in the corner and decided to pour himself a glass of brandy.

Kira looked out across the vast expanse of beach, covered with activity. Like Sean said, it *did* bring back a bunch of memories but that wasn't what she was excited about. Kira just loved watching Sean take in new experiences. He invariably got as excited as a little kid when he was confronted with something new and she positively *loved* being there when he did.

It made the whole experience new for her as well. She had given a lot of thought to all the experiences she had enjoyed through her modeling years and how much fun it was going to be to relive them all through Sean's experience.

"Oh my gosh!" Sean exclaimed causing Kira to grin ear to ear. His well-timed comment perfectly dovetailed with her thoughts.

"Surely you've seen this beach on TV or movies somewhere?" She asked, already knowing the answer.

"Well, of course I have, but it's nothing like actually being here."

Sean cast his eyes around and Kira followed his gaze. The sights were so familiar to her. The groups of muscle-bound weightlifters pumping iron, the skaters weaving in and out of the crowd as they zoomed along the sidewalk, the volleyball nets scattered off in the distance with a ball rebounding repeatedly above it, all wove together to create the beach scene the world always saw on TV. There were even surfers out this afternoon which, though not uncommon, wasn't always a part of the show.

"What's going on over there?" Sean asked, with his steps already following his pointing finger. Kira just smiled and followed.

A crowd was gathering around a man who was juggling. Normally juggling wouldn't garner such a gathering, especially on a beach with this much diversity, but this guy wasn't just juggling. He was juggling items of different shapes and weights. At the moment Sean glanced over at him he was juggling a glass, an egg and a bowling ball.

"Oh my gosh!" Sean said as he moved up into the crowd.

Kira stayed beside him relishing in the expression on his face, just like a kid at his first Mardi Gras parade. It was wonder that she saw on his face, pure wonder. That expression on the face of a full-grown man was an extraordinary sight to behold, and she never tired of seeing it on this particular face.

"This guy has been here for years," Kira commented as she slipped an arm around Sean's waist, "I'm really kind of surprised he's still here."

"He's fantastic," Sean replied vacantly.

"I'll be interested to see if he still juggles the thing he was really famous for."

"What's that?" Sean asked pulling his eyes away from the juggler.

"Just keep watching. I'll tell you if he doesn't do it."

The guy took a break to thank the crowd and pass around the hat. Kira wondered what kind of a living this guy made off donations for his performances.

After numerous pats on the back and no small amount of money being thrown in the hat, the juggler turned around to a black leather trunk. He reached in, blocking most of the view with his body and then pulled out a chainsaw which he promptly started. The crowd flowed backwards in reflex to the raucous noise with mouths hung open. Apparently, there were still a bunch of people who had never seen this act before.

The chainsaw had a small steel rod welded along the top of the handle that stuck out behind it about six inches giving it a somewhat easier means to snatch out of the air. Without any further preamble, the juggler threw it up into the air and began to juggle it along with an apple and a china cup. The applause was spontaneous, and only increased as the performer nodded and snatched a bite of the apple he was manipulating without missing a single beat.

"That must be what you were talking about, right?"

"Yep," Kira answered, "He's been doing the same act for close to forty years."

"Wow. Is there much more?"

"Usually the chainsaw is his finale."

"Wow," Sean said again. "Let's go get something to eat."

Kira laughed at the abrupt change of subject. "What made you think of that all of a sudden?"

Sean turned to her and grinned as he began to pull her through the crowd. "The apple."

Kira laughed harder as they weaved their way out of the crowd.

"So, what is the best thing to have on the beach?"

Kira only had to think about it for a second. "Well, there are two things that a New York City street and a Los Angeles beach have in common."

She almost laughed again at his puzzled expression.

"You're kidding. What?"

"Crowds and amazing hot dog stands. We found one of those things, let's go find the other."

"Sounds great."

They headed off down the beach hand-in-hand dodging the skaters and the other walkers. The crashing surf overlaying all the other human sounds and the smell of the ocean lingering like a net beneath her other senses barely tweaked a few of Kira's memories. The new experiences with Sean and their easy conversation drowned out everything else and left her feeling almost giddy. Their love filled her heart so full; it occasionally muted everything else around her. Today was one of those days.

~

Sean's feelings closely matched Kira's. He knew this because hers were so strong that it was difficult to filter them from his own. Some moments he didn't even want to. It was a wonderful sensation to feel this close, this in tune, with another person. He had certainly never imagined love could be this way. That thought made him think of his marriage, and the ring on her left hand, being held by his right, rose to the top of his senses. He couldn't imagine being happier.

"Aye!" Sean exclaimed suddenly grabbing his head. After the briefest of pauses Sean's eyes shot up followed by a scowl, and he began searching the crowd.

"What?" Kira asked her concern thick in her voice.

"It can't be, that's what," Sean said. There was lightning in his gaze and steel in his voice.

It didn't take him long to find his target. He walked directly to the hotdog stand he and Kira had already been heading toward. It seemed to be unmanned but Sean wasn't looking *at* the hotdog stand, he was looking *around* it. He veered slightly toward the beach with Kira following. He could sense her bewilderment as he dodged people in an effort to go faster. It was that guy again, the one from the museum. Sean could see the oily black hair on top of his skinny frame walking quickly away.

"Hey," Sean called breaking into a jog. The guy didn't react, so Sean tried again, louder this time. "Hey you, with the black hair!" Several people turned toward him before his target finally did. Once he did, Sean was certain it was the same guy from the museum. What were the chances of running across the same guy twice in two days in Los Angeles? Astronomical, he decided. The look on the guy's face convinced Sean he had been recognized as well and that was followed, a bare second later, by a thought from the guy.

Not him again, Sean received, as clear as if it had been uttered by vocal cords, followed by, *I'll stop this asshole.*

"Aye!" Sean exclaimed again as a pain lanced across his forehead. Again, like in the museum, it felt similar to thought but with some other quality. More intense somehow, and more tangible was the only way Sean could think to describe it, and in this case slightly more intense than he had experienced at the museum. It was accompanied by a thought from the guy.

Talus 3 millimeters clockwise.

Sean wondered what a talus was as he ignored the sudden pounding in his head and continued to pick up speed. Instinctively, and for no reason he could understand, Sean felt the need to defend himself as if someone had just thrown a knife at him. Although he couldn't visibly see any danger one of those intense, tangible thoughts seemed to be flying his direction with lightning speed and malicious intent. As a reflex, and without even being fully aware of what he was doing,

Sean used the will of his mind to deflect the mental knife being aimed at him like using a racquet to deflect a deadly tennis ball. There was a look of surprise on the guy's face when Sean continued his advance undeterred, and then he garnered a sensation of fear followed by yet another thought.

The girl is with him.

Another wave of pain streamed into Sean's mind and those same words again.

Talus 3 millimeters clockwise.

This time, however, the words were accompanied by a scream and Sean spun in shock to find and feel Kira go down in a heap, pain emanating from her as she reached for her ankle.

The fleeing man was instantly forgotten as Sean reached for Kira. Sean could still feel vestiges of the skinny man's thought lingering around Kira.

He could feel it moving in a certain direction in almost the same way that someone knows without being told if an elevator is going up or down. The intense quality was fading, but it was still tangible enough for him to grab wisps of it with his mind. His protective instincts toward Kira made him act without thinking, and he reversed the momentum of the tangible thought.

Talus 3 millimeters counterclockwise, Sean thought for no reason he was aware of. The sensation of pain abruptly disappeared from Kira's mind, even as her yell was cut short.

The crowd parted as Sean bent down to help Kira up but otherwise paid them no attention. He guessed nothing qualified as unusual on this beach.

"You OK?" Sean asked.

"I am now. What happened and why did it stop?"

"Kira, it was that same freak from the museum."

"That's impossible. There's no way we could run into the same guy in two days in this town by accident."

"That's what I was thinking. But if you think back, it seems we have a tendency to get drawn into these impossible situations. Maybe it wasn't an accident. Maybe we're supposed to cross paths with this guy."

"But Sean, this doesn't even have anything to do with my painting."

"I know. Maybe it has something to do with me. Because of my . . . uh . . . gift growing. That guy is doing something to people using his mind, and I can feel it if I'm anywhere near."

"But you started chasing him. Why didn't he do something to you?"

"I think he tried. I felt the thought like an attacker coming for me, but somehow, I think I defended myself. It was a reflex; I'm not exactly sure what I did. Maybe that's why he did something to you. To stop me when acting directly toward me didn't work."

"This is just too strange," Kira said. They were standing now, facing each other on the sidewalk beside the beach. The people continued to flow by them, giving them irritated glances.

"Let's get off this sidewalk," Sean said, taking Kira's hand, "These annoyed sensations from everyone are distracting me."

Kira let herself be led, looking pensive. "If the guy did something to me, Sean, why did it stop?"

"Um, I don't know."

"Did you sense a thought from him?"

"Yeah."

"Well, what was it?"

Sean thought for just a second. "Talus three centimeters . . . no, not centimeters, millimeters clockwise. What's a talus?"

"I don't know, but I think we should go back to Brian's and get on the computer and find out."

"Sounds like a plan. Should we call Jackson, or do you think he'll be there already?"

"Let's give him a ring. I'm getting antsy to get back to work on that painting, too. I don't want Brian to think we're just using him."

"Once he gets a glimpse of your work, I don't think you'll have to worry about that. You got a *lot* done."

Jackson showed up fifteen minutes later. He must have made a point of staying in the area. The ride back was uneventful or at least as uneventful as it gets when riding through LA traffic. Sean and Kira were both lost in their own thoughts.

A rthur was burning with rage. Every footstep he took as he strode down the paved sidewalk felt like he was pounding a nail in the concrete with his shoe. This was the second time in two days he had run into that couple. How was that even possible in a city the size of Los Angeles? The mild heat from the afternoon sun paled next to the furnace burning within him. Who was this guy and how was he managing to interfere? He had tried to stop the boy and it hadn't worked. It *always* worked. Did that guy do something? Maybe, like he did at the museum? His thought had worked on the girl just fine . . . at least it had at first. Something strange was definitely going on.

He continued to walk rapidly, considering possibilities. After turning away from the beach, a block or so from the encounter, Arthur unconsciously headed back up hill toward his apartment. It was a cool afternoon, but he was sweating. He didn't even notice the sounds of the passing cars, familiar as he was with the area. He wiped his brow, wondering if it was from the exertion or his emotional state.

He thought briefly about just leaving California, but he liked it here, and he had possibilities here for his headaches. Also, moving would require money, a commodity of which he was in short supply. That turned his thoughts back to financial considerations.

Now he not only wanted to find a way to use his gift to gain some much-needed cash, he was going to find that guy again and find a way to punish him, or if not him, at least he could punish his girlfriend. He had no idea *how* he was going to find the guy, but it didn't worry him. He had a feeling they would meet again whether he did anything or not.

Thoughts of vengeance soothed his raging temper. Nobody treated him like that. No one was going to take advantage of him or take away any of the things he wanted to do. The little tendril of fear that slithered through the back of his mind was pointedly ignored.

Strolling past one of the many shops on Rodeo Drive he saw a woman emerge from the back of a Cadillac limousine. She was moving awkwardly as her belly was heavily swollen. She was at least seven months pregnant. She looked and moved like a cow, but a cow covered in jewelry. The thought crossed Arthur's mind to walk by her and trip her. That would teach the bitch. Maybe he could even snatch some of that jewelry off her neck. It must be worth ...

Suddenly, he had it. He knew how he was going to get the money he needed to do whatever he wanted. A nearby bus stop bench provided just what he needed most right now, a place to wait. The woman would certainly come back to the same place to be picked up, whether the driver waited in the area or just returned when she called, and in her condition, it was a cinch she wasn't going to be strolling around for very long. A smile crept across his face that made him seem almost attractive, that is unless you knew what was going on behind it. In that case that smile would seem more like the frozen faux smile of a viper patiently awaiting its approaching prey.

Arthur rehearsed in his mind what needed to be done. He would need to approach the woman quickly and convince her that she was going to have to listen to him. That would be the easy part. Then he would need to get into the back of the limo with her and have her convince the driver to leave them alone. Maybe even roll up the intervening privacy glass. Then the coercion could really begin. He just needed to convince her what he could do, and to accomplish that convincing, quickly. To that end, he spent the next few moments reviewing images in his mind of the medical texts he had read referring to women.

As he anticipated, he didn't have to wait long. The woman came waddling down from his left with both hands full of shopping bags. Clothes it looked like, probably something to augment her rapidly changing pregnancy wardrobe. To Arthur's surprise the woman walked up and sat beside him on the bench pausing only to grace him with a sneer of disgust as she heaved her bulk onto the bench with a very un-lady-like grunt.

"Surely, you're not waiting for a bus," Arthur began in his most charming tone. On the rare occasions when he wanted to be pleasant his smile and his crystal blue eyes worked to good effect.

"Of course, I'm not," she replied, the sneer in her tone easily matching the visual one she had cast upon him prior to sitting. "I'm waiting for my car."

With that last she had returned her gaze to the street, dismissing him as completely as if she'd told him to scurry along. Her disinterested look was disturbed, however, by the sudden approach of a bus. The breeze, fumes, and dust of the approaching city transport brought an absolute scowl to her countenance that reminded Arthur of some sort of disgruntled Disney caricature. The mental image actually made him smile.

People shuffled off the large transport with no one getting on, though the driver stared at the two of them expectantly for a moment before shrugging and closing the door. Seconds later, the bus hissed off to its next stop leaving them in relative quiet.

"Weren't you waiting on the bus?" The lady asked obviously disconcerted at his continued presence.

"Why no," he replied, the smile dropping completely from his face as he continued, "I was waiting for you."

"Me? What do you mean? I have no idea . . ." The woman winced in sudden pain as Arthur stimulated a pressure point in the side of her neck.

"Shut up," he said simultaneously, "Or you're going to experience a whole new level of pain. Do you understand me?"

"No . . . How did you . . . ooooow!" He tweaked another nerve, this time beneath her ear.

"I said shut up. If you say another word other than answering my questions, I'll make you wish you were dead. Do you understand?"

"Yes," she answered, her voice quivering and her eyes wide with both shock and fear.

"When your car arrives, we are both going to get in the back, and you're going to have the driver roll up the privacy screen. Do you understand?"

"Yes. But . . ." Her next words were cut off by a little scream as she jerked her head and reached for her eye where he had pinched a nerve.

"Only answer my questions. GOT IT?"

"Yes." She was almost whimpering now.

"What's your name?"

"Julia," she answered carefully

At that moment the long black limo pulled up to the bus stop directly in front of them, and the driver began to get out.

"Introduce me as your friend Sam," Arthur said in a barely discernable whisper. "And don't you dare make a mistake."

Her head was bobbing in the affirmative as she heaved her bulk from the bench at her driver's approach.

The driver was efficient and agile. He had his large torso out of the limo almost before Julia could get to a full standing position. He briskly moved around the car to open the door. The man was large, but his eyes burned with intelligence. He immediately fixed his dark eyes on Arthur with a suspicious glare. Apparently, Julia didn't miss the look.

"Oscar, this is my friend Sam. He saw me struggling with my packages and stopped to help. We'll give him a lift."

Oscar's eyes shifted to Julia then back to Arthur with only a minute lessening of suspicion. "Yes, Ma'am," he responded as he opened the door and took her hand to help her in.

Arthur took her packages and held her other hand. Once she was inside, he slid in beside her and turned to reach for the door. Oscar was still there perusing him as though looking for the bulge of a weapon. Satisfied he moved to close the door while Arthur managed a smile.

"Thanks, Oscar."

Oscar closed the door without responding. While he walked around to the other side of the car Arthur turned back to Julia.

"Quick. How far is it to your house?"

"Uh . . . twenty minutes or so up in the Hills."

"Good. Now tell him to roll up the center divider."

"I can do that from here," she said reaching for a button on the side console.

Oscar got into the car and closed his door. "Where may I take you, Sam?"

Arthur had already been considering that question, and he was prepared. "You can drop me at the Beverly Hills Hotel. I think it's on the way." He turned his gaze back to Julia and looked meaningfully at her hand on the console. "Thank you, Oscar," she said as she depressed the button. The intervening opaque privacy divider slid up quietly.

She looked back at Arthur questioningly but too afraid to speak.

Arthur hesitated while the privacy screen finished its cycle. "How much is the jewelry you're wearing worth?"

Her eyes widened again. "Um, I'm not sure."

The end of her sentence was punctuated with a sharp squeak as she grabbed the far side of her neck. Arthur had made a point of crossing his arms so that both hands would be in view to her.

"Wrong answer. You must have some idea. Now tell me," he said as his eyes scanned down to the huge diamond on her finger.

"The necklace and bracelets are insured for seventy-five thousand."

"What about the ring?"

"Oh, please don't take my wedding . . . oww!"

"How much?"

"Maybe a hundred thousand."

"OK. Here's what you're going to do. Let me see your driver's license."

"But . . ." This time just a look from Arthur stopped her, and she reached down for her purse. Arthur looked at the address on the front and told her to put it back.

"Now. After you drop me off at the hotel you will go straight home, put that jewelry in a plain bag, wait one hour and place it under something on the left side of your porch. Do you have something on the porch?"

"Yes. There is a concrete lion there."

"Fine so you understand what to do?"

Julia just nodded.

"And to make sure we understand each other, if you don't do what I say, or if you alert anyone, I will hurt your child." Arthur punctuated the statement with a momentary restriction of the umbilical cord which apparently caused the baby to kick.

Julia's hands flew to her abdomen as she looked down reflexively. Her eyes widened with shock and tears welled. Terror lay transparent in them as she looked back up.

"No no! Please don't hurt my child." Her voice rose to a near shriek.

"Do as I say, and you'll both be fine. Just remember, that was merely a taste of what I can do. I could just as easily separate your placenta from its wall, and I can do it from any distance. So, don't test me." Arthur hadn't studied pregnancy enough he realized; it was a mistake he would soon remedy.

Now her tear-filled eyes widened even further, and the terror converted to horror as she nodded back to Arthur.

The rest was a breeze. Oscar dropped Arthur off at the Beverly Hills hotel, though not without some strange looks in his rearview mirror, which Arthur pointedly ignored. He watched them drive off and glanced at his wrist to check the time.

An hour and fifteen minutes later Arthur showed up at Julia's house in a taxi. The cab waited at the street while Arthur walked the hundred yards up the finely manicured driveway. True to her word, there was a small plastic grocery bag behind the large stone lion to the left of the front door. Arthur wasn't surprised. No mother would risk her child, and even though he had lied about his distance limitation, she didn't know that.

A rare smile garnished Arthur's face as he strolled back toward the cab. He had a few things to learn about fencing stolen jewelry, but he had just discovered a virtually unlimited source for income. He also needed to find more wealthy, pregnant women. He knew exactly where to do that.

Kira was still preoccupied when they pulled into Brian's driveway. So much so that she didn't even notice that Brian's car was in the garage, well one of them anyway.

The more she rehearsed events in her mind, the more she was certain that Sean had done something. The black-haired guy had done something to her, but then it stopped so suddenly that she felt certain Sean must have *done* something. But he had no idea of what he might have done.

"Brian's home," Sean said absently as Jackson pulled the car to a stop in front of the main door.

Kira looked up again. "Well, I guess we're going to find out what he thinks of the painting so far."

"He's going to be amazed," Sean muttered as he opened his door and reached for Kira's hand to help her out.

"I certainly hope so."

They walked hand in hand to the door which opened just as Sean was reaching for the handle.

"Well hello there," Brian said as he pulled the door back wide, "Did Jackson take care of you alright?"

"Oh, he was wonderful," Kira answered before Sean could get words out. Kira caught a look in his eye and suspected that his hesitation had something to do with thoughts he was picking up from Brian.

"Told you so," Sean said as if on cue. He said it too low for Brian's ears, then raised his voice. "Yeah Brian, I can't tell you how glad I am he was doing the driving around this town and not me. I thought traffic in Kansas City was bad. Sheesh!"

"Did you get a chance to look at my work?" Kira said as she stepped by Brian and into the house. Sean was right behind her.

"I certainly did, but let's get a drink and sit down, and we can talk about it."

Brian led them into the great den area where the painting still stood on its easel. Prior to getting to that side of the room, he veered straight to the bar.

"What do you like to drink, Kira?"

"White wine if you have it."

"Certainly. What about you, Sean?"

"Do you have any ginger ale?"

Brian hesitated for just an instant at the non-alcoholic request, and Sean reflexively picked up his thought. *Don't they drink alcohol in Kansas?*

"As a matter of fact, I do," Brian said out loud.

"Great," Sean began, "then maybe you could pour a little over some rum." The words were hardly out of his mouth when he sensed Brian's touch of regret regarding his previous thought.

I have to get out of his head, Sean thought to himself.

~

Kira let her smile slip onto her face. She knew Sean so well that she imagined she knew most of what just happened. Brian's hesitation must have been regarding Sean's question about the ginger ale, and it had prompted Sean to read his thoughts. She would have bet a crisp fifty that Sean's next thought was about staying out of the poor guy's head.

What a chore it must be to have to deal with that all the time, she thought. Surely, at least a percentage of his thought garnering was instinctive. From what she knew, *not* reading thoughts took a conscious effort while the sensing itself came automatically.

Sean and Kira had seated themselves side by side on the large leather couch across from the windows. The painting was at an angle, so it was visible from the couch. It was currently backlit by the afternoon sun flowing through the giant windows. The sea stretched beyond in the distance.

Brian brought the drinks over to them, then sat down in a chair facing them. He read their faces for a moment before shifting his gaze to the painting. He began speaking without turning his head from the canvas.

"I must admit, I was amazed at not only how much you have accomplished already but at the material itself. How did you choose that setting?"

"You recognize it then," Kira responded.

"Yes; though, until recently I hadn't seen it in a long time. It was Angelie's before we got married. How did you know about it? I mean, it is where we found Angelie, but I know the paper didn't reveal that, and there were no pictures taken."

"I didn't," Kira answered, "It is just what I saw when I started. I have a question for you though, Brian. Who the heck is Lisa?"

Brian's head snapped back to Kira's eyes and for a brief instant you could have heard a pin drop in the room. She felt Sean's senses go on high alert while Brian's mouth opened, as if to speak. Still, for a couple of seconds, nothing came out.

At that instant Kira wished she *did* have Sean's abilities. What had her question triggered? She was almost jealous of the several second head-start she knew Sean was getting in answer to her question.

"Where did you get that name? I don't think she has ever revealed that to the press."

"You mean, Lisa is Angelie?" Kira began.

"Yes," Brian answered, "You mean you didn't know that?"

"No. It was a name I got while I was beginning to paint. I had no idea who it was."

"Oh my God," Brian virtually gasped, "Your abilities really are astounding."

Kira hesitated. What she was about to say next concerned her, but in the end the truth was the only way to proceed.

"Also, Brian, I'm pretty sure she is in that place in the painting for a meeting with somebody. I don't know who yet, but I imagine we'll find out when I start painting next. I get the impression it's someone she's excited about, too."

"Really?" Brian began, then paused.

~

Sean's curiosity got the better of him, and he let Brian's thoughts flow into his mind. The first thought was a flash of jealousy, followed closely by self-deprecation at even considering such a thought about Angelie.

Next, curiosity filled his mind which flowed naturally into his next question, which for Sean was an easy transition from mental awareness to audio recognition.

"So, you think you'll know who this is when you paint next? And if there was someone else there, why wouldn't they have reported Angelie's death? As it was, *nobody*, reported it. I found her by tracking her phone when I couldn't reach her unexpectedly after I got back in town."

Sean tried to back pedal out of Brian's mind as fast as he could, but he wasn't fast enough. The image of finding her cold, dead body bounded into his awareness, and he could even smell the odor that had accosted Brian along with the horror of his wife being dead.

"Excuse me," Sean said suddenly as he virtually jumped to his feet. "I have to go to the restroom."

He was holding his hand over his mouth as he bolted out of the room, hoping desperately that everyone would suspect simple nausea.

Kira guessed what had happened and intervened smoothly. "I guess his country boy stomach was no match for a good old-fashioned hot dog stand hot dog. I just hope it doesn't get me too."

"I hope he's OK. Should I go check on him?"

"I'm sure he'll be fine as long as he can act like no one knows he has a sensitive stomach."

"Well, OK. But if you think I can do anything to help, let me know."

"Thanks Brian, if he's not back shortly, I'll go check on him."

They both sat quietly for a moment before Brian spoke again. "When do you expect to work some more on the painting? Now you have me intrigued and more than just a little curious. Surely this person she was going to meet never made it to her house before the . . . uh . . . incident."

"I'll probably do some more tonight or start fresh in the morning."

"Kira, do you really not know what you are going to paint before you start? I mean each and every session you don't know before hand?"

"The only time I know before hand is on the very first session. I usually get a sense of the setting before I first begin the tribute."

"Tribute?"

"Oh. Yeah. Did I not mention that I refer to them as Tributes? As in tribute paintings: a tribute to the deceased for the living. To me that's what they are."

"I guess that was in your literature somewhere. It just hadn't really registered. I like it, actually."

About that time Sean entered the far end of the room and Kira, to her own surprise, sent an urgent thought to him.

I blamed it on the street vendor hot dog. He had told her that he got her directed thoughts quite clearly. Well, here was a chance for him to prove it.

His eyes flickered to her pointedly and the hint of smile touched the corners of his mouth.

He got it, she thought. Her next thought was how cool that was.

Sean's eyes shifted to Brian. "I'm sorry to race off Brian. I think that street vendor hot dog got to me," He paused for a second. "Dang, it sure tasted good going down though."

"Gross! No more details please," Kira blurted out.

Brian was just laughing. "Isn't that the truth? I've had a similar experience in the past. I keep going back though."

Sean laughed conspiratorially. "I know, right? They're just a little too good to give up on. Give me two days and I'm sure I'll be blaming something else for the stomach issue so I can have another one."

Brian laughed again, "That's exactly what I did."

They all had a brief laugh as Sean sat down by Kira and graced her with a very brief thankful look. She didn't miss it.

"Well, I hate to rush off, but I need to shower and change. I have a meeting with a director to go over this new movie. I guess we're having dinner after that, so once again, make yourself at home, there's food here, or feel free to have Jackson take you to dinner. He's a great resource to suggest places as well."

"Thanks, Brian," Kira piped in. "I think we've been out and about enough today. I think we'll stay in and eat. That way if I get the urge to jump back into the painting this evening we'll be right here."

"Sounds great. I wanted to thank you again, Kira and reiterate how much I love what you're doing. This feels *so* right. It already seems to be giving me some closure I didn't get from the service."

"And maybe answer a few questions," she added.

Brian's smile faded slightly. "That, too."

With that, he rose from the chair and headed toward the door.

Sean watched him go and took a moment to drink in the man's thoughts. He really was tremendously pleased with Kira's work. It was gratifying, almost as if it was Sean's own accomplishment.

They both sat in silence briefly as Brian disappeared down the hall.

"Well that was interesting," Kira began, "I'm gathering that something Brian thought sent you racing to the restroom?"

"Yeah. Great cover by the way, and kudos to you for sending me the thought. That was a good idea."

When Sean didn't continue, she prompted, "Well, don't leave me hanging. What thought caused that sudden bathroom sprint?"

"Oh. Well, I couldn't back out of his mind quick enough to avoid getting the image of him finding Angelie. She had been dead a couple of days, and it was a wicked combination of disgusting physical sensations and the emotional horror of her being gone. Kira, I think I'm going to have to die before you. I don't think I could stand it."

"We'll go together."

"Fine," he answered smiling.

"In the meantime, why don't we go for a swim, then see what we can dig up in the kitchen?"

"Sounds like a plan."

CHAPTER

The swim was delightful. They managed to catch the sun dip into the ocean before they dressed and headed for the kitchen. Sean was delighted to find a couple of gourmet chicken potpies in the freezer, and dinner had been a simple matter of putting them in the oven. They took their time eating and chatting before retiring again to the den.

Sean stared out at the evening sky through the giant windows, waiting for Kira to be ready.

Kira sat down on the stool. A casual glance told her Sean was settling in on the couch. She began to mix, reflecting on the memory of Sean being with her when she painted. At those times, when brush was working canvas, she had a sense of how it must feel for Sean all the time. At those moments, she could feel him with her, sense his emotions, and largely be aware of even his thoughts. She poured most of the remaining ashes into her paint mixture and stole another glance at Sean.

His eyes were closed as if he was napping, but she knew better. At that instant his eyes popped open again and he smiled.

"Are our thoughts wandering a bit?" He asked, with an engaging smirk on his face.

She knew he had sensed her thoughts, and therefore she knew that he knew she had sensed his as well. It was all so confusing sometimes.

"You know one of the advantages of conversation?" She asked, smiling back at him and concentrating on her next sentence.

For the briefest of instances, he had a look of concentration on his face, then he laughed at the thought he had snagged.

"It has a stopping point?" He laughed again.

"Yeah," she answered adding a slightly serious tone. "You can stop. Don't you get tired of having a nonstop rendition of everyone's thoughts playing through your head like a recording you can't shut off?"

Now it was Sean's turn to become earnest. "Now you know why I was such a recluse for all those years on the farm. Even before I could pick up on people's thoughts, their emotions were just like that for me, a constant thread of sensation pulling my own emotions back and forth in response to theirs. The truth of the matter is that these sessions with you and your paintings have helped me to gain a new level of control I never thought I'd have.

I don't know why but working with you has helped me improve my filter for blocking that constant flow. I think maybe it's because that is what I'm trying to do for you, be a filter between you and the reality you create with your brush and canvas." Sean fell silent for a moment. Pensive with the concept he had just expressed.

"The reality I create?" She finally responded. "You think I'm creating reality when I paint?"

Sean looked sharply up at her. "Don't you?"

Now it was Kira's turn to become pensive. The silence hung softly in the cavernous room; her mixing bowl forgotten in her hands.

"I certainly never thought of it that way," she finally responded.

"Well you absolutely do. Think of all the changes that have come about as a result of your paintings. Not just people finding peace with the loss of their loved ones.

Kira, twenty-year-old murders have been discovered, lost bodies recovered and laid to rest, an arsonist stopped, and her secret discovered, not to mention lives saved. Yes, you absolutely create a new reality with that paintbrush of yours. And from my perspective it is a very positive one." The concept was quite a revelation for her. She couldn't deny the logic of his words but the notion of creating reality was almost too ponderous to entertain. He apparently sensed her thoughts . . .

"Oh, I don't mean like God. But in a smaller way we all create reality by the choices we make and the way we interact with the people and the world around us. Walt Disney created cartoons that made children happy. Wasn't he improving their reality and that of their parents if in no other way than providing entertainment to give their parents a break from constantly monitoring them? Yours is just a bit more direct than that."

Kira smiled. "Well when you put it that way it doesn't sound near as intimidating. However, it's still a little intimidating to be compared to Walt Disney."

"OK, I might be a tad biased."

"You think?" She replied. "Well maybe I ought to do a little reality creating right now before this paint dries in the bowl."

"Sounds good to me."

Kira applied the paint from the bowl in her hands and then that of several smaller bowls to the palette sitting on the little TV tray table beside her and her face lost all expression as she lifted the brush to the canvas.

~

Sean again had the sensation of Kira's emotions becoming fuzzy and now a sensation of falling. Images blurred giving the impression of great speed which suddenly cleared, and Sean found himself in the living room that Kira had partially painted. This image wasn't incomplete however, it was finished in great detail; at least the room itself was detailed. Beautiful burgundy drapes covered large windows and a plush mauve carpet covered the floor. There were paintings featured around the walls, but as his glance continued, Sean realized that several of them were still depicted as frames-only. He was sitting on the couch looking in the direction of the door into the room.

It was open and there was a figure in the doorway. It was a man and he had an unusual expression on his face.

Maybe it was an amalgam of more than one emotion. Excitement, fear, joy, and concern all seemed to be battling for dominance on his features. He had blue eyes and light hair and was raising his right hand in a gesture of greeting. Sean got a bit of a shock when he, instinctively, tried to access the guy's thoughts and got nothing. It took him aback for a moment until he remembered this was just a vision and not even his vision at that but Kira's.

His attention was distracted from the man, however, as one of the empty picture frames suddenly acquired a composition. It was a skiff on a rock and sandy shore with a calm ocean behind it. Sean thought he'd seen that picture before and imagined that it was near a lighthouse that was still absent from the scene.

Meanwhile the man entering the room took another step forward. The entryway had a bit of a foyer-like construction with walls on both sides of the doorway, which opened to the left. Sean could just barely see the edge of another frame on the wall to the right of the door, another, currently empty, painting. Then the man spoke.

"Hello again, Lisa," he said tentatively.

"Hi, Elliot," she replied, a touch of excitement in her voice.

The female voice was a bit of a shock for Sean as it felt as though it came from him, sitting there on the couch. It took a moment to clarify in his mind that he *was* that female character on the couch at the moment. Sean quickly reminded himself that Lisa was in fact Angelie? It was all rather confusing.

"I wasn't sure when you'd make it over, or even if you would," she continued.

"Why wouldn't I come by? I'm thrilled to really start getting to know you. And I'm a scientist. I'm always on time." He countered, continuing to move into the room.

Sean sensed, through Kira, from Elliot an underlying nervousness. Elliot was struggling with something. It didn't seem to be Lisa that was causing the problem. However, Sean couldn't pick up anything else to tell him what it was. It was frustrating. The very thing he was trying to accomplish in real life was happening here in this recreation of the past beneath Kira's hands.

He *couldn't* just turn it back on and discern what Elliot was thinking. Here, in this world, he was limited by the strokes of Kira's brush and for once, he wasn't enjoying it. It suddenly gave him quite a different perspective about his feelings for his abilities.

They *were* a part of him and when that part was taken away, he felt a sense of loss.

An illuminating concept to remember and consider later, he thought, as Elliot continued speaking.

"Why did you have us meet here?" Elliot asked. His voice was almost trembling now. "Is there some reason you don't want me to meet your husband?"

"Nothing so sinister as that," Lisa replied, with an easy placating tone. It was almost a giggle. "The fact is I wasn't sure I would even be able to find you to begin with and how you would feel when I did, so I've kept it as kind of a secret. More like a surprise actually. I wanted to surprise him, and I wanted to wait to do it until I had met you and you felt comfortable."

Sean's eyes shifted to a slight movement in the edge of the room, near the door. The other painting on the wall. The one that had been empty a moment ago was developing an image, or rather an image was moving into it. At that instant the rest of the image in the frame resolved into a mirror. It wasn't a painting at all.

Was Kira drawing that mirror at this very instant? The wonder changed quickly to concern as a small bit more of an image slid into the frame. It was someone else; someone was standing just outside of view behind the door frame, and the angle of the mirror was allowing his reflection to move into view. Why was someone else there and why was Elliot not mentioning him? Was he just there to listen? Suddenly, a chill spidered up Sean's spine and he wrenched . . .

~

Kira's paintbrush dropped to the floor, and she gasped. Her eyes focused, and she turned sharply to Sean who was staring at her vacantly. "Why did you do that? That was almost painful."

"I . . . I'm not sure. Something . . ." As he spoke Sean got up off the couch and moved toward the canvas. "Look Kira, there on the wall. I thought that frame was going to be a painting, but it's a mirror. See? And there is an image coming into view. It has to be reflecting someone just outside the door. Had you not noticed it?"

Kira's eyes tracked Sean's. "No, I hadn't, but I see now. So why did you pull us out?"

"I didn't really mean to. It was just an instinct. I'm sorry."

"No. It's fine. If you had an instinct to pull us out, then I'm glad you did.

That's why you're there with me to begin with, remember? As for the image in the mirror, I'm really curious. If this is the first or second time she has met this Elliot, why the heck would he bring someone with him. It doesn't make any sense."

A silence settled between them as they both took in the new revelations.

"Sometimes being the main character in the scenes you are creating is a bit unnerving," Sean ventured.

"You should have tried it when it was Jason in the act of committing murder."

Her tone was dead flat causing Sean's eyes to shift abruptly up to hers. He shivered. "I'm sorry," he said, opening himself momentarily to her remembered terror.

She just smiled back at him and reached a reassuring hand for his shoulder. "Ancient history," she began, "Now can we please get back to the business of painting?"

"We should probably clean up Brian's carpet first," Sean said, glancing down at the spot remaining from the dropped paintbrush.

Kira smiled and reached into her bag of art supplies. "This should do it," she said handing him a small squeeze bottle and a little rag. "I've done this before," She added. She had already retrieved her paintbrush and never actually dropped the palette. While Sean cleaned, Kira turned and resituated herself on the stool. She glanced back at Sean.

"You ready?"

"As I'll ever be," he replied, as he finished the small cleanup.

Kira lifted her brush to the canvas and the room once again disappeared.

~

The living room reappeared but this time from a third person's perspective. Sean was looking at Elliot on his left and Angelie on his right. Apparently, they were now outside observers in the scene and not in the body of one of the characters. Angelie was even more beautiful than the photos he had seen, and her face held his gaze for a brief moment.

Sean felt a sudden ripping sensation, and the room seemed to accelerate into a blur. Sean's stomach reacted as though he had just crested the highest climb of a rollercoaster and was now starting down.

The sensation of speed was dizzying, but just as it seemed it was about to crescendo, the feeling stopped.

Abruptly.

He was now in another room. It seemed like a study with broad windows and Angelie sitting behind a grand piano with a music stand right beside it.

For a brief second the entire scene was frozen like a picture. It was the strangest sensation. Sean imagined Kira sitting still on her stool while she took in the new scene, undecided momentarily as to what stroke of her brush was required next. Then the scene jerked and moved, stopped, then jerked and moved again. Several times the jerking started and stopped until finally the room returned to normal motion. Angelie was writing something on a music tablet beside her, and the thin grey curtains on the windows were moving from some gentle breeze. Sean realized that the broad windows were open, and he tried to peer out of them. All he could discern was a variety of foliage. And then he heard it.

Music.

She played a few bars on the piano then stopped and wrote on the staff paper she kept close at hand. It had the five lines already drawn on it for music notation. She was in the middle of writing a song.

~

Kira was enthralled. She wondered if this was a song no one else had heard. She felt Sean wondering the same thing. Here inside her painting experiences, she was aware of Sean's thoughts just like he was aware of hers. It was an interesting situation and yet another tremendous insight into what it must be like for Sean all the time. Angelie continued to work on the song as she pondered. She wondered briefly if this room was in the same house as the one in which she was currently painting. Whether it was or wasn't this was a room she hadn't seen.

The scene shifted suddenly with Angelie in the middle of writing on the tablet. They were now back in the living room with the open door and Elliot standing there smiling.

It was also the same perspective as before, to the side where she could see both Angelie and Elliot. Kira could almost sense her hand moving on the canvas . . . but not quite. Her attention refocused when Elliot spoke.

He picked up right where he had left off the last time Sean and Kira were in the room with them, as if they had never left.

"I would feel OK meeting him now I think," he responded, answering the comment Angelie had previously made.

"That would be great. We can do that next time we meet. Take a seat and make yourself comfortable."

Elliot started to move toward a chair, but that wasn't what caught Kira's attention. There was a hint of movement near the door. Her eyes turned that way landing on the mirror on the wall. It was the partial profile she had seen earlier when Sean yanked himself and her from the trance. It was slowly moving further into view.

Arthur's eyes opened abruptly. He had been sitting in bed and must have dozed off. What had awakened him? He had the sensation that he was being watched. But that couldn't be. The room had blackout blinds on all the windows. He lay there for a moment pondering. He had the sensation that something important had happened, but he couldn't for the life of him think of what it might be. Moments later his eyes slipped closed again, bringing with them a repeated and unwanted dream. It was only one of many.

~

"Arthur, go to your room!"

Just the sound of his mother's voice made is stomach drop. The content, even more so. "Mom, I'm sorry! They wouldn't let me stay! The nurse called you before I could talk her out of it."

"I don't care, Arthur!" She screamed as she slammed the front door hard enough to make the room rattle.

"It's not my fault! I tried to tell her you had a friend over. She didn't listen. She said kids with 101-degree fevers weren't allowed on school grounds. I didn't mean to bother you."

"Well you did! You've ruined my plans with your stupidity. Now I said go to your room!" she punctuated the command by throwing the nearest object at his head, which in this case was her set of car keys.

Arthur had expected this and ducked out of the way just in time to avoid having the weighty metal ridges connect with his face. That was a mistake. His mother's already contorted face flushed with fury, and she made a beeline for him with retribution burning in her eyes.

"OK, I'm going. I said I was sorry! I just don't want to be in my room all day again, please?"

It was mistake number two. Arthur should have known better, but he was too tired to think straight, and the fever was making him slightly dizzy, so he didn't move fast enough. In less than a second his mother had his hair clenched in her fist and shoved him against the wall. The smell of rotten breath from her decaying teeth made his stomach heave, but he stifled it. He'd made enough mistakes already. He didn't want to make it worse, and he knew from experience how much worse she could get.

"You're an insufferable little shit with your excuses and your demands. A real man would have stood up for himself and for me, to that idiotic little school nurse and not ruined everything. But you're too weak to do anything. Just like your pathetic father. You'll never be a real man. You're an embarrassment to me and to all men every-where. No woman could ever respect a spineless rat like you. You're lucky I keep you locked in your room and don't just send you away to be devoured by all the men and women of the world who would see you for the weakling that you really are."

And with that she threw him on the floor by his hair. The impact of it startled him, but not enough to keep him still. He scrambled down the short hallway to his bedroom without another word. Nevertheless, he heard his mother screeching behind him.

"Now I don't want to hear another word out of you this evening. I'm having more company over tonight, and if he even suspects that you exist, I'll make you wish you didn't."

Arthur began to suspect that she really had a different reason for wanting him to stay in his room.

The apartment was a small two-bedroom affair with dingy walls and poor lighting. It was located in the seedy end of Long Beach, California, but at least it wasn't some home belonging to his mom's man-du-jour. That would simply mean that as soon as the guy was through with his mother, they would be looking for somewhere else to live. The appliances worked most of the time except when the refriger-ator would go on the fritz and his mom would end up having to replace some food they couldn't afford because it had spoiled. They had been here for six months now and the little place felt more like home than any other place Arthur could remember, not that he wanted to remember the others . . .

Arthur closed his bedroom door with a mixture of depression and fury warring within him. His mother was mercurial at best, and he suspected that his frequent trips to his room had more to do with men his mother had coming over than with any real issues with his behavior.

He was thirty minutes into his enforced confinement when he heard the doorbell ring. His mother had known many men since his dad left a few years ago and at eight years old he hadn't understood some of what he had been going through living with her, but now, at ten, he was beginning to understand.

She was attractive enough to have suitors for her affections, but they always used her and left. He couldn't understand why none of them stayed. He was unfamiliar yet with the term prostitution and even as much as he was coming to hate her, he would have been hard pressed to attach that label to her even if he had.

He was barely starting to form the idea that the vitriol she released on him so frequently was more associated with her own sense of failure and her anger at men in general than anything else. Arthur was merely the available dog she kicked. Her lovely blue eyes lacked the flame of intelligence behind them and although the men she attracted seemed to be aware of this fact, she certainly wasn't. Nor was she capable of understanding the hatred she was breeding in her young son whose intellect at age ten was already far beyond hers.

Arthur set down the Sci-fi book he was reading and listened for a moment to the deep voice of the man who had just arrived. It had been two years since being bullied at the playground by Mike.

A giggle from the other room sent him back into his book. He had heard it before, and he didn't want to hear it again. Science fiction was a wonderful escape. He was quickly ensconced in Edger Rice Burroughs's world of Barsoom, and nothing else garnered his awareness.

Still, his rising hate lingered below the surface. The day was steadily approaching when it would rise to the top.

~

Arthur tossed his head in his sleep, breaking free from the grip of the unpleasant somnial memory. His dreams shifted to something more enjoyable, his recent successes with his abilities.

Sean was so intensely focused on the wall mirror that for a moment he forgot Kira completely. Just a little more and he might be able to recognize the face in the mirror.

Then, all of a sudden, his perspective shifted. It was dizzying, as though someone had spun him around repeatedly. When his eyes refocused, he was looking directly at Angelie. He was in the middle of the room. Elliot! He had shifted into Elliot's body. Was Kira here with him or still off to the side? He focused on Angelie and immediately noticed her eyes were looking past him. Of course! She must have already seen the third person in the room. Now he, too, would be able to see the features of the person standing in the threshold.

He spun to follow Angelie's gaze and shock coursed through him. It was the man from the museum!

"Well hello there," the man said, "I'm not a big movie buff, but unless I miss my guess, I believe you are Angelie Carrington the famous actress. Elliot, you didn't tell me your friend was famous. How convenient. Well, Miss Carrington, my name is Arthur, and Elliot here needs your help."

"No. How did you find this place?" Sean heard the words escape his lips and was confused only a moment before he remembered they were, in fact, Elliot's. The words continued, "You followed me?"

"Well there's certainly nothing wrong with your deductive abilities, Mr. Scientist. And all I had to do was walk right in after you."

Now Angelie spoke up, seeming to have recovered from her surprise. "Who are you and what do you want?" Her voice seethed, and Sean wondered briefly if the emotions were real or if she was just using the skills of her vocation. He quickly decided that even asking that question was ridiculous. Of course, they were real.

"As to who I am, I already told you, Arthur. As to what I want, that's simple, money. I want money from you. Not for me actually, or at least not directly. I want you to donate money to Elliot's lab so he can finish his research. You see I'm dying, and I think he might be the only one on Earth who can help me."

Sean sensed Kira's fear at that moment and realized two things. One, her perspective was coming from Angelie, which caused him to speculate as to how they got separated, and two, her fear was not proportional to the situation. He didn't have time to consider it further as Angelie spoke up again.

"Get out of here before I call the police."

"Oh, you're not going to do that," Arthur responded in a tone cold enough to chill a fireplace.

"And why not?" Angelie's tone was defiant and determined.

Several things happened next, almost simultaneously.

Elliot shouted, "No Arthur!"

Angelie yelped and grabbed her head.

A sharp pain lanced through Sean's head which he gauged came from Kira who was experiencing Angelie's anguish.

Sean yanked, and his and Kira's eyes opened abruptly.

~

"Oh my God," Kira began rubbing her temple with her free hand as she set her brush down. "What is it with that guy?"

"I guess now I have an idea how we managed to run across him in the art gallery and the hotdog stand. It apparently wasn't a coincidence . . . not that that even comes close to explaining *how*."

"It's beginning to seem that we get drawn to the real characters that show up in my paintings. Sean, this is a whole new world of weird."

Sean actually expected to sense fear from Kira but that wasn't what he was getting . . . determination was the strongest sensation he was getting from her. "So, what do you want to do now?" he asked.

Kira paused and turned back to her work. The figure on the couch was nearly done.

It was Angelie and she was looking toward the door, but between her and the door was Elliot. His outline was drawn but not finished. One hand was held out to Angelie as if entreating while the other was behind him as if warding off something. His face was going to be looking straight out of the canvas as though in the middle of shifting his gaze from Angelie, back to Arthur. The profile in the mirror on the wall was still a ghostly vague version of a profile, and Arthur himself was just beyond the threshold and therefore not in the painting at all.

Kira turned her head, her gaze coming back to rest on Sean's as he mimicked her action.

"We're going back in. That's what we're going to do. We're going to find out how this scene played out. After that, I'm betting we will need to talk to Brian, and then I believe we're going to have a villain that needs finding . . . again."

Sean smiled vaguely, pride welling for his lovely bride. "Then I guess we better get on with it my dear."

Kira picked her brush back up and reseated herself on her stool. Without turning her head from the canvas, she lifted her brush and said, "Let's get this bastard."

~

The room vanished.

The dropping sensation that Sean was beginning to expect was strong but brief. In the blink of an eye he was back in the living room. It was from the side. Unlike before, he now had a disembodied perspective that allowed him to see all three players in the room. His thoughts focused, and he suddenly knew that Kira was still seeing the scene through Angelie's eyes. So how did Kira perceive him here, or did she see him at all? He would have to remember to ask. And why the heck would the perspectives change? Was it random or was there some, as yet undiscovered dynamic?

Arthur took another step into the room. First his full profile filled the mirror then his complete form stepped from behind the door blocking the mirror completely. Sean saw his oily black hair and tall lanky frame; it was the same image burned into Sean's memory from the museum and the hot dog stand. He could feel his pulse accelerate.

"Well?" Arthur began, "Are you going to help me or are you going to get yourself hurt?"

Angelie was just lowering her hand down from her head where she had reached reflexively from Arthur's previous onslaught. "How did you do that you little maggot?"

Sean was a bit taken aback at her persistent defiance. Then again Arthur was turning an incredible moment in Angelie's life into a nightmare. Vitriol was probably not so out of place.

Angelie's hand flew back to her head and a small scream escaped her.

"Just like that," Arthur replied as he took another step into the room.

"Stop it!" Elliot yelled.

Elliot reflexively took a step toward Arthur only to drop to the ground with a yell of his own.

"Shut up, Elliot. As for you missy, you haven't answered my question. Before you do though, let me tell you that that pain in your head is nothing compared to how your chest will feel if I move something near your heart."

Angelie looked up at him with a tear forming in her eyes that looked out of place rolling down a visage of rising fury.

"I'm not giving you a damn thing you bastard!"

~

Kira's heart was racing too. This was too reminiscent of her episodes with Jason. Once again, she was deep in her painting mode with some form of pure evil. The only thing holding her together was the sensation of Sean close by. But he wasn't seeing things from the same perspective as she was . . .

"All right you asked for this you spoiled bitch."

Arthur's countenance displayed brief concentration followed by a blood curdling scream from Angelie, who bolted up toward Arthur as if to grab him with one hand while her other clutched her chest.

She took one step and one massive inhalation of breath then, before she could resume screaming, her eyes opened even wider and she collapsed to the floor.

"Lisa!" Elliot yelled lunging towards her.

"Oh shit!" Arthur began. He retreated a step with his eyes fixed on

Angelie lying quietly on the floor then shifted his gaze to Elliot who was cradling her head. "Come on, Elliot, we're getting out of here."

"I'm not going anywhere you maniac," Elliot sputtered, "I think she's dying."

"She's dead. She must have had a weak artery, but if you don't want to be lying there beside her then come on!"

Elliot didn't move. He seemed to be bordering on hysteria as if he'd just lost a piece of himself or the final piece of a life-changing puzzle.

"What did you do, you murderous bastard!" Elliot screamed as he grabbed his head with both hands.

Arthur reached for his collar and pulled him to his feet. "I said, let's go!" Elliot's eyes rolled back, and he collapsed.

"Shit," Arthur said as he turned for the door dragging an unconscious Elliot behind him.

Suddenly the room was still with Angelie lying on the floor.

~

Sean's eyes flew open only to find Kira already staring at him.

"He killed her," she said.

"That's what I saw," Sean responded in a muted tone. "Sounded like he tried to move something near her heart, and something went wrong."

"Whatever, it was still murder."

"Damn right it was," Sean responded, heat slipping into his tone, "And now I believe I'm on a mission to find the little shit."

"That could be dangerous, Sean."

"For him, maybe. I believe I already have his number, but regardless this guy has got to be stopped."

Kira gently nodded her head in agreement as they both fell silent for a moment. Kira looked up at the painting. It was frozen at the moment just before Arthur had spoken; there was a look of anger blooming on Angelie's gorgeous features and one of concern on Elliot's. Arthur was still just a profile in the mirror.

"I'm glad the painting froze there," Kira began, "But I'm still going to have to make some changes.

"Yeah and now I guess we have to find Brian and tell him the news."

"What if he calls the police?" Kira said returning her gaze to Sean.

"Might be about time to do that anyway, don't you think?"

Kira opened her mouth to reply then hesitated. "Maybe we better think this through. What proof do we have? We have a telekinetic psycho that murdered someone by accident, and we know this because I just painted a picture?"

"Ugh. You're right. When you lay it out that way it sounds more like we'll end up in those funny white jackets with the arms tied, and he'll get away. It's not like we have John to report it to . . . That only leaves one choice."

"We go after him," Kira finished.

"So . . . do we even tell Brian?" Sean countered.

"Well, he's going to ask some questions when he sees the painting even if we don't say anything. Let's sleep on it and figure it out in the morning. I doubt Brian will check it out tonight if we turn off the lights."

"Sounds like a plan," Sean answered. "Maybe we should go for a walk or a swim or something. I need to get these images out of my mind."

"Welcome to my world," Kira said with a chuckle of relief, "Come on, let's go."

~

Sean was already out by the pool when Kira came prancing out of the house. She looked like she might be concerned someone would see her, and she was hurrying on her tiptoes like she was trying to be quiet. With Brian potentially showing up at any time, Kira hadn't wanted to risk skinny dipping, but Sean couldn't manage to be disappointed when he saw her in her bikini.

"Wow. You should do some swimsuit modeling. I believe I'd buy anything you tried on."

"Been there, done that, remember?"

"Oh yeah," Sean said smiling, "Somehow I manage to forget that you were a world class model. Maybe it's just that I can't believe I got to marry one, Mrs. Easton."

"Flattery will get you everywhere," she said as she threw her arms around his neck and drug him into the pool.

The afternoon had slipped by quickly. It was the beginning of a warm, calm evening with a crescent moon rising over the dark Pacific. A gentle breeze stirred just enough to keep the bugs away. All in all, it was turning into a perfect Southern California night.

Five minutes later Sean found the light switch for the pool and even though Kira didn't want to walk out to the pool naked, laying their swimsuits beside the pool with the lights off didn't seem to bother her at all. For Sean's part he only concerned himself with the incredible feel of his new wife . . . and maybe some of their sounds . . .

All thoughts of the painting and its gruesome revelations were miles away from their minds by the time they slipped into bed an hour later.

~

Kira repositioned herself on the stool and raised her paintbrush to the canvas. But when she focused on the image in front of her she jumped. A pair of menacing blue eyes were overlaid on about a third of the entire picture. Her first thought was again of her experience with the computer sex fiend, Chang, but his eyes were brown. Also, those eyes had been leering, these were cold and scary. Suddenly, the eyes adjusted and focused on her. Kira would have sworn the blood in her veins had just frozen even while her pulse began to gallop.

"This is not going to work out well for you," said a cold minacious voice.

It seemed to be coming from the painting but not. The sound was huge and hollow like a speaker in an empty warehouse but without the echo. The penetrating gaze of those eyes was unmistakable. The voice could only be addressing her. Fear dimpled her skin and raised the hair on the back of her neck. Where was Sean? He was supposed to be here with her. She lifted her paintbrush away from the canvas intending to end the experience, but the voice arrested her movements.

"Oh no you don't!" It said with such vitriol that she could easily envision a malicious smile with lips drawn back dripping the words like acid.

With deliberate slowness a pair of pale fingers began to extrude from the surface of the painting, stretching the canvas like the surface of a giant balloon. She recoiled but the fingers shot out at her morphing into claw-like hands and boney veined arms.

She couldn't get away; she felt their cold, scratchy grip encircle her upper arms and drag her toward the surface of her work. She tried to scream, but it was choked off as she felt a silent force constricting her vocal cords.

"Nope. You're mine now. You don't get to scream." The malignant voice continued. "I don't know who you are or how you do what you do, but I'm tired of you interfering with me. It stops now."

Kira's face was inexorably drawn into the canvas as her horror continued to rise. This was an episode from Alice in Wonderland. Her painting was the mirror. Why wasn't Sean with her? He said he would always be there. This was the thing she had feared most.

She could now see inside the room she had been recreating. She felt completely powerless. She didn't want to be trapped in a world of paint and canvas. There had to be a way out! Vainly she struggled against the assailant, but to no avail. Angelie and Elliot were both there looking as afraid as she felt. Her continued attempts to scream only seemed to make the clamp on her vocal cords constrict all the more.

~

Sean had been so tired he was sleeping unusually heavy, but something was disturbing his dreams. A part of him was trying to discern what was bothering him while another facet of his subconscious was trying to ignore it. But it wouldn't go away. There was something . . .

KIRA!

His eyes popped open, and he turned to her. She seemed to be just lying there with her arms pinned at her side. It was only then he realized he wasn't receiving anything from her. No thoughts, no dreams, no emotions, nothing! The realization terrified him. Was this how if felt if she was dead?

With a panicked effort he used his new-found skill to dive into her mind. He was suddenly inside the room she had been painting. Kira was across the room from him with Arthur staring at her while holding her arms down by her side. But he was abnormally large with icy, dead eyes that seemed to take up the whole room. Angelie and Elliot were there as well, but they both seemed to be frozen in place, looks of horror evident on their faces.

Arthur was glaring into Kira's eyes and at first didn't seem to notice him. Without turning his head and in a terrifying voice that came from everywhere he began to speak.

"Stay back or I'll kill her," he said calmly.

"No. You won't," Sean responded, realizing that he was actually being seen inside this dream. He let the surprise pass, however, and with another effort of concentration he was suddenly in Kira's body with her. Now he sensed her stark terror and urgently sent her reassuring thoughts.

I'm here, Kira. It will be OK.

He sensed the effect of his words then heard her unspoken response.

Thank you, Sean.

Through her eyes, he looked up at Arthur just inches away from Kira's face. Fueled by a sudden roaring rage he yelled. "Let her go!" The voice, though it was coming from Kira's mouth, held all the power that would have issued from Sean's own lips.

There was a brief instant of Arthur's eyes widening before Sean, with Kira's hands, raised her arms suddenly to break Arthur's hold then stepped in to put an elbow in his face . . .

~

Kira's eyes popped open followed immediately by Sean's. Kira's eyes grew wider as tears welled up. "Oh Sean!"

"I'm so sorry, honey. I have no idea how you managed to slip into that dream without me being aware of it immediately. I guess maybe I just wasn't expecting it and let myself sleep too heavy."

Kira rolled into his arms and buried her face in his shoulder. "I haven't had a dream that horrible in so long. It felt so real!"

Sean felt certain that this was going to cause Kira to quit painting altogether, so he was surprised when the next emotion coming from her was anger.

"I'm not going to let this son-of-a-bitch get away with hurting anyone else."

To Sean, the fire in her voice was augmented by the emotions behind it, and he found himself being proud of her all over again.

"So, let's go get the bastard," he responded, eliciting an approving squeeze from Kira whose head was still on his chest.

"Do you think I'll have more dreams tonight?" she asked, her voice slightly muffled from its place against his body.

"Not if I can help it. I won't let myself be caught unawares again even if I have to stay up all night."

~

Arthur bolted awake for the second time that night with a sudden intake of breath. A frisson of fear coursed through him, but as he had unknowingly trained himself to do throughout his life, he turned his fear abruptly into anger, and anger elevated easily into rage. "Who the hell are these people, and why are they messing around in my life?"

The questions caused him to stop and think. Had he just been dreaming? Yes. He thought he had. What, then, was he dreaming about?

Arthur's poor ability to remember his dreams was nothing new, and he supposed that was a blessing because so many of them became nightmares about his mother and his childhood. It probably was best *not* to remember, except recollection was just what he wanted now.

He concentrated and amid the fuzziness he got an image of Elliot. He hadn't talked to Elliot since he had dragged his unconscious carcass with him after his mistake with the movie star. Damn, that had been unfortunate. All he had wanted to do was coerce her with pain to help him or, rather, to help Elliot help him. How the hell was he supposed to know the damn woman had a weak artery? And what was the relationship with her and Elliot anyway? Elliot had been so crazed when Arthur struck her down, that he'd had to restrict his carotid artery to knock him out, then physically drag him out of there.

Later, he had easily convinced him that he would appear guilty if he called the police. No one would believe him if he told them about Arthur, so he had thus far kept quiet. But it had certainly made an already tenuous relationship with the scientist noticeably more strained, so Arthur had kept his distance for the last month. That made Arthur nervous. It would be so much easier to just kill the guy and not worry about it, but he still needed him. The situation with the woman had unnerved him as well; he hadn't had to kill before. A death evoked a lot more questions.

You couldn't investigate a case of pain, but this had left something tangible. He'd already racked his brain as to whether he had touched anything in the place, but he was fairly sure he hadn't, neither had Elliot . . . except maybe the doorknob. Damn. It had all happened too quickly.

None of this resolved his first question. Who were these people who had shown up in his life and now in his dreams? How had they found him and what were they trying to do? It was something he was going to have to find out and deal with, but he had no way to accomplish that. That was OK, he decided again. He was confident they would find him again. They had found him twice. There was no reason to think they wouldn't. He just had to keep waiting. That bit of logic allowed his thoughts to quit gyrating, and he finally managed to roll over and fall back asleep.

CHAPTER

Brian was alone for a few moments in his dressing trailer. The meeting with the director had gone well, but the dinner had lasted longer than he'd anticipated. He'd felt disconnected somehow and decided to go pick up his copy of the new script before going home. Once he arrived, he'd been waylaid with another bout of tears. On the one hand he didn't want to go home; it held too many memories. On the other hand, he was anxious to see what progress, if any, Kira had made on the painting. He shook his head in remembered amazement. Her work was positively astounding, almost spooky. Did she really get her information from Angelie?

The little squeak from his remote sounded loud in the empty lot as he walked toward his favorite car. The four-seater Mercedes convertible was made for southern California. Even if the days were hot the nights were always perfect for a cruise with the top down.

By the time he pulled into his driveway it was late and the only thing he remembered about his evening drive was the warm air swirling around him. He glanced at the moon floating high in the sky as he entered the house through the front door.

Brian absently hung the keys on the peg in the kitchen while he continued to make a beeline straight for the den. The whole house was quiet, and he surmised that Sean and Kira were already asleep by now. Still, he wanted to see if she had finished any more of the painting and knew he wouldn't be able to sleep until he took a peek.

Flipping on the light in the den, Brian's eyes were instantly riveted on the canvas across the room. He was seeing it mostly from the back, but his eyes nevertheless remained glued to it as he approached the front.

He gasped before almost succumbing to yet another round of tears. There she was on the canvas, sitting on the sofa in her other house looking at someone in the middle of the room.

It was an incredible likeness. She had a strange look on her face, though. It was a combination of joy, excitement, and maybe a touch of surprise. What the heck was going on? Who was this guy anyway? And why was he meeting with Angelie in private in her old house? And once again, how the hell had Kira chosen this scene? Brian couldn't help but wonder if Kira had any of these answers.

He had a brief urge to find her and ask her now but judging by the pervasive quiet in the house he assumed it would have to wait until morning.

Damn, he thought. *I may not get any sleep at all tonight.*

CHAPTER

Sean's eyes popped open with a start. What had awakened him? Someone's emotions. It was Brian.

He was apparently in the kitchen having coffee and more than just a little impatient for he and Kira to wake up. That could only mean he had seen the painting already. Sean turned his head to face Kira only to find her eyes wide open looking at him intently. At his gaze her countenance sprouted a smile. For Sean it was a sight to put the sunrise to shame.

"Well good morning," he said, his voice slightly hoarse.

"Good morning to you. Did you sense something? I felt the little twitch when your eyes opened."

"Brian is home and seems to be more than a little anxious for us to appear. I think maybe he saw the painting last night after we went to bed."

"Yep. That would do it alright." She kissed him lightly on the cheek. "Well let's not make him stew any longer."

They both slipped on T-shirts and shorts and made their way to the kitchen. The coffee smell wafted out to meet them. Brian was sitting on a bar stool at the large kitchen island looking at a newspaper.

"Good morning," he greeted, setting down his coffee and paper. "How did you two sleep?"

They both hesitated slightly before Sean spoke up. "Like the dead." He sensed a snicker from Kira at his choice of words, but his quick glance revealed only stoicism on her features.

"Good. I was dying for you to wake up. I looked at the painting last night when I came in and, Kira, it is incredible. Your likeness of Angelie is simply remarkable. I love it. It did spark a question, though."

"I imagine it did," Kira interjected, smiling broadly.

"More than one actually," he answered, "But help yourself to some coffee first, and if you're interested there are some pastries in the cupboard."

"Just coffee for me," Sean replied, "And it smells great."

As they moved to serve themselves Brian could apparently wait no longer.

"So how did you pick Angelie's old house as a setting? For that matter how did you even know it existed, much less be able to recreate it? When I asked you that question before you only kind of answered."

There was a moment of silence in the room as Sean served himself, and Kira took a seat along with her first sip.

"Oh, this coffee is delicious," she began. "The answer to your question is that these scene selections come to me from the deceased. At least that's the only answer I've ever come up with that makes any sense. But they always are significant. I had no idea that was Angelie's old house or anything else about it for that matter."

"So, you're saying Angelie gave you that scene?" Brian's skepticism was evident.

"Yep. I'd certainly never seen it before and couldn't have even described it to you before I saw it on my canvas."

"So, you didn't know what you were going to paint when you sat down at your easel?"

"Never do," she replied simply.

"That's just incredible." Another silence ensued while Brian absorbed the information. Both Sean and Kira patiently sipped on their coffee. They both knew what was coming next.

"OK then. My second question is, who is that other guy in the picture?"

"All I can tell you," Kira offered, "is that his name is Elliot, he's some sort of scientist, and he is apparently someone that Angelie was excited to see."

"Nothing else?" The look on Brian's face was a study in amazement.

"Not yet. I might be able to tell you more after my next session."

"Well, whoever he is, it sure looks like she was excited to see him . . . How did you know his name by the way?"

Sean's coffee cup froze in mid sip, and he slowly lowered it. "She looked excited?" He asked, sensing the same question about to jump from Kira as well.

"Well yes. That expression on her face looks like that to me."

Sean and Kira turned to face each other briefly. The last expression she had seen on Angelie's face was one of anger.

"Why don't we all go take a look at the painting together?" Kira suggested, setting her cup down.

Sean followed suit while he sensed the confusion coming from Brian.

"Sure," Brian said and led the way back into the den.

Brian was the first one to reach the painting with Sean and Kira coming up behind him.

"See," Brian began, "She looks happy and excited at the same time. Kira it really is an astounding likeness. I've never even seen a photo of her that captured her so well."

Sean and Kira didn't respond. They were both stunned into silence. The last image they had seen on the canvas was one of blooming anger on Angelie's face, concern on Elliot's, and Arthur reflected in the mirror on the wall.

Kira had intended to change it, but now that didn't seem necessary . . . it had changed itself. Although this had happened with other paintings before, it didn't happen with every one and usually didn't bode well.

Arthur was nowhere to be seen and the look on Angelie's face was as Brian described. She looked happy and excited; Elliot's expression matched it.

Kira's thought jumped out to Sean.

This is just how I was going to change it, came surging from her mind.

"Are you two OK?" Brian asked. "What's wrong?"

Sean was unsure how much to share with Brian, but Kira made the decision for them both.

"This isn't the way I left the painting. I know it may sound hard to believe, but it has changed since I saw it last. And before you tell me I'm nuts, this isn't even the first time this has happened with my work."

While she spoke the words, Sean concentrated on Brian, gauging how he was handling the information. He was handling it better than most.

"This isn't the way it looked last time you saw it?" Brian repeated. The question was redundant but under the circumstances, not surprising.

Sean decided to take a turn. "Nope. Last time we saw it Angelie looked angry, Elliot looked scared, and there was a reflection of a third face in that mirror there on the wall."

"My God. That's incredible. Wait, who was the third guy in the mirror?"

Sean was increasingly impressed with Brian's ability to assimilate the unusual information he was receiving. He decided it was best to push ahead with the rest of it. He knew Kira was thinking the same thing and would probably tell Brian right now even if he didn't.

"Brian, why don't you have a seat and we'll tell you the story we have so far . . ." He began.

~

Kira watched Brian carefully as he slowly took a seat on the couch. She could see a touch of fear creeping onto his features and was certain Sean was more aware of it than she was.

He had also apparently decided that this was the best time to give him the whole story, and it occurred to her that it might be slightly easier coming from her, so she began even as Brian sat.

"Well, the truth is we don't really know. All we know is that this meeting was apparently arranged between Elliot and Angelie, and this guy, Arthur, who we saw in the mirror, showed up unexpectedly." At this point she paused, fully anticipating any of a number of questions from Brian, none of which she was going to be able to answer. But he remained sitting on the couch with a look of what could only be described as numb shock. When no questions were forthcoming, she plunged ahead.

"Here's where it really gets strange," she continued, "We have run into this Arthur guy twice since we've been here, and he apparently has an unusual ability. He can move things with his mind, especially very small things. Sean calls it micro-telekinesis. We think he uses it to force people to do what he wants, and it seems as though he followed Elliot to his meeting with Angelie then tried to force her to give him, or rather give Elliot, money that would somehow help Arthur. When Angelie said no, Arthur tried to force her with his ability, and something went wrong. We think he might have killed her by accident."

Brian's mouth was hanging open slightly, and the look of amazement was large on his features. Kira was just surprised that she couldn't detect any note of incredulity. She wondered if Sean could. She glanced up at Sean as she directed the thought at him and detected the slightest shake of his head. That was answer enough for her. Still, she wasn't sure what else she could say at this juncture, so she merely let the silence stretch.

"How the hell did you manage to run into this Arthur guy twice in the few days you've been here? You could hardly do that on purpose in LA much less by accident."

"I asked Kira the same question," Sean interjected, "And all we can figure is it has to do with the fact that this Arthur guy is affiliated with the painting she's doing."

"Someone should find this guy," Brian blurted out, then seemed to run out of steam.

"I intend to," Sean offered, "Both times we have come across this guy he has tried to hurt Kira, and I'm going to stop this asshole."

"How would you do that?" Brian asked glancing up at Sean. "Wouldn't he just hurt you too?"

~

Sean realized he had just backed himself into a corner. Letting people who were paying Kira know about her abilities was one thing but telling them about his was a whole new consideration altogether. And, Sean realized, it was one that definitely left him feeling uncomfortable. He was still trying to figure how to broach the subject or how to dodge it when Kira spoke up, making his considerations moot.

"Brian, Sean has an ability, too. It started off as simple empathy, albeit powerful empathy, for other's feelings and has grown into being able to read other's thoughts. I have a suspicion his gifts are developing as a result of being around me."

Now it was Sean's turn to be surprised. He had been so focused on Brian that Kira's statement had caught him unprepared. He turned to her; his thoughts rampant on his features.

"Who *are* you people?" Brian finally responded. "I had no idea I was inviting an entire supernatural circus into my house. Damn," he continued, "I need time to think."

With that he virtually jumped up from the couch and marched out of the room.

Sean and Kira were left there feeling dumbfounded and embarrassed as they watched him disappear through a doorway at the far end of the room.

"Well, that was fun," Kira said, still staring at the door through which Brian exited.

Sean turned to her slowly. His irritation at her for divulging his personal information was evident on his face. "Whatever made you decide to blurt that out?"

"What do you mean, blurt it out? It's not like it was some kind of secret."

"It was to me," Sean answered in a tone slightly more heated than he intended. His moment of anger began to fade as he sensed the sincere surprise coming from Kira, which she spoke to almost immediately.

"Really, Sean? I had no idea you felt that way."

"It's just that I've always been different, and before you it seemed that it was something to be embarrassed about. I mean all it ever did was get me in trouble, so I've grown used to hiding it, and . . . well, you and I have never discussed letting everyone know what I can do, so I guess it just caught me off guard."

Sean couldn't stay mad at Kira even if he wanted to.

"Oh, Honey," Kira began as she moved over and put her arms around Sean. "I'm sorry. I didn't stop to think. It's just that I'm proud of what you can do and telling someone else was just bragging on you from my point of view."

Sean didn't get the chance to respond before the door Brian had exited through opened again, and he walked back in. Sean was surprised to sense sheepishness even before he spoke.

"I'm sorry," Brian began, "That was rude of me. This is all kind of a lot to take in at once, what with everything you two can do and finding out that Angelie had been murdered. It feels like my entire world has just turned upside down, but I want to *do* something. And I think the best place for me to start is to figure out who this Elliot guy is. Angelie and I didn't have any secrets or at least I didn't think we did. Anyway, I have access to her computer and emails. I'll find out, and maybe that will lead us to finding this Arthur guy."

"That sounds like a great idea, Brian. And for our part, I'm sorry that we disturbed you so. It seems that Kira's talent almost always takes us somewhere we didn't expect to go. While you hunt for Elliot, we'll see if we can't learn more about Arthur. It seems like we keep getting drawn to him or him to us, so I have a feeling it won't be too long 'till we cross paths again."

Brian's eyes had been focused on the painting but now he looked up. "So exactly where did you run into this Arthur before?"

At that point Sean went on to explain their two incidents with Arthur at the museum and the hot dog stand. Brian listened with rapt attention, offering no comment at all as Sean relayed the episodes.

"And I thought my life was crazy," Brian began, "I can barely imagine what it would be like to live in your shoes." No one spoke when he paused and a moment later, he looked up at them again. "I really am sorry for flying off the handle. What you two are doing is giving me a closure I could have never hoped to find by myself. But I'm going to go.

I have some research to do, then I have to get back to the studio. I'll let you know what I find out."

Sean and Kira barely got out a goodbye before he was gone from the room.

Kira turned to Sean and put her hands on her hips. "Well, you were the one that told him that we could find Arthur. How do you propose we do that?"

"Easy," Sean said. "You go paint him back in that picture."

Brian took a hurried shower and went straight to the studio. Once he got there, he headed directly to his dressing room. He sat down at the counter beside the large mirror. He kept a laptop there and he turned it on. While it was booting up, he took stock of his feelings. His mind was whirling with so many emotions he could barely keep them straight. Intimidation from Sean, fear of their abilities, and worse, an unrelenting attraction to Kira that he had no idea how to handle. It had just come on him suddenly. The only other time he had felt an attraction that strong in his whole life was for Angelie, and this woman had a husband that could read his thoughts. Incredible. Scary.

At least he knew where he needed to start today. He had never tried to go through his wife's emails or her browsing history, but he certainly had her passwords just like she had his. He couldn't do anything about the browsing history at the moment. He'd have to be on her computer for that, but her email was online and that he could check.

There was a lot of spam. It had been weeks since Angelie had passed, so no one had cleared her email; it took Brian a while to trudge through it, especially since he didn't know what he was looking for and frankly he wasn't too tech savvy. It finally occurred to him to use the search feature and look for the name Elliot. That got results immediately.

It led him to a string of emails from a guy named Christopher at LA Investigations. He changed the search words and pulled up all the emails to LA Investigations, then started at the beginning.

Oh my God, Brian thought as he read. She had been hunting down her birth parents. He knew she was adopted, but she had never mentioned a desire to find her real parents. Her father had apparently passed away some time ago and according to their records her birthmother had passed away as well a little while back in Savannah, Georgia. Why had Angelie not told him any of this? As he continued to skim through the emails, tears welled up in his eyes. Was she afraid to tell him? Embarrassed? He would have been so glad to help her if she had only let him know.

Brian caught his breath. Elliot Drake was Angelie's brother! Like Kira had said, he was a scientist. Were they meeting for the first time? The email gave a phone number, but after that there was nothing connecting to Elliot. She must have used her phone from that point on. Brian thought for just a second. He knew where her phone was sitting. It was back at the house in a drawer beside his bed . . . her side of the bed, right where he had put it when the police gave it back to him. He hadn't touched it since, being reticent to hear her voice again so soon. He no longer wanted to be at the studio.

It was easy for Brian to let himself feel crushed and betrayed, but the more he considered it the more he realized that those feelings were wrong. They didn't jive with the relationship he had with his wife. As he pondered, he remembered how little time he and Angelie had had together over the last several months. Maybe that was the reason she hadn't told him, or maybe she just wanted it to be a surprise. For that matter she might have just been concerned about how their first meeting would go and didn't want to bring someone new into their life until she had at least met the man.

These thoughts finally brought a smile back to Brian's face. That's what happened. He was sure of it. He could imagine the smile on her face when she first surprised him with her new discovery. The memory brought tears to his eyes.

My poor Angelie, he thought.

Without giving the idea any thought at all Brian left the studio, drove straight home and poured himself a brandy. Even the brandy was virtually forgotten as he found a seat by one of his huge windows.

It was a seat where he and Angelie used to sit and watch the ocean. He let his other cares slip away as he slowly took a sip of his drink and with a tear slowly tracing its way down his cheek, he let himself just remember his sweet wife.

CHAPTER

"Kira," Sean began, "Why do you think we ran into Arthur twice? Could it possibly be because you were *about* to be painting him?" Kira gave Sean a quizzical look with a slight tilt of her head pondering his question.

"I don't know, Sean."

"OK then, tell me this, have you ever painted anyone while they were alive?"

Kira flashed back to a memory. "Well, not counting Elliot, I don't know if I've actually *painted* living people, but I did do several sketches of Poena when we were trying to catch her with some rather interesting results if you remember. And I guess I have continued to think that some of that connection had to do with the other connection Poena and I shared. I have no idea if it would work the same way with someone else. I have painted animals though and I probably should tell you the story of what stopped me from painting as a young pre-teenager.

"It's no secret how connected I get to everything I paint. It was true from the very beginning. Every time I slip into 'painting mode', everything and anything I paint takes on a life of its own. The extraordinary realism of my visions, even about things as mundane as a meadow by a stream, takes on a vivid reality in my mind that is invariably depicted in my work. I began with nature scenes which seemed innocuous enough, but there came a day when I wanted to try something else. Eventually, I incorporated animals into my work and when I did, the sensations of the animals I was drawing came home to me with such reality that the vividness of it scared me a little.

I persisted though, and finally, after seeing an animal special on TV about life in the African Veldt, I attempted to recreate a scene I had watched of a lion taking down a zebra.

My goal had been to simply duplicate the reality that I saw in that poignant scene, intending to recreate with paint a sense of motion to that single frozen instant in time. I did it and that was the beginning of my problems. While I was creating that canvas, I awoke several nights in a row screaming. In those dreams I *was* either the zebra or the lion. The terror and pain the zebra was experiencing washed through my dreams as vivid as reality; stopping the instant the zebra breathed its last. That was bad enough but what turned out to be harder to shake was the sense of satisfaction and power I felt when my dream body was the lion. In my last dream I felt the zebra's hot blood squirt into my mouth as my powerful jaws closed on its throat. I relished it.

The screaming I awoke to that time seemed to be coming from the zebra itself until my ears registered the sound of my own voice, and my eyes recognized my own hands stretched out in front of me curled like talons. When my mother rushed into my bedroom frantically asking me what the problem was, I was too shocked at age eleven to attempt to recount it. Nevertheless, I put down my paints and didn't return to them again until years later."

Sean was stunned. He had never heard this story before and the power of the emotions she was feeling while she recounted it struck him like a hammer blow. He felt his own throat constricting in symbiosis with hers at the power of the tale. For a moment he couldn't speak at all. As the memory faded from her mind, his emotions finally subsided as well.

"My Lord, Kira. Was that the last time you ever painted anything alive?"

"Well, there was one more time, but it's not worth mentioning now. After that last time though, I didn't pick up my paints again until after my mother died, for fear of what I might see. When I finally came up with the idea for this business, I thought it would be safe because I *wasn't* painting anything alive, and it had worked so well for my mom. Hah, so much for assuming."

Sean sat there in thought for a moment. He finally looked up into Kira's eyes and he knew that she knew what he was about to ask. "So, with me around to help, would you be willing to paint or draw someone alive again? I think it might be the surest way of finding this Arthur guy."

~

Just hearing the question, she had anticipated coming from Sean made her heart race. But something else was going on with her as well. Arthur's actions had actually angered her. Righteous indignation welled up in her like a tsunami. This guy hurt people on a regular basis for personal gain or just fun, and now he had actually killed at least one person. She couldn't let it stand if she could help it, and she thought she could. Somehow it seemed even worse than her experiences with Poena.

"You're damn right I would," she finally answered.

~

Sean hadn't thought he could feel more love for Kira than he already did, but this show of bravery filled his cup even more.

Tears of pride and love blurred his vision. "Then I say let's go find the bastard."

Sean smiled. "So, did you bring your sketch pad when you packed?"

"Sure, I did. I always do.

"Great," Sean responded. "Then why don't you find a comfortable place on the couch. I'll sit beside you, and let's see if we can locate the son-of-a-bitch right now."

Kira felt sure her grin matched his, which was bordering on feral, but for this occasion she supposed that that was the appropriate emotion. "Sounds good," she answered and headed for her suitcase.

Arthur awoke with the distinct feeling that he had been dreaming. Again. He recalled waking up in the night more than once, having been disturbed by visions from his subconscious, but the details were fuzzy.

He trudged the few steps to his little kitchen and started some coffee. The black painted walls gave the room a dark feeling, like backstage at a theatre.

As a matter of fact, that was one of the things he liked about this apartment, all the walls were painted black from the previous tenant. The owner had offered to have them repainted, but Arthur said no. He liked them as they were. They seemed to both engender his entire life and imbue a quality of creation just like a blank stage.

His hands moved mindlessly with the simple task, while bits and pieces of the dream came back to him. It was the day he had followed Elliot to Angelie's house. He had been excited to be following Elliot; it was a thrill and a challenge to track him unnoticed. He seldom drove his beat-up old Chevy Nova. He rarely had the money for gas, much less repairs, but it still seemed to run on the few occasions he needed it, which were few indeed. Another reason he liked his little apartment was its proximity to all his everyday needs.

He pushed the button to begin the brewing, then focused on his memories. In his dream he had been reliving that disastrous day when suddenly Angelie became the girl at the museum. The beauty with the dark-haired boy. Arthur's anger ignited. He needed to kill that woman and her boyfriend, too. He wanted to see her pretty features twist in fear at what he could do to her. He had no idea why they had come into his life, or how, but he knew somehow that it wouldn't be over with them until he did.

Arthur snapped out of his revelry to the sound of the coffeepot percolating. Why was he even having a dream about those two? Their mere presence in his mind made his hatred writhe like a pit of vipers. Try as he might he could conceive of no reasonable answer for their intrusion, so his thoughts wandered from memories of the dream to memories of the actual experience.

He had never killed anyone before. Hurt, yes. Maimed even, but killed, no. Until her . . . A rush of power surged through him as he recalled the look on her face when she grabbed her chest. It was an accident, of course, but it was also a sensation of power he'd never experienced before. Arthur had felt the tremendous sensation of being able to bring pain to others to force them to bend to his will or be punished for it. But taking a life, that was the ultimate expression of his abilities. He controlled the power of life and death. A previous thought resurfaced. What else could he do?

Could he break a bone? Maybe just a small one like a finger or a toe? And could he separate skin, produce a laceration?

The mental image of producing a schism in someone's flesh so excited him that he was becoming sexually aroused. Maybe he could snap a small bone in the boy's hand quickly enough to distract him while he produced a gash in the girl's throat. Now the sexual arousal was beginning to distract him, and his heart was pounding. Arthur realized that his breath was also getting ragged from the excitement. There were so many things he could do once he removed this cancer from his head. So why was he still living in squalor? A memory of the wealthy pregnant woman flashed through his mind. He still hadn't found a good place to fence the things he had taken from her. It would require using his car again. He didn't know much about turning stolen valuables into cash, but he knew enough to know not to try to do it in the neighborhood near where they had been taken.

That was a problem for later, however. He also knew he wanted to try a theft again today to see if he could garner a bigger score, and that was his first priority. He began to sip his coffee as he allowed himself to continue with his violent daydreams about upcoming opportunities.

A smile slid onto his features as he poured himself a cup of coffee. It was a grin that would have sent shivers up a preacher's back.

CHAPTER

Kira set the sketch pad on her lap and raised her pencil. She hesitated, wondering if this attempt would carry her into her creative fugue just like it did when her medium was oil paint and human ash. In her hesitation she thought of Sean and his awareness of her thoughts, which prompted a sidelong glance at him sitting near her on the couch reading a magazine. His smile was as reassuring as anything she could have hoped for or conjured for herself. She smiled back and turned to the pad, lifting her pencil. She visualized the face she had seen in the museum and let her hands take over from there.

Rodeo drive. It felt like Kira lifted her head to look around but there was a part of her that realized she was still sitting in that chair in Brian's den. That, in itself was a new experience. Before when she was painting with cremains, she was so engulfed in the scenes that she was completely unaware of herself being in the act of painting. She was simply *there.* This was one small sliver of detachment back from that total immersion, which made it less intimidating. She resumed perusing the scene around her in all its detail. Bustling people moving in and out of stores or progressing along whatever path was on their agenda today. The sense of purpose was almost palpable along with the unmistakable sensation of arrogance.

These people exuded superiority like a skunk exudes stench. Kira remembered briefly that she had been here herself in real life and never noticed that aura of preeminence before. Maybe it was because at that time she had been one of the people generating that sensation or perhaps because she was hyper aware of everything when she was in her creative mode.

Kira continued to walk down the street and observe. The experience was drastically different from when she had been sketching Poena, and she briefly wondered why. Maybe it had to do with Arthur's abilities or the difference in the connection she unconsciously made. When she had sketched Poena she had only been snatching fragments of the images that surrounded Poena, she was now *experiencing* the environment in full detail. Maybe it had to do with her own intent. When she sketched Poena, she was more focused on accurately depicting the face she had yet to see, but with Arthur her intent was to know where he was, not what he looked like.

The thought was still coalescing in her mind when she saw him. Tall, thin, shabby appearance, black hair, angular face, ice blue eyes, his attire consisted of some sort of rumpled black slacks and a dingy grey T-shirt, but nothing stood out as surprising on that street. Multimillionaires could dress any way they wanted and frequently did, from tuxes to rags, nothing was considered unusual in this area. He was walking on the other side of the street with his arms down by his side like some sort of robot. Kira glanced up to get her bearings. The palm trees and their shadows danced across the swirling stone pavement. The graceful arched front of the Versace store loomed in the distance.

It brought back memories of her modeling days, a few good ones even. She was just in front of Louis Vuitton. Her eyes refocused, and she saw Arthur turn in to Versace.

She pulled her mind back and glanced down at the sketch in front of her. There he was standing on Rodeo drive. The likeness of his face was amazing if she did say so herself, and even the detail of the street texture was much better than she would have expected.

"How long do you think it would take us to get to Rodeo drive?" She began, suddenly looking straight at Sean.

"You're asking me? This is your neck of the woods, not mine, but I can Google it. Your likeness of him is amazing, by the way."

"Thank you, but we need to go. I think he's there, and the sooner we get there the better the chance we have of catching him."

"It says an hour and four minutes. Do we have Jackson take us?"

"We may as well let him drop us off in the neighborhood. Just not too close. After that we could Uber," she answered reaching for her purse. "That should keep us from being overly obvious."

"Alrightythen," Sean answered. "I just hope we're not too late. Let me grab a different shirt and my shoes, and I'm ready."

"Hurry, Sean, I have no idea how long he'll be there. I'll grab my shoes too, and if you'll carry my backpack, I'll put my sketchbook in there."

"Sure," Sean answered absent mindedly. "This ought to be interesting," he mused.

Jackson took less than ten minutes to swing the limo around front. Sean and Kira were already there and hopped into the back.

"Where will we be going, folks?"

"Rodeo Drive," Kira spoke up. "Only we just want you to drop us off near there. We'll pick a spot when you get close."

"Will you need me to wait for you?"

"No thanks, Jackson. If you could just drop us off that would be great."

"No problem," he answered aiming the big car down the driveway.

Sean watched the scenery go by but both he and Kira were preoccupied. Finally, she spoke up.

You think he'll still be there?" Kira asked.

"No way of telling. I guess it depends on why he's there. Judging by his clothes in the sketch I don't think he's looking to upgrade his wardrobe."

"Isn't that the truth? What other reason could he have for going in there?"

Sean paused a moment. "Well, if he's not looking for some*thing*, he must be looking for some*one*." Sean sensed Kira picking up on his train of thought before he continued, so he let her speak next.

"And if he's on Rodeo Drive looking for someone... Sean, he's looking for someone wealthy!"

"Right. I'm thinking it's his next victim."

"So, if he's looking for a victim in that area of Beverly Hills, he either has a particular beef with wealthy people..."

"Or he wants to extort some money out of someone," Sean finished. "That's what he said he wanted in the painting. It didn't work with

Angelie. But I'm guessing her death hasn't stopped him from trying."

"Oh my God," Kira breathed. They both fell silent as the limo made like an ocean liner cruising along a calm sea, heading down the 405 toward the heart of Los Angeles wealth.

~

Arthur tried to look inconspicuous as he walked through the store looking for any signs of pregnancy, however, his clothing and his mannerisms both, made him stand out like a horsefly on vanilla ice cream. He didn't really care. Until he actually *did* something, all they could do was glare at him with their stupid looks of disdain. He wanted to hurt every one of them just like he'd always wanted to hurt his mother's procession of boyfriends.

Though he was tempted, he realized that in this case self-restraint was required. He had a goal to achieve or he wouldn't be in this dumb ass mecca for people with too much money and indulging his emotions wouldn't further that goal.

His eyes continued to rove, trying to vacillate between the people and his half-hearted attempt to seem interested in the merchandise. He was in a hurry though. He couldn't stay in a place like this too long just lingering or that, in itself, would be enough to motivate someone to at least call security.

He didn't really need to tarry for long, though; it wasn't like pregnant women were that hard to spot. It took him a bare few minutes to determine that this store was anything but a target rich environment. He began to walk to the exit then decided to try something new. He'd ask someone.

"Excuse me," he began as he crossed paths with a woman entering the store. He tried to be as pleasant as possible to the attractive young lady entering the store.

"Me?" She was both confused and instantly a little put off by his unkempt attire.

Arthur turned his smile up a notch, which was not totally ineffective and simply asked, "I was told there was a maternity shop in this area. I'm looking for something for my sister. Do you perhaps know of one?"

The woman's features softened slightly, but she didn't appear ready to stop walking altogether. She answered over her shoulder while she kept on moving.

"You're wanting A Pea in the Pod. It's on North Beverly between Brighton and Dayton."

"Thank you so much," Arthur answered sweetly. He turned to leave but not before tweaking a nerve in the lady's ankle. He smiled at the gasp of pain as he let the door close. Its waning echoes kept the unnatural smile on his face for blocks after leaving Versace. His entire mood brightened as he sauntered beneath the beautiful palm trees of Rodeo Drive. Reaching into his pocket, Arthur pulled out his phone and glanced at the map program while he continued to walk. The store she had suggested was only a short distance more. Once he had the location firmly fixed in his mind, he began to consider what method he might use on his next victim.

The technique he had used before had worked well, but it left him with merchandise to fence and that wasn't something he was particularly comfortable with doing. If he was going to accept the risks involved in this endeavor, he at least needed to maximize the rewards.

Arthur's mind, however evil, was fast and nimble, and walking was a wonderful technique for focusing all its capacity. He wondered how many of these women might have safety deposit boxes. If he could capture one of those, the reward should be substantially higher and possibly even easier to negotiate than trying to fence jewelry or hoping for a full pocketbook.

He was still toying with that idea when he approached the store some minutes later. He hadn't come up with any approach that would glean him a reasonable chance to find a victim with a safety deposit box. He felt stymied and frustrated. Pausing at the store front he continued to think until he noticed a lady a half a block over stop at an ATM.

Of course! He thought. He should have thought of that sooner. With a renewed grin his suddenly soured countenance sweetened once more. He opened the door and walked in.

~

The traffic was moving smoothly on the 405 and Sean remained continually entertained with the hustle and bustle of the city. Kira, however, was focusing her attention on her Google Maps program to determine the best place for Jackson to let them out that was neither too near nor to far from Versace. Sean casually sensed her thoughts but felt he would be of no help in that endeavor, so he let her continue and went back to his infatuation with the birthplace of the entertainment industry.

Certainly, the traffic didn't require a lot of attention, though Sean had never seen so many cars in his entire life. Mid-day traffic in Los Angeles was probably worse than rush hour traffic in Kansas City. And he'd thought Kansas City traffic was bad. It was hard to believe how many humans could choose to cram themselves into such a tight spot. It made him glad that he hadn't visited New York City.

Just thinking of those millions of people crammed onto an island that size was enough to give him claustrophobia. Signs for I-10, or "the 10" as he'd overheard locals call it, were getting more frequent. All those vehicles moving in various directions were hypnotic and Sean's thoughts wandered.

Since meeting Kira his life had become amazing. He had already been places and done things he couldn't have imagined two years ago; first his Dad, then Poena, and now they were in LA traffic trying to catch up with a killer that could apparently move things with his mind. How did he do that?

Sean thought back to the scene at the beach and the museum, and the nature of the thoughts he had picked up from Arthur. They had felt so different from any other thoughts he had ever sensed. But how? A thought like that was more substantial somehow that was for sure. Sean had had the sensation that he could almost touch it. It was a thought with force. Mental force. Obviously, if he was physically moving something with his mind, he was generating a force of some sort, and the more Sean thought about it, the more he realized that that was just how it had felt as well.

At that moment Sean recalled another image that had flashed

through his mind when he had confronted Arthur. He had ignored it at the time because it was disjointed and seemed unconnected to the action taking place. Now he focused on it. It had been nothing more than a passing flash of a schoolyard bully pushing him, and Arthur's reaction. Then something being thrown at the bully, maybe like a knife, then a nearby swing hitting the young bully. It was Arthur's thought! And it had moved that swing. That's exactly what it had felt like when he confronted Arthur. So how had he stopped the guy? Did he just convey a thought and distract him? If he did, that was a new experience in itself. To date, he had only received thoughts and feelings from others. He had never sent anything except to his dad or in Kira's trances or dreams. So, is that what he did? Or was it something more? Had he managed to send out some sort of compulsion of his own? Maybe even *forced* Arthur to stop what he was doing? Surely not. As a test, he began to concentrate on Kira putting her phone down and turning to him . . . nothing. She was engrossed in her current task.

Sean gave it up and concentrated on his memories from the museum and again at the hot-dog stand.

It occurred to Sean then that maybe his abilities were having some sort of reaction to Arthur's abilities, something he could only do when confronted with Arthur himself.

What he had done felt different somehow . . . but he couldn't repeat it, at least not now. What was he going to do when they caught up with this guy? Undoubtedly Arthur would try the same thing again. Would he be able to stop him again? Even though he had no idea what he had done or how he had done it? A mental image of Kira being hurt blossomed in his mind, and his heart jolted to a gallop.

No, he thought. *Whatever it is, if I stopped him once, I can do it again. He is not going to hurt Kira.*

"Jackson, just let us off at Bvlgari on Wilshire," Kira said. "That should get us close enough."

"Yes, ma'am. And are you sure you don't want me to wait somewhere?"

"I don't think so. We have no idea where or how long we'll be."

"Yes ma'am."

Kira's voice had yanked Sean out of his revelry, but his heart was still racing. He could feel the pounding of the artery in his neck when Kira turned to him.

"Are you alright?"

"Sure," he answered, a little too quickly.

"Uh huh . . . are you angry or scared maybe?"

Kira may not have his abilities, but she was still quite adroit at reading emotions. He decided to come clean. "I was just thinking about this Arthur guy and what he does, and how we might stop him. It's a bit intimidating to say the least."

Kira smiled. "Worse than facing Poena?"

That gave Sean pause. Thinking for a moment, he finally responded, "At least when we were facing Poena it was a physical threat. I know how to handle those. This is something different."

"I know," Kira answered, "But you already came up with something. I'm sure that when you need to, you'll figure it out."

"I hope you're right. If something happened to you, I'm not sure I could live with it."

Kira smiled again, put her phone down and grabbed his arm with both hands leaning her head into his shoulder.

"I know just how you feel."

There was no need for more, Sean sensed the rest, and Kira knew it. It was the best encouragement she could have possibly given him.

Jackson had already exited onto Santa Monica Boulevard by the time Sean and Kira paid attention again. He went north and turned right, so that he passed by Versace. All eyes from his passengers were glued to the right-hand window as they passed the store, though they saw nothing of their quarry.

When he turned right again on Wilshire and immediately pulled over in front of Bvlgari they were both bunched up by the passenger-side rear door.

"Thank you so much, Jackson," Kira offered.

"Just call me again if you need me," he replied but they were both already closing the door. Shaking his head slightly, Jackson checked his mirrors and reentered the traffic but even as he pulled away Sean caught his thoughts. He was thinking that there was not much he hadn't seen during his years in Los Angeles but still, there was something about that couple. Sean almost chuckled.

~

Maybe "glare" wasn't the exact word to describe the attention Arthur garnered as he strolled into A Pea in the Pod. "Regard with distaste", maybe described it better. If you threw in a smattering of distrust and even a pinch of disgust, you would have a good idea of the emotions bestowed on him by every pair of eyes in the place. Arthur could have cared less except for the simple fact that this kind of focus would guarantee that people would remember him. Fortunately, in this instance, he had no need or intention to do anything *inside* the store. He just needed the place to provide him with a candidate to attend to once she left the store. Since there was apparently only one exit, all he needed to do was choose a target, then wait outside.

A few moments passed before he spotted her; she was a middle aged, dark brunette, very attractive, maybe six months pregnant or more. She wore some sort of designer maternity dress and was a walking manikin for any nearby jewelry store.

The dark blue hue of her frock caused the expensive ornaments to stand out on her body like they would on the black velvet cloth of a display case. He'd seen enough and the looks from the other customers were already turning from distaste to concern. It was time to wait outside.

Arthur spun on his heels and made a beeline for the exit. Once outside, he looked to his left toward the ATM machine about fifteen feet away. His excitement was growing to the point that he was beginning to become aroused sexually. His psyche was twisted enough that the reaction didn't even strike him as strange, just inconvenient.

He adjusted his pants as he left the storefront. Next, to keep from seeming like a threat, he turned right and walked away from the ATM another twenty feet or so. At that point he leaned against the brick wall, crossed his legs at the heels and folded his arms. Now he would wait.

CHAPTER

Sean and Kira rounded the corner walking briskly. Versace was just half a block up. Sean was momentarily overwhelmed by all the thoughts and emotions coming from the crowds on the street. He stumbled a step before gathering himself and consciously blocking them out. Except for Kira.

"Sorry," he muttered, at Kira's concerned glance, "For a moment I forgot to filter. I'm good now."

Kira responded with a smile and reached for his hand.

I love you, she thought, which generated a wide grin from Sean. *Now let's find this bastard.*

Sean turned his head sharply. Kira was beginning to think at him more often rather than using her voice. He spent a moment trying to decide how he felt about that as they moved up the street.

~

Kira was trying not to think about the doubts she was having, which of course served to accomplish the opposite. She knew Sean could pick up on those thoughts, and she didn't want him to feel like she doubted him. At that instant he squeezed her hand gently, and she knew it would be alright anyway, though these were the type of instances when she wished he couldn't read her every thought. Interestingly enough, however, the fact that he could and was consistently OK with it generated an amazing level of trust.

How were they going to stop this guy if he tried to do something to them? Sean had done something but didn't know what, or if he could do it again when a more concerted attack was directed at them. She guessed she'd just have to believe what she told Sean. He'd figure something out . . .

The breeze coming in from the ocean was freshening, causing the rustling from the palm fronds overhead to rival the traffic noise and cast interesting shadows up and down the street.

"Here we are," Kira began as she looked up at the Versace sign. Memories swept through her. She used to model for Versace. At least this group of memories was pleasant.

"I guess we just go in and ask, if we don't see him, huh?" Sean offered.

"That's about it. I imagine if he's not there someone would remember him."

"Isn't that the truth?" Sean answered as he opened the door.

It took about two minutes to determine there was no strange looking man in the Versace store. They were turning to leave when Kira made eye contact with a tall woman glancing at them as she made for the door.

"Excuse me," Kira began, "Have you seen a tall lanky man with ice blue eyes in here in the last hour or so?" Kira felt a little strange asking, but the woman replied immediately.

"Sure have. As a matter of fact, that was why I was glancing at you two. Your husband is the only other man I've ever seen in here besides this guy a few minutes ago. Except, if you don't mind me saying, your husband is gorgeous, and this guy was poorly dressed and creepy."

Sean was flushing, too embarrassed to say anything, so Kira continued.

"You don't happen to know which way he went do you?"

"Well, I know he asked me if there was a maternity store around here and I told him about A Pea in the Pod."

"Up on North Beverly?" Kira asked.

"That's the one."

"Thanks a lot," Kira replied.

Sean opened the door for the two women. One step outside, though, the stranger turned back to them. "I know it's none of my business, but I sure wouldn't be following that creep if I could help it. There was something strange about him, and I got a sudden pain right when he walked away. It was spooky. I had the strangest sensation he had done something to me even though I know that's impossible."

"Maybe not," Sean muttered under his breath.

"Thanks a lot," Kira said at about the same time. "We'll be careful."

Kira turned to Sean as they started walking. "You think he did something?"

"Count on it," Sean answered, a shard of ice permeating his voice.

"Let's hurry," Kira said. "It's only a couple of blocks away."

"Let me look at your sketch pad again," Sean asked abruptly.

"It's in the backpack. Just reach in and grab it."

Sean swung the bag around to his side and fiddled with the straps on the pack for a second. Once he pulled it out, he began to study it as they walked, and after a few moments Kira's curiosity was piqued. "What are you looking for?"

"This," Sean answered with a note of triumph in his voice. As he spoke, he gestured forcing Kira to lean in to for a better view.

"A clock?" She exclaimed.

"Yep. That's what I was hoping for. I've been thinking about that time issue ever since you mentioned it."

"So, you think this might be the actual time he went into the store?"

"That's what I'm hoping," Sean replied. "Look."

Kira leaned in. "It looks like it says 1:30," she said gazing back up at Sean.

Sean glanced at his watch, then paused. "My watch says 1:35."

"So, he just left here five minutes ago just like the lady said."

"Right; now we know we're close. Let's go."

While he stood there leaning against the wall waiting for his victim, Arthur gave some more thought to his notion of killing someone. It was possible that he hadn't done it before because he couldn't, and the only reason he had killed Elliot's friend had been due to some congenital defect in her heart.

Exactly what would he need to move inside someone to cause death? He could move small bones, and tweak nerves, but what else could he do? Considering for a moment, it occurred to him that he could constrict the carotid artery to knock out the man but, in that case,, he would have to hold it closed for a longer period of time. A minute? Maybe more. That would work but would be difficult to accomplish unless someone was restrained. If they tried to attack him during that period his concentration would likely be broken, and he'd have to switch to a more instant tactic. His trick with pregnant women was to constrict the umbilical cord which caused both the baby and the mother to react violently but wasn't actually fatal to either unless he could shut that organ down for a period of time. So, what would work more quickly?

People flowed by him as he thought, completely unaware that the lanky unkempt man leaning passively against a wall was actively cogitating on creative forms of murder. Two possibilities came to mind. First, if he could burst a tiny vessel in the brain that would essentially be a forced aneurysm, which would do the trick but require more study. Secondly, if he could move the correct vertebrae or possibly a spinal disk that might kill as well or at least produce paralysis, but which vertebra would be easiest and how much movement would be required? Could he move that much? It remained to be seen, and in both cases, he needed more hours in front of a medical text.

His train of thought was interrupted when the woman he was waiting for emerged from the store with two large bags in tow. She turned away from him and toward the ATM nearby.

Good, he thought.

That would make it that much easier. Shrugging his shoulders back against the wall, he propelled himself upright and walked in quick pursuit. She wasn't walking very fast, so it took him just a few steps to catch up which left them both still several steps from being directly in front of the ATM.

"Excuse me, Miss?" His voice had an engaging quality and timbre that caused the lady to turn at once to see if she was the one being addressed. When she did, his eyes caught hers.

"Are you talking to me?" She asked gesturing with one bag-laden hand.

She was almost in front of the ATM when he approached.

"Why, yes. I ..." Arthur focused his concentration on pinching a nerve behind her eye and was rewarded with a sudden gasp from the woman, who dropped one of her bags as she reached for her head.

"Here let me help you," Arthur said using the moment to move in close. He retrieved her bag smoothly with one hand and put the other on her back as if to steady her.

"Listen to me woman," he whispered to her in a sinister growl, "What you just felt was nothing. If you want you and your baby to leave here unharmed, you'll do exactly what I tell you to. Do you understand?" He punctuated the statement with a tweak to a nerve in the side of her neck causing her to gasp. Before she could even reply, Arthur constricted her umbilical cord and both she and the baby jumped.

"Do you believe me?"

"Uh ... yes ... who are you and what do you want?" The woman's voice was trembling, and her eyes were darting about searching for help of some kind.

"For starters, I want you to stand in front of that ATM and withdraw all the cash you can."

"But," she began and then gasped in pain again.

"'But' is not a word I want to hear from you. Now do it." He again accosted that nerve in her eye while he continued speaking. "If you don't do exactly what I tell you to lady I'm going to blind you and kill your child."

This statement caused the woman to glance up at Arthur with the wild-eyed look of a horse spotting a rattlesnake.

"OK. Fine," she said, as she stepped up to the machine. It was incredible, or maybe in Beverly Hills, not so incredible that no one so much as glanced at their interaction. Arthur had been keeping his voice low and his mouth near the woman's ear, so his words were picked up only by her. And despite his words, his actions seemed innocuous enough, as though he was still trying to help steady the lady.

~

Kira and Sean were moving quickly up the street. They had already turned onto North Beverly and Kira was glancing at her GPS when Sean spoke.

"I see him," he announced in a tone so cold that it almost scared Kira. Her eyes jerked up from her phone in time to see Arthur move toward a seriously pregnant woman who was coming out of the maternity shop. She took several steps toward an ATM before Arthur apparently spoke to her briefly. Without warning she dropped a bag and grabbed her head in sudden pain while Arthur seemed to be trying to help or steady her.

"Is he about to force her to withdraw money?" Kira asked as her pace picked up.

"Sean felt the power of the thought. That's what he's doing," he replied, reflexively accelerating his own steps to match hers.

"That's a stupid way to rob someone. Look at the jewelry she's wearing."

Sean could see it from the rapidly diminishing distance. The woman virtually sparkled in the sunlight. He thought about breaking into a run but didn't. It would alert Arthur and maybe result in additional injury to the woman. His gaze remained fixed on the pair, however.

While they closed the distance, the woman shrugged and turned to the machine.

A few more steps, Sean thought, *and . . .* Suddenly he picked up another thought from Arthur . . .

Hurry the hell up woman or I'm really going to hurt you . . .

The thought hit Sean like a hammer. Without realizing it he had tuned out everyone else and focused on Arthur. This thought didn't contain the force Sean remembered sensing when he was hurting someone though. This one was just a thought.

The woman was finished pushing buttons, and both she and Arthur were staring down at the dispenser when Kira surprised Sean with a shout.

"Hey you! Leave that woman alone!"

So much for surprise, Sean thought, but it didn't matter now that they were getting so close.

Arthur and his victim both looked up at the same time. Sean received another thought as clear as a voice spoken to him.

Not these two again. Their timing is incredible. Damn them! Slow them down.

Then it happened. Sean again felt what to him seemed like a mental shove which was slightly different from an attack aimed at him. Which had to mean . . . Kira! At that same instant Kira screamed as Sean received another thought, *center metatarsal moving down.*

"Aaahhh!" was all she got out before she began to go down in a heap grabbing at her right ankle.

Due to the fraction of a second warning Sean had received, he turned to Kira and caught her by the waist as she went down thereby minimizing any additional damage from the fall. The powerful thought Sean had received stopped suddenly and so did Kira's pain.

"Are you alright?" Sean asked holding Kira up.

"I'm fine now. That son-of-a-bitch did that to me, didn't he?" she asked, her eyes blazing ahead at Arthur.

"Yeah, he did."

"Can you stop him from doing that again?"

"I . . . I don't know." At Kira's question, Sean refocused his attention on Arthur who was now busy shuffling the woman farther up the street.

She was handing money to Arthur and retrieving her cell phone from her purse. Sean and Kira broke into a run.

It came again. This time the thought, or mental shove as Sean perceived it, came in the form of an image of Kira's neck. As the thought crystalized, Sean did his best to mimic what he had felt coming from Arthur.

No! He thought with as much force as he could conjure.

Kira remained unscathed while the thought immediately stopped and Arthur himself straightened up and faced them directly.

Sean wondered what would happen next, but he didn't have to wait long. A thought began to surface in his mind along with the sensation of something being thrown at him, and as it hit him a searing pain shot through his temple. He stumbled, grabbing his head with both hands. Kira didn't have the early warning Sean had received and wasn't fast enough to help him as he fell, landing on his knees and evoking another bolt of pain.

~

The word, 'No' came like a shout in Arthur's mind, and it was accompanied by a wet sensation from his nose. Involuntarily he reached up to touch his philtrum, the two lines descending just below his nose. One of those two lines had a drop running down it.

When he drew his hand back, he saw it was blood. Whether this was a result of the shouted syllable in his brain or his own effort to stop the girl Arthur had no way of telling, but either way these people spelled trouble, and he was going to stop them.

Although it hadn't worked at the beach, Arthur knew the man was the real problem and aimed his next attack at his head. Meanwhile, at his direction, the pregnant woman was calling her limo back. If he could just stave these two off for another minute or so it would arrive, and they'd be gone.

~

The searing explosion of pain in his knees acted like a mental trigger and Sean experienced a rage like nothing he had ever known. He took that emotion and channeled it into duplicating the thought he had just received, the one that had caused him to stumble with the pain of it resulting in the lingering agony in his knees. It *had* been like a mental shove when it was directed at Kira, so this time Sean grabbed the memory of it and shoved back.

~

The limo was pulling up. The girl was getting in, and he was just getting in after her when it hit him. "Aaah!" He exclaimed, grabbing the side of his temple.

"What is it?" the terrified girl asked as she slid across the seat of the luxurious coach clutching both her packages and her stomach to protect her baby.

Arthur was clutching the side of his head with one hand as he growled, "Just tell the driver to go!"

Immediately the lady flipped a switch on the far door arm rest. "Take me home, Joshua."

"Are you alright ma'am?" Joshua asked, the look of concern clear even in the narrow field of the rearview mirror.

"Yes. I'm fine. Just drive please."

"Roll up the privacy screen," Arthur whispered.

The limo pulled away, and at once the pain left Arthur.

"Damn," he mumbled. "I think that boy just learned something."

"What?" The terrified mother asked.

"Shut up. I have to think."

~

Sean pushed himself up from the ground with Kira helping. His knees throbbed horribly but at least they were functioning.

"Are you alright?" Kira asked.

"Yep. I'm going to have some wicked bruises though."

"Why did you stay down so long? And what were you thinking? The look on your face was scaring me."

"Did you see Arthur grab his head before he ducked into that limo?"

"Not really. I was too worried about you."

"Well, I think I just gave our skinny little villain a taste of his own medicine."

"What do you . . ."

"I think I just managed a bit of micro-telekinesis myself." Sean turned away from the retreating limo and looked Kira in the eyes.

"Are you kidding?" She asked.

"Nope. I think we better call Jackson and you need to get your sketchpad ready again."

"What are you talking about? We're not some sort of psychic super-hero team. We need to call the police."

"And tell them what? We're right where we were before. You had a vision while you were doing a painting about a guy killing the subject of your art with a thought? Hell, they'd lock us up for loonies. No, Kira. I'm afraid that if someone is going to stop Arthur it's going to have to be you and me."

"But I . . ." Kira began only to stop mid-sentence because she realized Sean was right. She damn well didn't like it, but it was true. Instead, she lifted her phone and dialed Jackson.

~

Arthur was so deep in thought that he really wasn't paying attention to where the limo was heading. He'd made a few mistakes today, and he didn't want to make any more. The whole ATM idea had been stupid. He used those machines so seldom that it hadn't even occurred to him that they might have a dispensing limit. Certainly, he had never approached it. It made sense, though, one of those machines could only hold so much cash and if they were going to be of use to the average person, they would have to limit dispensed cash or it would require too frequent servicing to keep them filled. He had gleaned a measly $400 from his victim for his efforts.

But that was the least of his worries. Damn that couple and their inconvenient timing. As much as he'd wanted another chance to make them suffer for the interruptions and had been waiting for them to find him, he hadn't counted on it being then. Now they'd messed up his plans twice. His rage grew. Had that boy really used his own ability against him? It was almost too incredible to consider.

He glanced over at the pregnant bitch, who was trembling.

Good, he thought.

"Where do you live?" He asked tersely.

"Cartagena," she responded with a pronounced quiver in her voice.

The unexpected response caused Arthur to pause but he recovered quickly. "You're too far along to have been travelling on a plane recently. Where are you staying?"

"Onboard my husband's yacht in Marina Del Rey."

Arthur smiled, which did nothing to calm the poor woman. "Tell your driver to take us there. Is your husband there?"

The lady hesitated, and her trembling increased.

"Is he?" The volume of Arthur's voice increased slightly as he asked the question, but it was the underlying tone of menace that broke the poor woman's reticence.

"No."

"Perfect."

"We're already heading there," she continued.

"Good."

~

Kira looked up from the pavement as Jackson approached. He had apparently decided to wait in the area even after they said they wouldn't need him. She glanced up at Sean who had a smoldering, far-away look in his eyes. She'd have bet money that he wasn't reading her thoughts at the moment which was maybe for the best. She was a little freaked out. She'd spent the last year or so trying to tell herself that the strange things that had happened to her and Sean were just part of her art. She didn't believe in the occult or the supernatural or at least she hadn't before, but that was getting to be a harder and harder sell, especially to herself.

She had sketched a man, a living man, accurately placing him at the location he existed but almost an hour in the future. How was that possible? Could she have done this before? What else might she be able to do with her drawings and paintings? Maybe Brian was right. What kind of a freak was she?

"You do realize that I completely understand your feelings right now, don't you? I mean it's not like the same thing isn't happening to me."

Kira started slightly at the intrusion into her consciousness.

Seems like I would have lost that bet, she thought.

For the moment she just smiled at Sean as she slid into the car with Jackson smiling at the two of them while he held the door open. Sean glided in beside her and Jackson closed the door. The hum of the traffic disappeared at once, but it started right back up briefly while Jackson maneuvered his large frame into the driver's seat. He turned to them even as he closed the door, again bringing silence to the interior of the vehicle.

"Where to folks?" He asked.

Kira answered promptly, "For the moment could you just drive around the area?"

"Certainly, ma'am." Jackson turned his attention back to the road ahead and his side view mirrors while Kira unabashedly raised the privacy screen.

You know I do, Kira thought to him answering his previous question.

Sean started laughing. "Well, you do know how to make your point," he replied. "You're really beginning to enjoy this 'thinking at me' thing, aren't you?"

~

Kira's return smile made his heart soar. It was an effort not to grab her right there and take her clothes off.

Now, don't bug me for a minute. I have a crazy to find, she thought again, while she pulled out her sketch pad.

"I guess it makes sense," Sean continued. "If you're going to have a car chase in Beverly Hills it really should be in a couple of limos."

Kira snickered briefly, but her hand was already busy.

CHAPTER

At least the stupid bitch had stopped whimpering. Arthur's mind was racing, in sharp contrast to the caterpillar progress of the limo. LA traffic was seething, and the impatience it wrought in Arthur was causing his mind to seethe as well.

It had occurred to him that given the unexpected circumstances, the best method to maximize his mistake with the damn ATM was to ransom this woman. It wouldn't have been something he would have considered if the woman hadn't been living on a yacht. That little nugget of info spoke of wealth he hadn't yet imagined.

"Are you going to let me go?" the trembling woman managed to utter.

"Shut up," he snapped back, and augmented his words with a twinge to a nerve in her forearm. Her muted squeal and prompt acquiescence somewhat soothed Arthur's own ramped up nerves.

Marina Del Rey was an array for the senses. The myriad colorful boats jostling restlessly in their slips and the smell of the ocean mixed with the sound of the gulls overlaying the clanging of the sailboat's rigging. The combined effect sounded like a thousand chefs banging metal spoons softly against their pots above a throng of voices. All of which was completely lost on Arthur. It seemed that natural beauty was not something that impinged on the senses of the evil. Maybe that was an aspect of evil, never being able to perceive, much less appreciate, the simple beauty in the world.

"Does the driver usually come on the boat?" Arthur asked.

"No," the woman replied between snivels. "He was just hired for this area."

"Good. When we get there, you can just tell him you won't need him anymore."

In response the woman merely nodded, probably afraid to verbalize anything else.

As they approached the Marina, Arthur was already rethinking his plan. Kidnapping was not an endeavor he was familiar with and the more he thought about it, the more he realized it wouldn't work.

He was not prepared to wait onboard her boat while her husband assembled cash, and he recognized that having him wire money somewhere was also fraught with problems he was ill-equipped to handle. He didn't have some offshore account or a dummy corporation somewhere that the money could be sent to without identifying him.

It seemed like all he could do today was make mistakes. He wasn't thinking clearly, and he knew why. That damned couple. How could they possibly have been at the maternity store at that instant? It stretched the imagination too far to imagine that their appearance was yet another coincidence. Although he had been expecting to cross paths with them again the timing could not have been less convenient. And that boy . . .

The limo pulled to a stop in a parking lot by the Marina interrupting Arthur's train of thought.

"Do you have any valuables onboard the boat?"

"Please don't hurt my baby," the terrified woman managed to squeak out.

"Do you have any valuables onboard? If you do what I say I won't hurt your baby, now answer me!" Again, he punctuated his words with pain, this time to a nerve on the side of the woman's neck.

"Oww!" she yelped. "Yes, I have cash and jewelry."

"OK. Tell the driver to beat it and act natural. We're going to take a little walk down the dock."

The poor woman did as she was asked, but when she opened the door it took self-restraint on Arthur's part not to hurt her again as she took an extra few seconds to heave her swollen torso out of the vehicle.

He almost shoved her but decided at the last moment that she would probably just fall over, slowing him down even more. Finally, they were walking across the parking lot. Well, he was walking. She was waddling like an overweight duck.

CHAPTER

Within minutes Kira had a sketch.

"The Marina? You think he went to a Marina? Why would he go to a Marina?" Sean's incredulous tone grated on Kira's frayed nerves, but she refrained from responding, correctly assuming that what he could pick up of her thoughts was rebuke enough.

"Sorry," he said promptly. "I guess I'm pretty much on edge, too. Part of me just keeps screaming that we are not Mr. & Mrs. Smith super spies, and chasing down some dangerous degenerate is probably right up there with trying to beat a skunk with a stick . . . Only with worse consequences."

Kira was having similar misgivings but at the same time she was admiring her depiction of a scene she hadn't seen in years. For a quick sketch, it was pretty amazing in its detail. And right there in the parking lot in front of the boats were two figures, a lean male holding the arm of an obviously pregnant female. She was far enough along that her condition was apparent even from a very slight side view. She even recognized the parking lot. It was one she had used years ago when she and a bunch of other models boarded a yacht for a Coca-Cola shoot.

"Look," Kira began, finally responding to his words, "We can stop anytime you want. I agree this is crazy. We came here for me to create a commissioned piece of art, not play Tom Cruise in Mission Impossible."

The silence stretched for a moment before Sean responded. "No. I guess I couldn't live with myself if we left that poor woman in his clutches without even trying to help her. I really don't want to do this, but we are the only ones who can and again, I'd call the police in a heart-beat if I thought it would do any good."

"Agreed," Kira responded. Without further comment, she pushed a button on the side armrest. "Jackson, could you take us to Marina Del Rey as quickly as possible?"

"Yes Ma'am," Came the prompt reply.

The traffic had diminished significantly since Arthur and his abductee had traversed the same roads and unknown to Sean and Kira, they were gaining on them substantially. Also, Jackson was taking Kira's request seriously and was doing a brilliant job of keeping his foot planted on the accelerator in the thinning traffic.

"So, you think this woman might have a boat?" Sean ventured into the protracted silence.

"A yacht more likely," Kira responded.

"Why would Arthur go with her there?" he wondered out loud.

"I can only imagine she either has or he thinks she has something of value on board. I have a hard time imagining he was so stupid as to make her take cash from an ATM. Too much risk and not enough reward. Maybe he's trying to make up for that mistake."

"That makes sense at least."

A few tense minutes later, Kira glanced down again at her sketch then pushed the communication button again.

"Jackson, turn right onto Mindanao Way then into the parking lot on your left."

"Yes Ma'am." Was all he said, clearly concentrating on the road ahead.

CHAPTER

The woman was remaining quiet, so Arthur was able to think while they negotiated the small amount of blacktop and wooden dock between them and the gangplank

"Will it arouse suspicion if you call and tell the captain to prepare to leave?"

"No. I don't think so, but my husband might wonder what's going on."

"I thought you said he wasn't on board."

The poor lady's eyes looked like they belonged to a deer staring down a pack of wolves.

"Please don't hurt my husband!" She whined.

"Shut up! Just make the phone call." Actually, Arthur had a plan for that too. He was still working on quick and effective methods to kill with his ability, but he had already worked out a good way to incapacitate someone. It would work because he could be standing right in front of them and they'd have no idea that he was producing their condition.

"Which one is it?" Arthur asked realizing that he didn't know where they were headed. At that instant engines started somewhere down the pier, but they sounded more like those of a jet than propulsion for an ocean-going vessel.

"That one at the end of the pier," the lady offered as she pointed.

"That one?" Arthur asked, incredulous.

"Yes."

The boat she had pointed out was the most amazing thing Arthur had even seen. It was huge, and though it was black it looked for all the world like the profile of a blue whale with sharp, stealth lines. Sure enough, it was the source of the engine sound Arthur had heard.

"Walk quicker," Arthur goaded. "What the hell does your husband do?"

"He owns wholesale and retail diamond stores," she answered.

"Perfect," Arthur said for the second time in the last few minutes.

They were well down the dock when Arthur turned sharply to the sound of tires screeching behind him.

~

Jackson caused the tires to screech when he wheeled into the marina.

"Where would you like me to stop?" Came across the speaker in the back.

Kira rolled down the privacy screen and peered through the front windshield. She immediately saw the couple walking briskly down the dock. They were nearly to a monster of a yacht moored at the very end of one of the longest piers.

"There," she said, directing an extended arm. "Get us as close as you can to that pier."

Jackson responded wordlessly, maneuvering the big limo across the lot to where she had directed.

"We'll never catch them," Sean said.

"We will if they haven't already prepared the launch to sail."

Jackson swung to the edge of the parking lot right at the origination of the pier Kira had indicated. The big vehicle was barely stopped when Sean and Kira bailed out the same door.

"Wait here," she called to Jackson before her and Sean broke into a sprint.

Kira knew it was going to be a futile gesture before they were ten steps down the pier, because she could hear the distinctive engines of the behemoth they were headed toward.

"We're not going to make it," she said.

"Sure we can, they aren't even to the gangway yet, and that lady can't run."

Kira was keeping up with Sean's sprint while she answered.

"No, we won't. Hear those engines? They can pull that loading ramp up in seconds and they apparently called ahead."

Even as she spoke, Sean watched as their quarry approached the pier side of the gangplank.

"Damn," he said. They were still fifty yards away, and Arthur and his victim were stepping off the ramp. No sooner did their feet hit the deck than the walkway began to withdraw.

"Now what do we do?" Kira asked, disappointment thick in her voice.

"Well, it seems to me that we have about two choices. Either you can draw another sketch, and we can chase them, or we can go back to Brian's and talk to him."

"I think drawing a sketch would be useless. Did you see the size of that yacht? Their next stop could be Australia for all we know. For that matter even if they're headed for another state-side Marina, they will be there long before we could arrive."

"Brian's house it is then," Sean replied.

The strength of the disappointment in Kira's thoughts was depressing him, and he tried to think of something positive.

"On the bright side, we have figured out another ability that you didn't know you have. Sketching the location of someone in the present is one thing but sketching their whereabouts in the future is quite another."

Kira looked up at him. "Great," she answered simply, "One more chit for entrance into the grand society of freaks."

"Watch it," Sean said, taking her hand with a smile. "That society includes me, too."

Kira smiled back. "Well, at least we get to join it together."

"You know," Sean began," More and more I'm beginning to suspect that interaction with Arthur is causing some of the changes in our abilities."

Kira looked thoughtfully at Sean for a moment but didn't respond.

They both stood there a little longer and watched the incredible black behemoth sedately motor toward the exit of the harbor.

CHAPTER

Arthur stood by the railing and watched them pull away. He was feeling pretty pleased with himself until he heard a deep voice with an angry tone.

"Who the hell are you, and what are you doing on my yacht? And why are you with my wife."

It was the husband. He was a big man with dark, curly hair and an accent reminiscent of Greek lineage. Arthur and his victim had almost made it to the foredeck, so Arthur was prepared. He would have preferred picking a spot closer to the cabins, but he was not going to have that luxury.

Without saying a word in reply, Arthur began to focus on the man's carotid arteries, constricting them on both sides of his throat.

The burly husband reacted immediately grabbing at his throat as his eyes slowly began to bulge, while evincing a look of utter bewilderment.

"Stop!" The woman yelled stepping up to Arthur.

He shoved her back heard enough to cause her to stumble backward, just short of falling. "Shut up!" He yelled managing not to lose his focus on the man.

The push and the near fall terrified the woman more than his words, leaving her too petrified to offer any more resistance. She merely stared from where she was with widening eyes and a protective arm over her belly.

The burly man's legs gave out a couple of seconds later with him still having no idea what had just happened. It took about eight seconds for the man's face to begin to lose color and his eyes to roll back up in his head. Then came the hard part.

"Where is your cabin, and do you have some rope?" Arthur demanded.

The woman's eyes were as wide as saucers now, staring down at her inert husband. "Is he dead?" She asked.

"If he was dead, we wouldn't need the damn rope. He's just unconscious at the moment, but I can kill him easily enough if you don't answer my question. Now where is your cabin?"

"Through that next door and down the hall on the left."

Arthur was relieved the trek wasn't going to involve any stairs. He was pretty sure he didn't have the strength to drag the big man up those, and down seemed unlikely.

"Show me," Arthur replied grabbing a beefy arm and beginning to pull. "We have to get to your cabin before he wakes up, or I might actually have to kill him."

The woman must have truly loved her husband for she increased the speed of her waddle substantially. Arthur had to struggle to keep up. Fortunately, the floor in the hallway was some sort of polished wood and the big man's bulk slid easily along it. They were about seventy-five feet down the corridor when the woman finally turned to her left and opened a door. She moved into the room quickly, and Arthur turned to grab the man with both hands and pull him across the threshold.

The master stateroom was expansive and replete with dark wood, black lacquer, and steel. Its futuristic décor was a perfect match to the sci-fi exterior of the monstrous floating trophy.

Arthur rather liked it, but he didn't have time for appreciation.

"Now, what about the rope?" He asked.

"We don't have any I know of that isn't connected to something," the woman replied with a quivering voice. There was a brief moment's pause before she continued. "But I have handcuffs."

Arthur did a brief double-take before replying. "Get them," he ordered tersely, "And hurry!" Memories of his mother floated to the surface which he quashed immediately, but it was enough, quick as it was, to fuel his anger.

The woman complied while Arthur dragged the unconscious man across the room to a pole near the window. It was a sleek metal affair and Arthur imagined it was more decorative than useful, but when he yanked on it with both hands and all his weight, it didn't budge.

Maybe it's structural, he thought.

The woman returned from a large dresser on the other side of the chamber with the item he'd requested in hand. They were covered in pink fur. Arthur was at first disdainful but upon inspection he realized they were stout metal underneath. Once he had the man secured, he turned back to the woman.

"Where do you keep your valuables?" He asked in a low tone that brooked no denial.

"Upstairs in the viewing room," she answered with her eyes glued to her husband. He was beginning to grumble, and Arthur preferred not to deal with him again.

"Good. Show me." Arthur didn't bother to gag the man, both assuming that his voice wouldn't make any difference on this huge ship and just being too inexperienced with the whole idea of kidnapping.

They moved to a door that Arthur assumed was just a closet, but when the lady opened it a circular stairway loomed before them.

"This way," she said and began a metered assent up the narrow treads.

It seemed to Arthur they must have climbed four or five stories before the woman finally reached for a doorknob.

"Here," she said breathlessly as she opened the door.

This new room was even bigger than the massive bedroom they had just left. It possessed the same futuristic décor, and the lighting that covered the entire ceiling was a pale, indirect, iridescent blue. Instead of a bed and a closet, the room housed a pool table with black felt and a fully stocked mirrored bar. However, the amazing décor and lighting were overshadowed by the view. The bow end of the cabin was shaped in a curving 'V' and was all glass, or acrylic, or whatever transparent material they had used. Even given Arthur's general disinterest for things material, his eyes remained briefly riveted to the spectacular view of the ocean ahead and the city off to his left before his mind returned to the business at hand.

Suddenly, any vestigial twinge of remorse he might have felt vanished like smoke in a hurricane. Whatever he managed to steal from these people would never be missed.

"What's in here?" He demanded of the woman.

"A safe," she answered simply.

"You better tell me you can open it," he replied.

"I can open mine," she responded.

"Yours? You mean there's more than one?"

"Yes," she answered tentatively, "But I can't open the other one."

"Let's see what's in yours," Arthur stated while simultaneously con-stricting the umbilical cord for emphasis. The woman gasped reaching for her stomach as she moved quickly over to a painting on the wall. The painting was of haystacks in a field.

Who the hell would want a picture of hay, Arthur thought while the woman smoothly pulled back the frame which was apparently mounted on a hinge.

Behind it was a simple black safe with a silver keypad and a handle. The woman hesitated.

"Do it," Arthur urged seeing the woman's hesitation.

The lady manipulated a small black pad with her index finger and waited briefly for a beep before she keyed in what Arthur thought must have been a ten-digit code. The whole process took about fifteen sec-onds before there was a distinct click. The hapless socialite pulled the handle and stepped back.

"There," she said simply.

Arthur looked past her and gasped. The small safe held several stacks of currency and several velvet boxes that even unopened screamed of jewels. Arthur reached for the first stack of currency. Fifty-dollar bills, twenty-five hundred dollars per stack.

He grabbed a second. This one was currency from another coun-try. Arthur didn't give it a second glance but reached for a third stack which proved to be hundreds. Five thousand dollars. There was several of each. Arthur's pulse was racing as he reached over them to the first jewelry box. It was about nine inches long and two inches thick. He tried to anticipate what sort of jewelry it might be, but when he opened it, he was still surprised. His eyes widened perceptibly. There before him glistened dozens of loose diamonds in varying sizes. What he was staring at must be worth a fortune. This was enough money for Elliot. Arthur was looking at his salvation.

"Just take it and let us go," the woman offered, surprising Arthur.

"Fine," he said. "Find me a bag to put all this in."

The woman waddled across the room to a closet, opened it and produced what looked like a medium size gym bag. It was blue and flimsy. Why it was there or what it was for, Arthur had no idea, nor did he care.

"Where is the nearest port?" he snarled. "We can't go back to where we were."

The woman surprised him with a prompt and succinct answer.

"San Pedro Marina is just a short way down the coast next to the Port of Los Angeles. It's probably less than an hour away."

"Make it so," Arthur answered channeling his favorite Star Trek character.

The distraught pregnant woman gave him a strange look.

"Do it!" He rephrased. "Now."

She moved to the nearby wall and pressed a button on a comm panel.

"Albert, could you please direct us to San Pedro Marina? We'll be making a short stop there."

"Yes, Mrs. Marshall, I'll adjust course immediately."

CHAPTER

The ride back was silent for a while. Sean was deep in thought about Arthur's abilities and his own and the possible interrelation. The depth of his concentration effectively filtered out Kira's thoughts even though that was not his intent.

He found that he was a bit excited about the whole adventure. It had never occurred to him that he might come to like the danger that his new wife's profession seemed to manifest, but there was no doubt, the danger was exciting. He turned toward Kira feeling a fresh flush of love for his new bride but still kept himself out of her head.

As time progressed, Sean would become increasingly aware that he could filter any thoughts anytime he wished, but he wasn't quite there yet. It was analogous to a sniper's ability to ignore any other distractions while he focused on a difficult shot.

~

Kira was silent as well but rather than being lost in thought, she was lost in her art. Her hands were quite busy on her sketch pad and she was so drawn into the fugue of her creation that her eyes were virtually glazed over. For her there was no sketch; there was a scene.

Her first flash was another pier with another dock and the monstrous black yacht pulling up to the end of it. It was huge with a point of land on one side and a man-made concrete pier on the other. Between the two fingers of land sat row after row of boats in every shape and size imaginable. No sooner had the walkway extended from the floating extravagance than Arthur was walking off with a blue gym bag in his hand. He turned to speak to the pregnant woman Kira had just seen him abduct.

"Don't think I need to be close to you to hurt your baby. If I see or hear a siren, your baby is dead."

Even from what seemed like a moderate distance, Kira could see the woman tremble. She was even affecting the typical wringing of hands as he spoke.

"I won't," was all she said.

Arthur turned to go then hesitated, turned back and reached toward the terrified brunette, a strange look on his face.

"Here," he said and handed the terrified mother-to-be her wedding ring. He then strode quickly away.

At that moment Kira realized she was familiar with this marina as well. It was San Pedro Marina by Los Angeles.

But that wasn't possible, it was over an hour away, and she'd seen Arthur board the yacht mere minutes ago. She realized with sudden clarity, like the final piece of a giant puzzle falling into place, that she was undoubtedly experiencing a scene from the future. Despite what Sean had pointed out about the clock in her previous sketch she hadn't allowed herself to fully accept the idea. Even if she'd had the time to truly ponder the possibility, she knew she would have reasoned the idea away.

But now any skepticism she had been harboring about the sketch was banished. Awe and fear lanced through her about what this new skill could mean when she saw Arthur turn a corner and disappear out of sight. She pondered briefly if she should do anything, but before she could focus her thoughts the scene flashed to somewhere else. It was an apartment, or at least she thought it was. It was dark, dingy, and littered with belongings in complete disarray. She took a step, continuing to scan around the human pig sty. She had yet to make a third step when the door banged open and Arthur walked in.

"You!" he exclaimed. "What are you doing here?"

Kira was too shocked to answer and had no idea what to say if she did. She merely backed a step away from him as he surged forward. Kira was momentarily stunned at the change of circumstance. In the midst of this sketch she had not only fallen into a scene similar to what she experienced when she painted, but now the scene had changed and one of its characters was reacting to her presence.

"It doesn't matter," he continued in a low menacing tone. "This will give me a chance to get rid of you, bitch."

He took one more step forward, and the entire room blurred from black to gray then to white. Bewilderment overtook Kira but before she could react to the change, everything came back into focus.

She was in a lab. Beakers bubbled above small gas burners in nearly every direction and the place smelled faintly of ammonia. On one side a black device stood on a tripod.

It looked vaguely like an old-style movie camera and it was aimed at another beaker. She couldn't begin to imagine its purpose. While she continued to gaze around the room, the door opened.

She spent a few seconds trying to recall if she had ever entered a scene before anyone else showed up, but the thought disappeared as she recognized the slight looking fair-haired man that had just entered the room complete with white lab coat. It was Elliot. What was he doing here?

For that matter, Kira thought, *what am I doing here?*

The instant he stepped through the portal he turned and looked straight at her. Unlike her previous scene, however, Elliot appeared not to see her at all. In fact, he closed the door slowly and shuffled over to the table nearest the odd projector device, seemingly lost in thought.

"One more try," he muttered to himself.

Then the entire scene vanished again, and she was back in the limo with Sean staring intently at her.

"Did you have a nice trip dear?" he offered smiling.

It took her a second to wipe the look of awe and surprise from her face before responding to Sean's taunt.

"Several," she finally said. As she spoke her gaze drifted down to her sketchbook and Sean's eyes follow hers. It was an unusual sketch, two actually, side by side. One of them was of that monstrous yacht pulling into another harbor, and the other was of some kind of a laboratory.

"That's got to be the first time you've ever done that," Sean observed.

"What? You mean two works on one page? I think you might be right."

"Well, not only that, Kira, you got into your painting mode from just doing a sketch and if you were intending to sketch Arthur it's odd that you ended up drawing two separate scenes."

Sean paused then pointed to the left side of the page. "That's the boat Arthur got away on," he commented.

"Yep. And I recognize the place. It's San Pedro Harbor by the port of Los Angeles."

"So that's where he went?"

"Or where he's going. Sean, even by boat it would take almost an hour to get there and we just saw them not ten minutes ago."

Sean was thoughtful for a moment. "I guess there's nothing for us to do about that is there?"

"I don't think so." Kira's answer seemed distracted, and she assumed Sean was about to automatically tune in to her thoughts so she continued, "I know we kind of breezed by this revelation before because we were in a rush, but now that I'm having a chance to think about it . . . I was there, in the Marina as Arthur was getting off the yacht. I heard his words as clearly as any other vision in my paintings. But it's not physically possible for them to have happened yet. I guess this is what happens when I draw or paint a living being. To be honest I'm not sure how I feel about the fact that I'm drawing the future."

~

Sean had some other thoughts about what was going on with Kira's drawings, but at that moment he kept them to himself.

"So, what about the lab?" He asked, circling the conversation back to the images on her lap.

"It's Elliot's and he was really upset about something. He muttered something about trying one more time."

"To do what?"

"I have no idea," she answered still staring at the drawing. "But I have a suspicion that it's important."

The sun had set, and the lights of the city were in full bloom by the time Jackson eased back into Brian's driveway.

Kira was acting a bit nervous as she set the sketch pad down in her lap. Sean could feel the tension but rather than snag her thoughts he simply asked her.

"Are you OK, Hon?"

Kira's smile was a bit tentative as she reached up and took Sean's arm. "Yeah, I'm OK. I'm just trying to digest all these new experiences and what they might mean . . . for me or for us. I mean really, Sean, I'm drawing people in the future and you're . . . you're . . . well you're almost using Arthur's abilities against him, like sending thoughts. How can we be doing these things?"

Again, Sean had an idea but at that moment Jackson brought the limo to a stop. Brian's car was parked out front as was another vehicle that Sean and Kira didn't recognize. It was, however, not one of Brian's wealthier friends as the car was a somewhat beat up, older model, green Ford Focus.

Jackson pulled to a stop and Kira and Sean were out of the door before Jackson had a chance to come around and open it for them. He smiled at them anyway as he approached and closed the door behind them.

"Thanks, Jackson." Sean threw back over his shoulder before turning to Kira. "I have a feeling that this is going to be interesting."

"I have a feeling you're right." Kira responded focusing on the massive doors in front of them.

The door closed to Arthur's little flat, and he marched straight to the couch where he plopped down and dropped the gym bag full of valuables. He listened momentarily to the sounds of the city outside his door then wiped another trickle of blood from beneath his nose before lifting the fingertips of both hands to his temple. His head was pounding. He indulged the pain for just a moment before casting it aside. He had a lot to think about and was becoming increasingly certain that his time is running out.

Once he started thinking he couldn't help but be proud of himself for his recent heist. He had turned a stupid mistake into an incredibly lucky windfall. Now all he needed to do was turn all the jewels into cash and go find Elliot. He picked up the bag and emptied it out on the dingy little coffee table. It had a black lacquer surface and the jewels seem to jump out at him. He considered where to sell them. On the one hand he could probably sell them locally since the people he stole them from weren't even Americans. The issue with that was that he wanted to fence the other jewelry he'd stolen and that *was* from an American. As far as the foreign woman was concerned, they might have called the authorities even though he was convinced that the woman was way too scared to do that; truthfully, she might not even tell her husband what was stolen. Still, it was a chance that he'd rather not take.

At that point the stack of cash caught his eye. It was maybe fifty-thousand dollars; though not enough to jumpstart Elliot by itself, it was enough to get him out of town.

He could even buy a new car so as not to interact with any public transportation. But where should he go? Where would be the easiest place to fence a million or so in jewels? He concentrated on it for a moment and the pounding in his head reasserted itself.

The headaches were getting more frequent and more intense. If that wasn't bad enough, he'd had that nosebleed when he'd encountered that boy and they, too, were becoming a regular occurrence. Was that to do with the cancer, or his abilities or the boy, or what?

Dammit! He thought as he reached for his temples. He rubbed his head briefly, then turned resolute. He wasn't going to let this throbbing distract his concentration. This had to be done quickly if he was going to buy himself a chance to beat this cancer.

Wait, he thought, *chance . . . That's it!*

It was perfect! The throbbing almost subsided as he crystalized the thought. Las Vegas. It was the perfect place to fence stolen jewelry.

Arthur promptly lifted himself from the couch and headed to the shower. He had work to do and maybe a few aspirin and twenty minutes under some hot water would ease the pain enough for him to get going.

CHAPTER

S ean still felt a little strange about just opening the front door to
Brian's house, but it was what Brian had told them to do and fur-
thermore if the butler was busy or off duty, one could knock for hours
and not necessarily be heard, especially if Brian was in his gym or out
by his pool and patio.

This time, however, Sean was in for a surprise. While he quietly
closed the door, Brian came walking up, his pace just shy of a trot.

"Hi there. I'm glad your back."

Kira briefly looked puzzled but recovered quickly.

"Were there some dinner plans we forgot about?" Her radiant smile
brought a much larger response from Brian than her words would
require.

"Heavens no," he began, smiling expansively. "Though if you're
hungry I can have something whipped up in a jiffy."

The word 'jiffy' was familiar to Sean and he briefly wondered if
Brian was from the south. The word seemed oddly out of place in
this setting, but the warm feelings emanating from Brian toward Kira
promptly overrode the thought.

"No, we're fine," Kira continued. "We ate while we were out." Which
wasn't exactly true; Sean could sense she was anxious to hear why
Brian was so excited, so he didn't contradict her.

"Oh, OK," the movie-star said briefly and hurried on, "I've got
someone here I'm anxious for you to meet." Brian was already moving
back the way he had come and motioning with his hands for them to
follow.

They passed through the hall and straight back to the den where
Kira had been painting. Brian walked through the opening and began

to introduce them to the fair-haired fellow that was staring at Kira's painting.

"Sean and Kira, this is . . ."

"Elliot?" Kira interrupted astonishment thick in her voice. Sean's jaw hung slack.

"Yes. Elliot Drake. I forgot; of course, you would know that." Brian responded with astonishment matching theirs albeit for a different reason.

Elliot seemed to struggle to peel his eyes away from Kira's painting, and Sean knew why before he spoke. Apparently, Kira's depiction of their meeting was astoundingly accurate.

"Nice to meet you," Elliot replied somewhat distantly. "What I'd like to know is where the camera was?" Since dragging his eyes from the painting, Elliot had not torn his eyes away from Kira. Sean, however, was used to this reaction to Kira's beauty and stepped up to offer his hand before Kira did.

"Nice to meet you, Elliot." Sean made a point of locking eyes with Elliot as he spoke and if he was truthful with himself, gripped Elliot's hand a bit too hard. Kira promptly nudged him aside though and extended her own hand forcing Sean to step back slightly.

"Hello, Elliot," Kira offered while gauging the expression on his face, "And to answer your question there was no camera.

I am producing this painting with ashes from Angelie."

Their handshake lingered just a touch too long, but Sean knew it was not the attraction to Kira causing the momentary lingering but the shock at Kira's words.

"You created this with no other image to work from?" Elliot's eyebrows were raised, and his amazement was simply unabashed. He absently stroked his blonde hair back off his forehead as he released Kira's hand and stepped back a half-step.

"Oh yeah," she answered. "I never work from another image. I think it would affect the integrity of the work."

"Is that also how you knew my name? Brian told me you were talented, and I must admit I've scarcely seen a photograph of myself that looked more real, but is what he said true about you being a," Elliot hesitated and stole a glance at Brian as he forced himself to say the word, "well . . . a psychic?"

Kira cringed slightly at the term.

"I definitely would not call it that. But, yes, I do seem to get visions from the subjects of my work and that is how we already knew your name. I also know that you're a scientist and that Angelie was so excited about her meeting with you that she could scarcely focus. It's all she thought about since Starbucks."

Kira knew that last detail was unnecessary, but she was hoping it would be enough to ensure Elliot's belief. Judging by the way she saw his eyes widen and his jaw go slack, it seemed to work.

"How did . . . I haven't told anyone where we met. Lisa told me she hadn't either. You couldn't . . ."

The silence stretched for a small, uncomfortable moment.

~

Elliot was feeling a little shell shocked. He was not all that accustomed to meeting new people and just getting the call from his sister's husband had been a bolt out of the blue, but now this new couple and that amazing painting had him wandering off into the surreal. Not to mention he had a thousand questions, but for the life of him, he couldn't conceive where to start. There had to be some better explanation for the accuracy of the painting, but nothing came to mind, and her answer was certainly compelling. He didn't get to ponder too long though before Sean filled the void.

"So, my curiosity is killing me, Elliot. How did you happen to be there with Angelie that afternoon?"

Elliot turned his gaze on Sean.

~

Sean sensed a vast intelligence behind those bright eyes, but at the moment he was being overwhelmed by the emotions wafting off him in thick dark waves. Surprise, sadness, guilt, and even a little fear battled for dominance in Elliot's mind.

"She was my sister," He began simply, "And this was our second meeting since she first contacted me." At this point, Elliot turned sharply back to Kira. "How did you know about Arthur?"

Sean's eyes flew back to the canvas. All traces of Arthur had been removed.

Brian must have told him, Sean thought as he turned to Kira.

Kira's answer was simple and direct. "I didn't until I drew this, but for some reason we kept running into this jackass, and so we started tracking him ourselves."

Fear blossomed in Elliot's eyes. "Oh, you really don't want to do that. You don't know what he can do." His eyes were focused on Kira, but before she could respond Sean spoke up and all eyes turned to him.

"Unfortunately, we do know. And that's one of the reasons we are tracking him. Fortunately, we're a bit more equipped to deal with him than most. But what I'm curious about is why he was there with you the day you met with Angelie?" The answer floated up to him well before Elliot could form the words.

"He wants something from my research that I can't give him yet. I told him I didn't have the money to finish the research."

Sean and Kira responded simultaneously, and their words tumbled over each other.

"He wanted money from her," Kira surmised.

"What research?" Sean asked with slightly more panic to his voice than intended.

"You mean my wife was murdered for money?" Brian's statement was barely on the heels of Sean and Kira's comments, and poor Elliot was left glancing from one to the other unsure who to answer first or whether to answer at all.

"Well I . . . uh . . . the research is on a possible treatment for previously inoperable brain cancer." Elliot's choice of responses was a simple leaning toward the answer he knew best, but the reaction he received was totally unexpected.

"You think you might have something that actually works?" Sean virtually demanded.

Kira turned to Sean at the question. She knew that it was Sean's dad that was prompting the unexpectedly intense question.

Elliot was surprised by the intensity of the inquiry, and his momentary confusion led to a protracted silence in the room until he finally replied in a somewhat guarded tone: "Well, according to my tests I believe it should work ... I ..."

"How does it work?" Sean blurted out.

"Uh well ... I have been experimenting in getting gold molecules to either bond to or gravitate around a brain tumor, and then hit them with microwaves effectively frying the cancer cells with minimal effect to the healthy brain tissue around it. I've already successfully destroyed tumorous tissue without damaging the surrounding areas, but I'm having a hard time getting the molecules to gravitate to the necessary area without physically placing them there. That's the area of research I need more funding to continue. But once I solve that problem, it'll just be a matter of injecting the gold infused serum into the appropriate area, exposing it to microwaves, and letting science do the rest."

"That sounds like it should work," Sean continued. "Are there any limitations?" At this point, Brian who had begun glaring at Sean and his unexpected line of questioning interjected. "I think the more pertinent question here would be, does this lunatic plan to contact you again and if so, do you know when?"

Elliot's eyes flashed with frustration. "Unfortunately, I think the answers to both of those questions are intertwined. I'm sure he will contact me if he comes up with some money or thinks that I have. Apparently, his brain cancer is quite advanced. As far as when, though, that's anybody's guess. He doesn't exactly make appointments. But the problem with that, and what has me worried, is that it's becoming increasingly evident that money isn't really the problem slowing the success of my experiments. As of yet I have no solution to the placement dilemma. That's the limitation. Which I'm sure will infuriate him. It's frustrating the hell out of me and I'm not the one dying.

But there's not much I can do without more time to keep testing. My next step will be to try adding iron to the solution and then maybe do some work with a magnetic field. It's likely to be a difficult balance of timing with the microwaves, but it's still my best idea, currently."

~

Kira was barely listening to Elliot. She was busy taking in Brian's facial expressions and surmising his thoughts. Not to mention wondering how Sean could be so distracted that he wasn't picking up on Brian's thoughts himself. Nevertheless, she thought she might have the answer to Brian's last question.

"Judging from what we just saw, I have a feeling Arthur just came into some money. So, I'm guessing you'll be hearing from him rather soon. I also may have a better way of determining when he might show up."

Her response caused Sean to finally refocus his attention. He gave Kira a knowing glance and she knew he had picked up her meaning. She turned to Elliot.

"Is there somewhere near your lab that we could stay?"

"Well, yeah. There's a Holiday Inn Express about three blocks away."

"What is it you think you're going to do?" Brian cut in, a touch of heat still lingering in his voice. The sound of the air conditioning kicking on seemed to fill the room as everyone became momentarily silent. The moment pulsed in the large room just long enough for everyone to feel the tension from the silence.

"We're going to catch that bastard," Sean finally answered.

~

Sean saw that his response brought a somewhat feral grin to Brian's perfect features, and the thoughts Sean picked up from him included a violence that was fairly shocking. Before he let his concerns run away with him, Sean imagined how he would feel if Arthur hurt Kira. Brian's unspoken fury was something Sean could easily understand.

Brian redirected the moment by asking if anyone would like some wine. The last light of the day had faded, and at least in Sean's mind it sounded like a perfect idea for draining some of the pressure.

"I'd love some," Kira spoke up promptly.

"Me too," Sean added.

"I'd love to stay," Elliot began, "But I really need to get back to the lab."

"Are you sure?" Brian responded. "I'm opening a Silver Oak cabernet. It's really quite extraordinary."

"I wish I could," Elliot said as he stood and began inching toward the exit. "Sean and Kira if you need anything or want to drop by just let me know. Brian has my number."

"Thanks, Elliot." Sean offered, detecting the man's nervousness and paving the way for the slight man to leave. "You'll hear from us soon enough, I'm sure."

Brian had moved to the bar and was already uncorking the wine by the time Elliot was out of the room.

"So, what was up with all your questions about Elliot's research?" Brian asked. The distinctive pop of the cork seemed to punctuate his question.

Sean sensed the last remnant of annoyance in Brian's thoughts. He also sensed Kira's unspoken thought, pointedly telling him to tread lightly. Therefore, he took a moment to decide how much he wanted to even tell Brian as he approached with three glasses of wine.

Brian handed the first glass to Kira and the second to Sean before sitting down beside them on the oversized couch. The seating arrangement left all three of them in the right position to gaze at Kira's work still sitting on the easel.

"I think I'll need a second glass of wine before I get into that answer," Sean replied with a warmth and humor that disguised his evasiveness. It seemed to satisfy Brian.

"To a brilliant work of art," Brian offered holding his glass out for a toast.

"To a life well lived," Kira added.

"To a murderer brought to justice," Sean said clinking his glass gently with the other two.

CHAPTER

Several glasses and some pleasant conversation later Kira stood up abruptly and said, "I believe it is time for me to retire." As she seemed to be wavering where she stood, Sean agreed, and frankly he wasn't in much better shape. Brian seemed wholly unaffected but was ever the congenial host.

"Well you two, I want to thank you for the amazing piece of tribute art and the excellent sleuthing. You have given me two gifts both of which were way beyond my expectations."

"We're not quite done yet," Sean replied. Brian's eyes shifted to Kira and his lingering thoughts regarding her nearly prompted a response. Sean reminded himself for the ten thousandth time that thoughts weren't actions, and Brian had done nothing to warrant any retort. As he calmed himself Sean took comfort in the fact that Kira was gorgeous, and this famous movie star, so recently widowed, was taken with her. Sean just smiled

"With that I bid you good evening, Sir." Kira offered, turning toward the bedrooms. Sean responded more to her unsteadiness than her words and rose immediately.

Brian rose as well. "I'm not sure of your immediate plans or even if you are planning yet, but you are welcome at my home whenever and for however long you like. Oh, and by the way, your money will be wired to your account tomorrow. Everything else aside, I want to thank you for an incomparable gift."

Even in her current state, Kira blushed. "That's very kind of you Brian, and I'm so glad you like my work. We're certainly not sure as of yet when we will need to relocate close to Elliot, but we will need to come back here. I have a few small details to attend to on the painting, and I think I might have one last little surprise for you."

"Now you have my curiosity piqued."

"Well, let me make shurrre I actually have it, and then I'll let you know. But, if you'll accuse me I think I should toddle to my room." Somehow, coming from Kira, the slight slur in her speech was endearing, at least to Sean.

"I'm with her," Sean added simply, including a broad grin.

"Good night then," Brian finished. He stood there watching them leave the room as he sipped another sip from his glass. Sean's final thought from him was not of her beauty but of them both being extraordinary. He smiled as he followed Kira into their room.

Sean decided on a shower while Kira got ready for bed. The hot water was calling to him as his mind churned the events of the day, and his shower lasted longer than usual. All in all, he had too many things on his mind, and he didn't think sleep was going to be in the cards anytime soon. This Arthur guy was bad and needed to be stopped, but the new information he'd received about Elliot's research had sparked some hope for his Dad. That train of thought reminded Sean that he hadn't heard from his Dad in a few days and then came guilt for not calling him.

Was there any way that Elliot's research could help his Dad? Was it really just a matter of money? Something was still nagging him about the Elliot and Arthur combination as he finished toweling dry and headed for bed.

All those considerations took a sudden backseat, then disappeared altogether when Sean looked up and noticed all of Kira's sleeping clothes were in a neatly untouched pile on the floor on his side of the bed. He raised his eyes and took in the smile on Kira's face. He definitely didn't need his abilities to guess what was on his wife's mind; that smile spoke volumes. It was right about then that she raised the covers invitingly and left him with but a single thought.

He barely had time to register the warmth of the covers and the smoothness of her skin when Kira rolled on top of him. He was about to speak when her mouth covered his and removed all consideration of communication beyond the physical. For one brief second, he opened himself to her thoughts and a last attempt to share ideas with her, but the torrid torrent emanating from her absolutely derailed any sensations other than touch.

~

Some time later Sean rolled off Kira but remained as much in contact with her as humanly possible in their side-by-side position. They were both still panting.

"You are extraordinary," Kira breathed, staring at the ceiling.

"Just trying to keep up with you," Sean replied. "Also, I think you solved my problem."

"What problem?"

"Having too much on my mind to sleep. Now I think I'm too exhausted to stay awake."

"Was it just the day's events bugging you?"

"That and thoughts about my dad. I was wondering how he was and feeling guilty that I haven't called him. Also, something is bugging me about Elliot's research. It's like I have an idea about it, but I can't quite put it together."

Kira turned to face him in the dark putting a hand on his chest and draping a leg over his.

"Elliot's research is intriguing, isn't it?"

"Yep, which makes me think of Arthur. This is twice now we've found ourselves in the position of tracking down the bad guy. How did we ever manage to turn into some sort of CSI team?"

"It just happened that way," Kira answered. "You know we couldn't do anything different. Could you really just leave Arthur alone and let him do what he is doing when we're the only ones with the knowledge and means to stop him?"

"No. I know you're right. We couldn't have done any different with Poena either. But it puts me right in the middle of concern for your safety, a desire to follow this thread about Elliot's research, and feeling obligated to do something with Arthur."

"I know what you mean, so why worry with it? We'll just do what we have to do and see where it leads."

"At least now I'll be able to sleep," Sean began, "and thank you for that."

"Oh, you're most welcome, but I don't think you're going to get to sleep just yet..."

With that Kira kissed Sean again and, as predicted, it was some time before they both found slumber.

~

Wind whistling through the house awoke Kira. The sound slid up and down the scales with the velocity of the gusts, but it was a sound she would more associate with the old farmhouse in Kansas than with a mansion in California.

She lay there listening for several minutes and glancing over at Sean to see if the sound was disturbing his sleep as well. It apparently wasn't. Finally, she slipped out from under the covers and reached for her robe and slippers. The ululation didn't seem to be coming from their bedroom so she decided to see if she could find an open door that was the culprit.

In her slippers, she moved silently down the hall intending to merely follow the sound. Nightlights dotted the walls allowing her to see clearly with her night-adjusted eyes. There were doors on both sides of her, but the sound was coming from further away.

The noise suddenly stopped, and Kira paused. She had never noticed how many doors were in this hallway but before she could ponder it further the howling wind resumed. It was somewhere ahead, and it drew her like a dog on a scent. The hall seemed to stretch on and on before her until an opening on her right caused her to turn. The sound was definitely coming from that direction. It was the direction of the kitchen.

In her mind's eye she could visualize the trees bowing to the heavy wind. Images of palms bending before hurricane winds floated into her mind but surely this wind was nowhere near that strong.

The hall toward the kitchen was not as well-lit as the one she'd just left, and she stepped more cautiously through the darkness. It was just a few steps more with the siren song of the wind continuing to increase as she approached. Just as she made the turn to enter the room the lights switched on, and the wind stopped as completely as if had never existed. But this wasn't the kitchen; it was a laboratory complete with black obsidian counters, beakers, burners, and glass tubing everywhere. She barely had time to take in the extraordinary scene when Elliot turned from one of the counters and looked right at her.

"Well hello there," he offered. "I didn't expect to see you here."

"Not nearly as much as I didn't expect to *be* here," She replied. At that instant, staring at Elliot's sincere smile Kira realized she must be dreaming. Was she really still in bed next to Sean? It was all so real. Yet it wasn't scary, and it occurred to her that she wanted to ride with this unusual manifestation of her subconscious, if that was indeed the source of this little adventure.

Before Elliot had a chance to answer, Kira glanced around the room. Two things drew her attention. There were now no doors or windows and the sound of the wind that had awoken her had resumed.

"Do you hear that?" She asked of Elliot. Elliot's attention had returned to the glassware and microscope in front of him. Without lifting his head, he replied.

"Hear what? All I hear are the sounds of boiling solutions and your voice."

"That wind, don't you hear that?"

"No," He replied simply.

She started to move closer to Elliot but stopped abruptly as Arthur appeared next to him. Elliot seemed unconcerned with the sudden change. Indeed, he barely seemed to notice Arthur's sudden presence at all.

"Is it working yet?" Arthur demanded seemingly unaware of Kira on the other side of the room.

Elliot exploded into an unexpected rage. "No, it's not working yet dammit! I told you this on the phone."

"But I gave you the money you needed," Arthur retorted, a hint of danger in his voice.

"I know, Arthur. And that has purchased the resources I need to perform these experiments, but it didn't DO them for me."

"I need you to hurry," Arthur stated simply. As if to add emphasis to those words, blood began to trickle from Arthur's nose.

"I know you do and I'm trying, but you standing over my shoulder distracting me isn't helping the situation any."

Arthur crossed his arms in frustration and began to look around the room. His eyes fell on Kira, and she wondered briefly if he even saw her.

"You," he hissed, answering her unvoiced question.

Suddenly the room telescoped so that Arthur's face filled her vision. His expression changed and his eyes began to sweep down her body. Following his eyes Kira looked down. She was shocked to notice her attire was a very thin silky nightgown. It was thankfully more than she'd been wearing when Sean crawled in bed with her but still way more revealing than she would intend for this psychopath.

"No," she ordered and was abruptly swept back across the room at a much more comfortable distance.

His expression darkened but before he could say more Sean appeared beside her. She jumped slightly as she focused her eyes on him, but his gaze was riveted on Arthur. For a moment she simply stared, pondering her quandary. Was Sean actively entering her dream or did she somehow summon him? Whichever Sean he was, active participant or a figment of her dream, he kept his gaze lazered on Arthur.

While the staring match continued, Kira shifted her eyes toward Elliot who was totally oblivious. His attention remained steadfast upon whatever experiment he was wrestling. His back was blocking the view though of what his hands might be doing.

Without warning a pain lanced across her temple accompanied by the shouting of Sean's voice.

"No!" He yelled across the room at Arthur while he took several steps toward the skinny maniac.

Blood began to trickle from Arthur's nose, and he grabbed his own temple, effectively mimicking Kira's own reaction.

"You can't do that!" Arthur's voice was rife with anger, shock, and fear.

"Apparently, I can," came Sean's fierce reply.

And with that, Sean appeared at Kira's side . . . again. She blinked and turned her eyes slightly to include the other Sean.

"Well, I guess that answers my other question," she murmured.

"What?" the newly appeared Sean asked. "Oh yeah," he continued reading the balance of her thoughts but seemed a bit surprised, and even amused, to be looking at the dream version of himself. "I guess you get a dose of me squared. Weird, but I'm glad you're OK." With those words he turned his attention to the seeming duel going on between the other him and Arthur.

"I can't read the other me, or Arthur. What's going on?"

"I think Arthur was trying to hurt me and Sean . . . the other Sean, stopped him," Kira answered as though it was the most normal thing in the world.

"You two stop that pissing contest and get over here."

At those words, all eyes shifted to Elliot who had turned from his experiment.

"I am working hard here trying to find a way to accomplish this last step in my experiment, and I think you two might be the answer . . . or Arthur anyway."

Arthur gravitated promptly over to Elliot with dream-Sean following closely. Kira and, she assumed, the real Sean moved closer as well, but just enough to better view what was happening. They were still trying to remain as passive in the scene as possible.

Elliot turned sideways to reveal a rabbit in a clear plastic cage sitting in front of something that looked, surprisingly, like an old timey video projector. There was a wire running from the apparently sedated or dead hare to another device that was connected to a laptop screen. On the screen was an image of the inside of the furry creature. One of its organs was on display.

"That's an appendix," the Sean beside her declared, surprising even himself.

"How would you happen to know that?" Kira whispered.

"Mine was removed years ago, so I looked it up online to see what it looked like, but I didn't know rabbits had one."

"That's right," Elliot remarked, answering Kira's question as to whether the other characters in this little drama could still hear them.

Dream-Sean turned to real-Sean, briefly evincing a bit of surprise, then nodded as though to give assurance that he understood everything that was going on.

"Come closer, Arthur. I want you to help me with this part," Elliot stated as he reached for a rather large syringe lying beside him on the work bench.

Arthur moved tentatively toward Elliot, doubt and curiosity battling for control of his facial features.

"What do you need me for?" He asked.

As Arthur spoke, Elliot reached into the clear enclosure and injected the rabbit. The bunny exhibited no reaction whatsoever, but on the computer screen small particles appeared in the area of the displayed appendix.

"Those tiny particles are the gold molecules I infused into that solution. I want you to try to use your ability to move them over to the surface of the rabbit's appendix."

"What?" Arthur replied, skepticism dripping from his tone. "Why do you want me to do that?"

"Dammit, Arthur. Do you want me to cure you or not? If you do, then just try to do what I'm asking you."

Still looking tentative Arthur turned his gaze toward the image on the screen and stared at the still visible particles. Both Seans and Kira stared as well, fascinated.

Slowly the particles began to move one at a time. They gravitated toward, and settled on, the surface of the rabbit's appendix. A minute or two passed and it was done.

"There," Arthur said, "It's done."

All eyes turned to him and the new drop of blood he was wiping from beneath his nose.

"Now what?" Arthur continued.

Elliot merely smiled and reached for a switch that led to the projector looking thing on the other side of the lagomorph's cage.

"Now we watch," Elliot said. "Keep your eyes on the image on the screen."

While everyone moved closer the representation of the appendix changed. The edges where the gold particles resided began to shift to a reddish color. The color intensified until the appendix itself began to turn red. Then slowly, as they all stared on in fascination, the bunny's vestigial organ turned to a deep shade of black.

Elliot waited another few seconds then reached again for the switch to the projector. "Done," he said in satisfied tone.

"What did we just see?" Arthur asked.

"You just witnessed me using microwaves and gold particles to effectively remove that rabbit's appendix."

Arthur glanced back at the screen. "But it's still there." The contempt was thick in his tone.

"Not for long," Elliot answered still staring at the screen. "We just burned that tissue to a crisp without harming any of the surrounding tissue. Within a few days the dead organ will be absorbed into the rabbit's body. I'm confident I can do the very same thing with your brain tumor."

"Except for one thing," Arthur stated flatly, "I can't do this to myself. I've tried before to move something within my own body, and it doesn't work."

"And he can't be there for any other patients you might ever have. So, this isn't actually a solution," dream-Sean chimed in with frustration coloring his tone.

Sean, the real Sean, and Kira reached for each other's hands. This was almost like watching a 3-D movie. It was especially strange for Sean to stand and stare while listening to another version of himself have a conversation that could have easily been coming from his own mouth. The thoughts dream-Sean was expressing were actually occurring to him just slightly before they were being spoken by his doppelganger. He doubted he was causing it even as the possibility crossed his mind. His other self was in this vision when he arrived, and at that moment he had had other thoughts on his mind, like how he had let Kira slip into a dream again without him which from his perspective represented failure. When he first popped in, he was simply relieved that nothing particularly terrifying was going on. Now, however, he was enthralled. Another thought occurred to him.

Before anyone could say anything more, both Seans disappeared.

~

Kira felt the removal of his touch on her hand even before her eyes could take in his absence. A second later the lab disappeared as well. Kira opened her eyes to Arthur standing beside her bed. She gasped and immediately reached for Sean. He was gone.

"Where is he?" Arthur asked. His menacing tone didn't do anything for Kira's already jangled nerves.

"I . . . I don't know. What are you doing here and how did you find us?"

"That's not your problem." Arthur reached for her as he spoke, and she screamed. Instinctively she flinched back as best she could while lying there on the bed. Kira's eyes waxed huge as her pulse began to gallop. She continued to try to push herself away from her attacker but there was nowhere else to go. Her eyes closed reflexively against the looming terror and the room spun. A wave of nausea swept over her causing her to open her eyes again to steady herself. She was alone. She turned to Sean, but he was still strangely absent.

"Sean?" she called out tentatively. No answer. She tried again only louder but gleaned no more success. She slid from underneath the covers and was surprised again to find that she was completely dressed.

Putting her feet on the floor, she moved toward the bathroom and a sound that she thought might be Sean. One step through the threshold and she lost her footing. It felt as though she had stepped onto a surface covered with oil. While her feet flew, she tried to brace herself for the landing. There was nothing she could really do except try to protect her head. She even failed at that, and with a sickening crunch her head met the floor. Everything went black.

Kira opened her eyes. Again. She was back in bed. Again. This time she took inventory. Lifting the covers slightly she verified that indeed she was undressed as she had been when she first got into bed. Next, she turned to Sean who was there beside her, eyes closed peacefully.

"Sean, wake up." Her voice was barely a whisper that met no response. Reaching over she shook his shoulder gently and tried again. "Sean?"

With a gasp, Sean bolted upright and turned to Kira with a look of horror.

"Are you alright?" he asked breathlessly.

"Yeah, but I was having one crazy dream. You were there twice and then you were both gone. Where the heck did you go?"

"I never went anywhere. I was still talking to Arthur when you disappeared. Where did you go?"

"Well I thought I woke up, but it was one of those damn dreams where you dream you're waking up and then you're still in the dream. Except it happened to me three times, I think. I'm surprised that you didn't follow me when I left."

"I thought I did," Sean answered.

CHAPTER

Arthur opened his eyes. His room was dark. His black-out drapes were doing their job except for a little light escaping around the bottom of one window.

He had been dreaming which used to be unusual for him until this couple showed up in his life. Since meeting them at the museum, he seemed to run into them at every turn regardless of his state of consciousness, and there they were again in his latest dream. He had been dreaming of Elliot . . . Elliot had found a cure! Arthur remembered watching him perform it on a rabbit, but then Elliot said he couldn't do the same for Arthur without Arthur's assistance which was something he couldn't do . . .

It was crazy. And anyway, it was just a dream. Wasn't it? It felt so real, and the only dreams Arthur ever had that were real like that were nightmares about his mother. This was something new to him. But at least he knew what he was doing next. He was going to fence that jewelry and make a date to visit Elliot again . . .

Arthur trudged slowly out of bed and made his way across the few steps to his kitchen and his coffee maker. The dream was still haunting him, and he needed something to do to make him feel like he was helping his situation.

The coffee started to brew as he stood there thinking. He had intended to wait to see Elliot again until after he fenced the jewelry, but he had plenty of cash which could be a decent start. He decided he'd go see that idiot today.

Twenty minutes later Arthur sat down in the back of the cab and handed the driver a piece of paper with Elliot's lab address. Oddly, neither spoke, but Arthur caught the intent look from the driver through his rearview mirror after he read the address. Upon seeing the eye contact the driver simply nodded slightly and pulled away from the curb.

Arthur's head was already starting to pound as he continued to think about his plan. It had never occurred to him to consider that others in the world might possess psychic gifts, but now he had to accept the fact that he was confronted with someone who did. That boy. The kid seemed to be able to read his thoughts and even send his own. What's worse was the apparent ability to stop Arthur's attempts at using his telekinesis. Now it seemed that the kid also had some facility for tracking people. Meeting up with him and his girlfriend three times was certainly not coincidence. But what had alerted them to his presence at all? It was all quite a puzzle, and a challenge; one he had to win if he was going to survive.

The drive passed quickly and unattended by Arthur. He was too engrossed in his own thoughts. The first words spoken in the cab were when they arrived at Elliot's little lab.

"Wait here," Arthur said. "I'll just be a minute, and I'll tip you well."

The diver merely nodded his agreement.

Arthur marched into the lab without even knocking and placed several stacks of cash on the nearest work bench.

Elliot looked up at Arthur's entrance, glanced at the stacks of cash Arthur plopped onto the table and stood there with his mouth open as Arthur spoke.

"You better be making progress," Arthur stated in a menacing tone. His blue-eyed gaze conveyed the mal-intent better than his tone. "You're running out of time. I'll call you soon. I'll have more money for you if that's not enough."

Elliot looked at once startled and nervous. "Arthur, it's not just the money. That will fund more experiments, but right now I still have no idea how to fix a problem I'm having. Contrary to popular belief, medical advancements like this don't just magically happen by throwing money at them. Without a way to make the gold molecules adhere to the proper tissues the entire procedure is impossible. I'm going to need more time. Things like this can take years to . . ."

Arthur cut him off with a particularly unpleasant pinching of his vocal cords. Elliot's hand flew to his throat as Arthur's rage began to rise like bile.

"Well then you're out of luck," he hissed, "because I don't have more time, which means you don't have more time. You're the supposedly brilliant scientist, so figure it out. Now."

He released Elliot's vocal cords allowing the slight man to respond, albeit somewhat hoarsely.

"I'm doing my best!" Elliot practically screamed. The heat Arthur saw in his eyes was shocking and hinted at a level of frustration that delved far deeper than this little interaction. With barely contained rage Elliot continued to vent at his oppressor, "It's never been done before so there's no precedent for something like this. If you want it fixed now, then why don't you help? I'm open to suggestions because unlike you I can't just move things with my mind!"

Elliot's eyes widened as Arthur watched an idea hit the scientist like a mallet hitting a gong.

"Oh my god," he breathed, "*you* have to do it."

"I'll be damned," Arthur murmured as he reached the same conclusion. Maybe those irritating dreams with that couple had a purpose after all. As his memory raced through the images from his dreams, he remembered the fly in the ointment.

"I can't," Arthur said simply. "I can't move things within my own body; I've tried, and it didn't work."

Elliot's features hardened with stubbornness. "Well if you're too much of a coward to even try, then you'll most likely die waiting. As much as I hate it, right now, you're my best bet."

It was just the right combination of buttons to push. Arthur would not be proven a coward and the idea of being vitally needed for a medical miracle stroked his ego.

A look of satisfaction blossomed on his hawk-like features. He took a casual step closer to Elliot and condescendingly patted him on the cheek.

"Alright, Elliot, how's this for a suggestion? You find out a way to test this experiment on something that's not me, and *I'll* do the hard work. Then, if it works, we'll see about the next steps." His soft, metered tone screamed predator as he continued, "Either way, you have days to figure it out, or I'll just kill you and take your research to a more competent scientist.

~

Another wave of fear swept over Kira as she looked at Sean. "This is the first time you have ever tried to follow me in a dream and lost me."

"Yeah it was. And even then, it was because I thought I was staying with you."

"I hope that never happens again," Kira said with a slight tremor in her voice.

"I guess we have learned the one way to separate me from you in a dream. All it takes is more than one you."

"Or more than one dream. What time is it anyway?" Kira began. "I'm not sure I could sleep anymore."

Sean turned to the clock on the table on his side of the bed. "Oh my gosh. It's already 7:30AM. I *never* sleep this late."

Kira smiled, "It's the blackout drapes. They've done that to me before as well. Those of us who wake up with the light will only sleep in if that light's not there."

"Why would anyone want those things?" Sean asked.

The look of true curiosity on his innocent open features brought a laugh from deep inside her that made Sean look perplexed and almost hurt, which in turn made her laugh even louder.

"What's so funny?" Sean asked.

Now the twinge of hurt in his voice made her feel a bit guilty. "Sean, some people work at night and need to sleep during the day.

Also, people that travel overseas have their days turned around for a while and need to have lights out until their bodies adjust to the new time zone."

"Oh," he answered simply, "I guess I remember that. I've only been overseas that once."

There was a wistful lilt in his tone that drew Kira to him like a magnet.

"And that wasn't exactly for pleasure or under normal circumstances," she practically purred. "Doing it again when we're not chasing someone is just one more thing I get to look forward to sharing with you. Now why don't we . . ."

At that moment Kira's phone rang.

She reached for it and spoke as she raised it to her ear, "It's John."

Sean tensed immediately.

John was supposed to be keeping an eye on their house and Aubrey. If the good-old-boy detective from Kansas was calling them at 7:30 in the morning, she was afraid it didn't bode well.

"Hi, Kira," she heard before switching the phone to speaker.

"Good morning, John. I have you on speaker; Sean is here with me."

"It's kind of early for you isn't it?" Sean added

"What do you mean too early? It's 9:30 here."

"Oh, that's right, two hours difference."

"Still not much of a traveler, are you boy?" Even though John's tone was light, Sean detected an undercurrent which promoted an unconscious peek into his thoughts. It wasn't as easy over the phone, but Sean could do it now.

"It's my dad," Sean blurted out causing a gulf of silence from all three.

Finally, John continued. "Yeah, Sean. He went into the hospital this morning and when no one could reach your phone they called me."

Sean had a moment to feel sheepish. His phone was off. "Sorry about that," he offered. "It died last night, and I left it in the bathroom to charge."

"No problem. I'm just glad I had Kira's number. Sean, your dad's condition has taken a turn for the worse. I'm sorry to be the one to tell you, but you might have some decisions to make," John's voice had grown soft at the last sentence, conveying his empathy. Kira couldn't help but realize John had no idea just how high the stakes really were.

CHAPTER

S ean was pale when he hung up the phone.

"So, we need to head home," Kira started, putting a gentle hand on his shoulder.

"What about Arthur? I don't want to leave that psycho out there to hurt someone else."

"I know. I feel the same way. But, Sean, we can only do what we can do, and in this case, I think your dad comes first. Maybe we can come back after we see what we can do at home." If nothing else, just the set of his shoulders spoke volumes to Kira about his inner struggle. "I tell you what," she continued, "Why don't you take a shower and get us packed, and I'll finish a few details on the painting and say our good-byes to Brian if he's still here. I know he wants justice, but I'm sure he'll understand; he of all people knows how precious time can be."

"That sounds good. I'll check on flights as well." Sean turned to her and pulled her to him for a big hug. Speaking over her shoulder he continued, "I'm glad you're here with me."

"I'm glad to be anywhere with you," she answered softly.

When Kira made it to the kitchen, she was surprised to find Brian there making coffee.

"Well good morning," Brian volunteered. "I thought you two would be off to town this morning."

"We would have been, but we got a call from home. Sean's dad has cancer and it just took a turn for the worse so we're going to hurry back."

Kira saw Brian's eyes falter as his hopes for justice slipped away, but he quickly recovered and put on his actor-face before he responded.

"I'm so sorry to hear that. Jackson can take you to the airport anytime you need. I'm heading to the studio."

"Thanks again," Kira began, "Sorry to leave so suddenly. I am going to finish a few tweaks on the painting and sign it before we leave."

"It sure looked finished to me when I viewed it this morning. I love that smile you left on Angelie's face, even if it was directed at Elliot it still warms my heart and truly gives me the closure I was looking for. Kira, I can't thank you enough. Your work was well worth every penny." As he finished, he glided in quickly and gave a hug and a peck on the cheek, both of which caught her off guard and flustered her.

"Well . . . uh . . . you're most welcome. I'm glad you liked it." Kira, at that moment, was feeling glad that Sean hadn't been there. She wondered if he would have been upset with the quick physical demonstration of gratitude.

"Help yourself to coffee and whatever you can find for breakfast. I'm off to the studio."

And then he was gone.

Kira poured two cups of coffee and strolled back to the bedroom. Sean was just hanging up the phone as she walked in and handed him a cup.

"That was pretty quick," Sean began.

"Brian was up and already had the coffee made. He said Jackson could take us to the airport whenever we wanted."

"That's good, but it's going to be a few hours. I couldn't get us a flight until early afternoon."

"Good, that'll give me more time to make finishing touches on the painting."

"And maybe go for one last swim?" Sean added.

The expression on his face gave her the hint that maybe swimming wasn't really what was on his mind. But regardless it sounded like a great idea. "Sounds good," she said. "You can finish packing, and I'll meet you at the pool."

"You don't want me with you while you paint?" He asked.

"I'm sure I'll be fine. I don't even know if I'll actually make it into painting mode. I just have a little shading and adjustments I want to make before I sign it."

Sean looked a little skeptical but nodded. "OK. I'll meet you out in the pool shortly then."

Kira leaned in to give him a quick kiss, but Sean had more in mind. The lingering connection aroused them both. "Don't be too long," he said as he finally released her.

"If I might have been, I certainly won't be long now."

Kira made her way into the den. From Brian's words, she had a sneaking suspicion that something might have changed on the canvas since she last touched it, and she wasn't disappointed.

Angelie's smile had gained some depth of feeling that hadn't been there when Kira's brush was last withdrawn from the canvas. Even in profile as Angelie looked at Elliot the love virtually emanated from her features.

"Thank you, Angelie, for that bit of help," she murmured.

Two remaining small bowls of paint sat sealed on the floor by her stool along with one even smaller container of ashes. She held in her hand the very last of Angelie's remains. And that was the final detail; she wanted to use the balance of her ashes and have all of Angelie be in the painting.

Gazing at the canvas, Kira picked up one of the bowls of paint and looked at it again. Yes, this was the right color for what she needed. It would just be a small change and should only take a few minutes. She mixed paint and the last of the ashes together. Positioning herself on her stool she raised her brush to the canvas . . .

She felt as if she were being propelled backward through a vast black void. A part of her recognized that she had entered her "painting mode", but it had never felt like this before and for that matter with the little she had to accomplish she hadn't even expected to enter that state. The sensation seemed to last forever until it suddenly stopped. She was standing in a room. It looked like a small apartment with black painted walls. Who would paint their walls black? Clothes and dishes were scattered around everywhere.

The place didn't look unlived in, it looked *over* lived in, and by someone with no thought for tidiness or even hygiene for that matter. She had a growing sense of dread as recognition dawned on her. Her eyes had made nearly one full circle of the slovenly hovel when Arthur popped into view.

"YOU!" They both said in unison.

"How did you get here?" Arthur continued.

Kira knew exactly *how* she had arrived at this place. What she wanted to know was *why*? Her curiosity was piqued to such a degree that the sensation of fear hadn't even reared its ugly head . . . yet. She was on the verge of saying something flippant when the scene abruptly changed. She was in another small, dirty apartment. It was not as disgusting as Arthur's had been, but not far off, and this room was busy. A somewhat attractive if unkempt lady was leaning forward with her finger pointing at a young boy while some burly dockworker, if Kira had to guess, stood behind her glaring.

"I told you if you didn't eat everything on your plate you were going to have to stay in your room. Now get going!"

"This isn't about me eating all my food. You just want me out of the way so you can screw this jerk!"

At that point the boy's mother slapped him hard enough for him to stagger back a couple of steps.

"I told you not to do that again," the boy said in a tone filled with fury. Not to be intimidated by her child the woman lashed out and struck him again. "Well screw you, too, Mother!" With that the boy bolted toward the door where Kira was standing. She was startled to see such malicious fury on the young boy's face as he picked up speed. His mother quickly turned to stop his flight but abruptly screamed and fell grabbing her ankle. The burly dockworker also took an aggressive step toward the boy before he too yelled and grabbed at his temple. Kira quickly stole a glance over her shoulder at the receding form of the boy who she now assumed to be a young Arthur only to find he hadn't even turned around. She surmised he didn't even know what he had just done.

Before Kira could even close her mouth from the surprise, the scene snapped away.

Kira found herself back in the study she had seen once before. The broad windows were still open making the thin gray curtains gently dance behind Angelie who was, as before, situated at a grand piano.

She had her fingers on the keys and a pencil in her mouth with sheet music on the holder in front her. Kira stood enthralled as Angelie's fingers delicately tickled the keys, and a hauntingly sweet melody filled the room. This was what Kira had been hoping to see. Angelie paused for a moment and wrote notes on the paper in front of her.

"If I can just get this done before his birthday," she muttered to herself. At that moment a phone rang and Angelie grabbed it off the bench beside her. "Oh shit," she said as she looked at the incoming call. She answered and listened for a bare few seconds. "I know; yes, I know. Fine, I'm on my way now. I'll be there in fifteen minutes." She turned back to the piano grabbed the music and jumped up. Opening the top of the piano bench, she dropped the music inside . . .

~

"Kira!"

Sean was relieved to see his urgent voice blast through her awareness and her eyes snap open. She seemed surprised to see him standing beside her dripping wet.

"Are you alright?"

"Yeah. Why?"

"I thought you were coming right out?" The concern in Sean's tone was laced with a slight touch of annoyance.

"How long have I been in here?" Kira asked.

At this point Sean picked up her thoughts and read both her confusion and excitement. His irritated feelings evaporated like a water drop on a hot skillet, and he gravitated to her excitement as he replied, "About forty-five minutes."

"Wow," she answered, "I'm so sorry but . . . well you know . . ."

"Yeah, I understand; but what are you so excited about? And the painting looks fantastic by the way."

"Thanks. Let me pack up and hopefully we'll have time for that swim, or at least a shower," Her gaze spoke volumes, "And I'll tell you all about it on the way to the airport."

"Sounds great."

Jackson had the car waiting and the door open when they hurried out. Between Kira's painting and both of their newlywed lingerings in the shower they were running a bit late for their flight. Jackson loaded their bags in the trunk while they hopped in the back of the limo.

"I'm kind of sorry we didn't get to spend more time with Brian. He is an interesting fellow," Kira stated as she rolled up the privacy screen. Jackson seemed to take no notice. He simply glanced back and smiled then pulled the big vehicle out of the driveway.

"Yeah, me too. I actually liked that guy. Did you know Brian had the hots for you?" Sean replied.

The question so stunned Kira that for a moment she couldn't even speak. "No, he didn't. I didn't notice a thing, and I'm usually pretty sensitive to stuff like that."

"I didn't notice a thing either except for his thoughts. That's why I never said anything. It was weird, Kira. It's only the second time I've been faced with that situation, and it was difficult not to say something, but he was a perfect gentleman, and I had no right to take him to task for his thoughts. Actually, considering them, he was downright honorable, but being aware of his thoughts made it difficult for me not to be jealous."

"Wow. I had no idea. That must have been really tough on you. If it makes you feel better though, it also makes me even more proud of you . . . and turns me on too." She smiled and he leaned in to kiss her.

"OK, it was worth it then. Now tell me what happened with the painting."

Kira laid out the story in detail while Sean listened intently. He was focused on her face, and she assumed correctly that he was taking in her feelings and thoughts as well as the words she was speaking. When she finished, they both sat quietly for a while considering before Sean finally offered up an opinion.

"That sure explains a few things about why Arthur is the way he is. It also makes me think we need to get word to Brian as soon as possible about the music in the piano bench. Sounds like it might have been written for him."

"I was thinking the same thing. It also makes me more certain than ever that we're not through with Arthur. I was thinking that after we see to your dad we might come back and track him, but after that vision I have a feeling he might try to track us."

"Wouldn't that just be par for the course?" Sean couldn't help but recall how they had been tracked before by Poena and the result of that.

"You think we should increase our fire insurance?" Kira asked with a straight face. Sean, however, broke out laughing.

"Or our health insurance," he finally answered.

"Or both," Kira retorted causing them both to crack up.

They arrived late into Kansas City, and between the time change and the drive from the airport back to their place south of town, it was approaching midnight when they pulled into the driveway. The motion sensor light on the side of the house switched on as they pulled up and it was a warm and welcoming feeling to be home. They barely got their luggage into the bedroom before they both virtually collapsed on the bed.

"I might be too tired to even get undressed," Kira said.

"I can help with that." Sean said smiling. But he was exhausted as well, so five minutes later they were both out like a light.

Sean barely had time to fall asleep before dreams beset him, or maybe it was just one dream. This time, however, it was him and not Kira doing the dreaming, and just like Kira's early experiences there was no one there to help.

Things blurred as Sean turned to find his father lying on the bed in the hospital. As he looked, his father's eyes fluttered, then opened. A look of pain crossed his features followed promptly by the sensation of pain flowing into Sean's mind like a fresh flow of molten lava, his Dad's pain. Sean winced and grabbed at his own brow unconsciously mimicking his father's action.

"It's become that bad, Dad?" The question was rhetorical. Sean had already felt that anguish. His father's eyes widened, and a hint of a smile crept onto his features. He was about to reply when the scene suddenly jumped.

Sean found himself standing over the grave of Jason, his adopted dad, in the woods on the back of their property.

A bolt of fear from those memories slithered up his spine as he nevertheless began to kneel by the headstone... when he heard a sound coming from his left. He turned his attention to the source of the mournful noise.

He was staring at himself sitting on a hay bale in front of the horse barn with his elbows on his knees crying. Sean was frozen in place, trying to decide what to do next, as the scene continued.

He took one step forward and was accosted by one of the strangest sensations he had ever experienced. He was abruptly sensing his own emotions from the other him. It was akin to experiencing his own emotions but not... It was much more familiar and personal somehow. As he tried to take in the experience, he took another step forward and began to raise his hand toward himself. The other him had not even looked up. He just continued the shoulder-shaking bout of crying on the hay bale. The anguish he was sensing was so intense Sean had to struggle to breathe and not burst into empathetic sobs himself. It felt like drowning and being crushed to dust at the same time. Sean's throat constricted as he neared the broken man.

Then came the thoughts... his thoughts... his thoughts from the other him. Aubrey, his only connection to his heritage, had just died.

Then Arthur appeared beside him.

"It didn't have to be this way for your dad," he said, all the while staring down at the headstone." Sean turned back to the headstone of Jason, but it now bore Aubrey's name. A new bout of grief overtook him, then came Arthur's voice again. Sean turned his head to look at Arthur's accusing countenance.

"But you weren't fast enough. You weren't smart enough." Sean turned away from the condemning words. The headstone was gone. Aubrey was standing there smiling, but Arthur's voice continued.

"The signs were there. You just missed them."

Arthur slowly lifted his gaze to meet Sean's eyes.

Suddenly Sean found himself standing alone in their new house gazing into the fireplace. An ample blaze filled it, lending a cheerful light and warmth to the darkened room. The scene fluctuation was bewildering, and before he could collect his thoughts enough to take in the abrupt changes, Poena appeared beside him.

Confronting her had been a terrible ordeal, and his pulse accelerated as he turned to face her. Memories of the horrors she had caused blazed into his mind, but before he could even contemplate a response, she grabbed the back of his neck and kissed him soundly on the mouth.

"Don't worry," she began, "You never were one to admit defeat." With that she kissed him again with a passion that implied a plan. Sean was left feeling dirty from guilt, but his emotions were in such a maelstrom from the tornadic succession of powerful sentiments that he could barely register one more.

Sean's mind wrenched itself from the images, and his eyes opened, leaving him panting with a thudding pulse.

"NOOOOO!" Sean heard, only realizing a second later that the voice was his.

"Sean!" Kira's voice rang in his ears, and his eyes popped open. He was panting as he turned to Kira.

"Now I know how you feel," he gushed breathlessly. "That was horrible and incredible at the same time."

"Welcome to my world," Kira said half-smiling. "Are you OK?"

"I am now. Now I understand even better what it's like for you to have me there when you wake up. Even sensing your thoughts is not as powerful as experiencing it yourself."

"Can you tell me about it?"

"Can we get some coffee first?"

Kira evinced a lascivious smile, "Can we come back to bed afterwards?"

"Oh, that sounds like a deal. Now I'm in a hurry."

With that they threw back the covers and made their way to the kitchen.

The rendezvous back to their bedroom was not to happen anytime soon, however. On the way to the kitchen Sean remembered why they had hurried home, and the scene from his dream came roaring back to him as vivid as it was in his sleep. Guilt for forgetting his dad's condition for even a few moments waged war with his logic. The guilt won.

"How early do you think we could call my dad?" Sean asked as he sipped the coffee Kira had made them.

"Maybe a better question would be what time are visiting hours," Kira answered with her eyes glued to Sean's.

~

She could see the emotions waging war on his features, and it was reminding her of her mother's passing and how much pain she had felt.

Definitely not memories she cared to have dredged up, but at least they added an understanding of where Sean was at the moment. She longed to spare him this pain, knowing full well it was beyond her power.

They both sipped in silence for a moment.

"I guess we can call the hospital at any time to get that information," Sean said almost to himself.

"Well, they certainly don't close," Kira said bringing a half-hearted smile to Sean's face.

"We've already slept in more than I really wanted to; it's already 8:30."

Kira reflexively glanced at the clock on the wall as she took another sip of coffee. "It's the time change, Sean. Our bodies are still on California time. It's just 6:30 there."

"Oh, that's right. OK then maybe I don't feel so bad. Maybe we should . . ."

At that moment Sean's phone rang. It was John.

~

Sean felt a wave of dread course through him, and he silently prayed his dream hadn't been a premonition as he raised the phone to his ear.

"Are you two west coast travelers awake yet?" He began.

"Sitting here sipping our coffee wondering when visiting hours at the hospital are," Sean replied.

"I can answer that one for you. The official hours don't really matter. You need to get over there to see your dad." The tone in John's voice shifted from teasing to serious instantly.

"That bad, huh?" Sean responded.

"I don't think the physical circumstances are that dire, Sean. I just think it's really important for him to see you as soon as possible."

"OK, John. We'll finish our coffee and head over there. It might take us an hour to get there though, are you going over?"

"I think I'll let this first visit be just you and Kira. I'll swing by this afternoon."

"OK. Thanks for the heads up."

Sean's features were pensive as he slowly pushed the 'end' button on his phone. He sensed Kira wanted to ask him about the call but decided to hold off for a moment and let Sean absorb whatever John had said. He was grateful for her thoughtfulness but spoke up anyway.

"John thinks it's important for us to get the hospital as soon as we can."

"His condition has gotten worse?" Concern filled her voice.

"That's what I asked. John said not really, he just thinks it's important for Dad to see us as soon as we can manage it."

"I can be ready in ten minutes," Kira offered.

"Me too," Sean answered putting his coffee cup back on the table.

CHAPTER

The drive into KC was a bit tense. It was no fault of Sean or Kira's, but Kira knew Sean was worried, and he could pick up on her thoughts which made him feel a bit guilty for dragging her with him through this. It was a vicious circle, and one of many occasions when Sean wished he could turn his gift off entirely.

"I feel so helpless," Kira finally spoke into the silence.

"I'm just so sorry to drag you through this with me, but on the other hand having you here with me is the best thing you could do for me."

"Sean, you can't worry about dragging me through some difficulty you're having. We're married, and there is no place I'd rather be than beside you regardless of the reason. Not to mention it's not like I haven't drug you through the muck with all my needs. The only thing I had to get me through after I left modeling and my mother's death was my painting, and if I hadn't met you, I would have already been driven mad by those unexpected experiences."

"You mean like what I put you through with Jason?"

"Or what *I* put us through with Poena? Seriously, Sean do you really think there was even the slightest chance that Jason was going to be the only scare I got, doing what I'm doing? I have to admit if I had known where it would lead before I started I might have given the whole thing a second thought, or a third, or skipped it all together, but I didn't. Now, thanks to you, I see there is a balance for all the difficulty you and I have to deal with. Look at all the good we've done, and at how much peace we have brought to families. You're the one that reminded me of that."

For Sean the power in her words was underscored by the determination in her thoughts and the underlying closeness she was projecting through it all. It warmed his heart.

"I love you. And I'm the luckiest man in the world," was all he could manage as a response.

Kira reached for the back of his neck and ran her fingers leisurely through his hair. She could almost feel the tension drain from beneath her fingers. "Only because I'm the luckiest girl in the world," she murmured softly.

"I'm trying to imagine how to act at the hospital," Sean began, changing the subject.

Kira stared out the window at the Kansas countryside rolling by for a moment before responding, "John didn't give you much in the way of details about his condition, did he?"

"No, not really. I'm not even real sure what he meant by saying Dad really needed to see me. I thought about reading his thoughts, but it seemed wrong and besides he got off the phone too quickly anyway."

"Well, whatever it is, we'll know shortly. Did John say if he was going to be there?"

"Yeah. He said it would be better if it was just us this first time."

"I wonder what that means," Kira responded.

"Like you said, I guess we'll know shortly. I think I'm a little scared," Sean added timidly. "I just keep thinking that I wish we'd had more time. I feel like I only just met him."

"Sean, you're talking like he's already gone. There's still hope."

"I guess," Sean replied slowly. "But I feel like how much hope we have depends on how much time he has, which I presume we'll know shortly.

I imagine that's why I'm feeling so tense. I think I'm also feeling a bit guilty about not spending more time with him, too."

"Come on Sean don't beat yourself up. It's not like you haven't been busy. You've been dealing with wedding plans and building a house. And we've seen him as many times as we could. Plus, as soon as we knew, we had him move into the trailer and had several wonderful weeks with him before this whole mess with Arthur and Angelie. You can't discount that."

Sean knew she was right.

"Thanks, Kira," Sean said smiling as he took the exit toward

Shawnee Mission Hospital.

"Whatever happens I'll be there with you."

Their conversation faded. Both were busy with their own thoughts, though Sean was busy with both of theirs.

Arthur's headaches were continually getting worse, and the rough ride from the beat-up old piece of shit he was driving wasn't making it any better. On the bright side, he was away from the city and headed toward Las Vegas. Wind noise from rotted rubber seals and the drumming of the old engine were the only sounds on the nearly empty highway. The hours ahead of him were a great opportunity to think, which was convenient, because he had a lot to think about.

The dream with that boy and his girlfriend haunted him. Like a shadow dancing in his peripheral vision he felt like he was just barely missing something important about the two of them. Arthur didn't like not having answers, and he still had a powerful desire to make them pay for their interference. But how would he do that?

How would he even find them? Speaking of which, how had they managed that little trick in Beverly Hills, and then again at the Marina? It was incredible.

If he didn't know better, he'd swear they had planted some sort of tracking device on him, but that was impossible. They had never even been near him or anything he owned. It was crazy . . . and worrisome.

Still, it was a problem for later. Right now, he had to think about fencing all this jewelry, and before he did that, he had to find out what it was worth. He pondered that for a moment. He'd either have to go to a jewelry store and find things similar to what he had, but no, that wouldn't work. There were too many nuances. He didn't know a good diamond cut from a bad one, much less be able to discern something like diamond clarity or color, or telling silver from platinum, so hiring an appraiser was going to be his only route. He had to believe they wouldn't be hard to find in Vegas. But finding an honest one might be. Arthur snickered to himself. The irony of him having to concern himself with the honesty of the jeweler appraising his stolen jewels wasn't lost on him.

Even living as close as he did, Arthur had never had occasion to visit Las Vegas or for that matter drive in the desert, much less at night. The dark emptiness appealed to him and seemed to make his thoughts come clearer. He was actually beginning to believe that his plan could work. He had already done a little research on possible places to fence the jewelry.

The thought caused him to glance over at the small bag on the passenger seat, but his train of thought was interrupted by a little stutter from his worn-out engine. He really didn't need his car to give out at night in the desert with a load of stolen jewelry on his front seat.

~

It only took him a day to move the stolen goods, and he had way more money than he expected and a much newer car. It cost him three or four pushes on some jewelry dealers and a couple of aggressive prostitutes to get the job done, but that shouldn't have bothered him. And it wouldn't have if each successive use of his ability hadn't begun producing more and more bloody nose episodes. He once again sensed his time was growing short.

He reasoned this was more of an inconvenience than anything else though because now he could go straight to Elliot and as long as Elliot produced, he'd be just fine. The other concern was that he had another part to play in his own healing. The one Elliot had already outlined. Arthur had serious reservations as to whether he could do his own part. He had a feeling the missing piece that escaped him about that couple was somehow becoming relevant. The obscurity of it infuriated him but he couldn't shake the feeling.

There was one way to find out, and it produced a consideration that haunted him. There was a route he did not want to have to take, both due to time involved and the complexity of it. It involved finding them first, but if that's what it took to save himself that's what he'd do, and to that end he had one more thing he'd picked up in Vegas for emergencies, and there was a pretty good chance that couple might just be such an emergency.

They pulled into the parking lot of the Shawnee Mission Medical Center which included Shawnee Mission Hospital. The artist in Kira couldn't help but register the multiple floors of glass windows rising before them that reflected the sun and lent an aura of the infinite to the complex. Kira wondered briefly if that had been the purpose. The only other detail that stood out in her mind as they entered the building was the large registration desk with its bright yellow panels inlaid in dark wood. It was striking, standing out against the white corridors in every other direction. She turned her attention to her husband. Sean hated hospitals even though he had only been in one once to get about ten stitches in his knee. She figured he was learning that their entry into the place was causing Kira some anxiety as well. Her thoughts didn't drift to why at that moment, but she figured he'd pick it up later. If not, he could resort to actually asking her. Instead, he just gripped her hand tighter to which she responded in kind.

"Aubrey Johnston's room please," Kira asked of the woman at the front desk.

"Room 344; you can take the elevators down the hall to your left. The nurse on that floor can direct you from there."

"Thank you," Kira responded leading Sean in the indicated direction. He seemed a bit overwhelmed by the whole building.

"Are you OK?" She asked.

"Yeah. I just don't like hospitals, and I'm worried about my dad."

"I understand. I don't really like them either. I can't imagine anyone does, come to think of it. It makes me really appreciate the people that work here, especially the oncologists. I think working with people who have cancer would be very depressing."

"I agree," Sean replied quickly. "I guess I have to remind myself that they are winning the battle more often these days. It must have really been difficult years ago when virtually every patient you saw was facing a death sentence."

The elevator dinged, and they stepped inside. Kira pressed the button for the third floor, and they rode up in silence.

"Aubrey Johnston?" Kira began again as they reached the nurse's station on the third floor. "We are his son and daughter-in-law."

"It's down the hall to your right then about halfway on your left."

"Thank you," Kira replied absently as she led Sean down the hall.

Kira felt the slightest hesitation as they approached the room. The door was ajar, and Kira knocked gently as they entered.

"Aubrey?" Kira said softly as they walked through the threshold. Sean was strangely withdrawn, and Kira could feel his hesitancy as clearly as Sean could have read hers. There was no response from Aubrey who was on the other side of a partially drawn curtain. The room was a study in hospital drab with light green and gray on the walls, and that patina of odor that could be labeled on a bottle as "hospital room." Kira plastered a smile on her face, and still holding on to Sean's hand, she pulled the curtain back. Sean's grip became uncomfortably tight as they both took in the sight of his father on the bed.

His eyes were closed and there was an obvious pallor to his skin. He had no tubes down his throat, but he did have the little tube running under his nose providing oxygen and he was hooked to a heart monitor. For a moment it was the only sound in the room.

Kira glanced at Sean's face, trying to discern his emotions so she could better support him. His features conveyed a combination of fear and concern, but his words spoke to his pervasive curiosity.

"Why the heart monitor?" Sean asked absently, "And is he really so ill that he needs oxygen? I thought this was brain cancer not lung. What does that have to do with his breathing and his heart?"

"I don't know," Kira answered softly. "But we can certainly ask the doctor. Do you want me to go find him?"

"Please," Sean replied as he released her hand and moved over to the bed.

"I'll be right back," Kira said moving toward the door.

~

Sean didn't like any of this. He didn't like the smell. He didn't like the sound of the equipment. But most of all he didn't like the way his dad looked. His new dad. His real father. The one he had only known for a couple of years now. This couldn't be happening.

"Aubrey?" Sean said tentatively. "Dad?" Nothing happened save for the sounds of the machine and the very slight hiss of the oxygen tube doing its work. Sean felt anxiety rising like steam from a pressure cooker. He responded with a gentle hand to the shoulder and a several-decibel increase in his voice.

"Dad?" Sean tried again. Aubrey's eyes fluttered and then opened. It took them another few seconds to focus and turn to him.

I'm OK, son, Sean heard in his mind. *I'm just tired.*

Sean smiled at his father's use of his abilities to reply without having to expend the effort to speak. It was a warm and wonderful bond they shared that had helped tremendously to bridge all the lost years they had as a result of Sean's so-called adopted dad's treachery.

Are you in pain? Sean responded mentally.

No. not really. I think they have me drugged up so that I won't be uncomfortable.

Doesn't that hurt your body's ability to fight the cancer?

I don't think it matters, son. Ask the doctor about that one. He'll give you a better answer, and I'm feeling a little woozy anyway.

Aubrey's eyes fluttered, and the steady beep of the heart monitor became erratic, then steadied. Aubrey drew a deep breath and settled into sleep. Seconds later the nurse came in followed shortly by the doctor. The nurse was a short, round woman with dark features and a face that reflected a frequent smile. The doctor was virtually the opposite. He was tall and thin, and though his features were also dark, his face looked more attuned to the delivery of bad news.

"What's going on?" Sean asked. He could read the concern on the doctor's features as easily as he could read it in his thoughts.

Kira silently re-grabbed Sean's hand while she eased in closer. Sean sensed the whole experience was reminding her too much of her mother's last days in the hospital which was elevating her anxiety substantially.

"The tumor is in an area of the brain where its growth is creating pressure on the hypothalamus and in turn affecting the autonomic nervous center. That's why you just saw his heartbeat become erratic and why we are supplementing his oxygen."

"Isn't there anything you can do to get rid of it or at least shrink it?"

The doctor turned to face Sean. "Your name is Sean, right?"

"Yes."

"Sean, I'm sorry but tumors like this are so deep in the brain there is very little we can do to affect it that won't have side effects nearly as bad, or worse, than what the tumor is causing.

I'm afraid all we can do is keep him comfortable."

The nurse was jotting something down from the monitor, seemingly trying to disguise the distress she was feeling at the news being delivered.

"So how long does he have?" Sean blurted out. His voice was shaky as he asked the question, and Kira sidled in even closer.

"It's hard to tell in these cases. He could have days or maybe weeks but not more than that."

"I see," Sean answered distantly. Sean's gaze shifted slowly back to Aubrey, who now appeared to be sleeping peacefully. "Is he in pain?" Sean asked.

"Not at all," the doctor answered quickly.

"Thank you, Doctor. We'll be in touch."

With that Sean turned toward the door pulling Kira behind him. His senses were too overwhelmed to even be aware of her bewilderment. It seemed to be all he could do to direct one foot in front of the other and head for the door. To her credit she didn't try to resist or add anything.

Sean's daze persisted as they walked down the busy hallway toward the elevators. Even the gurney being raced down the hall and narrowly avoiding a collision hardly elicited a flinch. Three other people crowded into the elevator before the door closed. Two of them were nurses and the third was a rough looking fellow with his arm in a sling. Sean's gaze lifted as far as the elevator keypad before locking there.

~

Kira watched him intently, unnoticed. The elevator descended, and as she watched she detected a change. Sean's gaze changed qualities from shock and dejection to what, to Kira, looked like the birth of an idea shifting to a hint of determination. By the time they exited the elevator Kira knew Sean had a mission. It was all she could do not to burst in on his thoughts with a question. His gaze flicked toward her as they exited the building, and suddenly she knew she already had.

"Give me another minute," Sean murmured, "and I'll tell you."

The air outside was crisp and the trees were in full fall array. Sean had mentioned before that this was his favorite time of the year in Kansas and Kira could easily see why.

The freshening breeze and the rustle of the leaves in the trees around the parking lot occupied her senses while she waited patiently.

When they got to the car Sean wordlessly opened the door for her and went around to the other side.

"OK," he began as he started the engine, "I'm NOT going to let my dad die that way. There has to be something else we can do."

"I don't know what it would be," Kira began. "Even if we or the doctor has an idea, we are just about out of time to do anything."

Sean pulled into the traffic and began to head south. The wind was picking up causing the trees to sway and shed showers of brightly colored leaves across the scenery.

"Something will come up. In fact, I think just maybe it already has..."

~

Aubrey's eyes fluttered. Sean was gone. He struggled to take a breath and thought how easy it would be to just give up. But Sean had come to see him. Through the fog of his painkillers he was certain of it. It wasn't just a dream. And he had sensed determination from him. That was reason enough for him to fight a little while longer. He wanted more time with his son...

265

CHAPTER

Elliot was having mixed emotions. Usually when he was in his lab nothing distracted him, but today, as his hands accomplished the work he knew so well, his mind wandered. It wasn't surprising. In the last two months he had been accosted by some maniac . . . repeatedly.

As if that weren't distracting enough, he'd also found out he had, and then met with, his full sister only to promptly have to deal with her sudden loss.

His life had never been this complicated, and to make it worse he most certainly had another rendezvous with the maniac to look forward to, and he didn't even know when.

Still there was a small voice in the back of Elliot's mind that wanted Arthur to show back up. He really wanted to have the opportunity to try out his theory on Arthur's tumor. The drawback to the theory was having to have the patient also be involved in the procedure. It felt unethical and problematic, but who the hell was he kidding, the very notion of experimenting on a human at this stage of the game was medically outrageous anyway. Why not add another little wrinkle and have the patient be part of making the procedure work? For that matter, as far as recriminations were concerned, he was reasonably certain that Arthur wasn't going to give him a choice anyway.

But the problem there was, if the patient died who was going to testify that the scientist in charge was forced into early experimentation by the patient himself? Maybe he could get Arthur to sign some kind release, except that Arthur would not be likely to agree to anything that might lessen Elliot's desire to see the process succeed. Elliot sighed. It seemed like his life was most likely going to take a turn for the worse and there wasn't a damn thing he could do about it.

An alarm made a ding at the end of the table. His solution was ready. Maybe he could occupy himself with his other projects enough to stop thinking about it. Maybe Arthur would never contact him again. He chuckled at his own wishful thinking. He had a better chance of that happening if the procedure worked and destroyed Arthur's tumor. But what then? Arthur still might kill him, if for no other reason than to just keep his mouth shut.

In the midst of that inconvenient thought Arthur opened the door to his lab and entered quickly with a determined look on his face.

"We need to have something to try soon," Arthur began, without so much as a hello. "Here is the money you said you needed to keep things moving ahead." With that, Arthur shocked Elliot a second time by plopping a very large sack of cash on his table. Stacks of currency spilled out. They were hundreds. If the whole bag was the same, it had to be over a quarter of a million.

"Where did you get that?" Elliot stammered.

"None of your damn business," Arthur replied heatedly. "Are you close to something we can try or not?"

"I . . . I . . . I believe I am. In fact, I believe we can move straight to doing the procedure on you. I've seen what you can do, and I've accounted for that in my plans; doing any other experiments would just take more time. If we skip the demonstration, then I'll only need a little time to buy some supplies and set things up."

"How much time?"

"Maybe Wednesday afternoon? Say 3:00PM?"

"Fine," Arthur said. "I'll see you then. Make damn sure everything is ready." With that, Arthur turned around and left as abruptly as he had entered.

"Damn," Elliot said out loud. "I don't know whether to hope it works or hope it kills that useless hunk of flesh." Then Elliot remembered his sister. "I guess I'm rooting for it to kill him." He couldn't linger on that thought, though. He only had two days and a lot of preparations to make.

Wednesday came up way too fast.

Arthur walked into the lab and Elliot was immediately aware of the change in demeanor. Gone was the patina of arrogance. Gone was the underlying anger. What remained as Arthur entered, and was so apparent to Elliot's eyes, was fear which was something Elliot could completely understand. He ran his hand through his blond hair as he focused on Arthur striding across the room. A moment passed before either spoke.

It was late afternoon. Arthur had shown up exactly when Elliot said he should. Elliot had all the preparations made that he possibly could. He had bought an easy chair that would serve as Arthur's for the procedure. All the equipment was set up.

"You really think this can work?" Arthur asked in a flat tone, seemingly devoid of emotion even while his eyes locked with Elliot's burning with intensity.

"I believe it can," he said. "No guarantees, but if you can do your part, I believe it can."

There was a window AC unit in the small lab that droned sonorously in the silence following Elliot's words. The white noise seemed to have a calming effect on both of them, drowning out all the other usual sounds in the lab.

In front of the easy chair a screen stood on a table and a device that looked like an old-timey projector.

"What do you need me to do?" Arthur asked.

"For starters, have a seat in the chair. What I'm going to do is arrange some sensors on your head and project on the screen the image of your brain. Then I need you to relax. I'm going to give you a topical anesthesia, then inject some microscopic gold particles into your carotid artery. I don't want to use a sedative for fear of affecting your ability. You will see the particles on the screen as your blood carries them up into your brain. The darker area you will see on the screen will be the tumor. It will be your job to gather those particles around the tumor and hold them there, so I can heat them and destroy the tumor. The entire procedure, other than the injection should be painless, and you just have to hold those particles in place for a few seconds. Do you think you can do that?"

"I told you before I've never been able to move anything inside my own body but that was always some piece of me, a nerve or bone. I've certainly never tried to move something foreign inside my own body. So maybe it'll work."

"Let's hope so," Elliot said before the doubts chased his words across his mind. "I'm going to have to shave your ahead to affix the electrodes," Elliot continued.

There was a brief pause.

~

Arthur had very little vanity within him, but he was proud of his raven colored hair. "Just do it," Arthur said, evincing a tone of disgust.

Having hair isn't much good if you're dead, he thought to himself.

Elliot moved efficiently and in moments Arthur heard an electric trimmer buzzing followed by the feathery sensation of hair falling on his shoulders and chest. What he didn't anticipate was the wet sensation he experienced next as Elliot applied shaving cream to his head.

"Is that necessary?" Arthur asked while holding stone still in the chair. Wiggling was a bad idea when someone had a razor against your skin. Visions of Lex Luther floated up in his imagination causing a smile. "Never mind."

~

Arthur's smile nearly brought chills to Elliot. It was such an unfamiliar appearance on that countenance that Elliot couldn't help but wonder what had precipitated it.

On second thought, he decided he didn't want to know. He

proceeded to attach other electrodes to Arthur's chest from the heart monitor.

The whole process just took a few minutes before Elliot was swabbing a bit of Lidocaine on Arthur's carotid artery. "Are you ready?" He asked Arthur.

"Yes," Arthur replied simply.

The solution in the syringe was clear. The gold particles were too small to see with the naked eye, but they still gave the impression of sparkling as the overhead light reflected off them. Arthur didn't flinch when Elliot began the injection, but he did make a very slight groan as Elliot depressed the plunger of the oversized syringe.

"That should be the worst of it as far as what you'll be able to feel. Just concentrate on the screen."

Arthur and Elliot both watched on the screen that was connected to a scanning device as the microscopic gold particles ascended Arthur's circulatory system. The magnification was such that the particles were just barely visible and therefore the entire image was too large to see all at once. What they initially saw was just the gold and a section of the artery they were moving through. Elliot's scientific mind was completely focused and left no room for discussion as he watched his life's work unfold. It was simultaneously daunting and exhilarating. Then the particles passed up into Arthur's lower brain stem.

"Ok Arthur, when you can see the dark area on the edge of the screen that will be your cue to begin trying to gather the particles around the entire circumference of the tumor. If you can actually settle them on the tumor, that would be even better. I will reduce the magnification slightly so that we will be able to see the entire mass at once."

Arthur frowned with concentration. "I've also never tried to control several objects at the same time." Arthur's voice was low and steady. The sensation of his concentration was almost palpable to Elliot.

"OK I'm reducing the magnification. There Arthur, that is the entire growth and you can clearly see the gold."

~

Arthur focused on a single particle and silently willed it to settle onto the tumor. As they watched, it moved. The visual feedback was also something Arthur had never had before, and he was surprised at how much it helped. It smoothly settled into place and Arthur methodically moved on to the second one. It, too, began to move. There were so many particles Arthur realized he wouldn't be able to concentrate on holding them all in place at once. He tentatively released his focus on one of the previously moved molecules and watched. Much to his surprise the molecule didn't revert to its original location. It stayed nestled against the black mass as if it had been glued there. A wave of relief and hope washed over him. This could actually work; he might truly be rid of this thing. He began to try to move each molecule faster as his hope for survival rose. He focused his attention on the next molecule, ignoring the rising pain in his head. One after the other he moved and released them. With each successful movement he felt his headache coalesce, but he ignored it. He was making progress. He just had to keep focusing.

~

Elliot stared at the screen with rapt interest. It was absolutely amazing to watch Arthur work. But very quickly Elliot began to understand that the way he was doing it, the whole process was going to take too long. There were just too many particles for Arthur to keep moving them one by one.

"You're doing great Arthur, but this will take too long. Do you think you can do groups of particles at once?" Elliot's attention had been glued to the screen but after asking the question he glanced down at Arthur and was jolted to see blood dripping from Arthur's nose.

"Arthur, Stop!" Elliot yelled as he reached for a towel.

Arthur seemed frozen in place and did not respond, but the particles on the screen were moving faster.

Elliot watched in horror as the blood became a steady stream flowing on to Arthur's shirt.

"Arthur," Elliot repeated fervently, "You have to stop!"

"I . . . ," Arthur began then suddenly sagged to the side simultaneously triggering the alarm on the heart monitor.

~

Arthur felt his consciousness slip away in a red haze. He didn't feel his heart stop. It was like he went somewhere else. He was concentrating on the gold particles realizing that this might be his only chance to save himself, and the next thing he knew he was in a field in the country somewhere. The trees were swaying and the air was cool. Arthur made a slow circle until his gaze encountered a house. New, by the look of it, but older styled architecture. His eyes were still sweeping the unexpected scene when the front door opened on the dwelling and out came a man.

No. Damn! It was the boy from the museum, and Beverly Hills, and the hotdog stand. What the hell was it with this guy? The guy walked toward him with an easy gait and confident step. Once he was within earshot, he stopped and locked eyes with Arthur. There was a simplicity about his demeanor that was confusing and infuriating, but he had no time to consider it as the boy spoke.

"You need me," the guy said.

"Screw you! I don't need anybody," Arthur spat out.

"You need me," the boy calmly repeated, "Ask Elliot," and Arthur suddenly felt a sharp stab in his chest.

His eyes popped open to find himself looking up at Elliot standing over him with a look of grave concern. Literally, grave concern he decided. Elliot was holding a huge syringe in one hand and at that moment Arthur realized how much his chest hurt.

"Ow," he said reaching up to his chest. "What did you do to me?"

"Your heart stopped," Elliot answered his eyes still wide with concern and fear. "I didn't have anything handy to shock you with, but I did have adrenaline here, so I injected your heart."

Arthur was still trying to gather his thoughts and understand the vision he had seen. "Did the experiment work?" He asked.

"It was working, at least until you passed out and your heart stopped, but it was going too slow. You were just managing one or two particles at a time. I don't know if we can even try again. Apparently, the strain was too much for you."

Arthur suddenly remembered his last vision and blurted out. "What do you know about a couple with abilities like mine?"

"What?" The question was so unexpected that Elliot stood there flustered for a moment before he could respond.

"A man and a woman. She looks like a damn model and at least one of them can do things with their minds like I can. You know them, don't you? What can you tell me about them?"

"I don't know. What makes you ask that question?"

"Do you know where they live?" Arthur continued.

"What? Why are you asking me this?"

"Just answer the question."

"I think Brian mentioned Kansas, but I don't know any more than that."

"Call Brian," Arthur said as he leaned forward in the chair. "I'm going to need an address."

"But . . ."

"Just call him. You have his number, right?"

"Well yes, but I can't just . . ."

"Call him, Elliot. Now."

The menace in Arthur's tone was unmistakable but Elliot was unsure whether Arthur would be able to do anything to act on his veiled threat after the effort he had just expended. He decided he didn't want to find out. "Fine. I'll call him."

Elliot moved over to his desk and rooted around with the things laying there until he muttered a soft "Ah" while picking up a piece of paper.

CHAPTER

There had been no change in Aubrey's condition. Since arriving back home, Sean and Kira's life returned to a semblance of normality, or at least as normal as it ever got. Sean worked with the horses or went to his martial art classes, anything to keep his mind off his dad. He and Kira had spent quite a bit of time just enjoying each other, but she was feeling the need to get back to work.

Some ashes had arrived while they had been in California, and they seemed as innocuous as possible. A lady in Tennessee wanted to memorialize her husband who was a career postman and had died suddenly from a brain aneurysm.

The urn was calling to her, and Sean understood.

"You're sure you don't want me with you on this one?" Sean asked.

"Really, a career postman? I think I'll be fine; unless, of course, someone trained killer dogs to attack him and the fear caused the aneurysm."

"OK. I get it. I'll head back out to the barn."

Kira just smiled at him as he turned to leave.

Sean's thoughts immediately returned to their trip to California. It had been bizarre. Just imagining running into someone that could move things with their mind. It was too incredible. The smell of the horses and their soft nickering distracted him briefly as he approached the barn. Once inside, the sensation of contentment that emanated from the horses brought a smile to his face. This was one of the favorite parts of his gift, his connection to the horses. He reached for the nose of one of his favorite ones, Cocoa.

It was then that Sean recalled the sensation in the museum when he had stopped Arthur from hurting Kira and what it felt like when he was confronted with one of those telekinetic thoughts. He hated the idea of that sadist running free, but he couldn't possibly be that far away from his dad right now. Cocoa bobbed her head beneath his hands which refocused his attention to the horse. It seemed that this line of thought disturbed the sensitive animal.

Sean stroked her nose more attentively. "It's OK, girl. It's not you; it's me, and my stupid human thoughts. I'll pay more attention to you." With that, he led her out of her stall and into the corral where he dedicated his attention to saddling her up.

~

Kira's thoughts were distracted as well. She wanted and needed to focus her attention on the task in front of her if she was going to do this tribute the justice it deserved, but even while she was mixing paints her thoughts were drifting back to California and Arthur. She had already received an image from the ashes anyway. It was a simple country road with a line of autumn trees shedding leaves in a breeze across a line of mailboxes and a lonely figure walking down the path with a bag over one shoulder.

The image reminded her of a Carl Sandberg painting. It would be a nice mixture of memories and old-world charm, hopefully something that would be meaningful to his survivors.

~

It was late afternoon when Sean finally opened the back door and came in the house. That door opened into a small utility room with the washer and dryer which led into the kitchen where Sean found Kira busy over the stove.

"Are you practicing your housewife skills?" He asked with a bit of a smirk on his face. He snatched a quick snippet of her emotions before she spoke. It was a good thing too, because her words were portraying annoyance while her emotions were reading playful.

"Don't try to lump me into your prehistoric image of the 'little wifey.'"

"Whoa there. I just asked a simple question. I think you need an attitude adjustment." He moved in to tickle her as he finished.

"No, no, no. You better not unless you want boiling pasta sauce all over both of us."

Sean desisted promptly but moved in close over her shoulder.

"Which smells fabulous by the way. What is it?"

"I've marinated some salmon and I'm going to broil it and serve it over a lemon and garlic linguini."

"Yum. OK. I'm not going to interrupt you. Is there anything I can do to help?"

"As a matter of fact, there is. Could you put those rolls in the oven? And after that, feel free to grab a bottle of that Sauvignon Blanc out of the refrigerator. I prefer to drink while I'm cooking."

"A woman after my own heart," Sean replied.

"A woman that already HAS your heart," she retorted.

"Ain't that the truth?" he said as he opened the fridge door.

The meal which included a fabulous orange-glazed asparagus, turned into a wonderful dinner, and the bottle of white wine turned into three. They considered dessert but jointly decided that the best dessert would be one spent in bed.

"I'll just carry these glasses upstairs," Kira stated as she deftly swooped up the glasses and virtually danced toward the staircase.

"I'll bring the bottle," Sean replied. "There's at least a little left we wouldn't want to waste."

Kira had been anticipating this interlude all afternoon, to the extent that it had been an effort to not rush the dinner.

~

Sean sensed Kira's anxious, amorous, fervor, and it ratcheted up his own desires to a matching fever pitch. As quickly as Sean had followed her, she was still already in bed when he arrived and set the wine down.

"Welcome to our boudoir, Mr. Easton," she offered as she lifted the sheet. She was already naked, and he pondered how she had done that so fast.

"Not that I don't positively *live* to see you naked, but could you let *me* undress you on occasion?"

"You're too slow," she answered smiling coyly.

"And that's a bad thing?" He answered, undressing quickly. "Well it's certainly not something I'm going to argue about," he added as he slid under the sheet.

The smell of her and the fineness of her skin overtook his senses, heightened by his own burgeoning desire. Thoughts gave way to sensation and sometime later sensation gave way to satiation and then sleep, nestled in each other's arms.

~

Kira's eyes popped open and Sean's musky scent filled her nostrils. She wasn't sure what had awakened her but after trying for several minutes she realized she couldn't go back to sleep. For some reason Arthur was weighing on her mind, and it occurred to her she wanted to do another sketch of him and see if it revealed his location. What good this might do she had no ideas, but once the idea formed it wouldn't go away.

What the heck, she thought.

She'd give it try then maybe she could go back to sleep.

She eased out of Sean's embrace being extra careful not to wake him. Just because she was having a momentary bout of insomnia didn't mean she needed to inflict that on him. Besides, she didn't plan on being up very long. She chilled at the cool touch of the sheets on the far side of the bed and reached for her robe as she stood up.

For some reason she felt like she didn't want to leave the room, however, and her solution was to quietly drag her chair into their huge walk-in closet. She then retrieved her sketch pad and pencils and partially closed the door before turning on the light.

An unbidden smile slipped across her features as she raised her pencil.

Pencil touched pad and her surroundings fell away.

The sensation of her environment returned, but she wasn't in the closet. She was sitting in an oversized stuffed chair in Brian's large den. The lights were very dim. A sketch pad was still in her hand marked with the beginning of Arthur's face. The countenance looked angry causing Kira to lower her pencil and stare for a moment. She turned to peer about the room which was empty. The moon shone through one of the huge ocean-facing picture windows. Its sharp sickle in the sky stood out over the deep darkness of the Pacific, bordered to its right by a bright planet. Jupiter, she guessed, as she continued to slide her gaze around the room. It looked just the same as it had the last time she had sat in here with Brian and Sean.

She shifted her attention back to her sketch pad and raised her pencil once again, and as lead contacted paper her surroundings again fell away with a great sucking sensation. She felt as though she were being yanked into a gigantic vacuum cleaner, complete with roaring wind noise.

Quiet returned and her surroundings again refocused into a cohesive image. Her sketch pad was no longer in her hand. She was now sitting on her stool holding a paintbrush in the air above Angelie's painting, specifically over the mirror on the wall that had revealed Arthur's face. She pulled her hand back and looked around again. She was in a small dark room she had seen before. It appeared to be Arthur's shabby apartment with black painted walls and a decidedly dirty look to it. The smell that came to her matched the info she was receiving from her eyes. Rotting food? Unemptied trash? It almost smelled like an old refrigerator that had been turned off with food left in it and reopened months later. Putrid was the word that came to mind. She looked around more carefully but saw nothing that should be emanating such an odor. What she did see were several volumes of medical texts sitting on the coffee table. Before she could reach for one, however, something changed.

Of its own accord and increasingly against her will, Kira's hand moved toward the surface of the canvas.

She didn't want to touch that canvas again with her brush, but it seemed her mind had lost control of her entire arm while it floated inexorably toward the canvas' surface.

It touched.

Blackness.

She was being drug by her arm as though she were permanently attached to, and being pulled by, the paintbrush in her hand.

Then with a swooshing sound she plopped into a chair again with her sketchbook returned to her lap and a bubbling sound around her. She lifted her chin and as she did, light returned. She was in a lab. A little gasp must have escaped her for the only other person in the room turned to face her. It was Elliot. He smiled.

"What are you doing here?" He asked.

But before she could respond a snarl emanated from her lap jerking her eyes downward in time to see a pair of arms reaching up out of her sketchpad framing the now completed face of Arthur.

"Leave me alone!" The face screamed. The hands angled toward her throat, and in a primal reflex Kira screamed back, jumping up from the chair and dropping her pad. But the hands had already secured a grip on her throat choking off her next scream. Her eyes dropped down to stare in horror at the sketch pad swinging in the air below her, supported only by the phantom-like pair of arms.

Horror quickly morphed into anger, and Kira swung her arm down and across Arthur's arms knocking them free from her throat.

"Let me go!" She yelled simultaneously. Then blackness returned.

Suddenly she was sitting on a couch in the dingy apartment she had so recently left. But before she could think anything, Arthur came running out of the bedroom straight for her yelling again.

"I said, LEAVE ME ALONE!" He continued yelling as his arms once more reached for her throat.

This time neither her stool, easel, nor sketch pad were anywhere in evidence leaving her free to jump up off the couch in an attempt to evade the charging maniac. As she stood, she realized her paintbrush was now in her hand.

Arthur came straight at her. She leaned back toward the couch, put her free hand on the back cushions, and swung her legs over, effectively putting it between her and what had now shifted into a furious carica-ture of Arthur.

Normal body lines had become a series of connected geometric shapes with the oil-painted profile from Brian's painting sitting on top of them. Picasso came to mind.

She was dimly aware that she was still in a dream or vision but remembering the very real consequences of her experience with Jason, she knew she still had to do something to protect herself. When Arthur came racing around the couch like a fugitive from Alice in Wonderland, she deftly flipped the paintbrush in her hand and swung the pointy end at Arthur's cartoon-looking neck. It sunk in and Arthur screamed. Simultaneously, the lights went out.

Bare seconds passed before her vision returned to reveal Brian's den again. She was back on her stool in front of Angelie's painting, and her paintbrush was once more in her hand. She glanced down at the painting and watched in shock yet again while Arthur's profile turned to face her.

"LEAVE ME ALONE!" The face yelled.

"I'm trying!" She yelled back as she bounded up off the stool knocking it down. "You leave *me* alone!"

A look of concentration focused Arthur's features, and a sharp pain lanced across her temple.

"NO!" Sean yelled suddenly popping into the room. "Leave her alone!" A similar look of concentration centered on his face and the pain stopped

In response, Arthur moaned in pain and a splash of blood flooded from his nose. His hands came up to catch the red tide and his expression changed. "Help me," he said quietly. The whipped puppy look on his face matched the sensation of defeat that rolled over Sean just before everything went black once again.

Kira's eyes opened. She was back in her chair in her closet, and she jumped at Sean's grip on her shoulders from behind.

"Easy there," he said. "Are you OK?"

"I am now. What took you so long?"

"If you wanted me there sooner you might have started by telling me before you sat down to draw. As it was, I was having my own weird dreams about Arthur."

"You were asleep, and I didn't want to wake you. Besides, it was just a sketch. Sketching doesn't normally produce visions and I thought since we weren't even in the same state as Arthur, his augmenting of my abilities wouldn't apply.

I guess I was wrong. It seems that all I have to do is think about Arthur for that connection to magnify. Although, I don't think I was seeing the future this time. It was just an all-encompassing vision, like I would have if I were painting. I have to tell you, it's weird not knowing what to expect. I mean, I never know exactly what to expect from my abilities, but this breaks every rule I've come to know, so I didn't anticipate it would be worth waking you."

"Uh-huh. And how did that work out for you?"

"OK fine. I messed up. What were your dreams about?"

"Well, Arthur was . . . hey wait a minute . . . OK just so you know I noticed, nice subject change. Anyway, Arthur was at our house threatening us if we didn't help him."

"Help him do what?" Kira asked. "He asked for help in my dream, too. Actually, he asked you for help in my vision."

"I was in your vision?"

"Yeah, I thought you'd put yourself there intentionally." Kira's eyes narrowed. "You didn't do that?"

"No. I didn't. But isn't it interesting that I was asked the same thing in mine? Maybe we should find him again and ask him what he wants?"

"I don't think we're going to have to find him. I still have a feeling he's going to find us. I also have a growing suspicion about me doing paintings of living people. I ended up with a connection similar to this when I painted Poena, too. And if I'm right, I think maybe I need to quit doing art involving living people."

"Hmmm," Sean responded. "That's a lot to think about. Why don't we see if we can't get a bit more sleep before the sun comes up, and we'll think about it tomorrow?"

"Sounds like a good idea if we can get back to sleep."

"Maybe we just weren't tired enough. Possibly a bit more exercise would help."

Kira smiled. "Well I think it's certainly worth a try."

"But this time don't get up and try to do anything art-related without me, please."

"Deal," she answered.

They exercised as only newlyweds can.

It worked fabulously.

~

The phone jarred them from sleep at 7:00AM the next morning. Kira didn't even hear it, but a groggy Sean managed to retrieve his phone from the nightstand. After a couple of attempts to clear his throat he managed to get his voice to accommodate him.

"Hello?" he croaked slightly.

"May I speak to Sean Easton?"

The official tone in the lady's voice cleared Sean's head instantly. Instinctively he tried to read her thoughts, but that seldom worked on the phone unless it was someone he already knew well. So, he resorted to a more normal reaction.

"This is he," he responded trying to add a bit more of business tone to his voice.

"Hi, I'm sorry to call you so early. This is Alicia with Shawnee Mission Hospital. There has been a change in your dad's condition, and the doctor has requested to meet with you at your earliest convenience."

Sean knew instantly that this could be nothing good. His hand tightened on his phone. "I can be there in about an hour if you don't care how I'm dressed."

The phone ringing and even Sean's initial voice hadn't roused Kira, but the tone in his voice as he gave that last response jolted her out of sleep as surely as cold water on her face.

"I'm sure the doctor won't take note of your appearance, Mr. Easton. He understands that this is an early hour and short notice. An hour you say?"

"Better make it an hour and a half and I'll try for quicker."

"That will be fine, just meet us in your father's room."

"He's still OK, isn't he?"

"As well as can be expected. He will probably seem the same to you as he did last time you were here."

"OK," Sean said, too anxious to ask more questions. "I'm on my way."

"We'll see you soon then." With that she hung up.

"What's wrong?" Kira asked, sitting up and reaching for his shoulder.

"It's my Dad. Something has changed and the doctor wants me there right away."

"Us," Kira corrected. "Let's get going." She sprang out of bed and headed for the bathroom.

Sean was almost too flustered to even notice her emotions. He still picked up concern and warmth as he slid out of bed after her, smiling.

They were in the car in twenty minutes racing toward the hospital.

The drive took longer than Sean expected mostly due to getting stuck behind a farm tractor on one of the county roads. He was glad he had given himself the extra half hour.

Sean and Kira held hands in silence as they went into the hospital and up the elevator, at least it was silent verbally. Sean was picking powerful sensations of Kira's support and compassion amidst the silence and almost desperate hand holding. Sometimes he was amazed that he could feel even more in love with her than he already did.

We'll get through this, he sensed her thinking as the elevator doors opened.

"Thank you for all your support," Sean replied. Kira was way past being surprised when Sean verbally responded to something she had merely thought.

"You're very welcome," she answered smiling. "Helping take care of you is a job I enjoy quite a lot."

The doctor's looming height drew Sean's gaze up to his frowning dark complexion. He was standing in the room reading his chart when Sean and Kira walked in. Aubrey was unconscious or asleep. On an impulse Sean focused on Aubrey's thoughts and was surprised when he received something coherent.

I love you, son, Sean sensed, *And I trust whatever decisions you make.*

Sean wasn't aware that people could have cogent thoughts about their surroundings when they were asleep or sedated, that is unless he was entering his dad's dream, and he'd never tried that with anyone other than Kira. He made a mental note and turned to the doctor.

Only a few seconds had passed but the doctor was silently watching, showing a respect for Sean's diverted attention.

"How is he?" Sean began, diving straight to the point.

"The tumor is growing faster than we expected. I don't know how long he can last this way, but I suspect not too long. Not with that tumor pressing against the autonomic nervous system area of his brain."

"So, what do we do?" Sean asked forcing himself not to read the man's thoughts. He almost didn't want the answer to the question he was asking.

"Well, that's why I called you in. There is a new viral therapy that is still experimental but has presented some phenomenal success in early trials. Basically, they are injecting a mild version of the polio virus in the tumor, and it attacks the tumor cells without affecting the normal brain cells. The biggest drawback is that it has only been tried a very few times and the results have ranged from incredible to useless."

Sean absorbed this information then asked, "How many trials have they done so far?"

"Maybe five or six. And to do this we need to transport your dad to a cancer facility in Los Angeles, California. That, in itself, would be very dangerous in his condition."

Sean couldn't help but smile at the crazy juxtaposition of events. "What a coincidence. We just came back from there. When would you want to send him?"

"As soon as possible, two days, maybe three."

Sean considered the thoughts he had garnered from his dad. It was what his dad would want him to do. "OK, let's do it."

The doctor simply nodded, and Sean turned to face Kira, who had been particularly quiet throughout. "Does it sound like the right move to you?"

"At this point, Honey, every option is a best-guess scenario. If you feel like it's the best choice, I'm here to support you." She hesitated, smiled, then added, "I'm still packed anyway."

Sean returned her smile then turned back to the doctor. "So, what is the name of this place?"

"It's the Beverly Hills Cancer Center," he stated simply.

"That sounds expensive," Sean said.

"Well ordinarily it would be but, in this situation, they are looking for candidates for the new therapy, and so they are minimizing costs and have negotiated with the insurance companies to pay for the procedure."

"That's surprising," Kira piped in.

"Not really," the doctor responded, "They have made it less expensive than other procedures that the insurers would have to underwrite otherwise, so it's a win for them as well."

"OK, we'll make arrangements to get there in a couple of days if you'll just have someone contact us with particulars for when we arrive."

"I'll have the nurse take care of it, and she'll contact you tomorrow with the information."

I love you, son, floated into Sean's mind again causing him to turn sharply to his dad. He sent a loving thought back to him knowing that his dad didn't have his abilities but hoping that at least the emotion would get across to him.

The doctor observed the behavior and asked, "Is something wrong?"

Sean knew Kira had picked up on what was going on but kept her silence.

Sean answered simply, "Just had a sudden memory. It's nothing. Will you be travelling out there with him?"

"I'm afraid not. You'll be dealing with Dr. Morton Anderson. His information will be included in what the nurse sends you tomorrow."

"OK, Doc, thanks for everything."

"You're very welcome, and best of luck to you and your dad."

Sean smiled, nodded his head, and turned with Kira to leave. He opened his mind to the doctor as an afterthought and caught the wave of sympathy. He didn't think highly of their chances.

"You'll have to tell me what happened there with your dad," Kira began.

"Just received a little positive affirmation from my dad via his thoughts. It surprised me, but it also helped me feel comfortable with this decision."

"Well great. I guess we're travelling again," she answered.

"That's not so bad, is it?" He asked grinning.

"Not with you," she answered.

CHAPTER

60

"Ahhh!" Arthur bellowed, as he bolted upright in his bed reaching for his face. His hand came away bloody, and the dream connected to it came flooding back. That couple again. He was tired of their interference in his sleep and his life, and he figured a little pain might convince them to leave him alone. Not to mention, the mystery of his lethal heart attack vision being a growing concern. If he really did need that damn boy to survive, he was going to have a list of problems to solve. There was no clock near his bed, but a quick glance through the darkened curtains told him it was still dark out. He got up and went to the bathroom, cleaned his hands and face, and decided to try for a few more hours of sleep.

When his eyes opened again, what little light that ever made it through his darkened drapes was filtering in steadily.

Time to get up, he thought. This was going to be a busy day.

He was trying to puzzle out how all of this might work. Earlier he had considered kidnapping Elliot and bringing him along, but the more he thought about it, the more he understood that he would have to get them back to Elliot's lab. It wasn't reasonable to believe he could snatch Elliot and all the necessary apparatus to do what needed done. No, he was definitely going to have to bring those two back here.

In that case all he needed from Elliot was that address. Elliot should have already gleaned it from whoever Brian was but hadn't been able to for three days due to the man being so hard to get in touch with. He should have it by now, though. Elliot thought they were from Kansas, so something must have brought them into the area and given them reason to contact Elliot in the first place. They certainly didn't seem like detectives, so what the heck were they doing in the area anyway?

He hadn't thought to ask, but it was a detail Elliot probably knew.

He would find out that little tidbit when he got the address, and that was something he was going to get done this morning. With that little bit of planning handled, Arthur hoisted himself out of bed and made for the bathroom. He needed a cup of coffee, but he needed the bathroom first.

~

"Good morning, Elliot," a familiar voice said from the doorway as he walked into the lab. Without moving, Elliot glanced at the menace. He watched the skinny intruder cast a cursory glance around at the plethora of equipment all over the room. Numerous tables held beakers, microscopes, and any number of other apparatus Arthur probably didn't recognize. Elliot cringed slightly. There was a look of disdain bordering on disgust etched onto Arthur's features. He feared it boded ill for this unexpected meeting.

Elliot had initially jumped slightly at the voice, then recovered. "How nice of you, to barge in unannounced . . . again," Elliot responded.

"Did you get the information I wanted?" Arthur stated flatly, completely ignoring Elliot's statement.

Elliot turned his head, looking up from the laptop he was typing on and paused briefly. His reluctance was plain on his face. Emotions coursed through him. The primary one being guilt. He felt like it was totally his fault that Arthur had found and then killed his only sister. If he hadn't gone to see her that day, she would still be alive. And that line of thought led directly to his next emotion: fury. He was mad enough at Arthur to kill the man himself if he thought he could do it, but he didn't believe for a second that he could and so both emotions just simmered inside him. They were taking their toll on his work as well. He was having a difficult time focusing on his research, which of course just made matters worse.

The extended pause was noticeably grating on Arthur's already meager patience. "Come on, Elliot; do we have to go through this again? You know you're going to tell me what I want to know, so why don't you save yourself the pain and me the time. Or are you really going to make me hurt you again?"

"Fine," Elliot said. "I remembered correctly; they live in Kansas. I can write down the address."

"Very good, thank you. While you're at it why don't you tell me why they were out here in the first place?"

"The girl is a painter. Angelie's husband hired them to do a painting using Angelie's ashes."

"What?" Arthur asked.

~

Arthur was uncharacteristically shocked. There were any number of possibilities that had crossed his mind, but this certainly wasn't any of them. "You're saying that girl actually paints with human ashes? Then who's the guy?"

"Yes, that's what she does, and the guy is her husband."

"So how does that have anything to do with me?"

"Apparently the scene she painted depicted me meeting Angelie at that little house and your face was shown reflecting in the mirror on the wall from where you stood behind me."

"She painted me?" Arthur's voice was raising, and his heartbeat was accelerating. This was getting a little too weird for words, and the more he heard about this woman and her husband the more he didn't like it. But it didn't matter because regardless, he was headed out there to meet them. He could scarcely believe that she had abilities as well as the boy. What were the odds of that? Arthur's rapid-fire mind whirled to assimilate the revelation. The pieces were beginning to fit together. Maybe she was the one tracking him somehow.

"What are their names?" Arthur asked tersely.

"Uh Sean and Kira," Elliot responded. Arthur saw guilt cross the young man's eyes to even offer up that much. It irritated him to have to deal with this type of reluctance, so he pressed further.

"Last names?" Arthur continued.

"Easton, they are married." Arthur examined the man's features, looking for any sign of deception. He saw none. What he did see was a twinge of hopefulness that Arthur didn't understand. Maybe Elliot wanted these two freaks dead just as much as he did. That wasn't likely, though. Arthur knew how much the scientist hated him. He'd seen it on his face at every one of their little meetings including this one.

It was more likely the scientist was hopeful that the couple would kill him instead. Arthur almost laughed at the thought. Elliot's hopefulness was wishful thinking. Arthur had contingencies to make sure of that.

He was becoming more and more certain that this Sean guy could help him, and sensed he was running out of time. The nosebleeds and the headaches were getting more frequent, and they most certainly had to do with his brain tumor.

"Why are you so interested in those two anyway?"

"It's none of your damn business," Arthur snapped back, but then thought better of his response. "I think that boy can help me with your experiment."

"To get rid of your tumor?" The incredulity in Elliot's voice was unmistakable. "How would you propose he do that?"

Arthur's head turned slowly to look into Elliot's intelligent eyes. His intense focus caused Elliot to take an involuntary step back.

The pounding in Arthur's head caused his features to look even more grim. Fear and desperation were doing nothing to help him, so he turned those emotions to anger. He'd get what he needed from that damn couple then watch them die screaming. The thought generated enough pleasure to ease the pounding in his head. He nearly smiled.

The emotions crossing Arthur's features were apparently unnerving Elliot. So much so that he even ventured a comment. "I can't decide if you are a maniac, or a genius, or both," Elliot offered softly.

Arthur smiled a wicked smile at what he considered to be a compliment and continued.

"Let's just take this one step at a time. First, I need to convince the couple to come back here. Thank you for the information."

With that Arthur turned and walked straight out of the door, leaving Elliot standing with his mouth slightly agape and his emotions boiling over.

CHAPTER

A rthur was thinking furiously. He was about to embark on any number of things he'd never done before: buy a plane ticket, rent a car, kidnap someone . . . wait he had already done that recently . . . but never two people.

And then what? Force them to come back to LA with him and help him with an operation to save his life? When he thought it through like that it didn't seem plausible at all, but he had no choice. He couldn't conceive of any other solution that had even a meager chance at saving his life. Therefore, that was exactly what he was going to do. If he had to figure out some of the details as he went, well, so be it. That's what he'd do.

As it turned out buying the plane ticket wasn't much of a big deal. The car rental was another situation entirely. In the end it had only taken a couple of hundred dollars extra and nearly blinding the car rental guy in one eye to overcome typical protocol about only paying with a credit card.

The flight was surprisingly difficult. Although the flight was smooth, Arthur was surrounded by an entourage of young women flying together for a bachelorette party. He wanted to hurt them all but knew it would cause problems. So, to make resisting temptation easier, he turned his head toward the window and stared at the scenery flowing by below him. He finally managed to doze in the cramped seat.

According to the GPS it was over an hour drive from the airport to the little town south of Kansas City where Sean and Kira lived. While he drove, he tried to decide if there was any reason to delay the trip or if any particular time would be better for his arrival. At the very least he was going to need to stop at a pawn shop and get another gun. He wasn't completely confident that he could use his abilities to control these two, and he didn't intend to take any chances. He had been pretty sure the one he bought in Vegas wouldn't make it through security even in his checked bag. And since he wasn't sure and didn't want to ask, he had decided to just get another one here in Kansas. His GPS accommodated him there as well, coming up with several that were at least indirectly on his path south.

He ended up purchasing the gun at a dingy little shop from some guy with an eye patch and a naked woman tattooed on his forearm. The tattoo disgusted Arthur, and he delighted in the opportunity to make the man yelp when he tried to haggle the price.

Their home was definitely out in the country. Arthur hated the country. He didn't like animals, he didn't like bugs, and the wide-open spaces made him uncomfortable in general.

He didn't see green pastures and lazy herds of cattle ambling from one patch of grass to another, he saw nothing. Why the hell anyone would want to live so far away from the nearest fast food restaurant was simply beyond him.

He made a left on a gravel road and drove a mile to the first stop sign. A cloud of dust trailed after him and blew across the car and past while he looked in both directions, not that any cars were going to be coming down any of these hick-ass farm roads, but he looked anyway. He consulted his GPS again and made a right. The house was a half mile down on the right.

~

"So, was that all your dad conveyed to you?" Kira asked as they trekked mindlessly back toward Louisburg and home. From Shawnee Mission Medical Center to Louisburg Kansas was a straight shot down highway 69, and they were getting out of town a bit before the rush hour, so the journey was neither complicated nor busy.

"Yeah, pretty much. But, Kira, it wasn't so much the words he conveyed as the feelings of warmth, love, and trust. He trusts me to make the right decision, and the right decision is getting him out to LA as quickly as possible."

Kira hesitated to ask her next question but knew Sean could sense it anyway.

"Do you think he's strong enough to make the trip?" Kira asked.

Her concern was stronger than her words conveyed.

"He has to be," Sean answered.

Kira was a bit overwhelmed by this entire experience. The only family loss that she had ever endured as an adult was her mother, and that had nearly shattered her. There was also her cousin who she had never known before, so that experience had merely left her with a strange empty feeling. There was a part of her that harbored a growing concern that this whole scenario with Sean's birth father would have some sort of negative effect on her relationship with Sean. What if he blamed her for bad advice?

~

There was a brief pause in the conversation before Sean turned to her sharply and simply said, "Never. It's not going to happen." And to punctuate his words a bug smacked the windshield with a big wet splat like a tablespoon of warm peanut butter.

A puckered facial expression preceded a second of confusion then led to a broad smile on Kira's face. "Do you realize how difficult it is to remind myself how completely you can read my thoughts? I mean I *know* what you can do. I accepted it sometime back, and even enjoy it, but it's still an easy thing to forget on a day to day basis. And to make matters worse, I've caught myself having flashes of thinking that maybe somebody else either just did or could read my thoughts as well. Boy, do you have me spoiled. I could never be happy with another man after being accustomed to what you can do."

"That's a good thing, right?" Sean said looking up from the road.

"With you it is," she said, repeating her statement from earlier.

The smile he responded with was answer enough for both of them.

"I'm so glad I have you with me," he said, returning his eyes to the road. They were almost to their exit.

"I love you, too," she answered.

~

The house came into view up on his right and Arthur slowed down. He studied it carefully for any signs of occupancy.

There was a big red barn visible, a typical looking brown trailer home, and a large house that appeared to be brand new. Someone could be inside any one of those buildings, but there were no vehicles that he could see, and Arthur had a feeling the place wasn't inhabited at the moment. Perfect. Still, the whole situation required caution, so he drove past the residence to the corner about a hundred yards away, made a right, and found a place to park his car in a shallow bar ditch in the shade. From here he would walk back.

He slipped the small 380 Beretta under his belt behind his back.

It was uncomfortable there but at least it would stay and not hinder his walking.

Horses whinnied as he approached the property from behind bringing him near the horse barn. The sound made him jump as he was unfamiliar with horses; therefore, the scent of them as he approached the barn had gone unrecognized. He chided himself for his jumpiness and then decided it was a good thing to have discovered this while the place was still empty.

Cautiously peering around the barn, he surveyed the landscape. The well-kept trailer was slightly off to the right but was still between him and the house. He decided it was ideal cover. The air was brisk and there was a slight breeze. He hadn't thought to bring clothes for cooler weather, so he had to ignore the chills that beset him while he headed for the trailer house. It turned out to be a perfect screen to get him to the new dwelling where he slipped around back. Crossing up and onto the porch he kept his eyes focused on the windows for any sign of movement, but the place was quiet and completely still. He moved his gaze from the windows and focused on the back door while he drew the gun from behind his back. It was at that moment he noticed the other door on the back side of the house, one of those lean-to affairs.

Basement entrance, he thought. It wasn't until later that thought sparked an idea though.

The white screen door was so new that it didn't even squeak, and, on a whim, he tried the doorknob before using the gun to break the glass. The door opened soundlessly into the kitchen.

"Country hicks," he mumbled. "Not even locking their doors. How stupid could you be?"

He barely managed to close the door before he heard the crunching of gravel from the driveway. *Just in time*, he thought as he scanned the room considering his best method of surprising them. The only door in the kitchen was the pantry and it was too small to accommodate even Arthur's gaunt frame. The next room was the dining room with no closets at all. Unwillingly, Arthur moved further into the house, encountering a large living area in front of him and what looked like a combination office and library to his left. He heard the crunching gravel go silent. He needed a place to hide right now. In spite of his rush he paused a moment. In the living area were a wooden easel and what looked like a bar stool. That was where the girl painted.

The girl that had painted him. A chill slowly crept down his spine. His shoulders shook. The idea of her drawing his likeness from the memories of the woman he had never meant to kill left him more than a little spooked.

A muffled male voice yanked him back to the present, "I'm going to go check on the horses real quick," Arthur couldn't make out the first words, but their presence alone startled him into action. His ears adjusted for the second sentence, "I'll be inside in just a few minutes."

Arthur silently turned to his left. The office featured a closet that turned out to be of a decent size, and Arthur quickly ensconced himself in there. Now he would just have to wait.

~

Kira moved on into the house evincing a bit of irritation at the door being unlocked. Sean never locked the doors, and it was a small point of contention between them. He had grown up in the country and un-locked doors were more the norm than the exception, but her years of living in the cities made such a careless attitude seem like nothing less than blatant irresponsibility.

The door closed behind her while she reached for the refrigerator door. There was a half full bottle of dry rosé in there and a glass of wine sounded like the perfect tonic for a less than perfect day. She grabbed a glass out of the cabinet and was pouring herself a small amount when she thought she heard a sound.

~

Damn, Arthur thought. He was trying to get a bit more comfortable in the cramped space when his butt bumped something behind him startling him enough to flinch forward and bump into the door.

It wasn't that much of a sound. Surely no one had heard it. If the girl discovered him now, he was going to have to hurt her, and as much as he would enjoy that it didn't serve his purposes at the moment.

~

Kira listened carefully for a moment, but she couldn't keep her attention focused. She had no real reason to believe or expect any problems in her own house, so the thought slipped away like a hazy memory. Even new houses made random noises sometimes. But it did drive thoughts of food from her mind. She took a sip of her wine. The rose was light, dry and crisp.

It relaxed her as it went down. Sean was looming large in her thoughts. He had gone through many trials since she had met him and finding his birth father had been a high point he had focused upon. To now have to consider the possibility of losing him was surely striking deep in his heart. Sean had been such a godsend to her whole life that she wanted to do everything she could to be that for him. Whatever it took, she resolved, she would find a way.

~

A little bead of sweat was slowly making its way down Arthur's nose. The house was air conditioned, but it wasn't reaching into this closet and he guessed the rest of it had to do with his nerves. He really needed the woman to come closer if he was going to have any luck taking her by surprise and even though he had the gun he had no intention of using it. He needed Sean, and he was guessing that threatening his wife was going to be the way to get him to cooperate. He was fairly certain that Sean could stop him from using his abilities, which was sort of why Arthur needed him. Having heard no other sounds other than the woman Arthur surmised that Sean was still outside which made this an opportune moment, but Arthur didn't know what to do next. His inexperience at kidnapping was suddenly a noticeable problem.

~

Kira busied herself with making sandwiches while she sipped her wine. Thoughts of the trip and her last painting occupied her mind. There was definitely something to be learned from the experience. For one thing the idea that painting live subjects was something she should avoid was a revelation with ramifications. Had she only realized this little tidbit when she was a kid, she could have saved herself a number of nightmares.

On the other hand, if she hadn't become afraid of her painting, she may never have attempted her modeling career and even though her feelings for that opportunity were less than stellar in hindsight, as a whole the experience was something she wouldn't have really wanted to miss. It had forced her to grow up fast and appreciate the fact that not everyone out in the world is as they seem. That applied for both good and bad.

She went back to the refrigerator to put the ham and cheese away and get out the mustard and ketchup. She still couldn't imagine how Sean could put ketchup on a ham and cheese sandwich but chose to find it an endearing quirk.

When she turned back to the kitchen table, she caught sight of one of her sketchpads where she had laid it and a thought struck her.

She figured she still had plenty of time before Sean came back to the house. It was always difficult to tear him away from those horses, especially when he hadn't seen them in a while. She reached for the pad with one hand and pulled a chair out from the table with the other. She had some pencils in her purse which she had set on the table as well. Reaching for one, she let her mind wander and the pencil approached the surface of the drawing table.

She felt herself slip away though not nearly as completely as she had the night before. Still it was similar to her sensations when painting with ashes. She was again aware of her surroundings even as her pencil began to move. Images of their encounter in the museum came floating back to her, and the look of intensity in Arthur's eyes when he had been concentrating on what she later learned was his effort to hurt that girl. The scene played in her mind and continuing to be aware of her surroundings didn't prevent the memory from standing out vividly in her imagination.

~

It had gone suddenly quiet in the house. The noises from the kitchen had stopped entirely. Arthur strained his ears while he forced himself to remain as still as possible, which was definitely not his strong suit. He leaned his ear up against the closet door and listened while he held his breath. He was pretty sure she hadn't left the house, but he was half-tempted to crack the door open and peer out. He didn't want to be wrong and blow his cover, though. He needed to do something. His hand traced the edges of the gun. If he could get within eyeshot, he could threaten her from a distance with that.

If she ran or screamed, then shooting her in the leg would stop her and shouldn't be lethal. And it would definitely get Sean inside, not to mention convince the boy how serious he was about getting them back to LA. But then again, he didn't know the layout of the house, and she could be anywhere. While his exceptional mind raced through all the options, he felt his window of opportunity shrinking.

~

She wasn't aware how much time had passed when she at last glanced down at the work her hands and subconscious had been creating. It was Arthur in close-up with his eyebrows knitted and a look of anxious anger marking his features.

It was dark though, and he was in some enclosed space. There were vague outlines of shapes on what looked like shelves behind him, and she spent a moment staring at those. They looked familiar somehow. She continued to stare until one of the slender shapes resolved itself into something recognizable. It was a football trophy. It looked a lot like one of the ones Sean kept in his closet in his study. Then she made out a word where a reflected beam of light shown on the base of the trophy making it legible.

Easton.

Then it hit her; what she had been attempting to do was locate Arthur. And she had just drawn him in the closet in Sean's study. Her heart jumped to a gallop as she drew in a sharp breath and held it. But surely that was impossible. Still, she wasn't going to scream for help or call for Sean until she took a look for herself. If it was just her imagination, she'd be too embarrassed to look at Sean for weeks.

Carefully, she placed the sketchpad on the table and slowly glided out of the kitchen looking for something to use as a weapon as she did. Not calling for Sean was one thing but doing nothing to protect herself was something else entirely. She strained to listen through the silence but all she could hear was the sound of her own pulse hammering in her ears. The butcher knife in the knife block was close enough to grab without even slowing her stride. It slid out with a quiet hiss as she walked through the doorway. Her palms were sweaty enough to cause concern of the smooth black knife handle slipping from her grasp, despite her white-knuckled grip.

~

Arthur was suddenly alarmed. Were those steps he was hearing? He closed his eyes and listened even harder. Yes. Someone was not only walking his way, but they were trying to be quiet as well. A creak in the floor confirmed what he had just deduced, but it wasn't possible. How could she know he was there? With a string of internal vitriol, he chided himself for waiting too long.

What occurred to him next was that if she knew where he was, remaining in the closet was actually a disadvantage for him. He hesitated just another moment before making his move. Suddenly he threw open the closet door and raised his gun. The room was empty, but before he could even release his breath, the girl rounded the corner holding a big knife.

~

Kira screamed, saw the gun, and raised the knife to strike. Arthur, by instinct, used his ability rather than the gun and pinched a nerve in her hand. She yelped again as the knife clanged onto the floor.

"What do you want?" Kira asked fiercely. But even as she spoke another idea came to her.

SEAN! she thought furiously.

"I want you and your husband's help," Arthur answered with a menacing determined quality waving the gun unsteadily.

"He's not a criminal," she replied matching his tone.

Sean, Arthur is here. We are in your library. Come in from your secret entrance and you'll be behind him. She had no way of knowing if he was receiving her thoughts, but she made herself believe he was, and so she stalled.

"I don't give a shit who he is," Arthur answered, "As long as he does what I want."

"And what is that?" Kira asked. She was concentrating on staying calm and preparing whatever she could think of to keep him talking.

"Where is he, anyway?" Arthur asked, completely ignoring her question.

Kira's tension was ramping up quickly. She could feel her pulse continuing to accelerate. There was no way to know if Sean had gotten her message, and she would be running out of ways to stall soon. She deliberately hesitated before answering.

"He's in the barn with the horses," she finally replied.

"Does he have his cell phone with him?"

Kira pretended to be thinking. She knew damn good and well it was in his back pocket, but she didn't have to tell this jerk. "I don't know. He might have left it in the truck."

~

Sean was getting grain for the horses when Kira's thought hit him.

Sean!

The thought roared through his head like a train whistle. He dropped the bucket he was holding. The power of the thought rattled him. It was from Kira, and it screamed fear. He was already moving toward the house when the second thought came.

Sean, Arthur is here. We are in your library. Come in from your secret entrance and you'll be behind him.

Bless her heart, that wife of his was no dummy. Now his own

thoughts were racing. The secret entrance to the library went to the upstairs bedroom and the basement. So, he sprinted across the intervening grass toward the storm door basement entrance built on back. Besides the fear that was coursing through him, Sean felt a twinge of satisfaction at having a real reason to use his hidden passage. He had thought of it as just a cool thing to have, not something he would ever need. Well, maybe the memory of Poena had sparked more than just a bit of his desire for it.

The storm shelter door was one of those lean-to looking affairs, and it had a lock, but it wasn't engaged, so Sean's main concern was to be quiet and not let it bang shut after he entered. The basement was too new to smell musty, but it was certainly as dark as any other basement. Fortunately, even though the house was new to him, he had had a lot to do with designing it so finding the light switch in the lightless space was no chore at all. Reaching up and to his left the lights sprang on at his touch, and he continued to his left toward the hidden entrance.

There were two sections of work bench down the left-hand wall, and the crack between the two marked the secret entrance. Reaching under the second section, Sean slid the catch toward him and pulled gently. The door flowed back revealing the stairs behind it. Now all he had to do was make sure it didn't thump when he closed it.

It didn't. He headed up. He was close enough now to sense Kira's fear which promptly quickened his steps. If that jackass hurt her . . .

~

"Well try him and see!" Arthur nearly yelled. His patience was wearing thin, and his head was pounding. He thought he felt the beginning of a trickle from his nose. Holding a gun was not something he was familiar with; he had never needed one before. He wasn't a poker player either, so the bluff he was running was also new to him. Again, it wasn't something that he'd needed in the past. He realized he couldn't shoot her, or he would lose his leverage with the boy. The girl, however, seemed agreeable enough, at least she wasn't arguing with him.

He watched while she slowly pulled her own phone from her back pocket. "No tricks. If I see you trying to dial 911, I'll shoot your knee and take the phone."

"Alright, already," Kira answered lifting the phone with exaggerated deliberateness. The thought had already crossed her mind that if the phone rang while Sean was coming up the secret passage, Arthur would hear it, so she played clumsy, and as she began to dial, she dropped the phone.

"Sorry," she said, "I'm nervous."

~

If you're there, Sean, now would be the time. He heard as clearly as if it were spoken. He had already stepped into the closet that Arthur had just vacated, and he took her words to heart. He burst through the opening like a sprinter off the blocks.

~

Kira was only slightly surprised when her thought brought the very action she was hoping for, and she'd already considered her best course of action if it did. As Arthur spun to face the noise behind him, she bolted up from her squatting position straight toward the gun which was slowing swinging away from her. He would have never brought it around fast enough to engage Sean, but she wasn't about to wait to find out. Kira yanked the thing away from him at almost the same instant Sean slammed into him from behind wrapping his arms around Arthur's arms as he did.

~

Arthur was so startled his reflexes were slowed. He sensed the woman moving up from the floor toward him, but he had to turn to face the new threat. He did attempt to tweak the nerve in her hand again, but the boy apparently caught the thought and shouted, "NO!" even as he grabbed Arthur's shirt to spin him around.

The action had the same effect as it had before and stopped Arthur's attempt, but this time it went a step further and suddenly the nerve in Arthur's hand flashed with pain.

"Ahhhh!" Arthur yelled even before Sean's right hook connected with his jaw. Arthur went down in a heap nursing his hand more than his jaw.

"Get up," Kira said pointing Arthur's own pistol at him.

301

"Do you know how to use that thing?" Sean asked, surprised.

"Oh yeah," Kira answered. "I made a point of getting trained. I used to carry one with me when I travelled for modelling. It caused more than just a little trouble getting into some countries. You'd be surprised what models can get away with though."

Sean turned his attention back to Arthur who was just raising himself from the floor. Now he was nursing the jaw. Apparently, that pain lingered whereas the other did not.

"What the hell are you doing here?" Sean asked. Asking the question, however, brought the answer to Arthur's mind, and Sean had it way before Arthur got the words out.

Arthur looked up with the strangest expression in his eyes.

~

"I need your help," he said simply. This was a new experience for Arthur. As the words left his mouth, it occurred to him that he had never uttered those syllables before in his entire life. He just took what he wanted, and he very seldom wanted anything from anyone else anyway. Come to think of it, he very seldom even talked to anyone. Ever.

~

Arthur's thoughts were rattling around in Sean's head almost faster than he could process them.

Never asked for help.

Hate people.

Hate women especially.

Doesn't want to die.

Loathing of he and Kira.

Memories of hurting people.

It was very nearly too much for Sean to handle. Not only were the thoughts coming fast, but it was worse than having worms crawling around in your mind. It gave Sean the same sensation one would get from plunging both hands into an old outhouse toilet. Revulsion, pure and simple.

Finally, he summoned up some words. A question, even though he already knew the answer.

"Our help? Are you kidding me? How the hell do you expect to get our help when you bring a gun into our home?"

"I was going to make you help me . . . if I could. I didn't think you would do it willingly."

"Well, you got that right," Sean replied glancing again up at Kira who was still holding the gun in a more or less ready position, while trying to stop the bile rising in his throat. "Kira, step back a step, and I think you can lower the gun. Arthur here isn't going to be doing anything else."

"You know my name?" Arthur asked.

"Yeah, from Elliot," Sean said. His curiosity promptly got the better of him though. "What the hell is it you think we can help you with anyway?" This was so much worse than even Poena's twisted mind. Sean yanked his thoughts away from this maniac and slammed the door, leaving him actually needing to hear Arthur's answers.

"You," Arthur began. "I think you can help me because of what you did in the museum, and at the beach, and then again just now."

"What are you talking about?"

"Moving things with your mind."

"Are you crazy? I can't move things with my mind. That's your trick. All I can do is read thoughts and emotions"

"You just did it when I tried to move a nerve in her hand. You not only stopped me, you actually moved one in mine. Didn't you hear me yell? Wait a minute. You can read thoughts?"

"You yelled when I slugged you. And yes, I can." Sean immediately regretted the inadvertent admission, but it was too late now.

"No. Just *before* you slugged me."

Sean thought for a second and realized Arthur was telling the truth, and now that he thought about it, he had tried to imitate the thought Arthur was directing at Kira. So, he guessed it must have worked. With that realization, curiosity now took over Sean's thoughts.

"So, what is it you want me to move with my mind?"

"Well, it'll take me a second to explain, but basically I have brain cancer. I think it might be connected to my ability, but if I don't get this tumor removed it is going to kill me, and it's inoperable."

Sean's father popped into his mind immediately. Suddenly he was intensely interested in Arthur's next words.

"What is it you think I can do to help?"

"Well, Elliot has developed a new procedure to inject gold molecules into the brain then gather them around the tumor and hit them with microwaves. It does nothing to the healthy brain tissue but heats up the gold surrounding the tumor thereby burning it up or at least heating it enough to kill it."

"I know. Elliot told us, but last we heard he said he's having issues with his research. So why do you need me?"

"It seems that Elliot hasn't had much luck trying to get the gold in place around the tumor chemically. Not exactly sure what that means, but it hasn't worked. Recently he mentioned that I might be able to move the gold molecules with my mind. So, I've already tried the procedure and it seems as though I can't move things within my own body or at least not enough to accomplish the cure. In fact, it nearly killed me."

"OK," Sean began, while sensing the powerful emotions Arthur felt in connection with the incident. It caused him to pause a moment before continuing. "Even if we agree to go with you, how the hell did you expect to get me to help you with a medical procedure? I'm pretty sure Elliot is no friend of yours and even if you got us there, you can't very well control me while surgery is being done to you."

"I know," Arthur answered. "I hadn't figured that part out yet. I thought I might be able to come up with something on the trip back."

Fortunately for Arthur, Sean already had an idea.

"OK, we'll help you, but on one condition."

The surprise on Arthur's face was matched by the same expression on Kira's followed quickly by a comment.

"We will?" Kira began.

"If he meets my condition, yes," Sean answered.

Sean didn't need to go on because at that moment he sensed Kira deducing his train of thought.

Your father, she thought clearly.

"Exactly." Sean said out loud, producing a further look of confusion on Arthur's face.

"What are you talking about?" Arthur asked after the briefest of pauses. "What condition?"

"You have to help my dad first."

"With what?"

"My father has inoperable brain cancer as well. We were in the process of moving him out to California for an experimental procedure there, but I think I like your idea better."

"Your father has brain cancer?" This was a turn of events that even Arthur could not have imagined, but it immediately occurred to him that this was a way to get what he needed without having to try to force these two, which he was becoming increasingly convinced would have been impossible anyway.

"Yes, he does," Sean answered simply.

"Then I'll do it," Arthur responded simply, surprising both Sean and Kira alike.

"Fine. We'll meet you in California in two days," Sean said decisively.

"Aren't you afraid I might bolt?" Arthur asked.

This time Kira spoke up. "No," she said, "For two reasons. One, you need us at least as much as we need you and secondly, I can find you anytime I want."

Arthur's eyes grew wide. "You *were* the one tracking me! Who the hell are you people?"

The echo of Brian's words from a few days ago caused Sean and Kira to turn to each other and break out in laughter.

"We seem to be getting that a lot lately," Sean answered, returning a wide grin to Arthur's perplexed one. Arthur was baffled at the couple's sudden exchange.

"Give us your phone number," Kira added.

"I don't have one," Arthur answered almost sheepishly.

Kira scribbled something on the bottom of her pad, tore it off, and handed it to Arthur. "Then get one," she said, "And call us in two days. We'll be in LA by then."

Arthur just nodded as he glanced down at the paper. He was struggling to smother his thoughts of hate toward Kira. Just another bitch ordering him around. Silence ensued as they all just stood there. No one seemed to have any idea what to say or do next. Kira finally broke the silence.

"Well, go on then and get out of here. My husband and I have things to do. And by the way my name is Kira, Kira Easton."

Sean smiled.

Arthur nodded, his face now a blank mask. Rage was sitting on his brain like a still pool of molten lava ready to blow.

"The front door is that way in case you haven't used it yet," Kira added, punctuating her words with a pointed finger.

"OK," was all Arthur could manage as he followed Kira's direction and walked out. His thoughts were a muddle of anger, confusion and, much to his surprise, relief.

~

A minute or two passed after the front door closed before either of them spoke.

"If that wasn't the strangest conversation I've ever had," Sean began, "It's dang near the top."

"You think he'll really call us?" Kira asked.

"As if his life depends on it," Sean said, smiling again. "I just hope that this works for my father, too," Sean's voice trailed off with the last sentence, and Kira stepped in to hug him.

"It will, Sean. I'm sure of it."

Elliot's guilt sat like a stone hanging from his neck. He was trying to work on several projects, not the least of which was his potential cancer cure, but visions of his sister and the look of horror on her face as she grabbed her chest haunted him. It was his fault. His research had brought Arthur into his life and therefore into Angelie's which resulted in her death.

His fault.

He had no other family, and now he assumed he never would. Several times he had picked up the phone to call Brian but lost his nerve in mid-dial. Brian probably hated him, and Elliot couldn't blame him for it.

He had ended up making the one call to Brian to locate Sean and Kira, again he almost spoke up to apologize, but his resolve failed him. Brian was nothing but cordial and helpful. Now his weakness had allowed Arthur the chance to find Sean and Kira and because of him they were in danger.

He pushed back from his large, black, obsidian work bench unable to get the images and guilt from his mind. He only wished there were something else he could do to make it right. It was at that moment that the phone rang, disrupting the bubbling hum of the equipment around him. Elliot didn't feel like talking to anybody, but right now any distraction was a good distraction.

"Hello?" he began simply.

"Elliot? This is Sean Easton."

Elliot was stunned into silence for a moment at the coincidence. He pushed his hair back absently from his forehead as his thoughts raced to catch up with his pounding heart. It was long enough to have Sean doubt the connection.

"Elliot, are you there?"

"Uh, yes. Sorry, Sean. I am just surprised to hear from you. Are you alright?"

Now it was Sean's turn to hesitate. "Why sure. Why wouldn't I be alright?"

"Oh, I don't know. I guess it was just the surprise. What can I do for you?"

"Well I just received a visit from Arthur and . . ."

"Are you alright?" Elliot blurted out a second time, his fears rising to a crescendo.

"Uh, well, yeah. Are *you* alright Elliot?" Elliot could hear the concern in Sean's voice and realized how transparent his emotions must be.

Elliot broke down, and his words came out in a rush. "I'm so sorry, Sean. Arthur forced me to help him find you. I was just afraid that he might have hurt you or Kira." His downcast eyes conveyed his guilt as easily as Sean could have read it.

"Oh, so that's how he found us, but how did you know?"

"I called Brian and asked him," Elliot answered with guilt continuing to color his tone.

"It's no problem. As a matter of fact, I'm glad you did, but we're all heading your way again and we wanted to talk to you about what's come up."

Elliot's curiosity took a rocket through the roof. "Sure, Sean. Anything I can do to help."

"I'm hoping you can. Is there any way we could get together tomorrow afternoon? Maybe at your lab if that's OK."

Now the rocket went suborbital. "Sure, what time is good for you?"

~

"Maybe around 4:00? Can you send the address to this number?"

"Perfect, and yes I can," Elliot said.

"Great. See you tomorrow then."

"Okay, Sean. See you tomorrow.

Elliot hung up the phone. He felt relieved. The guilt he had been harboring evaporated as his curiosity continued to grow.

I wonder what they have in mind? He thought.

The next morning Sean and Kira found themselves sitting at their breakfast table drinking coffee, both lost in thought. The only sounds were the muted hum of the air-conditioner, the singing of the birds outside, and the clinking of their wedding rings against their coffee cups.

"So, what's going on in your head?" Kira asked, finally breaking the silence. "You've been acting weird ever since the phone call with Elliot."

"It's not Elliot. It's Arthur."

"Do you think he was lying to us?"

"No that's not it, Kira. I was getting his thoughts from him for a while, and he was telling the truth. At the moment our interests coincide."

"OK. So, what's the problem?"

"Being in his head. It was horrible. It was even more of a keg of worms than Poena's twisted brain. He hates women, likes to hurt people, and all his memories are of something evil he's done or planning to do. I still have such a hard time believing there are people in this world that are so evil, even though I've seen it."

Kira scooted her chair closer and put her arm around him. "It is a sad truth. I've seen it many times but never as intimately as you must from being in their minds." She saw Sean's grip on his coffee mug tighten at the recollection.

"Yeah, I had to slam shut the connection to him just to keep my concentration."

"I'm so sorry, Honey. But hey while I'm thinking of it, you have to remind me to call Brian back. I need to tell him about the song Angelie was writing in my vision. I'm pretty certain she finished it. I'm afraid he may never find it unless I give him a heads up."

"Why don't we just call him now?"

"Honestly, I don't really feel like talking to anyone else at the moment, and we still have packing and planning to do before we leave this afternoon. Besides, it's still early there."

Sean simply nodded his agreement then went to make one more call to the hospital to confirm his dad's transportation and condition.

"Dad's apparently doing better," he told Kira when he hung up the phone. "He's actually been way more stable. I asked them why, but they said they're not really sure and it's not worth the money or the delay in schedule to do tests to figure it out."

"Oh," Kira answered. Surprise was evident in her tone. "Well, it least that makes it less scary to move him right now."

"That's true," Sean said, mentally thanking her for any morsel of optimism at this point. "He should be checked in at the Beverly Hills Cancer Center before we even get there."

~

Arthur still hadn't slept. He was driving his new car back from the airport paying almost no attention to the traffic.

The encounter with that couple had left him feeling more defenseless than he had felt since little Mike had pounded him on the playground.

He didn't like it.

Even though he didn't understand what had happened at the time, the incident with Mike all those years ago had led him to feel more self-assured than he had in all his young life. It was a feeling that morphed into one of superiority, which had never since been challenged, until now. As much as it irked him to admit it, even to himself, he was feeling somewhat scared of this couple and their abilities.

But during the long drive back to the airport, and the even longer flight home, he had been thinking about it and how to make them wish they had never crossed him even with their abilities. By the time the wheels squeaked on the tarmac at Los Angeles International he had a plan. He simply had to get rid of the cancer, all of the cancer. He felt better, giving rise to an evil grin. Now all he had to do was stop and get a damn phone, run a couple of other errands, and get some sleep. The next couple of days were going to be busy. As if on cue, the pain in his head made a crescendo causing both hands to fly up to his temples.

Damn, he thought, *not now.* The pain promptly faded as he considered the fact that this thing in his head would be gone soon.

CHAPTER

A nother set of wheels squeaked on the tarmac later that day. This time they were on the plane carrying Sean and Kira. Kira had been considering their situation all the way. While she looked out of the window and watched the decelerating plane whiz down the runway, she wondered how it happened that so many of her paintings led her and Sean into such drama. Was it merely a by-product of being so connected to the world of the spiritual? If so, maybe that was a good enough reason to quit.

Her thoughts meandered to the look on Brian's face when he saw the painting, she had done for him, and the one she wouldn't get to see when he found the song Angelie had written for him. No, it was worth it. She wouldn't rob people of a gift that only she could give. It really *was* worth it.

Sean turned to her right then, "You're damn right it is," he said grinning. She turned to him and planted a big kiss on him at the very instant the pilot switched to reverse thrust jerking them both forward and nearly, Kira was sure, chipping a tooth.

"I thought you were trying not to read my thoughts all the time," she teased as they both leaned back into their narrow leather seats.

"I am trying," he answered. "I'm just not succeeding all the time." That earned him yet another tentative kiss which in turn generated a few cautious smiles from several observant passengers.

~

Sean's gaze shifted to the giant crossed double arches of the LAX terminal they were about to be taxiing past. Their last flight into the area had taken them into John Wayne airport, therefore all these new city structures including the airport itself were once again fascinating him.

Pretty cool, huh, Kira thought at him, causing Sean's head to whip around from the window.

"You know on the one hand I love it when you do that, and on the other it continues to catch me off-guard. I don't know why."

"Probably something about having your wife in your head," Kira quipped. "Though that's something every newlywed husband has to get used to."

Sean laughed as the bell dinged signaling they were at their gate.

"Right, but that isn't usually a literal thing."

Kira just smiled back as they gathered their things.

"I guess you know your way around this airport?" Sean asked.

"Don't you know it."

"In that case I'll follow you to the car rental counter."

Right this way, she thought to him again, producing yet another smile from Sean.

While they walked Sean couldn't help but be awed by all the golden tones and high arched ceilings of the airport. It occurred to him that using gold in so much of the décor was not an accident. This was Los Angeles after all.

By the time they picked up their luggage it was 2PM local, two hours until their meeting with Elliot . . . and then with Arthur.

~

The multi-use research facility where Elliot worked was near Torrance and was a low unassuming building.

Had it been closer to the beach, it would have fit in perfectly as a stucco beach condo, but it was the only place he could find as an independent researcher that he could afford.

As a single scientist, it was the place he felt the most comfortable. Just not today. Sean and Kira would be there in a couple of hours, and he had no idea what they wanted. Sean didn't sound on the phone like he was angry for giving Arthur their location. As a matter of fact, he sounded excited to talk, and Sean had even thanked him. And this was after they talked to Arthur. How could anyone be in a chipper mood after talking to that psychopath? Elliot guessed it didn't matter.

313

He would find out soon enough.

A bubbling beaker to his left snagged his attention. Absently he got up, walked over to it, and used a nearby lighter to ignite the fumes floating above it. Burning hydrogen from microwaved sea water always fascinated him even if it was inefficient. There had to be a better way.

His thoughts trailed off to several possibilities he had considered, and in moments his later meeting was forgotten.

~

Ensconced in their Hampton Inn just outside of Torrance, but not too far from the beach, Sean and Kira decided to walk back up to the front desk and see if the coffee they had seen as they walked in was as good as it smelled. It had already been a long day, and the important part was yet to come.

"Do you really think we can do this, Sean? I mean where are we going to do it? At your dad's hospital? At Elliot's lab? Could we even get your dad out of the hospital to do that?"

"I've been thinking about the same thing, and I guess I'm hoping Elliot's got an idea. I don't even know how large his equipment is or how portable. It almost makes me tired just to think about it, but I don't see where we have any other choices."

"We could just let the hospital do the treatment that's currently planned." Kira offered.

"Yeah, I know, but somehow that just doesn't feel right, and if things don't work out with Elliot and Arthur the hospital procedure is still an option, right?"

"Sure, if they don't kick us out first." Her tone was teasing, and she followed her statement with a brief, reassuring smile.

"Which reminds me," Sean added, "I need to call the hospital and see how Dad is doing."

Sean held the door for Kira and followed her into the office area. The coffee was as good as it had smelled, and they took two cups to go along with a couple of complimentary muffins. It was 2:45 PM with about a twenty-minute drive to Elliot's lab.

Elliot was as nervous as a teenager on a first date. He wasn't sure why. Maybe it was the guilt still playing havoc with his emotions, or maybe he was afraid Arthur would show up, or even worse that they would bring Arthur with them. He shook his head. This was ridiculous. It was a simple meeting, but what for? He had spent a fair amount of time trying to resolve that little puzzle.

He looked down at his hands and realized he had stopped cold with one hand holding a test tube and another holding a beaker.

Damn! He thought. Now he was going to have to reheat the beaker as the solution he was adding required that the mixture be heated to near boiling. He started to glance at his watch when he heard a knock on his lab door. Ever since Arthur's intrusions he had been keeping it locked even when he was inside.

Setting the test tube back in its holder he called out, "Just a minute. I'm coming."

~

"This guy is nervous. I can feel it all the way through the door. What would he be nervous about?"

"He doesn't really know us, Sean. His most recent experience with a stranger was Arthur."

"And Angelie," Sean responded.

"Right and look how that turned out."

"OK fine. I'll just . . ."

At that moment the door opened. Elliot seemed even more slender than before, and his slightly glistening forehead indicated his nerves were having physical ramifications. They were a bit surprised to see him in a white lab-coat, though they should have expected it. When he met Sean's gaze Sean felt his nervousness so intensely that his own heartbeat began to accelerate. It was all Sean could do to not break down in a panic.

"Oh, hi Kira; hi Sean. You are right on time. I should have guessed who was at the door." Elliot stepped back opening the heavy gray door wide and motioning them inside.

"Thanks, Elliot," Sean said.

"Wow," Kira added, "This place is cool. I don't think I've been inside a real laboratory before. Reminds me of something from a Frankenstein movie."

Elliot snickered as he closed the door behind them.

"You've heard it a hundred times before," Kira responded.

"Not as many as you might think. I don't have that many visitors. We can sit over at that empty worktable if you like," he gestured to the big black obsidian work table as he moved toward it himself. "I must admit, I'm more than a little curious what brings you all the way out here to talk to me."

There was a moment's silence as they settled at the sole unoccupied table in the room accompanied by the hum, bubbling, and hiss emanating from the other tables all around them. Sean wondered just how many different experiments Elliot was running at once, or if these were all part of the same work somehow. As he moved to sit, he caught a thought from Kira and had to grin. She had noticed his fascination and as usual was tickled to be a part of him discovering the world, only in this case it was pretty new to her, too.

Elliot sat and promptly placed both hands on the table.

"OK," he began, "What can I do for you?"

Sean looked briefly at Kira then turned back to Elliot.

"To put it simply, we are hoping you can help us."

"You mentioned that on the phone. How so?"

"Arthur told us about your attempt to cure his cancer with your microwave treatment."

"That's right; he was, let's say, somewhat less than happy when it didn't work out. But what does that have to do with you, and why did he come to you?"

Elliot's dark brows furrowed slightly as he asked the question. Curiosity was being tempered by concern about any dealings involving Arthur.

"Well, two things really, Elliot. One, Arthur came to us because he thinks I might be able to help him with his treatment, and we're here talking to you because . . . well . . . as it turns out my father has a similar brain cancer, and we think Arthur might be able to help him using your treatment."

Silence hung in the air at Sean's pause and the flurry of questions rushing about Elliot's mind was almost making Sean dizzy. He had never encountered someone whose thoughts moved so fast. It was no wonder this man was a brilliant scientist.

"Arthur must have told you that my treatment didn't work on him. What makes you think another try would be any different? And with that in mind, why would you want me to try this on your father?"

There was another pause, and this time Kira stepped in, "Those are good questions, Elliot, but the answers are going to require you to have an open mind. Can you do that?"

"I pride myself on it," he answered simply.

"Great. Well you're somewhat familiar with my abilities with paintings already, but what you don't know is that Sean has an ability of his own. What started off as intense empathy on his part has grown into telepathy, and it's growing daily. Just by the accident of running across Arthur's path and him attempting to use his ability on me, we discovered that Sean can affect Arthur's abilities, stop them if necessary, or even turn them back on him. Essentially, we think that's where we can help Arthur. Arthur believes that your treatment didn't work on him because he can't use his abilities very well on himself. With Sean's help he thinks it will work."

"But why the hell would you want to help that evil bastard . . ." Elliot began with a mix of anger and incredulity on his face. As his lightning fast mind raced, his expression softened and he answered his own question in a matter of milliseconds, "oh wait . . . your dad," Elliot finished turning his gaze to Sean.

"Right," Sean said, "He has to help me save my dad before we help you to save him."

"Ah," Elliot responded then paused. Everyone waited while he weighed the ramifications of the information Sean had just imparted. Again, Sean's senses allowed him to pick up the man's tremendous velocity of thought as he processed the possibilities. Sean snagged his next thought just before Elliot could voice it, and more to prove a point than anything else, answered the question just before Elliot could utter a syllable.

"You wouldn't have to move your stuff very far. He's already at a cancer facility here in the Los Angeles area."

Elliot's mouth was just opening to speak when Sean said this, and at the telepathic response his mouth snapped shut again. The shock was evident on his face. Kira realized what had just happened, so she spoke next.

"Just in case you didn't believe us," she stated smiling. Her smile was nearly as convincing as Sean's demonstration. To his credit Elliot took all of it in stride and continued with the line of thought.

"So what facility is he in?"

"The Beverly Hills Cancer Center," Sean replied.

"Hmm. Well that would be convenient at least. I am good friends with the director there. Still, I'm pretty sure they won't just let me waltz in there with my equipment and perform an experimental procedure on one of their patients."

"Would they let you in to examine the patient and evaluate him as a candidate for your procedure?" Sean asked.

It was at that point that Kira realized how much more of this Sean had thought through than he had bothered to share with her.

"Hmmm . . . Since I know Dr. Moritz, the hospital director and with his family requesting it, I bet he would."

"And how much equipment would you actually need to carry in to really *do* the treatment?"

"Well just this scanner to let us see where the gold was going and this small microwave projector . . . Oh I see where you're going."

"Right," Sean continued, "all that would fit in the extra suitcase we brought of his clothes and things. Of course, we can take the clothes out and bring them in later."

"You realize we could all be arrested for this," Elliot pointed out flatly.

"Yep," Sean said, "I'm sure it's not an issue for Kira and I, and I'm hoping it won't be for you either. What happens if the treatment doesn't work?"

"The tumor doesn't die. That's it. As long as I'm careful with the emitter, which is pretty easy, the only ramification is failure to kill the tumor, unless of course, your dad has some other kind of metal in his head and we can scan for that while we are watching the gold migrate to the tumor. What kind of tumor is it anyway?"

Sean, much to Kira's surprise, responded immediately, "The word the doctor was thinking was some sort of glioma and it's affecting his autonomic nervous system."

"That means it's down in or by the brain stem. That's good actually. It should be easier to get to for what we want to do and also explains why they can't remove it surgically. Too much risk of heart or lung failure . . ."

"So, does that mean you'll do it?" Sean asked.

"Truthfully, I'm not nearly as concerned about the legal ramifications as I am of having to be in the same room with that maniac."

"Don't worry about him," Kira offered. "Sean can handle him. Already has been, as a matter of fact. Sean can sense when Arthur is about to use his ability and, like we said, can stop it, even turn it back on Arthur from what we've seen so far."

"And after we treat your father, what are you thinking? We'll come back to my lab and try it again on Arthur with your help?"

"That's about it," Sean replied.

"And then what? Let the bastard go?"

"I've been thinking about that too," Sean offered. "My first thought was to turn him into the police, but can you imagine trying to explain to them what Arthur can do, what he did to your sister, and how we know all this? I'm afraid we'd end up in the coo-coo house ourselves."

"I see your point. So, we just let him get away?"

"Unless we can come up with a better idea, I guess so."

"I really don't like that idea," Elliot said flatly.

"Me either," Kira chimed in. "Isn't there some way we can double-cross him?" Sean glanced at her somewhat surprised. From her mind he snagged an image of Arthur with the gun in her face. That must be what slanted her thoughts in such an uncharacteristic direction.

"I kind of figure he'll be expecting that. I just don't know what he might try to do about it." Sean finished.

"Well regardless, whatever we do we need to do it quick," Kira said, her eyebrows furrowing slightly. "They're not going to leave Aubrey, that's Sean's dad, sitting in that hospital room for very long before getting on with the viral procedure we ostensibly sent him there for. As much as I want Arthur to pay for what he did, I think Sean's dad comes first."

Sean could sense the passion in her words, and he loved her all the more for it; not to mention she was dead right. He also sensed Elliot's general agreement. It was a nebulous thing that led straight to Elliot analyzing logistics of actually accomplishing the task.

"OK," Elliot began, "I'll call Dr. Moritz this afternoon and see about setting an appointment for tomorrow and start getting the equipment packed up. Is that too soon to get Arthur cued up?"

"I don't think so," Sean offered. "He is really struggling with his headaches; I could feel the intensity of them when we last spoke. I think he's as anxious to get this over with as we are. Maybe try to make the appointment for tomorrow afternoon though, if you can. We're waiting on him to get a phone and call us, but I don't anticipate any delays. He can't afford them."

"Sounds good. The entire thing should take less than about twenty minutes as long as we don't have any complications, and unlike surgery, the number of things that could possibly go wrong is pretty miniscule."

"Good," Sean began.

"We'll head back to the hotel and get a suitcase ready," Kira added. "Sean, we also need to give Aubrey a call and see how his transfer went."

"You're right. Elliot, we'll go get settled in and give you a call as soon as we hear from Arthur tomorrow, and you can tell us what the director said and firm up an appointment."

"I believe we have a plan," Elliot said smiling. "Honestly, I'm really glad to have an opportunity to help you guys regardless of what it means for Arthur."

"Thanks Elliot. I have a feeling something appropriate will happen with Arthur one way or another."

They made for the door and five minutes later Sean and Kira were on the highway heading back toward the beach and their hotel. Fortunately, the traffic was mostly heading the other way giving them both time to think as the sights of the city flowed quickly past.

"OK," Kira began, "I can't read your mind so spill it. What's going on in that brain of yours?"

"Oh, I was just thinking about my dad and hoping this thing works. Also, it makes me nervous as hell to be doing anything with Arthur regardless of what I said to Elliot. He hates you, Kira. He hates women in general, but now he hates you especially. Mark my words, if he can find a way to hurt you, he will, and the fact that it would hurt me as well is just a bonus in that nut job's mind."

"Why don't we go for a walk on the beach before dinner?" Kira suggested.

"Wow. Nothing wrong with your changing-the-subject skills," Sean retorted with a smile.

"I'm not really changing the subject, just recognizing that you and I both need a bit of a break. We've got plenty to worry about and some time to kill until tomorrow, so why not de-stress a little. After all we *are* still newlyweds, or had you forgotten?" Her faux annoyance was undermined by her accompanying mischievous smile.

Sean's face lit up like a beacon through the fog. "Hell no, I haven't forgotten, but you're right a little *us* time sounds wonderful and would improve my outlook substantially."

They ended up stopping back by the hotel to change into something a little more "beachy", which Sean was eager to do even before it occurred to him to ask Kira where they were going.

"We're going to the Redondo Beach Pier and maybe eat at Tony's if it's not too packed."

Their communication was so utterly unique. She was excited to show him something new and without saying another word he sensed both her excitement and his own. His joy was then greatly enhanced by hers and both of their anticipation as well. It made almost all their experiences so much deeper and richer, a thing that would be lost without Sean's gift and Kira's acceptance of the ramifications of that gift.

Within about an hour, they were back out of the hotel and down on the beach.

To Sean's continued surprise the Redondo Beach pier didn't just extend out straight into the surf. It was more of an enhanced double triangle with material mounted on poles shaped like sails, ostensibly, he surmised, to provide some shade but more likely just to enhance the ocean motif. Before ascending the stairs up onto the boardwalk, they decided to stroll the beach itself for a while.

"It's gorgeous isn't it?" Kira offered. The breeze was in their faces, and the smell of the ocean was strong. Gulls added their incessant cries to the ambience as did the sand squishing between their toes.

"I don't know how you could ever get tired of it," Sean answered. While he spoke, he was busy soaking up the happiness wafting off Kira in waves. Reflecting their relaxation, their shoes dangled lazily from Sean's left hand while his right was pleasantly occupied encircling Kira's waist.

"Sean, do you get tired of all the drama my paintings seem to draw?"

"Are you kidding me? I'm having the time of my life experiencing all this with you. I'm just so grateful it's you I'm with while my own abilities are growing. What I'm experiencing could be horrible and isolating with just about anyone else."

Sean halted his steps and turned to face Kira. He stroked her thick, long hair from her face as he leaned to kiss her. She leaned in as well wrapping her arms around his waist and pulling him even closer. Moments passed unnoticed.

"I love you, Mrs. Easton."

"I love you too, Mr. Easton." The electricity generated from their loving stares could have powered a building.

Silently they both turned to face the blossoming variegated sunset. Hues of orange jumped to azure below where the sun was dipping into the Pacific and magenta radiated above. It was glorious.

"It's going to be dark soon, Mrs. Easton. Maybe we could slip off under the pier and practice being newlyweds."

"That sounds both uncomfortable and dangerous," she purred and then smiled, "But, I like the way you're thinking. Why don't we go grab a bite at Tony's and then head back to the hotel?"

"Hmm . . . Not as adventurous but it sounds equally brilliant."

The breeze picked up as they meandered along the darkening beach towards the glowing lights dotting Tony's on the pier.

The lights and thrum of Tony's was a bit more of an unwelcome change from the peace on the beach than either one of them had expected. They quickly adjusted, however, and the food was excellent. They started a bottle of wine then decided to take the rest of it back to their room. Being alone was looming large on both of their minds.

The short walk back to the car was also idyllic, even though the lights from the stars were muted by the glowing corona of the beach-front lights, and the sounds of traffic inevitably overtook the sweet susurration of the ocean.

"Do you think all this is going to work, Sean?" Kira asked for the umpteenth time.

"We are going to make it work."

The hotel was quiet when they arrived, and from the moment they entered the building they walked straight to their room in silence.

Sean slid the key card into the slot and eased the door open.

"I need to go the bathroom," he announced as he entered.

"I'll alert the media," she retorted smiling, "But can I have a kiss first?"

"Always," Sean answered, stepping into her arms.

The heat in her kiss quickened his pulse noticeably, and as he pulled her tighter, he not only sensed her growing desire but felt her pulse accelerate as well.

"I'll be right back," Sean said, finally pulling away.

"Hurry," she answered almost breathlessly.

His moments in the bathroom stretched on forever, but he wanted to brush his teeth and rinse his face from the salt smell of the ocean.

When he opened the door to the bedroom his breath caught as his eyes lifted taking in the vision of Kira completely naked standing with one leg straight and the other crossed demurely, bent at the knee, and poised up on the ball of her foot. Her arms were open as in a welcoming gesture, and in each of her hands she held a half full wine glass.

"Nightcap, Mr. Easton?" She asked.

Sean swallowed hard and stepped toward her with the grin blooming broadly across his features. Kira offered one glass to him as he approached, then used the free hand to begin unbuttoning his Hawaiian shirt. He paused briefly as she did.

"To the most amazing wife in the world," he offered, raising his glass.

She finished his buttons then stepped in to hook arms with him and lift the glass to her mouth. He mirrored her move, pulling them even closer to each other.

"To the love of my life," she murmured as she took a sip.

Both glasses found the bedside table seconds later whereupon Sean swept Kira into his arms and lowered her into the bed she had already turned down. Their lips met again within seconds and the heat of his passion was echoed by his sensation of hers. Bodies intertwined while the rest of the world disappeared to the newlyweds.

~

Kira walked out of the back door calling Sean's name as she did. He was supposed to come back to the house but since he hadn't, and hadn't answered his phone, she decided to go out and look for him. It was a cold, crisp Kansas morning. As she approached the barn, she could hear the restless horses in their stalls.

They shouldn't be so restless with Sean in there, she thought as she pulled her robe a little tighter around her. From her vantage point she could only see the long side of the barn as the entrance was off to the left, facing the eastern hay field. It was at that moment she noticed how quiet everything was.

The horses stepping about and snorting were the only sounds anywhere. No birds. No bugs. No breeze. Nothing. It was odd. Tentatively, she continued her steps to the barn.

"Sean?" she called out. Her voice seemed to fall dead in the air and received no response. More chills slid down her spine unrelated to the chill in the air. She pulled at her robe again anyway. "Sean?" she repeated as she neared the entrance-side of the barn. Still no answer. Placing her hand on the edge of the building she rounded the corner.

The huge door was open, and what she saw froze her in her tracks. The horses in stalls on both sides still shuffled nervously, but there in the middle of the barn standing side by side in a stair-step fashion on the hay floor stood three of her works on their easels.

She recognized them all immediately. She had painted them. The first and furthest back was the painting of the old farmhouse that Poena had burned to the ground. It was the first one she had created for Sean. The memories of the terror associated with that painting chilled her even more as she refocused her eyes on the second one in the middle which was an oversized version of a sketch. It was the one she had made of Poena with her dead black eyes staring out at her. Lastly, the nearest, was the painting she had just finished of Angelie except instead of Arthur's face being slightly reflected in the mirror by the door, he was standing behind Elliot facing out as if looking directly at Kira.

Instinctively she took a step back, suddenly very aware of being alone with those three paintings that shouldn't be there at all. As she did, a movement seemed to occur in all three paintings. At first, she wasn't sure what it was, like a deer running through a forest, she perceived the movement but couldn't identify the source.

She concentrated on the first painting and immediately saw an orange dot in two of the house windows. She realized at once that the dots were growing and in seconds she perceived them as eyes. Eyes that were growing. Wanting to look away, she shifted her gaze to the second easel only to realize that Poena's eyes were also growing and leaving the surface of the painting to move toward her. The motion from the third painting yanked her eyes in that direction only to see an impossibly large version of Arthur's pale blue orbs growing as well and moving in her direction. She gasped and stepped back again.

The eyes from the first painting were now larger than a human head, and she could discern why they had looked orange when they appeared in the house windows. Fingers of flame flickered within the pupils giving them a decidedly satanic quality and evoking memories of past terror.

All three sets of eyes continued to grow and advance in her direction. With a breathless gasp, she turned to run only to find that she was no longer at the edge of the barn but in the middle. The gaping door through which she had entered was now closed. She raced toward it anyway and grabbed the old metal handle but it wouldn't budge. She threw a quick glance behind her and terror filled her gaze. All three sets of eyes were now half the size of a horse and almost upon her.

She backed up as a blood curdling scream accosted her ears.

~

She felt being shaken before she discerned a voice.

"Kira! Kira!" Sean yelled at her as he continued to shake her shoulders. "Wake up!"

With a final gasp Kira opened her eyes and flinched as she found herself staring into Sean's eyes with his face pulled close.

"Ahh!" She yelled one last time still trying to pull back for a split second before realizing she was safe. She immediately reversed her efforts and threw herself into Sean's arms.

"Oh my God. That was horrible, Sean. Just horrible. Why weren't you there to help me?"

"Did you have some sort of vision?" Sean asked urgently. "Or was it another nightmare? What happened?"

As her breathing slowed and the warmth of Sean's caress sank in, she considered his question. "I guess it was just a nightmare," she began. "It was three paintings on easels in the barn. One of the old farmhouse, one of Poena, and a variation of the one I just painted for Brian. While I watched, eyes detached from each of them and began to grow and come at me. Oh, Sean it was the worst."

He hugged her closer. "I'm so sorry, Kira, and I'm sorry I wasn't there to help. It seems that I'm aware when you are having visions about your paintings even in your sleep, but if it's just a dream or a nightmare I have to be expecting it to be aware of it when I'm sleeping. I'm so sorry."

"What do you think it means?" She asked, lifting her eyes from his chest to see his face.

"I think it means your subconscious is on edge about our meeting tomorrow with Arthur, but nothing is going to go on in that hospital except my dad getting better. It's the meeting after that that has me a bit on edge."

"You think he'll try something then?"

"If he's going to try anything that's when he'll have to do it, but I can't imagine what he might think he can do with me there reading his thoughts."

~

Sean twisted slightly so he could look into Kira's eyes. The dim moonlight drifting in through the curtains created shadows across her face that only made her even more beautiful. It made Sean smile. His smile was greeted with one in return.

"Do you think you can get back to sleep? I'll be on guard this time."

"Only if you hold me very close," Kira said locking eyes with him.

"Hmmm. I think I can probably do that." Sean sensed the lingering effects of her fear. It evoked his protective instincts at the same time it made him swell with pride at her bravery.

Sean pulled Kira close to his chest and eased back onto his side. Again, the delight of feeling her so close to him was augmented by the sensation of pleasure wafting in from her. It was amazing. They were both back to sleep in moments.

The phone rang promptly at 7AM waking them both. They had barely moved since returning to sleep in the middle of the night. The phone was on the bedside table behind Kira and it took her a minute to disentangle enough to turn and reach it.

"Hello?" she said. It came out a bit gravelly. She cleared her throat.

"What time do we meet with Elliot and where?" Arthur's voice was flat and menacing. It was the quintessential rude awakening, and it jarred the cobwebs out of Kira's head.

"Sometime this afternoon," She began tersely. "I can let you know the time later this morning as to exactly where, but it's at the Beverly Hills Cancer Center. Do you know where that is?"

"Yes," he answered. "You have my number now; call me back when you have a time."

And with that he hung up.

"Arthur, I presume." Sean stated.

"Yep. And rude as ever. He just said to call him back when we know the time, then hung up."

"Perfect. You didn't want to chat with that jackass anyway." Sean replied.

"Well, that's true enough. What do you say we go get some breakfast and go for another walk on the beach? After that we can call Elliot and firm up the time then go visit your dad."

"Aren't you the little planner this morning?" Sean said grinning broadly. "That sounds like a perfect idea. Come take a shower with me."

"Sounds great."

It turned out that a little in-room couple's exercise preceded the shower, which preceded the walk, which preceded breakfast, and they were both happier for it. As they walked back to the hotel room Sean pulled out his phone.

"So, did you get a hold of the director, Elliot?" Sean asked. He had to pull back the phone and adjust the volume to hear Elliot's reply. "Say that again, please?"

"I said yes, I did get a hold of him, and if I didn't know better, I'd say he was a bit suspicious. But he agreed to let me do the evaluation this afternoon at 3PM. Did Arthur call?"

"He woke us up at 7AM this morning and is waiting for us to call him back with a time."

"No doubt with a cheerful tone in his voice."

Sean could sense the smile that must be on Elliot's face from the emotions he was receiving. "Don't you know it. It took me several minutes to get the scowl off Kira's face after talking to him."

"She talked to him? I can imagine. He especially hates women."

Sean paused briefly thinking about the comment. He knew from the few thoughts he had gleaned from Arthur that it was absolutely the truth. A real misogynist. "At any rate," Sean began, "We'll go ahead and call him back when we're heading over to the hospital to just visit with my dad until you get there. If he's awake, that is . . ."

"That sounds good." Elliot answered simply.

"Unless you need any help getting anything over there."

"No. I'll text you when I'm in the parking lot and you can meet me down there with the suitcase you brought to load everything into."

"Perfect," Sean answered. "See you then, and if anything changes, we'll call you back."

"Great," Elliot answered.

Sean hit the end button on his phone while he considered the conversation.

"Sounds like that went smooth," Kira said as she moved up behind Sean and planted her hands on his shoulders.

CHAPTER

Before they left the hotel room, they decided to get the undoubtedly annoying call to Arthur out of the way. It was Kira's phone number Arthur had, so they agreed on using it, but Sean didn't want her to have to talk to that maniac again, so he volunteered to make the call.

It only rang twice before Arthur picked up.

"So, what time?" he said in a harsh voice.

"Good morning to you too, jackass. Room 304 at the Beverly Hills Cancer Center 3PM," with that Sean hung up but not before he caught a dose of the nastiness raging through Arthur's thoughts. He slammed his mind shut even faster than he had hung up the phone.

"Ugh," Sean said handing the phone back to Kira. "The closest thing to a non-vile thought that jerk had was surprise that it was me on the phone instead of you. From there on it was strictly mental garbage."

"But you think he'll still show up?"

"He has to, Kira. He needs me to help him save himself, and he's not going to screw that up."

"Yeah. I'm sure you're right. If there is one thing we can probably count on with this guy it's for him to serve his own interests."

"Isn't that the truth? Let's head over to the hospital."

"Sounds like a plan," Sean answered sensing the undercurrent of tension in her mind lying just below the surface. He took the opportunity to lean in and plant a lingering kiss on her lips.

~

Kira decided that the Beverly Hills Cancer Center was slightly different than a regular hospital.

Or at least it had a different feel. Patients there were mostly terminal ones looking to try some experimental procedure to save their lives.

She was admiring the building as Sean maneuvered their car into the parking lot. It was a five-story affair which made it quite a bit shorter than many of the commercial buildings in the area, but it still had the southwest flair, being comprised of large pink granite blocks sitting on a white stone base. It had nice brown stone touches around the windows and although the roof was nearly flat it still possessed the half-cylinder, ceramic tile, shingles that were so common in the area. To complete the picture the landscape sported at least two palm trees. To Kira it seemed a bit forced, but had a nice feel, nevertheless.

"Are you ready for this?" Sean asked snatching Kira's attention from the architecture.

"The more important question is, are you?" She responded.

"As ready as I'll ever be."

They strolled into the building hand in hand and headed straight to the front desk. They knew what room Aubrey was in but had no clue if there was more than one section or set of elevators. As it turned out the obvious ones to their immediate left were the only set, so they thanked the bored looking, rotund lady with the vacuous smile and turned in the direction she had pointed.

"She was thinking about the bad grades on her son's report card," Sean said casually.

"That would explain the distance in her demeanor," Kira replied, blithely accepting Sean's statement. It was amazing what you could get used to.

The elevator hummed its way up to the third floor with no more conversation between them. Even Kira could sense Sean's tension and was well aware of her own. Even the oversized elevator smelled like hospital. The ding from the elevator preceded the opening doors, and they stepped directly to the floor nurse's station. The nurse this time was bright and cheerful and directed them to her left.

"That's almost funny," Sean began.

"What?"

"She was thinking about her child's report card as well; only her daughter had just gotten straight 'A's. It's weird that I picked two peo-ple's thoughts in a row that were on the same topic at about the same time, don't you think?"

"So yesterday was report card day at the local high school. What's so unusual about that?"

~

Sean simply shrugged and turned his attention to the numbers on the hospital doors. He had seldom been in hospitals and had been too keyed up to pay attention to the one in Kansas City. The wide, blond-wood doors with their oversized handles that were left partially open unnerved him slightly. It prompted him to make double sure he didn't pick up any stray thoughts.

"Why do they leave so many of the doors open?" He asked.

"I don't know; maybe it makes the rooms feel a bit less stuffy, or maybe it's just easier to hear if there is a problem with a patient. Here's our stop."

Aubrey's room door was closed. They knocked softly as they gently pushed it open.

"Dad?" Sean offered as they eased into the room. It smelled like a typical hospital room with the lingering smell of cleaning products and the beeping of medical equipment greeting them. There was a thin curtain that separated the room into two halves and though there was no one on the near side the curtain was drawn anyway.

"Dad?" Sean tried one more time before gently pulling back the curtain.

The reason for the lack of response from Aubrey was immediately apparent. He was intubated and apparently sedated, or asleep at the very least.

Sean had been unaware that his dad had been intubated, and the surprise caused an immediate reaction. In Sean's case that reaction was to reach for his father's thoughts. It was almost an instinct, and yet it felt a bit strange. His father was dreaming of some house in the country somewhere that Sean didn't recognize.

"What is it?" Kira asked noting the look on Sean's face.

"He's dreaming, and it's weird. I have never been in anyone's dreams but yours. Wherever he is it's a peaceful place in the country some-where."

Kira was thoughtful for a moment, then smiled and leaned over to put her arm around Sean's waist. "Sounds like what his son might dream," she said smiling broadly.

Any reply Sean might have made was interrupted by a soft noise at the door.

"Hello there. I'm Susan Dieters the floor nurse. Are you Aubrey's son?"

"Yes," Sean answered. "And I'm surprised to find he was intubated. What happened?"

"The tumor is just exerting a little more force on the autonomic nervous system, and he was having difficulty breathing, so until we get started with the treatment, we thought it better to sedate and intubate him."

"I see," Sean answered distantly.

"I understand you have another doctor coming in this afternoon to evaluate his condition for another possible treatment. Is that right?"

Sean didn't answer immediately. Too many thoughts were racing through his brain, so Kira filled in the silence. "That's correct Susan, and I'm Kira, Sean's wife, by the way."

"Nice to meet you," she answered blandly. The smile on her face didn't touch her eyes as they moved up to the computer screen beside Aubrey's bed.

"Well, it looks like he's doing fine. If you need anything let me know. There is a concessions room on this floor and a full cafeteria in the basement."

"Thank you so much," Kira responded. The words were barely out of Kira's mouth before Susan flowed out of the room.

"Well she seems efficient, at least," Kira said turning back to Sean. The distant look on his face apparently bothered her. "Hey are you, OK?"

"Yeah," Sean answered jerking his attention back to the room. "I was just concerned about Dad, so I was reading his thoughts again and trying to decide if I recognized the place he was dreaming about. It looked like the farm . . . but not."

"Sounds like a typical dream to me," Kira offered.

"So now, since we can't talk to him, I guess we just wait," Sean said.

Tension oozed from Sean in waves that he figured even Kira could sense.

"I guess," Kira replied. "Not my favorite thing."

Sean focused on Kira's feelings as a reprieve from his own. She wished there was something more she could do. Instead she simply focused on her desire to be there for him and hoped that was enough.

"Mine either." Sean answered belatedly, then smiled and put his hand on her shoulder

Arthur was in a constant state of fury since his last phone call with that couple. He had taken a stroll down to the beach to hurt a few of the passersby just to make him feel better. He was walking back from that outing now. It had been much less gratifying than he had hoped for and had done nothing to assuage his anger.

Sean made him a little afraid, and he hated being afraid. And since that morning phone call with Kira ordering him around all he could think of was his mother and how much she had tormented him all his life. He had even had one of his nightmares about his mother last night only this time his mother had Kira's face. He ground his teeth just thinking about how he had woken up sweating and scared.

Now he had to get home, change, and go meet those assholes to save the boy's dad. That was fine.

Today was going to be their day, but tomorrow or the next day they were going to save him, and then he was going to have a little surprise for them. He just had to get rid of all the cancer. The thought made him smile.

And if they decided not to help him after he'd done what they wanted, well, he had a couple of ideas about that as well.

One bridge at a time, he thought, *one bridge at a time.*

~

Elliot had already loaded everything he would need for the procedure in his car the night before. He had awoken early with ugly dreams about confronting Arthur again. Confrontation was not his forte, and even though he trusted Sean and Kira to be able to handle the situation he was still torn.

His lingering fear seemed to be doing battle with the underlying hatred for the man who had killed his newly found sister. It was amazing how someone you just met for the first time in your life could garner such a dear place in your heart. He surprised himself by spontaneously having thoughts of how to undermine Arthur's procedure, but he knew he didn't have it in him. He was no killer, however much he'd been wronged. All he could do was cling to the words Sean had said and pray that some justice found its way into the upcoming situation in the next couple of days.

With a deep sigh he turned his attention back to another experiment he was trying to finish before making the drive to the hospital. Surprisingly, there was barely any part of him that was anxious about the experiment itself. Somehow, he just seemed to know it would work. He spent a moment trying to support his confidence logically, but there was nothing to support it except his own intuition. Maybe that was enough.

The morning slipped into the afternoon with no particular change in Aubrey. Sean had been saddened that he hadn't been able to speak with him, but with about two hours left before Arthur and Elliot were due to show up Aubrey's eyes slowly opened. Neither Sean nor Kira saw it at first as they were deep into a conversation about what would come next after this little adventure.

Sean.

"What?" Kira asked reacting to the sudden loss of Sean's attention.

Sean. Sean heard again in his mind.

"Dad? Are you OK?"

Uncomfortable but fine. What's going on?

"Sean is your dad talking to you?"

"Yes. Just like you like to do. Directing thoughts at me," Sean answered briefly then lowered his voice and moved on.

"Dad we have arranged to try a procedure this afternoon to kill your cancer."

I thought they said you can't do surgery on what I have.

"You can't, and this isn't surgery; it's a procedure using microwaves and gold particles to kill the tumor."

~

This was a unique moment for Kira. Sean was actually speaking his side of the conversation, but Aubrey was only thinking his. It was a lot like listening to a phone conversation where you can only here the speaker with you, not the one on the other end of the line. Except in this case Kira wanted badly to know what Aubrey was saying, though she also had no desire to interrupt. At any rate she was sure Sean would relate it to her in a moment. In the interim all she could do was listen to Sean and stare at Aubrey's kind eyes which were turned at a sharp angle to view Sean. Kira figured that moving his head with the breathing tube in place might be painful. Instinctively she moved closer to the bed and put her hand on Aubrey's forearm and squeezed. He was the closest thing she had to a parent and seeing him in this condition was having more of an effect on her than she had realized.

She held her breath to ward off the flood of emotions trying to seep through her tear ducts. She had to be strong. She had to be strong for both of these men. She gently squeezed Aubrey's thin arm in support and listened raptly to Sean's words.

~

How do you get the gold where you need it to go?

Sean couldn't help but smile at his dad's astute question. "Well that's the tough part. Because of one of Kira's commissions we ran across a guy that can move small things with his mind, and he's going to come here to help."

That's very kind of him.

"Not really, Dad, but that's a whole different story. You just need to rest a little while longer. They'll be here in another couple of hours."

Getting drowsy again anyway. I love you, Sean. Tell Kira I love her as well.

"I will, Dad." Sean watched his dad's eyes flutter then gently close again.

"OK, so tell me," Kira asked anxiously.

"You pretty much heard it from my side, but he did want me to relay that he loves you."

"He's such a sweetheart," Kira replied. "Did he seem scared?"

"No. I think he was too sedated to get too emotional about anything. And frankly unless Elliot tells me different, I'm hoping he stays out through the whole thing. I'd just as soon he not experience Arthur's presence at all."

"Isn't that the truth? I wish we didn't either."

"Yeah, right?"

There was a little grey-green couch in the hospital room that would have qualified for a love seat, so Sean and Kira availed themselves of it and tried to nap.

Arthur was still fuming while he drove himself to the hospital, but he realized that he needed to get his thoughts under control before he had to face that boy.

His head was aching terribly though, and that wasn't helping matters. It was, however, reminding him that he was doing this to help himself not these other jackasses, and he needed this thing out of his own head so he could get back to what was about to become a very wealthy life.

He just had to get rid of all the cancer then things would be fine. But Sean's abilities still made him nervous. It affected his choices. He wanted to cause them pain, lots of pain; images of that Kira bitch lying on the ground screaming and covered in blood danced through his mind like his own twisted sugar plum fairies. He could see her gorgeous eyes bulging in terror and her disgustingly sensuous curves contorting in pain. It made his mouth water. He'd even envisioned blinding Sean or bursting a vein in his brain. He'd love to see that bastard's eyes and nose drip blood.

As much as he'd rather unleash his depravity on Kira, Sean was becoming an increasingly enticing target as well. But he couldn't make any of that happen without Sean seeing it coming and turning it back on him. Hell, he probably couldn't even fantasize about it without causing some problems with that damn mind-reader. He'd never had to control his thoughts before and the entire idea of it was annoying enough to undermine the clear thinking he needed. He had given the problem a lot of thought and had already considered a list of things to think about that wouldn't alert Sean too much, not the least of which was the procedure itself and how maybe it could be improved when it came to his own treatment. That was also the point at which he would be working the closest to the boy and therefore when he would be most vulnerable, but he was quite sure that at that point focusing on saving his own life wouldn't be an issue.

Looking up from the road he could see the sign for the hospital just past the next exit.

It was almost time for round one.

~

Elliot's previous confidence about this upcoming procedure had dissipated like morning fog. As a matter of fact, he hadn't been this nervous since he had turned in his doctoral thesis, or when he met Angelie for the first time.

The memory brought a renewed wave of sadness, followed by another rush of anger at the detestable excuse for a human being that had caused him such pain. The very thought of actually helping the son-of-a-bitch still rankled, but Elliot calmed himself by remembering that today he was going to save Sean's dad.

His pulse was racing, though, as he pulled into the parking lot. He had made a point of being a half hour early so as to have everything ready to go when Arthur arrived. The less time he had to be around that recalcitrant chunk of evil, the better.

Parking the car, he reached for his cell phone to have Sean bring the luggage down.

~

The phone ringing jarred Sean awake, and his sudden movement did the same for Kira who had her head on his chest.

"This is Sean," Sean said without bothering to look at the caller ID first.

"Sean, Elliot here. Can you bring the suitcase down? I'm in the parking lot. I'll be just to your right as you come out of the door. It's a green Ford Focus."

"On my way," Sean answered hanging up.

"Surely that's not Arthur coming early,"

"Elliot," Sean answered. "I need to take the luggage down to him."

"Need any help?"

"No, I've got it. Just stay with Dad and keep praying."

"Why am I even surprised you knew I was praying? Even after all this time I occasionally forget," Kira just smiled as he left.

When Sean reached the parking lot Elliot waved, so he could walk straight to him which he did after making a quick detour to the rental car to retrieve the suitcase.

Elliot opened the trunk as Sean approached.

"Is this all there is?" Sean asked setting the suitcase on the ground beside the trunk of the car.

"Yep. The screen looking thing is for the fluoroscope, and the thing that looks like an oversized hair dryer is the microwave emitter. The little case has syringes and a few other things I'll need."

"I guess I didn't pay attention when I was in your lab, or maybe I just didn't bother to see which of all your equipment you were actually using when you did the experiment,"

Sean paused as he mulled over the memory of the experiment then softly chuckled, "Oh wait, never mind that was just a dream."

Elliot stopped and stared at Sean for a second and then drew a breath as if to ask a question. Instead he did a nearly visible shake of his head and continued with what he had intended to say. Sean snagged the quick thought in his mind.

Nope, not asking.

He grinned slightly as Elliot continued.

"It's amazingly simple when I have something to get the gold to go where I need it. That has been the hurdle I can't cross, at least not without Arthur."

Sean didn't need to read Elliot's thoughts to hear the change of tone when he said the name Arthur. It was just an echo of what they all felt.

"OK. Let's get this stuff loaded up and in there then," Sean said enthusiastically.

~

Kira stood up reflexively when Sean and Elliot entered the room. Elliot was carrying a little brown case, and Sean was lugging the large suitcase.

"So, what now?" she asked.

"I've been thinking about that. We could hook everything up and wait for Arthur, but I don't want another doctor or nurse waltzing in here and asking questions, so maybe it's better if we wait until Arthur actually arrives."

"You think he'll be on time?" Kira asked. She was as nervous as she used to be just before a big photo shoot. She cast a half-hearted smile up at Sean knowing full well that he could see through it.

"We'll get this done and be through with this guy as quickly as possible," Sean said responding to what he sensed from Kira.

Sean glanced over at Aubrey who was still sleeping soundly. Whatever it was they had given him certainly hadn't worn off yet.

"What if Dad wakes up while we're doing the procedure?" Sean asked.

"I'll check him before we begin. I know what they gave him, and I can administer a bit more if needed. We really would like for him to remain asleep. It's not that he would feel anything, but the more motionless we can keep him, the better."

The conversation died after that. Everyone was tense for so many different reasons that Kira could almost imagine the walls vibrating with the nervous energy floating around the room.

At 3:00PM sharp Arthur stole into the room like an evil wraith. Everyone froze and turned to him.

"Well, don't just stare let's get this circus going. I want to get this done, then we can discuss when I get my turn."

Sean and Kira just stared for a moment, but Elliot flinched into action, possibly remembering the pain that hesitating had caused him on other occasions involving Arthur. Arthur in turn moved casually back to the door and swung it closed. He cast a brief glance at the door latch, recognizing the lack of a lock, then moved closer to the bed and drew the dividing curtain as well.

"This will give us at least a little notice if someone decides to traipse into the room." He muttered.

~

While Elliot finished setting up equipment Arthur turned to Sean, pointedly ignoring Kira.

"OK here is what you need to do. When I begin working, you're going to have to be reading my mind or whatever it is you do, so you can do as much of this as possible the next time. I don't really know how far I'll get, working on myself before I just can't do anymore. You got it?"

Sean was a bit surprised at the calm business tone coming from Arthur. In another life this man could have been a business manager.

What a shame, he thought.

"Yeah, I got it," Sean finally replied. "You just make sure you get your part done."

Sean paused there snagging the overwhelming feelings of doubt and fear streaming off Kira. He turned to her.

"Don't worry, Sweetie, I got this." He punctuated his words with a steady gaze, eliciting an accepting nod and a tentative smile.

"Isn't that sweet?" Arthur began sarcastically. "Now are you about ready, Doc?"

"Another couple of minutes," Elliot answered, not even looking up from the microwave emitter he was positioning.

Everyone nearly held their breath for the next couple of minutes until Elliot turned to them.

"OK. We're ready to go."

Sean could sense everything in the room. Elliot was nervous, Kira was anxious, as was he, but Arthur was nothing but intent. And he kept focusing on getting rid of all the cancer. As a matter of fact, he was focusing on getting rid of the cancer so completely that Sean couldn't really pick up anything else from him except a vague visualization of what he was going to be trying to do. It was an odd sensation. Sean moved in beside his dad, increasing his proximity to Arthur. Most people's thoughts he picked up tended to flow like a stream bubbling over various topics and feelings, but Arthur's seemed to be locked in place. Maybe it was that focus that allowed him to do what he did.

"I'll sit here by the screen where I can see the gold particles more clearly," Arthur announced as he drug a chair over to the position he'd selected.

Wordlessly, Sean eased over to stand behind Arthur. The position allowed him to better view the screen. What he intended was to be tuned into Arthur's thoughts, not only seeing his progress but gauging what Arthur was doing as he was doing it. Whether he liked the idea or not he was going to be attempting to help Arthur do this to himself in the near future and the better he understood it the more likely that was to be successful.

"OK, I'm just about ready," Elliot announced, "Arthur, are you ready?"

Arthur merely nodded his head.

Arthur was still thinking about killing all the cancer, Sean sensed.

Instead of continuing to focus on Arthur, however, Sean turned his attention to Kira's anxiety only to find she was staring at him and wondering what it was he was thinking.

~

Kira's intuition was no match for Sean's abilities, but she knew her husband and something had caught his attention. Judging by the tilt of his head, she was betting it was Arthur.

Just when she was thinking of asking him what it was, he turned to her and smiled. With the tiniest shake of his head he alerted her that her question should wait. Kira had a bad feeling. Arthur was being a little too quiet, Elliot was a little too nervous, and Sean was much more intent than normal. She couldn't shake the feeling that more was going on here than was obvious on the surface. There was nothing she could do either.

The stage was set with the characters in place, and she was just the audience. She shuffled her feet and clasped her hands behind her back trying to manage her fidgety nerves. She didn't want to be a distraction to Sean.

"OK here goes," Elliot began. She watched him move over closer to one of the IV bags beside Aubrey, check his vitals on the monitors above one more time, then proceed to inject the syringe of gold molecules into the line protruding from his arm.

345

The whole room went quiet as they watched Elliot and then the screen he had set up by Aubrey. It took just a few seconds before the gold molecules became visible in one of the arteries going up toward Aubrey's brain.

"You're on," Elliot said simply, looking back at Arthur.

~

Arthur's expression barely changed. A slight furrowing of his brows was about all the emotion he showed. Sean, however, felt the increase in concentration and then suddenly there it was— that strange feeling of power as Arthur began to direct the little molecules of gold.

Move up this way, Sean sensed from Arthur's thoughts.

Sean had still not managed to get a label on the sensation he got when Arthur was using his ability, but he was certainly aware of it. As before it definitely had its own nature, somehow different than other thoughts Sean had learned to perceive, and just like his previous brief encounters, he had the sensation that he could emulate what he was sensing.

The tumor on the screen pulsed like a dark shadow at the heart of Aubrey's brain.

Towards there, Sean found himself thinking and was rewarded by tiny darker specs gravitating toward the tumor.

"Good," Arthur said simply as the particles angled in the direction of the tumor. "That is actually helping. Keep doing that. This is what I'll need you to do later when it's me on the table. I can do some, but the closer those particles get the more difficult it will become for me to concentrate. So, keep helping just like that."

Sean wasn't quite sure how he was doing what he was doing. All he could think of was to try to do what Arthur was doing. Making his thoughts like Arthur's.

Everyone's eyes were glued to the screen and for a few moments as the particles entered Aubrey's brain, the only sound in the room came from the vitals-monitoring equipment which kept its steady, even beeping.

The particles continued to move slowly toward the shadow that was the tumor. Sean sensed Arthur's concentration shifting slightly and one group of particles paused in their forward motion while another began to move more quickly. Arthur maneuvered that group into position around the shadow where they became still. He next shifted his concentration to the other group and a portion of those started proceeding to the periphery of the shadow. A moment or two later all the particles were in position hovering closely to the circumference of Aubrey's tumor.

"Is that close enough?" Arthur asked.

Sean almost jumped at Arthur's voice.

He had been so engrossed with the movement of the particles; he hadn't even noticed Arthur's intention to speak. That oversight caused him concern. He had assumed Arthur couldn't conceal any thought from him when he was connected like this, but apparently there was some limitation to how much he could sense from someone at once, or at least there was under these circumstances. If Arthur could keep things from him then none of them were as safe as they thought they were.

"Yes," Elliot answered moving his hands over to the microwave emitter. "Just keep things right there for another few seconds."

Hold them steady. That was the continuous thought emanating from Arthur. Sean could see Elliot's hands working with the emitter and the particles themselves were doing just as Arthur intended. Sean tried to discern if any of his interaction was helping or not. How was he supposed to tell?

He was trying to perceive a sensation he had never had before, so even if he was sensing something, how the hell would he know?

Sean blinked and stared more closely at the screen. Were those magnified particles beginning to vibrate? Concern lanced through him like an icicle to the heart. If something went wrong at this stage his dad could die. Sean blinked again. They were indeed starting to vibrate. As the miniscule motion continued, the shadow in Aubrey's brain seemed to darken.

"What's happening?" Sean asked.

"It's working," Elliot said simply continuing to manipulate dials on the emitter.

"How do you know when it's done?" Sean continued.

347

"Be quiet," Elliot answered, obviously irritated at the distraction.

Sean looked back at the screen and saw the shadow that was Aubrey's tumor continue to darken. It went from a shadow to a darker shadow and then began to look like a solid black obelisk lying in the middle of his dad's brain.

"There," Elliot said finally, pulling his hands away from the dials on the emitter. "I believe we did it," he continued.

"Are you sure?" Kira asked.

"Impossible to be sure right now, but we'll know pretty quick when the tumor size begins to diminish as the body absorbs the dead tissue and that should be visible in just a few hours. We would probably know quicker if we could remove the breathing tube. I'm guessing we have already diminished the pressure on his autonomic nervous system, but I'm not about to remove that breathing tube or stop his sedative. That means we're going to have to wait until his doctor figures it out."

"I hate having to wait," Sean said. "I'm going to wait until after you leave and call his doctor. I'm sure Dad would want that tube out of his throat as soon as possible. Also, I'll know when he wakes up before anyone else." He felt a question arise from Elliot, but the slight man voiced nothing and simply nodded his head.

Kill all the cancer. Sean sensed again from Arthur before he suddenly stood up.

"OK. It worked. Now when are we going to handle mine?"

Silence fell over the room at Arthur's sudden outburst.

"Uh, well we should wait and see the results with Aubrey first, I would think," Elliot stammered.

"No. We shouldn't. I want to get this thing out of my head as soon as possible. Let's do it tomorrow at your lab."

Sean looked at Elliot and then back to Arthur.

Kill the cancer, he continued thinking. Elliot was thinking that he didn't know what to do. Sean was about to speak when, much to everyone's surprise, Kira spoke up.

"Fine. Elliot, if there's no reason to wait let's do it tomorrow. I'm as anxious to get this over with as Arthur."

Sean's attention swung back to Kira. She truly was nervous, and he couldn't quite understand why. Nothing new had really occurred.

Certainly, Arthur's impatience wasn't much of a surprise.

"We can't do it tomorrow," Elliot offered.

"Why not?" Arthur shot back. Sean sensed his desire to hurt the scientist and geared up to play defense when Arthur's outburst continued, "I knew you people would try to back out on me!"

His eyes darted to Sean's and abruptly the emotions were subdued.

"I'm not trying to back out," Elliot responded, throwing his hands up in the air. "I just don't have any more of the gold particle preparation made up, and it takes a little time to get it in the stable solution we need for the procedure."

"Then I suggest you head back to the lab and get some made because we're going to do my procedure tomorrow afternoon, or someone is going to be very unhappy about it." There was a hint of a sneer on Arthur's face that prompted Sean to scan his thoughts again. He was still thinking about getting rid of all the cancer but then . . .

"A bomb?" Sean blurted out, "What the hell do you mean, a bomb?"

Now the sneer dominated Arthur's features while Elliot looked dumbfounded, and Kira had a simple look of recognition. She knew what Sean had just done.

"Very good, Mr. Mind Reader. That's right. I planted a bomb at your nice new house. Two, actually. I added one in the barn for good measure. It ought to be plenty strong enough to take out those damn foul-smelling horses. And if I don't get back there in time to disarm them, you'll not only be rebuilding again, you'll be picking up horse parts for weeks."

"You lousy son-of-a . . ." Sean lurched toward Arthur as he spoke and reached for his thoughts as well.

Kill all the cancer, was all he got. That phrase was beginning to ring wrong in Sean's mind, but at the moment he was too angry to consider it.

"Sean, wait!" Kira yelped as she reached for his shoulder. "It won't do any good now anyway."

"Good thinking, girl. We wouldn't want your nice new house blown up, now would we?"

"How do we know you would keep your end of the deal once we help you?" Kira continued, still gripping Sean's shoulder.

"You don't," Arthur said unleashing his particular smile that was guaranteed to frighten children. "But we can't do much about that, can we?"

"As a matter of fact, we can," she said and turned to Elliot. "Elliot, can you do this at our house in Kansas?"

Elliot was taken by surprise, and the current dialogue was already overwhelming him. "Uh..well . . . yeah, if I have enough time."

"You don't," Kira said. "How about if we all pitch in to get things prepared tonight and get on a flight out of here in the morning?

And before you even think about protesting, Arthur, if you don't agree then we'll lose our house again, but you'll lose your life. Elliot, what do you need from us?"

Sean kept having the sensation that he should interject something, but Kira was doing such a marvelous job that he couldn't think of anything of value to add. As a matter of fact, he realized, it was pride he was feeling, not fear.

Elliot on the other hand was nearly at a loss. His emotions were interfering with his ability to estimate time limitations. To make matters worse, after Kira's direct question, the entire room fell silent waiting on his response, making him the absolute center of attention, another thing at which he did not excel. Still, the moments stretched.

"Uh . . . yes," he finally said. "If we get back to my lab right away and work through the night, I could have the solution ready to go in the morning if we can get a flight."

"Leave that to me," Sean stated. "But what about my dad?"

This was something Elliot was prepared to answer. "He'll be fine, Sean. When they come in to check on him later, they'll see the improvement in his vitals and remove the breathing tube before the sedative wears off. We couldn't do anything better if we stayed, even if we were allowed, which we aren't."

Once again, the metronomic beeping from the machinery monitoring Aubrey became the only sound in the hospital room, like the precursor to some awakening of a new alien life in a sci-fi movie, until Kira spoke into the silence. "So why are we still standing here? Let's go. Arthur you can ride with us."

~

Arthur's eyes turned sharply to Kira. The last thing he wanted was to spend an extended time in a confined space with this damn mind reader. He wouldn't be able to keep control of his thoughts for that length of time.

"No," he said flatly, "I'll take my car. I'll pack a few things and meet you at the airport." Then he quickly shifted his thoughts back to killing all the cancer. He hoped that little slip in his concentration hadn't already caused him problems. He cast a surreptitious glance at Sean. No emotions registered.

Good, Arthur thought.

No one questioned whether Arthur would show up or not. It was his life that was on the line here.

"You can call me with the flight arrangements, and I'll be there." Arthur hurried from the room with a scowl on his face and a determination in his step. As he did so Elliot was the first to move, wordlessly beginning to repack the equipment back into the suitcase that Sean had brought.

"This all feels just too weird to me," Kira said as she snuggled in next to Sean in their hotel room bed. It was 2:00AM and they had just returned from Elliot's lab.

They had helped as much as they could, but eventually Elliot told them he'd have to finish the rest himself. He had sent them off with a tired smile and an assurance that he'd have the solution done in time to make their 10:00AM flight.

"I don't think there is any way that it wouldn't feel weird dealing with that crazy monster," Sean answered.

"I know. It's just that something feels off. Didn't you feel it Sean? Did you pick up any weird thoughts from him?"

"Sean?" She asked again after waiting a moment for a response, but it was too late. He was already asleep.

Her last thought was that she hoped she didn't have any more dreams of that lunatic.

~

Elliot finished the serum preparation at 3:30AM. He was exhausted and wasn't going to get much sleep before the flight tomorrow. He could have accomplished the task a couple of hours sooner, but his thoughts were holding him back. A big part of him did not *want* to do this.

He felt certain that his procedure would prove successful on Sean's dad, and he just didn't want to give that kind of help to Arthur. Here was a man who had no business being allowed to continue walking this Earth, and he was about to help save him. It was wrong. That evil should just be allowed to die and not only because of what he had done to his sister.

Now, other lives were in jeopardy, however, and it wouldn't be right to make Sean and Kira suffer for Arthur's misdeeds. Elliot breathed a deep sigh as he loaded the last of his equipment, including the sealed beaker with the serum in it, into the suitcase Sean had left for him. It should travel well on the plane. He noticed the uncharacteristic shake in his hands as he closed the latch. This entire situation was so far out of his wheelhouse . . . he would just be glad when it was all over. A flash of Angelie's smile swept through him bringing a tear to his eye. His sister. If he had only had a little more time . . .

He shook off the memory. Gripping the suitcase, Elliot took one last look around the lab trying to think of anything he might have forgotten and made one last sigh. Tomorrow was going to be a long and troublesome day. He hoped he survived it.

~

Arthur was back in his little apartment, and he was smiling. This smile might even have seemed pleasant from the outside unless you knew the reason for it. His plan was going well.

So far, he had managed to accomplish what was needed without that damn mind reading boy or his bitch wife being any the wiser. He had been forced to test the limitations of Sean's abilities and had found the gaps for which he had hoped. The boy could read his thoughts at will, but he couldn't do that consistently or at least he didn't. Arthur had reasoned that when others were in the range of Sean's abilities that he wouldn't be able to take in everyone's thoughts all the time. It would be too confusing for one thing, and damn annoying for another. The boy must have developed some method of selectively tuning people out, so thoughts weren't flooding him all the time. That is what Arthur had hoped for, and it had proved fruitful.

Tomorrow he would have that abominable tumor out of his brain, and he would be done with that horrible couple, especially that bitch that reminded him more and more of his whore of a mother. The thought made him smile once more. This grin, though, would probably frighten even dogs.

The stage is set, Kira thought. This whole day had felt like some monstrous choreography preparing for this afternoon. She had texted the flight information to Arthur with no acknowledgment . . . which was worrisome.

They had met Elliot at the airport then made the uneventful flight back to Kansas and the subsequent drive back out to the farm. They hadn't seen Arthur at the airport and Kira was beginning to wonder if he had slept through the flight or simply changed his mind. Sean had spent his spare time trying to locate the bombs Arthur had hidden but to no avail.

"Well Damn," Sean said as he sat down at the kitchen table.

"Still no luck, huh?" Kira asked.

"No. I thought about calling John and seeing if he had any connections to somebody with a bomb dog, but I don't even know when Arthur is going to show up, and it certainly wouldn't do to have the police sniffing around when he drove in the driveway. I'm afraid we're just going to have to play this out Arthur's way for now."

"But you don't trust him?" she said.

"Hell no, I don't trust him! I just don't see a better option yet. We'll see what he's thinking when he gets here. Yesterday all he was focused on was 'killing all the cancer' which I guess is probably all I would be thinking about in his position, but it wasn't very helpful in anticipating his steps, so hopefully his thoughts are more illuminating today."

~

Elliot was busy setting things up in the den. It was 2:30PM. His goal was to be ready a bit before 3:00PM. Anything he could do to accelerate things and be done with this Crazy, the better.

"How's it going, Elliot?" Sean asked for about the third time. Apparently, Sean was as tense about the upcoming rendezvous and procedure as he was himself.

"I'll be ready in just a few minutes," Elliot answered.

"I think we could all use a glass of wine," Kira called from the kitchen.

"Amen to that," Elliot answered.

~

For Sean that suggestion immediately triggered memories of all the times Kira had served them both wine completely naked. "Just make sure you're dressed for the occasion," Sean called back eliciting a bit of a giggle from the kitchen.

"Don't worry," she yelled in reply, "I always dress appropriately."

"Don't I know it," he barely mumbled evincing a smile of his own and turned his attention back to watching Elliot make his preparations.

At 2:53PM Arthur walked in the front door without so much as a knock, accompanied by a brisk breeze and a smattering of leaves. He all but slammed the door and turned to face the little group. His expression was a mixture of anxiety, anger, and anticipation.

"How nice of you to knock," Sean commented dourly.

"Let's get this over with," Arthur answered favoring Kira, who was now sitting on the couch with her glass of wine in hand, with a particular scowl.

"Everything is ready," Elliot said. "Just come sit over here, and we can get started."

"Good," Arthur said moving in the direction Elliot indicated.

"But first," Sean interrupted, "I think we should discuss the elephant in the room, or more to the point, the bomb in the house."

Arthur smiled. "There is no bomb in the house. I made that up. There isn't one in the barn either. I needed some insurance that you wouldn't try to double cross me, so I invented planting some bombs to make sure we all got here. I figured since it was a newly built home it might mean enough to you sentimental idiots to work in my favor.

I had to convince you to bring us all here somehow. I knew if I delivered the threat as a thought, you'd pick it up and think it was a secret you'd stolen and be more likely to act on it. After that, I just had to get here early enough to scout the place for a weakness. While you took a 10:00AM flight I took the red eye, and it worked. I loosened a pipe to cause a small gas leak in the basement and set a lighter beneath it; now that I'm here I can strike that lighter from where I stand."

~

Sean immediately focused his thoughts on Arthur's. Arthur was thinking about the lighter and his proximity to it. A hundred yards. That was what Arthur believed his range was for moving things with his mind. This was a revelation for Sean who had been under the impression that Arthur would have to be in the same room. Examining the idea, Sean realized he had no basis for such a supposition. Abruptly he refocused on Arthur's thoughts which were now firmly planted on simply killing all the cancer.

Over and over Arthur repeated that phrase to himself. Sean stayed focused, intent on Arthur's thoughts for several seconds before wrenching his mind away. Sean stared in Arthur's eyes for a moment before speaking. "You're a real bastard, you know that?" Arthur just smiled.

~

Kira was disgusted, but not shocked. She had felt something was off about the way events had unfolded, and now she knew why. They'd been tricked. Besides the initial wave of disgust, she was surprisingly calm at Arthur's confession.

She set the wine glass down on the end table, turned her eyes from the predominately silent struggle going on between Arthur and Sean, and glanced at the snow outside. It was early for snowfall, but the flakes were big and heavy. The scene took her away for a moment to other times she had enjoyed the snowfall with Sean. She had spent so much of her life in the warmer climes that snow was particularly magical for her. At the moment she was just wishing this whole ordeal was over and this maniac was out of her house. She was still deep in her thoughts when Sean's phone rang.

He glanced down then hurriedly answered. "This is Sean. Oh, hi Dr.

Moritz. This is good news I hope." Sean listened intently, and a smile blossomed across his features. He shifted his eyes to Kira and smiled even more.

"That's fantastic," he said. "Well, maybe it is a miracle, but regardless I'm just happy to get the news. No. I understand, but when do you think you can release him? OK great. Thanks Doc, I'll relay the news. Right . . . Bye."

All eyes were glued to Sean as he hung up his phone. Kira was the first to ask what everyone was thinking.

"So? I'm guessing that was good news from your dad?"

Sean went over and hugged her. "The tumor is apparently dead and has already quit pressing on his autonomic nervous system. They removed the breathing tube about two hours ago. He is sleeping comfortably. The doc says they want to keep him for 24 hours of observation, and then he'll be on a flight home tomorrow."

"Great," Arthur said flatly. "The damn procedure works. Now let's get this thing out of my head." He moved to the chair Elliot had previously indicated as he spoke.

Elliot had remained quiet but was smiling broadly at the news from Sean. Once Arthur seated himself Elliot began quickly arranging the equipment around him.

"Sean, in this case you need to stand close so you can see the screen clearly. If this happens like it did before, once the particles begin to get close to the tumor, Arthur will have difficulty continuing to place them. If this is going to work, you will have to help him right near the end of the final placement while I turn on the projector."

"Got it," Sean answered moving into the position Elliot had suggested. Kira wordlessly moved up behind him and put her hands on his shoulders.

"I love you," she whispered into his ear.

Elliot picked up the syringe and moved toward Arthur. "Here goes everyone. Time for the show."

"No tricks," Arthur commented acerbically, not even glancing at Elliot as he approached.

"The trick will be to simply make this work," Elliot responded.

~

Kira watched over Sean's shoulder as Elliot administered the syringe of clear liquid and depressed the plunger. She was more nervous than any photo shoot she could ever remember, and all she could think of was how badly she wanted this maniac out of her house and her life.

"It'll be alright," Sean said quietly without taking his eyes off Arthur.

~

Sean saw Arthur wince slightly at the injection and sensed his twinge of pain, then the gold particles appeared on the screen. Just like with Aubrey, they moved up the carotid arteries and into Arthur's brain. Sean could feel Arthur's thoughts. He was incredibly focused on sending those little particles to the shadow in the outline of his brain. It was in a very different location than Aubrey's had been but roughly the same size. That same quality of thought Sean had detected before filled Arthur's thoughts— the relative intensity that marked Arthur using his abilities. Sean tuned in to those thoughts and tried to mimic them both in quality and intent.

Move those little particles, he thought.

"Yes," Arthur said simply.

As the gold approached the tumor Sean felt a lessening of the intensity in Arthur's concentration. Sean sensed pain coming from Arthur and attempted to pick up the slack. The particles slowed at first then accelerated as Sean concentrated.

"It's working," Elliot relayed calmly. "Is it just Arthur or are you helping, Sean?"

"Hush," Kira interjected. "He's concentrating. Don't distract him."

Sean felt Arthur's concentration continue to slip as the particles drew closer and closer to their target.

Pain.

The sensation of pain coming from Arthur almost caused Sean to retreat. This was why Arthur couldn't do this himself. Something about approaching this tumor with the little molecules of gold was causing Arthur pain. Sean had no idea why that would be, but it didn't matter. He was locked into Arthur's thoughts, and it was allowing him to finish the job which Arthur couldn't.

"Excellent," Elliot began. "Now just hold them there." Elliot proceeded to turn on the microwave projector, and as before with Aubrey, the tumor began to darken.

Suddenly, Arthur's consciousness slipped away, and Sean nearly lost his grip on the tiny specks of metal. Arthur had passed out. Fortunately, Elliot had anticipated this possibility. Arthur's head barely moved against the headrest Elliot had set up.

Trying to maintain his grip on the particles without Arthur's thoughts being connected to his was exponentially more difficult than it had been just seconds ago. Sean focused even more. He felt beads of sweat begin to appear on his forehead. He was distantly aware that his wife must have noticed when she alerted Elliot.

"Hurry," she said, urgency thick in her voice. "I don't think he can hold it much longer."

"Almost done," Elliot answered.

Sean's head was pounding, and he felt his grip on the particles slipping.

Just a little more he told himself as the pressure in his head increased. He was beginning to worry that he might cause some kind of rupture in his own brain when Elliot called out.

"Done! Sean you can relax now."

But to his surprise it wasn't as easy to let go as Sean had anticipated. It was like trying to untangle himself from a net, each strand seemed to pull from a different direction, and Sean had to remove or unwind one strand to get at the next. He remained silent while he mentally disentangled himself.

Finally, with a deep sigh, Sean leaned back into Kira who was still standing behind him and slumped into her arms. "That better have worked," he began. "Because I don't know if I could ever do it again even if I wanted to ... and I don't."

Kira grabbed Sean in a tremendous hug and guided him to sit on the couch.

"You did it, Sean," she said.

Sean glanced over at Arthur who was still apparently unconscious. "Is he OK?" Sean asked, lifting his eyes up to Elliot without moving from Kira's comforting embrace.

"I'm sure he'll be fine. I think he pushed himself too far trying to do this."

"Yeah," Sean added. "I could feel the pain he was enduring as the particles got closer to the tumor. It was incredible. Just sensing it almost broke my concentration."

Arthur's eyes fluttered and opened. He rubbed his temples then promptly focused and turned sharply to Elliot. "So, did it work?" He asked in a distrustful and menacing tone.

"As a matter of fact, I believe it did. The results look better than what we got with Aubrey even."

~

"Great." Arthur said flatly. His thoughts immediately turned to his next objective. Getting rid of the last of the cancer. The cancer that was infecting the world, and had been degrading his life since childhood, was going to be eliminated. Killing that cancer would become his life's goal. And he was going to start with that last bit of cancer in the room— Kira. Even more than he despised Sean, he loathed Kira. She reminded him too much of his mother. She represented all the disgusting, self-important women that were imposing their selfish will on the world and destroying it piece by piece like a disease. If he could just get rid of her his task would be complete, and his real work could begin. Once it was done, he could bolt in the confusion or actually blow up the house like he had threatened, igniting the lighter was a simple enough task.

He began to gather his thoughts and focus on Kira; eliminating the cancer of women on the world would start now.

Sean's head snapped up with deadly speed and violence in his eyes.

"What?!" Sean yelled. "What do you mean Kira is the last of the cancer? Why, you miserable little bastard! I'll see you dead first!"

Chaos ensued.

Kira was stunned for a second by Sean's side of the communication before she could piece together what was happening.

Elliot didn't know Sean well enough to deduce what Kira just had, but Sean's actions gave him enough of a hint to back pedal away from the two.

Sean bolted toward the chair Arthur was just rising from, but before he could grab Arthur, Arthur flicked a thought at the lamp on the table beside him knocking it off into Sean's path. He didn't waste any time with that distraction either. He immediately began to drag other objects in the room off the walls and tables instantly making the entire room a melee of distractions. He considered lighting the gas in the basement, but wasn't sure he could still escape, so his next thought was directed at Kira. A single artery in the heart was his target. The right-side coronary artery. The very same one he had intended to use to cause pain to Angelie when it had unexpectedly given way, but this time he wanted it to fail, and he directed his ability with many times the force with which he had assaulted Angelie.

"Aaaah!" Kira yelled reaching for her chest and gasping. She was beginning to stumble backward when Sean screamed yet again.

"NO! You will not!"

~

Sean felt the pressure of Arthur's unusual thought. The ones Sean had sensed so many times now. He directed his concentration on them and with an effort of pure will that he would never really understand, he bent the thought and the force resulting from it back on Arthur using what he had just learned while trying to save Arthur's life to not only rebound it but to increase it as well.

Arthur's eyes swung wildly back toward Sean, widening by the second. "NO!" He screamed reaching for his own heart. "You can't!" Arthur tried to increase the force of his attack, but a second pain burst in his head. Instantly blood flooded from his nose.

In that same instant all cries of pain disappeared from Kira, and she stared in shock as Arthur fell clutching both his heart and his head.

~

As it turned out Arthur's abilities were stronger than he'd known and being amplified by Sean made Arthur's lethal intent more gruesomely effective than he could have possibly anticipated. The bottom portion of the artery actually tore away from where it connected to the aorta, immediately flooding Arthur's chest cavity with blood. Had he been in an operating room with a team of cardiac surgeons standing by they would not have been fast enough to deliver Arthur from such a massive separation.

And even if they had, the damage his effort had precipitated on his brain would have been lethal as well. With a final gasp Arthur hit the floor.

~

Unfortunately for Sean, he was still connected to Arthur's thoughts, and he bellowed with the mere echo of the pain that was shooting through Arthur's chest and brain.

"Sean, Sean! Are you all right?" Kira shouted back as she flew to his side.

Elliot had stumbled to the floor and was staring in utter shock, unable even to gather his thoughts enough to regain his feet. "Somebody want to tell me what just happened?"

"I think he's still connected to Arthur!" Kira yelled.

Almost in response to Kira's supposition Sean's eyes got momentarily wider, and a hand moved involuntarily toward his chest, but it never made it. With a sensation like a snap in his mind the world went black and the pain disappeared.

For Sean, the room reappeared seconds later, and he was suddenly pain free with Kira's arm around his waist. Exhaustion overtook him. He gave Elliot a strange look for a moment then answered his question.

"Arthur just tried to do intentionally to Kira what he did accidentally to Angelie. In shielding her I made it rebound on him."

~

Kira stared into his eyes and saw the pain leave him but, for a brief second, she saw something else she couldn't understand. Shock maybe? Horror? But it was so brief she couldn't be sure.

All she knew is what she glimpsed briefly in Sean's eyes reminded her of visions of Sean's adopted dad Jason and the horror she had experienced there.

"And yes, Kira I'm fine . . . I think," Sean began drawing in a slow deep breath. "That was . . . strange . . . to say the least. I was connected to him when he died. I've certainly never done that before, and I'm pretty sure I don't want to ever do it again, at least not with someone evil."

"What did you see?" Kira prompted still reeling from her own sensations.

"Black mostly, but it was more what I felt. It was a sense of evil and not the one emanating from Arthur but of something coming . . . I . . ." Sean shivered. "I don't ever want to feel that again."

In unison Sean and Kira's eyes slid back down to the body of Arthur. Elliot was already staring vacantly at the still form on the floor, and he was the first to speak.

"So now what do we do? We have a dead body on the floor of your home." As if his words had broken some spell, Elliot gathered himself off the floor and began to pack up his equipment.

"I know who we should call, anyway," Kira answered, "John."

Sean was already nodding to her suggestion, but no one seemed able to speak for a few moments.

"Who's John?" Elliot finally asked vacantly.

"He's the Sheriff," Sean answered. "And he's also a good friend. He'll understand and know what to do, I'm sure."

Sean's voice was distant; it matched the look on Kira's face and the tone in Elliot's voice. She was filled with a sense of disorientation that she was sure Sean sensed and shared. What do you do with a dead body in your house when that person died under circumstances that you couldn't explain? Micro-telekinesis? Telepathy? Yeah right.

"I think the sooner we call John, the better," Kira offered.

"I'll grab my phone," Sean responded then did so and began dialing.

~

He was trying to sort out his emotions, clear the fog from his head, and decide what he would say when the call connected.

"Hi, John," Sean opened.

John replied with a tone of emotional support, "Hi Sean. How's your dad?"

"Well, I can catch you up on all that later. Right now, I need you to get over here as quick as you can."

John's tone changed immediately from friendly to business and with a sheriff, business was almost never a good thing. "What's going on Sean? Have you looked out the window lately? It's still snowing. Hell, you'd think it was late December the way it's coming down. I'll have to round up the county SUV just to get over there."

"Well, I have a dead body over here."

There was silence on the line for a brief moment before John replied. "A murder?" John finally asked.

"Well, no. As far as anyone is going to be able to tell it's going to be a heart attack and maybe a brain aneurysm."

"What the hell does that mean? No, never mind. I'll be there as quickly as I can. I'll call the coroner on the way, too."

John hung up the phone almost before the last word could leave his mouth. Sean heard and sensed the concern in John's voice, just as he knew he would. He turned back to Kira and Elliot who were both standing in rapt attention staring at him.

"He's on his way, and he's calling the coroner to come too. He said it would take a while because of the snow."

All eyes shifted to the still form of Arthur. His pale blue eyes retained their dead stare. No one had thought to close them and probably wouldn't. Everyone in the room was reticent to go near him, much less touch him . . . for any number of reasons.

Silence fell in the room. The fire in the fireplace crackled while everyone continually tried to avoid Arthur's glaring, vacant eyes. They now seemed to be fixed upon Elliot.

Elliot glanced slowly around the room at the mess Arthur had created "Can we at least go in another room to wait?" Elliot asked.

Sean realized that however much he and Kira were shaken it wasn't nearly as bad as his plight. At the very least their past experiences had given them some basis as to how to act in the face of such unusual circumstances. Sean tuned in to Elliot and found the poor man to be just short of quivering inside

"Let's go in the kitchen," Kira offered as she picked up the broken wine glasses lying by the end table, another consequence of Arthur's rage. "We can pour some more wine. I think all our nerves could use it."

"Maybe it would be a good idea to clean some of this mess up first," Sean suggested. Kira nodded and she and Elliot promptly began picking up what they could.

Moments later nobody even commented as they followed Kira into the kitchen.

"How can you two be so damn calm?" Elliot asked between sips of the dry J. Lohr cabernet Kira had served.

Kira was the first to speak. "The paintings I do," she began. "They often come with unexpected results."

"Like this?" Elliot asked evincing a look of shock and wonder.

"Well, not exactly. But there have been some that were even worse," Kira continued. "I don't think you'd want me to get into it, and at the moment I don't want to anyway. Just suffice it to say, we have had other run-ins with death coming back to haunt us somehow."

Elliot was simply shaking his head. "So why do you do it?"

"We ask ourselves that question a lot," Sean said shaking his head. "But in the end every bad thing we deal with is accompanied with something of great good. The painting Kira did for Brian is giving him some much-needed closure, and in this case, we caught a killer which brought about a little justice. Not to mention, saved some other people's lives. In the moments before he attacked Kira I picked up his thoughts. He viewed all women as a disease, Killing the world like a cancer. He wanted to start with Kira, but I picked up on his serial killer cogitations. Any woman that crossed his path would have been met with the same horrifying fate as your poor sister. Who else was going to catch Arthur? And how would anyone else prove anything against him? Moving things with his mind? I mean really, he was virtually untouchable."

"I guess I see your point," Elliot answered, "But it puts Kira at risk."

Kira set down her glass. "Both of us really, but me especially. When I've had these conversations with Sean it just seems to come down to one thing. God gave us these unique abilities, and we both feel it would be something of a sin not to use them to help others. It's like your calling to be a scientist. Would you quit just because it became dangerous?"

Elliot quietly shook his head and took another sip of wine.

CHAPTER

John still managed to arrive before the coroner. Sean heard the crunching of the SUV in the snow before he caught the opening and closing of its door and sensed John's thoughts. He was worried.

Kira got up to go look out the window. She turned back to Elliot. "It's our friend, John, the sheriff." Elliot simply nodded and continued to work on his wine. Kira felt sorry for him. This was not something he was accustomed to or prepared to handle. His life day in and day out was working with inanimate things or the occasional rat.

Knowing them as well as he did, John didn't bother with the front door and trudged through the deepening snow toward the back door. Seeing his progress through the window, she moved to the back door to greet him and turned on the outside light. The sun wasn't down yet, but the shadows were lengthening and the cloud cover from the snow made it pretty dark on the path to the house. As he came up the three steps to the door, Kira opened it and caught him in a hug.

"Thanks for coming so quickly, John. We have quite a story and a mess to catch you up on."

John returned the hug and grinned. His scarred face twisting one side of his expression. He never complained about the scar or mentioned it, but it was a mark that reminded Kira of what a hero the gentle old country cop was.

"Glad I was so handy," he began, "But I think you better show me the body and catch me up before the coroner arrives."

Sean came into the room, shook John's hand warmly, and started walking back toward the den. "This way," he said simply. "Oh, and by the way this is Elliot Drake. He's a scientist and a doctor-friend of ours."

John looked briefly puzzled but reached out to shake hands with

Elliot. "Nice to meet you," he offered.

"Likewise," Elliot answered tentatively.

"So, who is the dead guy?" John asked as they walked down the hall.

"It was a guy we ran across when Kira was doing this last painting."

"The one for the guy in Hollywood?"

"Yep. That's the one. Angelie was the name of the guy's wife who had died of a heart attack. You might have heard of her. She was a pretty big star as well."

"Of course, I have. It was in the news for over a week when she died. I specifically remember the heart attack part." As he said the words heart attack John sensed he was about to hear of some kind of connection.

Sean continued with the blow by blow of the story as John walked slowly around the scene taking in every detail. Anyone who deduced that due to his age John would have lost some of his skills as a detective would have found themselves dead wrong. He absorbed Sean's entire rendition without slowing down his observations. He only interrupted a few times to ask Sean specific questions.

~

"How do you know it was a heart attack?" John asked as he reached down for a pulse and closed the guy's eyes. He stood back up before turning to face Sean. "And why's there blood on his nose?"

Sean glanced at Kira then turned back to John. "The heart attack was because he was trying to give Kira one, and I sensed it and sort of turned it back on him. The blood on his nose I'm guessing was an aneurysm from the impact of our interaction."

"Sort of turned it back on him? Seems to me your abilities have been doing a bit of growing don't you think?" John paused there for just a second then continued before Sean could answer.

"Kira's abilities have been growing as well," Sean added. "She was able to sketch him in Los Angeles at a place he was going to be at a later time. That's how we caught back up to him. Ironically enough, he also had a brain tumor. That's how Elliot got involved."

John paused and glanced over at Kira. "You two make quite a pair, you know that?" After thinking for just a moment John asked again,

"So he really did have a heart attack, you're sure? The coroner won't be able to tell anything else? Well besides the aneurysm."

"Don't know how he could. That's what actually happened. I just can't explain to anyone else how it happened. They'd think I was nuts, and there's nothing physical to prove otherwise."

"So . . . he came here to threaten you?" John asked.

"Well, that's where we get into some of the good news."

Sean started to explain about his dad and the cancer, but John cut him off. "You can give me that story later."

Sean became distracted anyway when he sensed, then heard, the Coroner's vehicle coming up the driveway.

"The Coroner's here," Sean offered.

"OK let me do the talking here. No need for you two to say anything unless he asks. If he does ask, just tell him you think it was a heart attack and you called me instead of 911 because you panicked and know me. If they want to know why he was here, just say he was a perspective client. As for you, Dr. Drake, you're here because of your connection with Kira's previous commission and you wanted to meet the artist. Everyone got all that?"

"Got it," Sean said for all of them. Kira and Elliot were nodding their heads.

It had been just like a dream. The Coroner had listened to the story from John, nodded, quietly taken the body, and left.

"This should all be fine as long as they don't find any cause of death other than traumatic heart failure and the aneurysm," John said, "And don't think you're going to get off without telling me this whole story." He retorted smiling. "I'll be back tomorrow or the next day when Aubrey gets home, and you can tell me all the juicy details." With that he left, whereupon they drove Elliot back to the airport.

~

Elliot was strangely silent causing Sean to zero in on his thoughts. He was thinking of Angelie.

"I'm sorry for your loss," Sean offered. "It is especially terrible that you had just found her, but, for what it's worth I want to thank you profoundly for saving my dad."

Elliot looked at them both for a moment before replying. "And I want to thank you for helping me bring justice to the one who took her from me," he said simply.

That little exchange seemed to be the balance of what the three had to share with each other until they dropped him off at the airport. As he pulled his suitcase from the back of the truck, he leaned back toward the window which Kira rolled down.

"Let me know if your dad needs anything else," he offered. "But I'm pretty certain he'll be just fine."

"Thank you," Kira answered with Sean just nodding, and then he was gone.

Sean pulled away from the curb and they were both silent for quite a while.

"It seems weird that that was the end of it," Kira said absently.

"Except that Dad will be home tomorrow." Sean looked across at Kira and decided to ask her what she was thinking rather than just snagging it from her mind. He liked to hear her voice. "So how do you feel about this little adventure? Did it resurrect any reservations about doing more paintings?"

~

Kira was silent for a moment, completely ignoring the fact that Sean had asked her the question out loud.

"Nah," she finally said, "I think I'm over that. I like doing my paintings and I like helping other people. If it puts us in danger from time to time, I guess I'm just ready to deal with it." She looked at Sean for a moment. "At least as long as I have you with me that is."

Sean smiled back at her. "Ditto," he replied. The loving smile in his hazel eyes gave her an idea.

"I think we've had a long enough day, Sean. Why don't we get some more wine when we get home and call it an evening?"

"Sounds like a deal to me," he answered smiling. Sean didn't need telepathy to snag the undertones of that invitation.

~

After a glass of wine and making love the way only newlyweds can, Sean fell quickly asleep, but Kira found herself feeling just a bit restless. A curiosity was rolling around in her mind that wouldn't let go. After waiting until she was certain Sean was in deep sleep, she eased her way out of bed and tiptoed over to her little desk where she kept some art supplies.

In the bare light of the nightlight she picked up a sketchpad and began to draw from memory the face of Arthur as she had last seen it. She started with the hair and began working down but got only as far as his eyes before an overwhelming sense of dread began to settle over her. A ripple of chills that felt more like a mild electric shock shook her, reminiscent of her brushes with Sean's adopted dad, Jason. She quickly stopped drawing. Then with another moment of consideration she tore the sketch to pieces and tiptoed back over to bed slipping into the warm comfort of her new husband's side.

Some things aren't meant to be known, was the last thought she had before surrendering to exhaustion and the comfort of Sean's side.

~

Blackness encompassed all senses combined with a bare sensation of unimaginable depth. Then came the movement of air rushing away into the unfathomable abyss as though a gigantic soundless fan had been switched on from somewhere behind.

Next a glow like that of a dying ember emanated from the endless depths, followed by the sudden appearance of two blue eyes. Those pale orbs caused an instinctive recoil, as one would from the sight of an asp coiled to strike. The remainder of that all too familiar face resolved from the darkness punctuated by the formation of an over-sized mouth locked in the throes of a hideous scream. No sound broke the silence, however, and with the appearance of two hands reaching for her from the darkness, the entire presence of him became unan-chored in some fashion and sped away from her into the darkness and the glow beneath.

~

Kira bolted upright with a gasp, dragging Sean from his slumber a bare second behind her. Her ragged breathing frightened him even more.

"Kira, are you OK?"

Kira struggled for another brief moment to settle her breathing before answering as Sean held her shoulders and watched her eyes.

"I am now," she finally said. "But I think I just got another elemental lesson about the curious cat. Damn. I also think I got a taste of what you experienced right after Arthur died."

She related the experience to Sean who heartily agreed with her cat analogy, the similarity to his brief experience, and the general idiocy of what she had tried.

"But why should that be different than painting using the ashes of someone who has passed away?" She finally asked Sean.

"That's a good question," Sean responded. "Maybe it's as simple as someone that has been laid to rest properly with a loved one requesting a memento is a very different spiritual scenario from trying to track the location of someone evil that has recently passed."

Kira thought about that for a moment. It made good sense. Her sketches seemed destined to track someone's location whereas her paintings were meant to bring closure to the grieving. Now she realized she didn't want to know these spirit's locations. Ever. Time enough for that when she was gone.

Snuggling back into Sean, they both slipped back into slumber in seconds.

CHAPTER

Errr-eh-errr-eh-errrr

Sean's eyes popped open to the familiar morning alarm of his rooster. The sound brought a smile to his face as it marked the return of normalcy. He turned to gaze at Kira's beautiful face for a moment. He loved to watch her sleep. His gaze lingered for a moment longer before her eyes popped open. A smile bloomed on her face, and she reached up to grab Sean around the neck and kiss him, pulling him down to her in the process.

"Good morning," she said after releasing him. "Is my breath bad?"

"Sweet as a rose," Sean answered pointedly not asking her the same question though he could unfortunately sense her thought.

'Love requires sacrifice, always.' The quote floated up in his mind, and he actually snickered leaving Kira with a questioning look on her face that he chose not to answer.

"So, what's on tap today?" She asked, changing the subject.

"Well for one thing, Dad is coming home, and we'll be picking him up at the airport. This morning I need to get out to that barn and see how the horses fared while we were away. Not to mention I need to make a little foray into the basement for that lighter Arthur left. That will point out the gas leak he arranged."

"That's good. I have unpacking and laundry to do . . . mounds of it."

A couple of hours later the call came from the hospital in Los Angeles confirming Aubrey's return flight information.

"So, you're certain he's fine to fly by himself?" Sean asked deciding to err on the cautious side. The doctor's response was quick and concise.

"Most of his physical symptoms were the result of the pressure on his autonomic nervous system. The tumor had already shrunk by half and ceased exerting any deleterious effects long before I called you yesterday. He'll be fine I assure you."

Sean had taken the call from the barn, and he couldn't wait to get back in the house and tell Kira. He jogged back to the house just from the joy of it.

"Kira!" he shouted as he opened the back door. When no reply was forthcoming, he moved through the house finding her on the phone in the den near her easel.

"I understand Brian . . . No, I'm pretty sure that will be the last . . . No, thank you for the opportunity of helping. Oh, and one more thing; you need to go back over to Angelie's place and look under the piano bench. She left a song in there that she wrote for you. I saw her finish playing it in one of my visions. I think you'll really like it . . . No, really, it was my pleasure."

Hanging up she turned to Sean. Rather than grabbing her thoughts he waited patiently for her to fill him in.

"I guess you heard that was Brian. Apparently, his painting changed again. Arthur is no longer in the reflection, and the expression on Angelie's face is now a tremendous smile. He said he loves it and asked me if it would change again."

"What did you tell him?"

"You heard that part. I told him I figured it was done changing."

"I'm glad you remembered the part about the song. I bet he'll love that."

"So would you," Kira responded. "It's beautiful. I'm just sorry you couldn't hear it."

~

The remainder of the day flew past with both Sean and Kira attempting to reestablish some further semblance of normalcy around being back home. Kira only knew it was time to get ready to go to the airport when Sean returned from the barn smelling strongly of horses.

"Really Sean, as much as I love horses, do you really have to bring their smell back into our house?" Sean found the scrunched-face expression she was miming to be positively delightful.

"I do until I get a shower installed in the barn. Now if you'll pardon me, I'll go relieve myself of this delightful fragrance."

"The sooner the better," she said, nevertheless kissing him on his way by.

After that, the ride to the airport was again accomplished with a minimum of conversation, but even Kira could sense Sean's slight anxiety and excitement regarding seeing his dad again.

They parked the car and made their way into the airport. Kansas City International was a good airport for that as each terminal was part of a larger broken circle with a corresponding chunk of parking lot out in front of each. For short term parking it made for quite a short walk into the terminal though it was annoying as a traveler if you had to change terminals since you had to board a bus outside to ferry over to another one. This was a fine set up when the weather was nice and not-so-fine during rainy weather or the dead of winter.

Sean held Kira's hand in a grip that was much stronger than necessary. Kira would have mentioned it but was concentrating on keeping up with his accelerated pace. As they made it through the automated doors, she finally got a chance to speak.

"Anxious, are we? And you can ease up on the vice grip on my hand now if you don't mind."

"Oh, sorry," Sean answered distantly. "What gate was it? Forty-four? That's to the left." And with that his pace went back into overdrive nearly dragging Kira along.

"Hey, he doesn't get here for another thirty minutes. Why don't you ease up a bit?"

"Oh, sorry again. You're right again. I'm just a bit anxious."

"Ya think?" Kira replied and laughed.

Aubrey strolled out of the plane looking nothing like someone who had just been in the hospital and on Death's door with brain cancer. The only visible sign to someone who knew him was his weight. He was about ten pounds thinner since the last time Sean had seen him up and around. He caught their eyes standing behind the glass partition just outside of the security area and smiled, adjusting his direction toward the door closest to them. Hugs all around ensued even before words, which, for Sean at least, were unnecessary.

"It's so good to see you up and around," Kira said backing up from the warm hug.

"It's nice to be up and around, and strange too. I guess I am the recipient of both a miracle and a mystery."

Sean and Kira exchanged a glance.

"You don't remember?" Sean began as they walked toward the exit.

"What?"

"Well, I don't know about the mystery, but I'm pretty sure we're kind of responsible for the miracle. We told you about it briefly before it happened. We had a whole conversation of you sending thoughts to me."

Aubrey shrugged his shoulders. "I was pretty foggy. All I remember was dreaming about the country knowing I trusted you. But I'm here, so I'm grateful for whatever it was."

Sean went into detail about the procedure he had undergone and how it had come about. They were just back to the car by the time he finished.

"Well that explains the mystery, too." Aubrey said.

"What was the mystery?" Kira asked.

"They did a final MRI before they released me and noticed some gold particles in my brain near the tumor. They couldn't imagine how they had gotten there. I guess I know now."

"I'm just glad it all worked, Dad. It's good to have you back." As the conversation continued, they began driving home.

The roads were clear but everywhere else was still coated with a blanket of snow as they drove back to Louisburg. Aubrey kept asking details.

"You two really do make an amazing team," Aubrey continued.

"Who knew?" Sean said. "I tell you what though, Dad, Kira and I are both getting a bit weary of dealing with evil characters."

"To say the least," she added.

"So, stay at home. After what Brian paid, you can certainly afford it for a while," Aubrey answered staring out the window at the snow-covered landscape.

The balance of the drive was conducted in silence. Sean sensed Kira thinking about things she needed to do around the house, and Aubrey was pondering over the details of his new abode on the Easton farm.

None of it needed any addition from him, so he pointedly tuned out of the other's thoughts. He considered everything that had happened in the last few days and how the new developments might affect them. Mostly he was just happy to get his dad back and some alone time with his new bride.

~

It was two weeks later when Kira came running out of the house with her phone in her hand calling for Sean. It was cold outside and grey again, but she had run out without her jacket in her rush to find Sean.

"Sean, where are you? Hurry, you have to hear this!"

As she entered the barn, Sean dropped down from the hayloft with an anxious look on his face. "What's wrong? Are you OK?" He began breathlessly.

"Yeah, great. Just listen." With that she turned up the volume on her phone and the mellow strains of a saxophone blended with some guitar background leading into lyrics. It was a love song about old family and new.

"This is brand new, and it's topping the charts," she said in a whisper.

"It's beautiful, but why the rush for me to hear it?"

"This is the song Angelie wrote for Brian. He produced it."

"Wow," Sean said softly then just listened. When it ended Sean turned to Kira and gave her a long deep kiss. "Your art made this art possible," he said softly, and they kissed again.

When they came up for air Kira pushed Sean back gently. "I have one other bit of news. I got a call earlier from some official down in New Orleans. They are getting ready to start bulldozing some of the buildings destroyed by Katrina and a few of them have burned. They want me to come do a painting and see if I can help identify any of their missing people. I really want to help them."

"And so, the adventure continues," Sean answered with a mischievous smile before resuming their previous embrace.

THE END

Follow Kira's and Sean's mysterious brushes with supernatural evil in the first book in the series:

Find Out How It All Started!

A dead serial killer's spirit longs to kill again and Kira's canvas becomes its portal.

Evil Comes Alive When She Paints with Ashes of the Dead

A dead serial killer's spirit longs to kill again and an artist's canvas becomes its portal. It all started innocently enough when New Orleans painter Kira McGovern mixed some of her mother's cremated ashes into her oil paints. Entering an altered state, she channeled key moments of her mother's life into a breathtaking memorial work of art. Her new business, Canvas of Life, was begun, and commissions rolled in.

But things get strange when Kira meets Sean Easton, a Midwestern rancher, hiding a secret of his own. Both are unprepared for the horrific terrors that emerge with every brush stroke from an unexpected new commission. Even as the pair fall for each other, the evil in the painting grows more malevolent. Soon, the awakened entity isn't satisfied to just flood Kira's dreams with blood and murder. It wants her as its next victim. Can Kira and Sean unmask the horror—and stop Kira becoming its next possession—before it's too late?

About the Author

Born in New Orleans, Jody Summers' life has been filled with unconventionality. The adopted son of a prominent Texas restaurateur, Jody grew up in New Orleans, Memphis and then Houston, learning the restaurant business while he built a career as a competitive gymnast that propelled him to a scholarship at the University of Kansas.

After college, Jody followed in his father's footsteps owning, at one point, three 24 hour restaurant franchises along with four tanning salons in Tulsa. Finally leaving that business, he turned his entrepreneurial skills to everything from a patent in the Pet Industry to a Single's website.

A restaurateur, a gymnast, a stunt man, an entrepreneur, a pilot, skydiver, scuba diver, and an accomplished martial artist for twenty-five years, Jody Summers has tried it all. Now he brings all those experiences to paper in his exciting novels.